# Youthful Distractions

by

**Michael Kennard**

Grosvenor House
Publishing Limited

This book is published by
Grosvenor House Publishing Ltd
Link House
140 The Broadway, Tolworth, Surrey, KT6 7HT.
www.grosvenorhousepublishing.co.uk

This book is a work of fiction. Any resemblance to
people or events, past or present, is purely coincidental.

A CIP record for this book
is available from the British Library

ISBN 978-1-83615-270-5

# Dedication

To Brian, my oldest mate

# Acknowledgements

I'd like to thank my son Alan for his technical experience and serious knowledge of computers, without which I'd probably have gotten lost. I'd also like to thank all the staff at Grosvenor House Publishing that have been so help in creating 'Youthful Distractions.'

It was the summer of 66, of youthful rebellion, of new found freedoms. They say "If you remember the Sixties you weren't there!" Well guess again, unbeknown to Joe Dempsey and his friends, on the cusp of leaving behind their rebellious ways, they were about to embark on the long and perilous road of life.

Friday night started just like every other weekend, but before Monday rolled around Joe's life changed in an instant. A simple glance across the dance floor, catching the eye of Grace, the most stunning woman he'd ever seen was just the beginning of a journey strewn with love, friendship, heartache, deceit, blackmail, betrayal, prison and finally murder.

Yeah, the Sixties were swinging and memorable in more ways than one.

# 1966
# Chapter 1

He shielded his eyes from the early afternoon sun and stared up at the clock perched just below the tall steeple of St Andrew's.

"Bob's taking his time," he muttered to himself. Then averting his gaze he concentrated on the dregs of his first light and bitter. Downing it in one, Joe contemplated whether to wait for Bob or get another. 'Chances are he'll arrive just after I've finished at the bar, he mused. 'There's no rush, its pleasant enough sitting outside in this July sunlight.' Absentmindedly he toyed with one of the brightly coloured beer mats that adorned the wooden table. He placed it at the edge of the wooded bench and flipped it with the back of his fingers and caught it with his hand. He added a second, repeated the process, then a third, a fourth, a fifth. On the seventh flip he failed and the beer mats scattered across the wooden table and chairs before cascading to the ground.

World Cup Willie grinned up at him from every one of the Watney Mann beer mats. As he reached down to retrieve them he reflected that England were almost halfway there. A good result this afternoon would bring them one step closer to that coveted trophy. 'Another week and we'll know for sure,' he thought and he wasn't just talking about the World Cup. On the Friday before the final he had the dreaded driving test. Football was great, but the challenge of his third driving test eclipsed even that. What narked him the most, wasn't the fact he was a damn good driver, but as an Air Cadet during his teenage years he'd had the opportunity to fly a light aircraft. He gave all that up when girls took up most of his time and attention.

1

Joe was twenty one, he was to all intent and purpose mobile. A two tone maroon and grey Mark 2 Ford Zodiac sat outside his mum and dad's three bedroom council house. The chrome of the Lowline Zodiac sparkled like new, but then it would, he'd spent the best part of Saturday morning washing and waxing it. It was his pride and joy, a real eye catcher with the girls. He couldn't wait to cruise the surrounding towns, arm resting nonchalantly on the open window, a casual leer in his eye. The girls, well he'd be fighting them off, at least in his dreams, he added. Now all that stood between him and driving heaven was the examiner; a symbol of much hatred over the last couple of months.

"You're obviously doing something wrong," said Dad.

"No, I'm not," he'd snapped. "I'm a good driver, that's what my instructor said. It's just nerves, bloody nerves. I need a couple of pints inside me before I start."

"That's what you don't need," Dad said sternly.

"I was only joking," he shot back immediately.

"That's the trouble with you, you're always joking. You need to take things more seriously."

"Ah forget it." Joe hadn't meant to cause an argument, but there it was, and it wasn't as if his dad could drive. Grabbing his jacket, he stormed out.

Joe looked at World Cup Willie, and thought about England's game against Argentina. According to the papers they played dirty, "Nobby will give em a taste of their own medicine," he mouthed into his empty glass.

"Talking to yourself again, first sign of age that is," said Bob as he crept up behind Joe.

"Never mind me, it's your round," cried Joe, as he handed his friend the empty glass he'd been nursing.

Bob laughed good-humouredly, took the offered glass and hurried into the public bar. A couple of minutes later he emerged carrying two pints.

"Cheers," cried Joe as he lowered his head towards the pint and took a sip. "Did you get those shoes you were after?

"Yeah got them in tan," responded Bob.

"Jim will like these," said Joe referring to the Chelsea boots, he'd pulled out of Bob's bag.

"Yeah," grinned Bob, "He had his eye on them last week." Both chuckled. "We going back to mine to watch the match?"

"Yeah I reckon. Jim said he'd be here about one o'clock."

"It's ten too, now," said Bob as he glanced at his watch. "If he turns up. We can stay til chucking out time, otherwise we'll have to take the train and use Shanks's pony.

"He'll be here don't worry."

As if on cue, a Vauxhall Cresta sped into the car park of the Queen's Head and screeched to a halt.

"I wish he wouldn't do that, he's liable to get us all barred if he ain't careful," said Bob.

"Are you gonna tell him, I'll be fucked if I'm going too, said Joe, "I want a lift back to yours."

"So do I," replied Bob with a cheeky grin as he stood up and ventured into the bar to get Jim a pint of stout and cider. Their normal local was a few miles away in Ruislip, but on an occasion they'd do a bit of shopping in Uxbridge.

Jim grinned at Joe and sat down opposite. "Where did you get to last night?"

Joe laughed, "That would be telling!"

Bob reappeared seconds later with Jim's pint.

"Just quizzing Joe about where he disappeared too."

"Let's just say if I'd passed my test last month I'd have saved a lot of shoe leather."

"But was it worth it?" asked Jim.

"I ain't saying," replied Joe.

"That means you got none," laughed Bob.

"Sounds about right," Jim added.

Joe just grinned.

*****

Joe was right, the Argentina game was a bad tempered affair, resulting in Rattin being sent off. The booing's and swearing from Bob's parents small, but comfortable front room could be heard up and down the street. Bob's mum raced around the living room closing windows in a vain attempt to muffle the sound. "I wouldn't bother Marg," said Bob's dad, "I think I've got a couple of bottles of Brown Ale. I'll go and get them. Be a dear, and get some glasses." Marg gave her husband a mock look of disapproval, then dutifully walked into the kitchen to get them.

It was left to Jim to dampen their spirits as the friends and Bob's dad celebrated the England win. "They gotta beat Portugal on Tuesday, then maybe they'll have a chance. That Eusebio is pretty useful."

"Yeah," said Bob's dad, "we shouldn't count our chickens before they've hatched."

"We'll worry about that come Tuesday, in the meantime we've Saturday night." said Joe, his eyes sparkling with anticipation.

"Yeah, what time are we meeting," cried Bob.

"About seven, down the George," said Jim.

"I ain't staying there all night," groaned Bob. "Who fancies the Top Rank," he suggested.

"Nah, but I ain't staying in the pub all night, what about the Starlight?" said Joe.

"What about the Starlight," echoed Jim sarcastically?

"Yeah, we were there last night, when you disappeared," added Bob suspiciously.

"You pulled that old sort, didn't you," laughed Jim.

"Nah, she didn't want to know and she ain't old either, she's twenty eight," said Joe defensively.

"She'd eat you for breakfast," added Bob.

"I should be so lucky," said Joe and laughed, "the Clay then."

"The Clay," came the reply.

# Chapter 2

Joe stared into the mirror, his face all covered in lather. His thoughts were of that magical Friday night. *He'd seen her around the hall a couple of times, their eyes had locked then nothing. Fortified by six pints and a couple of whiskey chasers, his heart pounding, he finally asked her if she wanted to dance. To his surprise she said, "I'd love to."*

*The band was playing "A Groovy Kind of Love" Wow he thought as he placed his arms around her. She smiled at him, adjusting his position as they danced. Joe usually came out with one liners but found himself slightly out of his depth. The girls he'd dated and associated with were just girls. The lady in his arms was one classy chick.*

*"What's your name?" she asked?*

*"Joe," he replied.*

*"I'm Grace."*

*A little repartee between them ensued, then all too briefly the song ended. Letting her go was the hardest thing he'd had to do in a long time. He watched as she walked back to a small group of girls. His heart leapt when she looked back and smiled. Ribbed by his friends he made light of it, "Thought I'd give the girl a treat," he said, though deep down he hated himself for saying it.*

*The music was noisy and wild as the boys retired into the bar at the back of the stage. The usual suspects were seated around the bar, including a morose looking Keith Moon, staring into his drink. Eric Sullivan as dapper as ever was sitting in a back booth, a double scotch in his right hand, an expensive Rolex adorning his left wrist. He beckoned the boys over. Eric with his bespoke suits and handmade shoes was the epitome of a London gangster.*

*"Get the boys what they want," he motioned to the bartender. The boys huddled into the plush leatherette seating of the booth. "Okay lads, what's happening?"*

*"Just the usual, nothing special," replied Jim.*

*"Where's Terry tonight?" inquired Eric, "Understand he wants a word." "News to me," volunteered Jim.*

*"Family, I think," said Bob.*

*"Whatever it is, it'll wait I guess," said Eric, "Tell him to get in touch."*

*Within minutes the crew were talking about the ducking and diving they'd got up to since last they'd met. Eric regaled his friends with tales of daring do in the London Underworld, which the boys lapped up avariciously. At twenty nine Eric with his London underworld connections had become a local celebrity at the George. At twenty six he'd left the hustle and bustle of London and moved to the suburbs, with his wife Gloria. He'd bought a small shop and dealt in antiques. It was proving a smart move as things in London were turning vicious. In March there'd been the shooting at Mr Smith's night club in Catford: worse was to follow. A day later a known villain had been shot dead in the Blind Beggar pub in Whitechapel. Eric had his suspicions but he kept them to himself.*

*Joe had other things on his mind; namely the classy chick with the darkest shaggy mop of hair he'd ever seen. Without a word he casually wandered back into the ballroom. It was getting late and Joe hoped to ask her for another dance. If she knocked him back, he'd re-join Eric and the boys. Panic set in as he spied the crowd Grace had been with; she was nowhere to be seen. He scoured the room expecting to find her dancing too closely with another guy. Realising she wasn't anywhere to be seen on the dance floor he looked again at her small bunch of friends. She still wasn't there. He approached the girls and asked of her whereabouts.*

*"She's just left," said a tall blonde.*

*Instinctively Joe raced for the exit, he took the stairs three at a time. The cool of the evening air hit him and he realised he'd had too much to drink. He looked left then right.*

*"Shit!" he exclaimed, she was gone. Feeling a little unsteady on his feet he turned back to the club. Just as he was about to enter, from out of the periphery of his left eye he caught a glimpse of a figure across the road. He focused both eyes and saw it was the girl he'd danced with waiting at the bus stop. What he was going to say he couldn't hazard a guess. He only knew he couldn't go home without asking for a date. He staggered into the middle of the road, ignoring the honks of the occasional motorist.*

*"Be careful," she cried as he had a near miss with yet another motorist. "I'm not too late am I, the bus should be coming along about now," he lied.*

*"Its due in three minutes," Grace volunteered, "but this isn't your bus home, is it?"*

*Joe ignored the question, "Why is a pretty girl like you taking the bus home alone?"*

*"Because I'm a big girl now," she teased.*

*"Why aren't your friends with you?" he asked.*

*"They're not really my friends, they're girls I work with; they live in different directions from me."*

*"Okay, but you shouldn't be going home alone, it's dangerous for a young girl like you."*

*"Thanks for your concern," she mocked.*

*Just at that moment the bus pulled around the corner. "I think I should walk you home anyway," said Joe.*

*"That won't be necessary, go back in and join your friends," she said with a slight edge to her voice.*

*She stepped onto the bus and began to climb the stairs, leaving Joe standing on the pavement. The conductor dinged the bell. Which broke Joe's paralysis, he grabbed for the pole and swung himself forward, within a few seconds he was climbing the steep narrow stairs.*

Grace looked shocked as he emerged on the top deck. He smiled drunkenly. She smiled back, in truth she was a little flattered by his persistence.

Joe moved forward as the bus swayed and lurched. He reached for support and eventually swung into the seats opposite Grace. The bus conductor wearily climbed the stairs and asked where they were going. Joe insisted on buying both tickets. The moment the conductor descend the stairs Joe turned to Grace, "I'm a pest, I know, but I couldn't let you go without asking you out."

"We had one dance, I'm clearly much older than you."

"I'm twenty two going on twenty three," he lied.

"Yeah of course you are, I'm nearly thirty. Much as I find your attention flattering, I can't go out with you."

Joe looked crestfallen, and sat there for a moment thinking. "Okay I get it, you're older, but I really think we have a connection. Go out with me next Friday, as a friend. Let me talk to you when I'm sober. If after that you don't want to see me, I'll understand."

"Joe, you're a nice young man, but it's not possible."

She remembered my name, he thought. "Nothing's impossible Grace."

For the next ten minutes they sparred around each other, until Grace said, "This is my stop." She gathered her things and made to get up. Joe immediately started to rise, until Grace motioned for him to sit down. She smiled down at him then added, "No." It was the finality of that one word that made him slump down into his seat.

He watched as she swiftly reached the stairs, Joe asked her again just as Grace started to descend the stairs. It was the desperation in his voice that made her look back at him. He gave her a cheeky grin. Another step down and he would vanish from her life.

"Seven o'clock next Friday, this bus stop. Just talk okay."

*His heart leapt, "I knew you couldn't resist me," he laughed.*

*She smiled back at him, without saying another word. Her heart saying why not, her head saying this was all wrong.*

*Joe remained on the bus to the end, only to find he'd missed the last bus home.*

Wiping off the excess shaving lather, he stared at himself in the mirror. His image stared back at him. Did he look nearly twenty three, he mused? His hairstyle was more a throwback to the old Teddy Boys, albeit a little more refined, although the proverbial duck's arse was immaculate, his sideburns were more Presley than McCartney. His blue eyes which held a hint of mischief also betrayed the fact that to a keen eye he still had a lot to learn. Joe consoled himself that his five o'clock shadow and his dark hair compensated for his lack of years. He began to have doubts whether Grace would turn up. He'd truly been smitten, something that had only happened to him once before, a few years earlier.

# Chapter 3

The talk in the George was all about England's win over Argentina and the forthcoming match against Portugal. As usual Joe and Bob arrived first.

"Get them in," said Bob, "You might as well get Jim's while you're at it."

As Joe began his order at the bar Jim walked in with Terry.

"Mine's a pint of Red Barrel, said Terry with a grin.

"Full house tonight then," replied Joe.

The boys sat and chatted for nearly two hours, mainly about football, Joe's driving test and why Terry had been allowed out on a Saturday night.

"Her mum's come to stay for a couple of weeks," he volunteered.

Usually Terry made most Friday nights, but because he had to pick Heather's mum up from Euston he wasn't out. Which was just as well thought Joe. Terry was four years older and a couple of inches taller, more importantly he had an eye for the ladies. He'd been married to Heather for four years, had two kids and another on the way. Getting Heather up the duff at twenty wasn't what he'd planned, but then he'd always been a sucker for blondes. Things could have been worse. They had a three bedroom council house on a nearby estate, a two year old Rover 2000 and the best Blaupunkt radiogram that money could buy. At twenty five, Terry Richards took risks with everything, his job, his wife and his freedom. Getting a job as a warehouseman at B.O.A.C meant cheap flights to Spain and faraway places like Cyprus, it also meant he was in the land of temptation, and Terry was tempted.

"Eric was asking after you," said Jim, "something about a bit of business."

"He down here Sunday lunch?" asked Terry. "He didn't say."

"Well he knows where to find me."

"You gotta be careful Terry," warned Jim.

"I'm always careful."

"Yeah sure you are," added Bob.

The Clay Pigeon was a large pub, saloon and public bar, with a hall attached, which held dances every Saturday and Sunday nights. Jim swung the Vauxhall Cresta into the car park of the "Clay" and the boys poured out. Bob crouching down looked at his reflection in the passenger window of the Cresta. He reached for his comb and a couple of swift movements with it and his blonde locks were in place. At twenty one he was the youngest of the bunch by three months. Tall and wiry but rippling with muscles which he'd picked up on local building sites where he'd learned his craft as an hod carrier and general labourer.

"Yeah you're beautiful, you tart," quipped Terry.

"I don't know about you guys, I feel tonight I'm gonna pull."

"The only thing you're likely to pull is yah prick," laughed Jim.

Joe said nothing, him and Bob were best mates, having gone to the same primary and secondary schools. Bob, not thick by any means, just wasn't the learning type, whereas Joe was a tool maker. He'd studied hard, worked as an apprentice at a local factory, his apprenticeship over he was now earning reasonable money.

The place was alive with rhythm and blues, not the boys favourite, but the birds seemed to like it. With a couple of drinks inside them, they started to mingle. Chatting with other groups of lads and generally hustling the girls. Trouble could and did on an occasion flare up on the dance floor, but not that often. Most troublemakers were bounced out pretty sharpish. Because it was local most people knew each other or were on nodding terms.

Satisfying themselves that the music and the lack of action wasn't to their taste Joe, Jim and Terry retired to the saloon bar, while Bob hung back. Saturday night wouldn't be Saturday night without trying his luck on the dance floor. He'd had an eye on some ginger sort and asked her to dance, not that Bob was that much of a dancer.

"You fancy a dance?" he asked.

To his surprise she took him by the hand and led him onto the floor

"Hey," he cried, "My name's Bob, I've seen you around a few times." "Yeah, I've seen you too. I'm Rebecca, just call me Becky."

"What'da yah thing of the band, Becky?"

"They're alright I suppose," she replied.

"Not really my kind of music, Stones are all right, but I prefer the Searchers."

"I like Keith, not that keen on Mick. Hollies are good though," said Rebecca.

"Yeah, seen the Hollies at South Harrow, they were brill." Tired of endless chat about rock groups, he went for the jugular, "It's hot in ere innit," It was his standard chat up line.

"Yeah, it is a bit," Rebecca responded.

"Fancy getting a bit of night air?" 'Where did that come from?' thought Bob. 'I normally say, wanna go outside? I must be getting a bit refined in me old age.'

"Yeah okay, but no funny business."

'Get in my son,' thought Bob. "Yeah no funny business."

They had no sooner passed through the double doors when she grabbed a hold of Bob and tried to snog the face off him. He pushed her against the wall and responded.

"Not here," she said breathlessly. Bob took the lead and led her into the darkest corner of the car park. Quickly they found themselves in the shadows, their bodies thrusting against each other, their hands all over the place. She was a live on, thought Bob. He broke away from her and fumbled in his pocket.

"You won't need it," she cried.

He gave her a look of incredulity, and in that moment he caught a look at her in the street light from across the road, her long red hair framed her face giving her a gentle but wanton look, creating an air of mystery. He couldn't believe his luck, she wasn't half bad. "What the fuck," he cried as he undid his belt and shuffled forward with his trousers around his ankles. Within seconds he was inside her. He thought it would have been over in a flash, but the five or six pints helped to prolong his climax. When he felt the tell-tale signs, Rebecca shrieked with excitement and pressed her lips to his and thrust herself forward. Bob wanted to pull out but the sheer passion of their fucking made it impossible. Sweating and breathless they clung to each other until the euphoria seeped away.

A brief moment of quiet reflection followed as Becky fixed her clothing and Bob pulled up his pants and trousers.

"I'd better go and get cleaned up," said Rebecca, "See you in the dance hall."

"Yeah, I'll be there in a while, gotta pop into the saloon bar, people to see."

"I'll be waiting," she said, then slowly she walked back into the hall.

"Oh fuck!" cried Bob to himself. "What if I've got her pregnant?" He'd gone the whole hog, normally he'd have either used a Johnny or he'd have pulled out and cum against the car or down her leg. "Fuck, fuck, fuck." He lit up a cigarette, took a deep drag and tried putting his life into prospective. He was too young to get married. He laughed at even contemplating it, he'd known the girl five minutes. What did that tell you? It might not happen, but knowing his luck. On the flip side she was a pretty good looking girl and mores the point she fucked like crazy. He could either cut and run, then again he could go back in the dance hall and see where that took him. But first a pint with the lads to gather his thoughts.

"Well, did yah score?" came the cry from the boys.

"Possible, if I work at it," he lied.

"It was the tall ginger bird?" stated Terry. "I fancied having a go myself."

"Leave it," cried Bob too quickly, "I think I'm on a promise. Might walk her home." 'Where was all this coming from, normally I'd have breezes into the saloon bar, cocky as you like,' he thought.

"I might still have a go at it," continued Terry.

"Nah, leave it," said Joe, sensing his best friend wasn't telling all.

"I was only joking, wanted to wind him up."

"Looks to me like you done the business already!" exclaimed Jim, "Judging from the flushed look on your face."

Ignoring the comment, Bob said, "I'll see you boys later," then he grabbed his pint and walked out.

The coolness of the night air comforted him as he retraced the events that had so recently happened. She was a nice looking bird, and in truth he'd seen her down the Clay a few times. Yes he fancied her and if things hadn't happened so quickly he'd have asked her out. That she fucked like crazy was a plus, but also a minus. "Oh what the hell," he muttered as he took a swig and re-entered the dance hall

He spied her standing with some girls watching the group. "Oh, you came back," she said.

"I said I would, didn't I," he shouted through the din of the band, then as if on cue they slowed things down a bit.

"You'd Better Move On."

"Oh, I like this one," and before he could say shit she had him in a clinch and pulled him onto the dance floor again.

"I thought you didn't like Jagger?"

"I don't, but I love this song."

"Can I walk you home?"

"Where did that come from?" she exclaimed.

"What? Can I walk you home," he repeated.

"Have you got a car? I live on the Race Course," said Rebecca.

"Fuck," thought Bob. It was a long walk from the Clay, to a council housing estate in Northolt.

"Nah, not at the moment. But my mates could give us a lift, he said innocently, but in truth he didn't want that."

"You gotta be joking, I ain't getting in a car with four strangers."

"We weren't strangers a little while back," he retorted.

She smiled, "We can catch a bus across the road, but it's still a bit of a walk."

"Why don't we go now?" Bob said, nervous that she might change her mind.

Becky thought about it for a moment, "Yeah, why not!"

# Chapter 4

Jim's Vauxhall Cresta drove into the George car park and pulled in beside Terry's Rover. It was five minutes to twelve, Sunday lunchtime drinking, the best two hours of quality drinking time. Two hours of chewing the fat, drinking beer and reviewing the weekend, before turning to the forthcoming working week. The boys got out and walked across the car park and joined Joe outside the pub's double doors. Jim glanced at his watch as the sound of bolts being pulled back and the doors opened. "That's what I call timing," he announced as the boys walked through the open doorway.

"Anyone seen Bob since last night," asked Jim. "Not usually this late," he added glancing again at his watch. "A bit like you on Friday night," he added.

"He'll be here," said Joe as he pulled a chair out and sat down.

"Talk of the devil," cried Terry, as Bob breezed through the double doors, wearing the same dark blue suit he'd worn the night before. Seeing his mates he grinned before stepping up to the bar.

"Looks like he slept in that suit," remarked Joe with a grin.

"Cheap suits don't look much even when they ain't bin slept in," said Terry as he straightened his tie and brushed an imaginary piece of lint from his bespoke light grey suit. Nothing but the best for our Terry.

"Smug git," mumbled Joe.

"I wonder whether it was worth it?" said Jim, eyeing the crumbled suit.

Joe laughed, "He looks like the cat that got the cream, dirty lucky git."

Bob paid for his pint, turned and looked across to the table at an eagerly anticipating group that he called friends. He took a good swig of his frothy light and bitter, then poured in the rest of the bottle of light ale. He grinned to himself, they were sure going to be disappointed, thought Bob as he walked towards the table.

"I'll get that," said Jim as he handed Bob, half a crown.

"Cheers Jim."

At half twelve on the dot, in walked Eric. Tall and roguishly handsome yet a devoted husband to Gloria, much to the disappointment of the ladies he brushed shoulders with. He glanced across, nodded an acknowledgement, ordered a double scotch with a single cube of ice then walked across and joined the boys.

"Bob's holding out on us," laughed Joe.

"Oh yeah," cried Eric, "Come on Bob, put the boys out of their misery."

"Nothing to tell," replied Bob, enjoying the attention that last night's escapade awarded him.

"We're going to the flicks this afternoon," said Joe. "You fancy joining us Eric."

"No. Thanks for the offer, it's not really my scene."

"Count me out too," declared Bob.

"He's seeing that sort," exclaimed Terry.

"Might be," added Bob.

"He's giving her one," said Jim and Joe together. "There's no other explanation!"

It was just before chucking out time when Terry pulled Eric to one side. "Got a big shipment of booze, they won't miss a pallet. You interested?"

"How much are we talking about," said Eric?

"I'd reckon around five hundred quid's worth," said Terry.

"Fifty alright with you? I'll see to Harry's end," said Eric.

Terry was expecting a bit more, but he wasn't going to upset the applecart, "Yeah fifty's good." The job was a piece of piss, no security cameras, well none that were working, but, he still felt a little resentful.

Eric never got his hands dirty. Harry was an old lag that Eric knew from the old days. He'd been around the block and back again. It was money for old rope. Eric had a lockup, a garage on a small council estate. Harry would pick up the booze, and deliver it to the lock up. A couple of days later Harry would deliver it to whomever Eric had sold it too. Yeah, Eric might look like a gangster, but he was smart with it, where ever possible he never got his hands dirty. Getting nicked for petty theft, still meant bird. Since moving from London, Eric had cultivated an image of respectability. Not to put too finer point on it, he had a couple of London's finest, all too ready to do him a favour, plus the ear of certain members of the criminal underworld.

Eric liked Terry, he was a risk taker and in their game all you needed was nerve. He didn't ask any questions, so he didn't know any answers. Eric had big plans for Terry. The airport was ripe for abuse and getting riper. It was going through a transformation, a large cargo terminal was being built and should be up and running within a couple of years. There was big money to be had and Eric intended on getting his share, hopefully without breaking into a sweat.

# Chapter 5

Sunday afternoon pictures was a tradition for the boys going back to when they were barely teenagers. Through the years they'd watched every Hammer horror that had been filmed, every western, Carry on, and the triannual Elvis movies. Jim the most avid filmgoer loved Westerns, in fact his Vauxhall Cresta had two wing mirrors set into a framework of two six-gun handles; to Jim it looked pretty cool. He'd studied hard at school and then college. Now a qualified electrical engineer, he found himself stuck in a rut, albeit with a decent wage, but now he was restless and looking for new horizons. He wanted to travel, he'd even thought about getting a job with Terry at BOAC, but his father had advised against it. Jim was his own man at twenty four but still living at home so he listened to what his father had to say, not that he always took his advice. On this occasion he did. "Yeah, you may be right about BOAC, but I'm still gonna put out feelers for something different."

Jim picked Joe up a little after four o'clock and parked his car in the car park at the back of the Astoria. "Now we're two, first Terry, now Bob," he said as they paid for their tickets to see a double feature, "The Reptile" and "Rasputin, the Mad Monk."

Joe laughed, "Terry yeah, but Bob I don't think so. By this time next week he'll be telling us all the gory details."

"Yeah, I guess you're right," replied Jim.

They both laughed as they walked into the cinema. They were greeted in the darkness by an usherette neatly dressed in a maroon uniform. In silence she shone her torch on their tickets then motioned for the boys to follow the dim light of the torch as she proceeded to walk down the aisle. The unmistakeable smell of the cinema invading their nostrils as they stared up at the big screen. Shipman and King were showing a trailer of the following week's film. As they were being shown to their seats Jim asked Joe a question, "You've a decent job, have you ever felt like chucking it all in and doing something different?"

"All the time, but that won't happen, my dad would go mad," said Joe as he took his seat.

"Baby!" cried Jim.

The lights dimmed and the main features began. "You having a swift pint after," enquired Jim.

"Yeah, I suppose, but I ain't staying all night. Work in the morning."

"Exactly!" said Jim sarcastically.

Three and a half hours later, they emerged from the darkness, "Well that was crap!" exclaimed Jim.

"It weren't that bad," replied Joe.

"You need to raise your standards, now let's get that pint."

Joe just smiled, 'If Friday pans out the way I hope, my standards will go through the roof,' he thought secretly.

Little did Joe and Jim know that Bob and his new girlfriend were up in the balcony, in the far corner of the back row to be precise? As it happened neither of them could give an opinion on the double feature as they were too engrossed in each other. Bob was feeling a little more relaxed than he'd been on Saturday night. *On the bus home Rebecca had reassured him that it was the wrong time of the month to get pregnant, so he had no reason to worry.*

*"Can I see you again," asked Bob as they reached the front door of Rebecca's parents' council house?*

*"If you'd like. Do you want to come in for a coffee, it's a long walk home."*

*Bob thought about it for a moment, there was the chance of a late bus, then he looked at Becky. "Why not," he grinned as*

Rebecca made a shushing motion with her finger to her lips. She reached into her handbag and retrieved her door key. They both giggled as Rebecca fumbled with the key in the lock.

"Is that you Rebecca," came a voice from upstairs.

"Yeah, it's me Mum," replied Rebecca. "Gonna make myself a cup of coffee, then I'll be up."

"You tell that boy you're with, to behave himself."

"Bob walked me home, just making him a coffee," said Rebecca, "Anyway, how'd you know I wasn't alone?"

"I wasn't born yesterday. Don't be too late for your bed."

"Oh Mum."

"Goodnight."

It was two thirty in the morning before Rebecca came to bed, Bob had tried to join her. "Best not push it, Mum's pretty cool, but she don't like having the piss taken out of her. You can kip down on the sofa if you like, catch a bus in the morning."

Bob overslept, the smell of bacon awakened his nostrils. This wasn't what he was expecting, breakfast with the family. It seemed that seeing him asleep on the couch must have allayed Rebecca's Mum's fears. Sitting down to breakfast with the entire family was a bit daunting, but once Rebecca's father asked him what he did for a living, things took on a life of itself. Tom laughed, "Been in the building game most all my life. Being a good hod carrier is one thing, but you can't do that your whole life."

"I'm doing okay," replied Bob.

"You need to look to the future son. Learn a trade, electrician, plumber even a bricklayer, that's what I did. Staying a labourer in the building trade is a mugs game."

"I'll bear that in mind," he said.

After thanking Becky's mum for breakfast he made his excuses and said he had to be going. Becky walked him to the front door. He hesitated for a moment then asked, "Look Becky are you free this afternoon?"

*"Yeah, I guess so."*
*"Good, then meet me around 4 o'clock at Ruislip station."*

Bob caught the bus and after giving his blonde locks a final comb in a shop window, he walked into the George.

# Chapter 6

Much as beating Portugal 2-1 in the Semi Final was a reason to celebrate, Joe's mind was elsewhere. Passing his driving test that Friday morning was uppermost in his mind, that and meeting Grace at the bus stop near Wembley. He had one more lesson just prior to the test and the use of the instructor's car during the driving test. At a pound a lesson, driving a crappy Vauxhall Viva, Joe vowed that if he didn't pass, he'd use his Zodiac the next time.

"I'm gonna pass," he kept saying to himself. "I'm gonna pass."

'Oh shit,' he thought, 'that fucker failed me last time. I hate the bastard.'

The test was a nerve racking experience, Joe experienced a gambit of emotions, but although his inner self was raging, his outer remained calm.

A few questions at the end of the test and it was all over. The moment of truth was upon him. "You've passed!"

Joe stared at the examiner, unable to comprehend what he had said.

"You've passed," he repeated and handed Joe the coveted pink slip. "Goodbye," he added curtly and in one swift motion he was out of the car.

Joe could hardly believe it, he sat motionless staring at the pink slip. It was only when his instructor walked back to the car that Joe realised what had just happened.

"I passed!"

"Congratulations. Now shift over and I'll drive you home."

Joe wasted no time when the instructor dropped him off. He untied the two L plates attached to his gleaming Ford Zodiac.

Since leaving school at fifteen he'd put some of his meagre wages towards the purchase of this car. His dad had encouraged him to save and had matched Joe's savings in his Post Office account. For which Joe had been extremely grateful until the moment of truth when they arrived at the second-hand car showroom.

*"That's the car!" he said excitedly.*

*"Hmmm. It's a bit big, don't you thing," said dad.*

*"No, it's perfect," declared Joe, a slight hint of panic in his voice.*

*"What about that one," his father suggested.*

*"No way, I'm not buying a Ford Prefect."*

*"I'm not sure that car is right for you," his father insisted.*

*"Dad, you don't own a car! How do you know what's right for me?"*

*It took a stand up argument with his father before Jim who'd accompanied them to the showroom explained how much safer you were in a larger car. It was a hard fought victory.*

\*\*\*\*\*

Now sitting inside the Zodiac, he was on cloud nine. Knowing he could now legally drive without an experienced driver sitting next to him, made him feel on top of the world. His thoughts quickly turned to Grace. He'd thought about her all week; now with his driving test out of the way he started having doubts. She was a classy bird, older than him by five or six years, he guessed. Would she have given him more than a cursory thought, be flattered and then laughed the experience off, or would she turn up? At least, he thought, if she doesn't turn up, the boys would be none the wiser.

Washed and shaved, a dab of Cusson's Imperial Leather, suited and booted, Joe left his house around six thirty, to a chorus of "Be careful," from his mum, "keep your eyes on the road," from his brother Bill and the proverbial "Don't drink too much," from his dad.

The petrol gauge read full, he checked his wallet, he had eight pounds and a ten bob note, more than enough he hoped, to impress the girl of his dreams.

His excitement gave way to butterflies in his stomach as he drew nearer his destination. His week of dreams could possibly be about to go up in smoke. He'd panicked earlier as he'd been caught up in the remnants of Friday night's rush hour, but still arrived a few minutes early. She wasn't there, he thought as he looked down the road towards the bus stop, then his heart skipped a beat, he spied a solitary figure walking towards the stop. His heart leapt, it was her. He slowed down and brought the car to a gentle halt, then leaned across and wound down the window. "Hi, you showed," he said hoping to appear confident.

Grace looked taken aback, "You've a car!"

"Hop in," he pushed the door open.

"Joe, it is Joe isn't it." She looked upset, a little worried. "Last Friday was a mistake. I only came to apologise for leading you on."

Joe's euphoria disappeared. "Can't we just talk about it? At least give me five minutes."

"I don't think so Joe."

"This is where we were last Friday. Five minutes," he pleaded.

Grace looked up and down the street, "Five minutes," she said as she stepped inside. "Very swish," she remarked.

Joe was about to state his case when Grace said, "Drive, please drive." The urgency in her voice jolted Joe into action. He slipped the Zodiac into gear and drove up the road, "Take a right," she commanded. "Drive for a couple of hundred yards then turn into that car park."

Joe did what she told him. He put the car out of gear switched off the ignition and pulled on the brake. "What's with the cloak and dagger?"

"I'm married!"

Joe's world crumbled. "But, I thought."

"It's my fault Joe, I was out with the girls from work. I was enjoying myself for the first time in ages. I saw you looking at me and I felt flattered. You asked me to dance. To be honest I was over the moon. I was being treated like a lady for the first time in years. I didn't want the music to stop, when it did I felt very down. You were nice, you smiled at me and protocol told me to walk away. I glanced back and you smiled. I knew at that moment I shouldn't be there, I was a married woman.

"You had every right, you hadn't done anything wrong."

"In your eyes maybe. I went back to the girls, made my excuses and soon after I left. Then you miraculously appeared braving the traffic, I felt my heart leap."

"You still hadn't done anything wrong."

"Maybe so, but I did agree to see you, that's where I went wrong. I should have told you I was married, but I was frightened you'd walk away. I didn't want that. By saying no to your advances I believed I wasn't doing anything wrong, but deep down I knew."

"Okay, let me speak now. I'm a few years younger than you. I've been around the block a few times and like most of us I guess I'm searching for that one special somebody. That might not be you, I might have to search for a few more years before I meet my soul mate."

Grace's face twisted in anguish.

"What I do know is I've never met anyone like you and I'd like to get to know you better. If it means as a friend only, then so be it. Let the chips fall as they may. So how about using me as a sounding board and having a couple of drinks while you tell me all about you."

"Oh my God, you are such a smooth talker!" She smiled, reached across and planted a kiss upon his cheek. "I'll have that drink with you, but not here. Somewhere far, far, away."

"Okay, I know just the place, only joking!" He laughed at her. She smiled back. Thirty minutes of chit-chat mainly about nothing followed until they found a small quiet pub nestling in the hills of the Chilterns.

# Chapter 7

Terry, Jim and Bob glanced at the clock above the bar, it was just after eight and no Joe. They'd all heard the news about Joe passing his driving test, and half expected him to pick them up. When he didn't show Jim spoke to Bob, "Are you sure he didn't say anything to you."

"Of course I'm sure."

"Then something must've happened with that older bird last Friday, the dirty dog," concluded Jim.

"He didn't say anything to you on Sunday?" asked Bob.

"No, and where the fuck were you?

"He must have been screwing that ginger bird," said Terry as he placed a tray of drinks on the table.

"She's not ginger, her hair's a deep red, and her name's Rebecca," said Bob.

"Deep red, get you, you queer boy," laughed Terry. "I still might have a go at it!" he added.

"You can fuck right off Terry," snapped Bob, "Or else." The look he gave Terry spoke volumes.

"Easy, easy, just pulling your pisser!"

"Okay children! No point in falling out over crumpet," said Jim.

"She's got a name!" snapped Bob.

"Okay, change the subject, this bird Joe's seeing, what's she like?" asked Terry.

"Out of your league," said Bob, still smarting about Terry's remarks.

"Classy looking, not really Joe's type," said Jim.

"And you'd know all about classy birds," chipped in Bob, glad the attention had switched to Joe.

"Oh yeah, you had a crush on that girl from the big house that went to private school," added Terry.

"I ain't seen her in ages," replied Jim.

"You didn't even ask her out, did yah?" goaded Terry.

"No, I didn't, missed my chance."

"She'd probably have said no," said Bob.

"Probably, but I was young then, wasn't sure of myself."

Bob looked at the clock, it was quarter past nine and Joe hadn't shown. It was two or three minutes later when Eric walked in with Gloria by his side, both looking like movie stars. He nodded to the boys, before seating his wife at a small table.

"Flash git," said Terry.

"He owe you money?" asked Bob.

Terry ignored the question, "We staying here all night or are we going elsewhere?"

"If we win tomorrow, there's bound to be some celebration, so I reckon I'll stick here tonight," replied Jim.

"Yeah, me too. Might be a heavy night," agreed Bob.

"It's alright for you two, I'm gonna be stuck with the missus and her mother."

"Come off it Terry, if you wanted you could easily wrangle a night out," said Bob.

Everyone knew that Terry had it made. Heather wasn't a bad sort, quite nice looking really, her only flaw was she let Terry get away with murder

Half an hour later Eric rose from his seat and walked into the gents. Seconds later Terry got up, smiled and followed him.

"If I didn't know better I'd think they were a couple of poofs," said Jim. "As long as he's washed his hands when he come out, he can get the drinks in," laughed Bob.

# Chapter 8

In a quiet corner of the quaint little pub in Chalfont St Peter's, Joe listened intensely to Grace's tale of woe.

"When I first met Sean, I fell head over heels for him. He was tall, worldly and ten years older than me. He was everything a woman could wish for." Grace couldn't help but notice Joe's expression change. "Don't forget I was very impressionable, after all I was only just eighteen. A week before actually."

Joe smiled, "I can't imagine you a love struck teenager."

"Believe me, I was as green as grass, butter wouldn't melt."

For the next ten minutes Grace and Joe talked about the movies, the films they liked and just about anything than wasn't directly related to Grace and her wonderful husband.

"Do you need another," he indicated to her glass. "I'll just get us a refill." He walked across the flagstone floor, negotiating his way passed a couple of tables and stepped up to the bar. "Light and bitter and a vodka and lime, with just a cube of ice."

While he waited for his order he glance across and gave her a little wave. He cursed himself for being soft. She was even better looking than he'd first thought. He began to doubt himself, what the fuck was she wasting her time with him for. Gathering his drinks he steeled himself for the walk back. Act casual, he kept telling himself. He needn't have worried, she smiled as he placed her drink on the table.

"Right where were we?" he said, trying to appear worldly.

"I'm not going to lie to you Joe. Life with Sean was great. He took me to exclusive clubs and casinos in the West End. He showed me a side of life I'd never seen before. It was a whirlwind romance, he swept me off my feet. I loved him, he was so manly, so together."

Joe was beginning to feel inadequate as pangs of jealousy set in.

"Within a year he asked me to marry him. I said yes, who wouldn't, I felt like the luckiest girl alive. He was far more considerate than I expected. When my parents suggested we wait until I was twenty one Sean looked at me and said, "Why not, we've got the rest of our lives together. My parents loved him, he was the ideal prospective son-in-law."

Grace stopped for a moment gathering her thoughts, she choked back an involuntary sigh, reliving it was becoming painful. She steeled herself to go on. "We got married at Caxton Hall just over a year later. Our future looked assured, we had a detached house, small but comfortable. Sean was in line for a promotion, the future was looking bright. When Sean suggested we try for a baby I was over the moon." She smiled reassuringly at Joe, "Sorry."

Joe forced a smile. "Go on."

"We didn't panic when nothing happened, but as month followed month, I noticed subtle changes in his demeanour and the way he treated me. Sean was always agitated. I told myself it was down to the sheer frustration and disappointment. We rowed constantly, well actually it was more Sean flying into a rage."

"Just because you couldn't conceive?" asked Joe.

Grace nodded, "I'd tell him, it's nobody's fault and it'll happen in its own time. We just have to be patient." Joe could see by the look upon her face that she was hurting inside. He tried telling her it was enough, but she shushed away his protest.

"He'd come back at me with, I don't want parents at the school gates thinking I'm old enough to be a grandfather, fuck no!"

"Couldn't he see how much he was hurting you?"

"I don't think he cared. Things had begun to change between us, he'd stay out all night. At first he blamed it on the job, but as one disappointment followed another, he stopped with the reasons. I could smell the drink, the aroma of different perfumes. "It's the job," he'd cry. But I knew he was seeing other women. Then one night around two in the morning he burst into our bedroom, so drunk he could hardly stand. "I'm gonna make you pregnant even if it kills you!" Then he forced himself on me."

Joe let out an involuntary gasp.

"I'm sorry Joe, I have to finish telling you everything. In the morning he was sorry and begged my forgiveness. I recoiled from him. He was not the man I'd married. It was becoming a living hell. A week later he came to me and said we should seek help. He had contacts with doctors at a nearby clinic close to Harley Street."

Tears began forming in Grace's dusky brown eyes.

Joe placed a hand upon hers, employing her to stop. She gave a small shake of her head.

"I was given a thorough examination and physical and they took all sorts of x-rays. We went back again a week later, they said there was a slight concern, something to do with my ovaries. They did another series of tests. All this time Sean was the man I'd married, kind and attentive. We were sharing a new experience together. I thought we'd turned a corner and somehow forcing himself on me had brought him to his senses."

"I'm so sorry," replied Joe, feeling a little out of his depth. He noticed a nervous twitch and her tears fell gently down her cheeks. "Grace, you don't have to say anymore."

She took a deep breath, "Oh but I do. Two weeks later the clinic sent us their report. My fallopian tubes were not functioning properly, which caused the doctor some concern. The follow up examination had found one of my ovaries had stopped working while the other was damaged. The chance of me becoming pregnant was zero. I was devastated. But instead of giving me the support I needed Sean went into his shell. He didn't seem to understand or care how I was feeling. Our life hadn't been great up until then, now it came crashing down with a vengeance."

"The bastard," exclaimed Joe, a little too loud.

"Shush," she said and placed two fingers gently across his lips. "I understand your anger, but as my friend," she squeezed his hand gently, "you need to let me tell you all of it."

Joe nodded, took a sip of his beer and felt really foolish.

"The problems in our marriage spilled over into his job. Two or three cases folded partly because he'd dropped the ball. He was passed over for the promotion. His future career in the Metropolitan Police was put on hold."

"He's a copper!"

"Detective Sergeant in the Flying Squad. That's why I didn't want to meet you. He can be very bad news!"

"Okay, I understand. But why have you stayed with him. Has he changed?"

"He's changed alright. He's become cold and distant. He blames me for everything. He treats me like dirt, like I'm his property. Our marriage has become a sham. I'm nothing more to him than a charade. The Met's social gatherings are a place for him to mix with the top echelons of the force, networking he calls it. Having a sound marriage is important to the top brass and his chances of a promotion."

Grace's voice was rising almost hysterically, "Most of the time I'm living a lie, while he's hardly at home, spending most of his time either catching crooks or he's fucking any number of women."

A number of pub customers turned their heads. Grace rose from the table, her face flushed with embarrassment. "I think we should go, this has been a mistake!"

Joe looked stunned at the outburst. "Okay, he said, still a little shell-shocked from Grace's revelations.

Within seconds they exited the pub and ventured across the road to the car park. As Joe opened Grace's door she turned and faced him.

"So Joe now you know why I can't see you. He's a very dangerous man, you don't know what he's capable of."

She climbed inside and Joe quickly raced around to the driver's side, a dark thought entering his head.

"Has he hit you?" he asked as he closed the door.

Grace hesitated.

Joe fought to contain his rage, he knew that to go off half-cocked would show Grace his immaturity. "The fucker doesn't deserve you."

Grace gave half a smile.

"Don't take this the wrong way, I want you to be honest with me. How old are you?"

Grace looked puzzled, "I'm twenty eight. Why?"

"I'm twenty two" he lied, just a white lie he told himself, "I'm twenty three in September."

"The difference in our age doesn't matter, you're my friend."

"I want to be more than a friend. I've known you only a few hours, but I'm hooked."

"That's very sweet, but I don't think you understand."

"I understand enough. Daft as it sounds, I think I'm in love with you." The words were out, he'd been struggling to restrain them all evening.

Grace smiled, sighed and smiled again. "Yes it does sound daft, you can't possibly be in love with me. Joe you're a nice man, yes I believe we are attracted to each other, but attraction isn't love."

Joe had a wounded look in his eyes, his stomach churned. He wanted this woman more than life itself. He couldn't give up without a fight. In desperation he played his last hand. "Answer me one question. I haven't stopped thinking about you since we met, have you thought about me?"

Grace looked sad, uncertain and unsure what to say next. Through the illumination of the street light Joe saw Grace's eyes overflow with tears. Her guard was fully down, she looked vulnerable, his heart felt like breaking in two. "Yes," she said softly, "every day." Joe slid along the leather bench seat of the

Zodiac, put his arms around her and stared into those glistening dark eyes and leaned forward. Grace reciprocated his advance. Their lips grew closer, they were past the point of no return. Their lips met softly and their world changed in that unforgettable moment.

# Chapter 9

"They think it's all over, it is now," those words took on a life of their own. England had just won the World Cup Final, and the boys were going out to celebrate, along with millions of England fans up and down the country. Terry had told Heather he was going out with the boys to celebrate. As usual, as long as there was a good excuse she'd let him go.

Washed and shaved, Terry added the finishing touch as he combed his premature blue grey hair back and admired the distinguished look it gave him. "I could kiss you," he said to his reflection. His clothes for the night were all neatly lined up on his bed. He was looking to have a good time and if there was any chance of pulling a bird he was up for it. 'Nothing like a bit of stray,' he thought.

Heather was getting the kids their tea, while her mother was wearing out her welcome. There was nothing like your mother telling you what you already knew, Heather gave her a withering look.

"You let him have too much of his own way. Nothing good will come of it, mark my words."

"He's a good husband, he provides for me and the kids, said Heather.

"No more than he should."

"You shouldn't say that mum, he's taking us all for a meal at the Swan and Bottle in Uxbridge tomorrow evening, it's a Berni Inn," she said proudly.

"He's flush."

"He got a bonus in his pay last night, Terry works hard, shift work's no joke and nights are a killer," said Heather, with an edge of impatience creeping into her voice. 'Another six days,' she thought wistfully.

Joe picked Bob up at seven. "About time I got to be driven around in this heap," said Bob.

"Great game, weren't it?"

"Yeah, great game," replied Joe with no real enthusiasm.

"What's got into you?" asked Bob.

"I'll tell you down the pub."

"Can't wait," said Bob with a hint of sarcasm.

Minutes later they stepped into the George saloon bar. They ordered their drinks and sat down in a far corner, away from prying ears. "Okay, what gives? You were obviously seeing that bird from the Starlight."

"Yeah I was, but it's not what you're thinking. It's complicated," said Joe.

"Oh fuck! She's married!" exclaimed Bob.

"Why'd you say that?"

"I might not have the education that you have, but it don't take a genius to work that one out."

"You're my best mate, what I tell you, stays between us," said Joe

"That goes without saying."

"Bob, I've never met anyone like her. She's gorgeous!"

"Yeah, they all are, replied Bob. "Get on with it before Jim and Terry arrive."

"She's married, but not happily." Joe looked at Bob, he wasn't sure he should continue, but he needed to tell someone. "We haven't done anything yet. I've only kissed her," he paused for the briefest time, "it was the most wonderful moment of my life."

"Oh for fuck sake, have you heard yourself."

"Yeah, I know I sound daft, but I can't help it. I love her."

"You think you do, once you do the business you might think otherwise," said Bob. 'Who the fuck am I to give advice, no one's more cunt-struck than me,' he thought.

"You're wrong Bob, believe it or not, but she's the one."

"Okay, so I'll go along with you. First, you'll be involved in a messy divorce, then if you come out of that with anything more than pocket change, what happens then?"

"It's early days, we're taking it slow."

Bob laughed, "You might be taking it slow, but me, I'm in the fast lane."

Joe relaxed, "Yeah, I forgot, you've tied yourself up with a fiery redhead. Be careful, you don't want to end up like Terry.

"Did someone call my name, mine's a Guinness and bitter as you're in the chair," laughed Terry as he and Jim crashed through the double doors.

"And a stout and cider," echoed Jim.

Moments later they were all sitting huddled together talking about the match, "Stuffed the Germans good and proper," laughed Bob.

"Don't care what they say, Hurst's goal was over the line," said Terry.

"Didn't matter in the end," added Jim

"Time to decide where we're off too. I fancy the Oldfield," said Terry, "last time I was there, it was wall to wall crumpet."

"We ain't been to Top Rank in Watford for a while," suggested Jim.

"Chances are we're gonna have a skin-full, so I reckon we should stay close, maybe the Clay."

"You just want to check that your bird ain't putting it about!" laughed Terry.

"Fuck off," cried Bob. In truth, Terry had hit the nail on the head.

"I'll go along with where ever you decide," volunteered Joe. Since his night out with Grace, he'd no desire to chat up girls.

"The Oldfield, it is then," announced Terry, "Seeing as no one can decide, plus it's closer than Watford."

"Bob looked aggrieved, but said nothing.

"We'll go in my car," said Terry. "But I have to warn you, if I pull, you're all walking home."

"We'll meet you down there," said Joe. You ain't likely to pull, but if you do, I ain't walking. You riding with me Bob?"

"Yeah."

"Thanks a lot, leaving me with Romeo," cried Jim as he glanced at Terry.

The Oldfield was heaving. It was as Terry had predicted, wall to wall crumpet. He wasted no time chatting up the ladies, mainly because shift work and family life got in the way far more than he liked. At twenty five, Terry was tallish, good looking and above all confident. His looks and his easy charm, made him a hit with the ladies wherever he went. Dressed in the latest style, with his blue black hair swept back, exposing a manly forehead, he had it made.

'But,' as Bob reflected, 'he got caught at such an early age,' It amused him. Terry was a good mate, but he could irritate the fuck out of you, on an occasion.

After negotiating his way around the dance hall and the bars, searching for but hoping not to see Becky, he relaxed. She'd told him she was babysitting at her sister's. She'd even asked him if he wanted to join her, he declined, hoping the footie would live up to expectations. He'd told her he thought he and the boys would probably end up at the Clay, so ending up at the Oldfield and bumping into Becky would have been awkward. He'd known her barely a week, but had found himself looking forward to being with her. He thought of how Terry had messed his life up. He hoped his didn't end up the same way. Becky was wild and free; sexually her behaviour was exciting and he couldn't get enough of her. His only fear was that he didn't know whether he could trust her.

He looked at his best friends, there was Terry, trying to squeeze every bit out of his life, Jim the strong silent type, good job, earning decent, but of late, looking for something else, but what. Finally there was Joe, his mate since primary school, head over heels in love with a married woman, love-struck or what.

Then the inevitable happened. The evening was jumping, everyone was happy until Terry tried pulling this little blonde. He as usual was winning her over when her bloke a tall hefty Scotsman, came back from the bar. He took her by the arm and pushed her towards the bar. Terry realising the situation and not wanting to get his face smashed in, backed away.

"Sorry mate, my mistake!"

"Yeah it was pal!"

Terry never saw it coming, the Jock landed a haymaker to the side of Terry's jaw. He went down like a ton of bricks. The big Scotsman turned and had begun walking back to his girlfriend when Terry picked himself up.

"That the best you can do?"

"Oh fuck" thought Bob.

"What the fuck did you just say?"

"You heard. Besides your girlfriend has already given me her phone number," he lied.

The Jock glanced at his girlfriend, then in a mad rush, as Terry expected he charged. Terry cool as you like sidestepped and kicked the legs from under him. The Scotsman's momentum sending him crashing to the floor. Terry was on him in an instant, landing blow after blow. He needed to finish it as quickly as he could, before the big man got his second wind. The element of surprise only works once.

Before he could finish the man, a bouncer had lifted him off the Scotsman and was marching Terry to the exit.

"Time we went," said Joe as the three of them followed the bouncer to the car park.

Terry got a couple of smacks from the bouncer, before Bob grabbed the bouncer's arm. "That's enough, we're going."

The bouncer glared at Bob and saw the wild look in his eyes. His job was done, no point in escalating the situation. "Get on your way! That fucking mad Jock will be baying for your blood, now fuck off!"

Joe had already read the situation, and was now reversing his car back to the boys.

"Get in now!" he screamed.

"What about my car," shouted Terry?

"Fuck your car!" said Bob

"Jump in, we'll come back for it!" added Jim.

The Zodiac burning rubber sped out of the car park with the Scotsman and five of his mates shouting and hurling pint glasses at the speeding car.

The noise inside the Zodiac was deafening. The laugher and bravado took a while to calm down but eventually was replaced by a more sombre reflection of the night's events.

"If that fucker had got hold of you, we'd be visiting you in hospital!" laughed Jim.

"Why the fuck did you taunt him about his bird," asked Joe.

"It seemed like a good idea at the time, and besides the fucker hit me first. Now can't we circle back so I can get my car?"

"Give it a few minutes, then how's about a Chinese," suggested Joe.

"Yeah, a good idea, oh and by the way, I didn't think you had it in you," laughed Bob. "I suppose on the plus side we ain't visiting the Oldfield again anytime soon."

# Chapter 10

Jim pulled into the George car park and was surprised that Terry's Rover wasn't in its usual place. Then he remembered Terry was spending the entire day with his family. Joe should be arriving soon, he thought. When Bob breezed in at half past twelve Jim was feeling agitated. "Where is everybody?"

"Everybody is me," said Bob, "Terry's playing the family man and as for Joe, fucked if I know."

"Maybe he's seeing that new bird."

"Possibly, but I doubt it," said Bob.

"What do you know that I don't?"

"Nothing. All I know is it's a bit complicated."

"She's married. The dirty lucky git!" exclaimed Jim.

"He don't tell me anything anymore."

Jim was a thinker, a dreamer even, but above all he had an itch that needed to be scratched. His friends didn't see it, but each of them was going on their own journeys. He'd been thinking about it for some time, but with Terry domesticated, well at least as domesticated as Terry could be, Joe besotted by some woman that would eventually blow him out, the writing was on the wall. As for Bob, he didn't know it yet but he was very soon to follow Terry to that prison called marriage.

Eric walked in around twenty past one and sat down with the boys. "What's up?" he asked.

"The future," said Jim.

"Go on, I'm intrigued."

"You're married, you've a decent house, you're well dressed and money doesn't seem a problem. What's your secret?"

"Don't get caught," laughed Eric.

"No, I get that Eric, but what is it you're striving for?"

"Fuck me Bob, who pulled his chain?"

Jim ignored Eric's quip, "You don't get it. I don't want to be here in this boozer doing the same things, day in day out, in ten years' time."

"Ambition! That's what you're talking about. I get it," said Eric. He took a sip of his scotch, savouring the taste as the warming liquid went down. "I ain't knocking you guys, but you've had a relatively easy life. Me, I was brought up in the East End, didn't have two farthings to rub together. I started nicking when I was four years old. A clip round the ear, if I was lucky, the strap if I weren't, taught me one thing. If there's something I want, go out and get it, just don't get caught. Most of my mates did bird, partly because they couldn't care less or they were plain stupid. I learned early on the art of stealing. It's simple, look at the Great Train Robbers, where did they go wrong. The greatest heist in history, but their plans were flawed, they got caught!"

"I ain't talking about stealing, I'm talking about life," said Jim.

"It's the same Jim. Whatever you do in life, someone always gets hurt. The secret is making sure it ain't you."

"Who wants another beer?" cried Bob.

The theoretical discussion met its end.

Jim arrived home for Sunday roast with his mum, dad and his sister Pauline none the wiser. Apart from his desire to do something different. He'd always been a saver, in fact his pride and joy the Vauxhall Cresta, had been his first project in the art of saving. Jim had always worked. From the paper round, to sweeping up at the local shops, to being kitchen staff in a nearby hotel, all before his fourteenth birthday. He supplemented his wages as an apprentice with two or three different part-time jobs. Now earning a decent wage he'd spent most of his spare time with the boys, the occasional girlfriend, drinking, smoking and raising hell. One girl in particular had caught his eye, he'd first noticed her as a school girl, because her uniform was different to others from surrounding schools. He soon learned it was a private school, that and the fact she lived in a big house on one of Ruislip's prestigious roads. She was definitely out of his league. Years later he met up with her at a dance at Harrow Tech, where The Who were playing. They chatted for a while, she seemed nice and friendly, but just as he was getting into his stride she was swept away by some of her Hooray Henry friends. Out of her league, he might have felt, 'but one day, one day,' he thought.

"I've made a decision," he announced, just as mum served up the roast lamb.

"Oh!" exclaimed dad, "What's that then?"

"I've decided against giving up my job, at least for the foreseeable future."

"Glad you've come to your senses," said dad.

"I'm going to buy a house!"

Mum and dad looked at each other, then at Jim, a shocked expression on both of their faces.

"I thought you'd be pleased?"

"We are son, but it's a lot to take on."

"Does this mean I get your bedroom," said Pauline his soon to be teenage sister.

"Quiet!" said mum, "Let Jim explain."

"Yeah, I know, but I've been thinking, most people my age start thinking about getting married. No, before you jump to conclusions I think I'm a little too young to settle down yet."

"Oh, thank God for that," said his relieved mum.

"Some of my friends, like Terry either get a girl pregnant and apply for a council house, or they get married and take on a mortgage. My idea is different. First I'll apply for a mortgage, I've got my saving to put down on a deposit. My job is secure. That's my first step. Second step, find a suitable two, three bedroom terraced or semi at the right price, then do the place up.

Third step, once it's done up, I'll rent out a room or two, depending on how things are at the time."

"Blimey, you've given this some thought," said dad.

"Yeah I've been thinking of this kind of project for some time," he added. Having listened to Eric at lunchtime, he realised that following his example would either land you in prison or worse. He could see that within a couple of years things would begin to change and although he'd known the boys most of his life his idea of the future was vastly different.

*****

A few hours earlier Joe pulled up at the gates to a park in Wembley. He turned off the ignition, glanced at his watch and waited. He'd hastily said good night to Grace on Friday night and asked when she could see him next. A brief kiss, "Do you know the rear entrance to Barham Park,"

"No, but I'll find it," he'd whispered.

For five agonising minutes he worried that he'd got the wrong entrance. Then he spied a woman heading in his direction. 'That can't be her,' he thought, 'she's a dog walker.

His heart skipped a beat as he realised the woman with the headscarf was indeed Grace. Furtively she looked around then both her and the Corgi leapt into the front seat of the Zodiac. "I can't stay long, Sean's with a colleague at his club. He'll expect me home before he gets back."

"I'm so glad you came," he said as he put the column change into gear and drove away. Joe smiled at Grace and his heart turned to mush. He drove around for a time, wasting the precious minutes they had together, before pulling into a car park. He turned off the ignition, slipped the column change into neutral and pulled on the brake. He turned towards Grace and stared into two pairs of dark brown eyes.

"This is Dusty!" exclaimed Grace.

Within moments Dusty was transferred to the passenger foot well. Joe reached under the seat and pulled a lever which sent the bench seat sliding back. He moved close to Grace and she responded. They embraced and Joe kissed her softly. Their embrace and kiss lasted an eternity before both of them came up for air

"Oh Joe, if only we'd met years ago, things could have been so different." Joe grinned, "If we'd met years ago, I'd have been in short trousers."They both laughed, the elephant in the room long gone. "Seeing you is all I've thought about the whole weekend."

"Likewise," replied Joe.

"Seriously, this is madness. He'd kill you!"

"Madness, but worth it," said Joe. "You told me you feel nothing for him. Yet you're still with him? To me it's simple. File for a divorce, do whatever you have too."

"If only it was that easy. On the surface everyone thinks we're the perfect couple, but we're not. He's got lawyers in his pocket, he could tie me up with legislation for years."

"What if we make it public?"

"Don't even think like that!" she cried. Joe's outburst had suddenly brought clarity to their situation. Although a man in size his immaturity was clear for her to see. It was sheer madness. "We've known each other for a week, not even that. This isn't working. I thought you'd understand. It's my fault I should never have agreed to see you."

"Don't say that Grace."

"I'm sorry, you're a nice man, but I couldn't subject you to Sean, he'd eat you alive. I don't know what I was thinking. Take me back."

"Sorry! I'm sorry, it was a dumb thing to say. I want you, and I believe you want me. Please don't throw us away."

Tears fell from Grace's eyes, smudging her makeup. "If things had been different…" Words weren't enough. "Take me back."

At the gates of Barham Park, he tried one last time. "Don't give up on me."

She smiled leaned over and kissed his cheek. "I'm sorry." Then her and Dusty quickly climbed out and walked briskly through the gate entrance. Joe watched through teary eyes as his world was shattered into tiny pieces.

# Chapter 11

Friday 12<sup>th</sup> August changed many lives. It was all over the news by 6 o'clock. Three police officers had been gunned down on the streets of Acton. After the euphoria of the World Cup, England descended into darkness. Joe had never had bad thoughts about anyone, but for the briefest of moments as he scanned the newspapers, he hoped one of those police officers was Grace's husband. He'd been in a dark mood for the best part of two weeks. Bob had tried talking to him but to no avail, Jim was wrapped up with buying a property, but Terry seeing his mate so forlorn decided on direct action.

On the Saturday afternoon he contacted Eric.

"What the fuck are you calling me for? Have you read the papers?"

"Yeah, it's nothing like that. That bird Joe pulled at the Starlight, she's given him the elbow. But all he does is mope about."

"Tell him to grow up!"

"We've tried all that. You see, her husband is a copper, his first name is Sean and he's a detective sergeant in the Flying Squad: he's in his late thirties. Oh and his wife's name is Grace."

"So, what's that to me?"

"Can you make enquires as to what this geezer's full name is, and where they live."

"You want a lot!" exclaimed Eric. "My best advice is for you to tell Joe to forget about her. Coppers is bad news."

"Just make enquires, I'll owe you."

"You bet, you'll owe me. I ain't making promises, I'll see what I can do."

48

A massive manhunt had begun. Two of the three men suspected of the murders were apprehended within a couple of days. Harry Roberts's name was on every policeman's lips. He'd gone to ground literally. Police leave was cancelled for the foreseeable future as they began the search.

"Bob, a word!" cried Terry

"Yeah, what do you want?

"It's Joe, I asked Eric if he had any contacts who could find out where this bird lives."

"What good will that do?"

"If Eric comes up with the goods it might help Joe to realise he's backing a loser."

"Okay, but don't mention this to anyone, least of all Joe."

"Do you think I'm daft?"

"I won't answer that," laughed Bob.

*****

Jim had made tentative enquires with his bank and a local building society. He met with negativity at his branch, the manager of his bank said, "Usually we have young couples coming to see me. They have what they believe is enough of a deposit. Sometimes the hard facts put them off. It is an important step and shouldn't be taken lightly."

'Pompous old git,' thought Jim. "How far will one thousand go towards a deposit?" The bank manager looked surprised. "Check my account."

The bank manager excused himself and left the office, returning a few minutes later full of bluster. "Mr Newton, Jim is it. Looking at our files I see, you have more than enough to cover a deposit. What kind of property are we talking about?"

Ten minutes later Jim and his dad left the bank and crossed the road and entered the Leeds Building Society. "No way am I going to be talked down too by some old git," said Jim.

"He assumed," said Dad.

"He assumed wrong, didn't he."

Jim's dad was beginning to notice a change in his son, the boy was waking up. His son had been in the wilderness since leaving grammar school. He'd studied for his engineering degree, and was holding on to a decent job, but as of yet he hadn't shown any ambition to better himself, until now.

Within half an hour, they walked out of the building society with the promise of a mortgage offer. "Next stop, the estate agents," said Dad.

"Wow!" exclaimed Jim, "that was easier than I'd thought." An idea began to form inside Jim's head.

*****

The hunt for Harry Roberts was in its first full week, there had been sighting of him in various places, but so far there was no real trace. The boys were drinking in the George.

"I suppose Bob's seeing his bird," said Jim.

"Don't know, don't really care," said Joe, a wounded look still in his eyes.

"What you need is a kick up the arse," said Terry angrily. "Get out there and find yourself a bit of stray. Give her a good seeing too. It's the only way."

"Yeah, I hate to say it but I think Terry's right. When you fall off a horse you get back on it as quickly as possible," said Jim.

"Grace ain't a horse," replied Joe defensively. Then Eric walked in. He was alone, dapper as usual. He casually nodded across, ordered a double scotch and stayed at the bar.

"Who's he waiting for?" said Jim.

"Fucked if I know," added Joe morosely.

"You're gonna have to pull yourself together sooner rather than later," said Terry.

"You don't understand, we had chemistry. She was into me as much as I was into her."

"All of four inches then," laughed Jim.

"Fuck off!"

"Only joking, there was a time when you had a sense of humour."

"It just hurts."

Terry looked across to Eric wondering who he was waiting for, when he was beckoned over. Grabbing his pint he said, "Excuse me a moment, bit of business." He stood up and smiled before walking across to the bar.

"You owe me big time," said Eric. "Do you want the good news or the bad news?

"The good news," said Terry.

"The good news is there is no good news. Your little mate over there has just avoided a hornet's nest. Detective Sergeant Sean Fallon, hot shot high flyer of the Flying Squad is one bad fucker. Messing with that bastard's wife, could in the worst case scenario get him killed. He's one corrupt cunt. He's connected to some highly dangerous individuals, as well as allegedly having the ear of one of the top brass."

"Fuck me, I wish I hadn't asked."

"Forget you did," replied Eric, "Joe's a nice guy. He doesn't deserve a shit storm."

"I've never seen him like this, in fact he's getting to be a bit of a pain. Joe's not stupid, perhaps knowing who he's up against, might make him forget about her," said Terry.

"People do the dumbest things in the cause of love. Personally I'd leave things lie."

"Joe ain't like us," said Terry.

"Okay, but it's his funeral."

# Chapter 12

It was a sunny Sunday afternoon, a little humid, but under the shade of a willow tree at Ruislip Lido it was just perfect. Rebecca had suggested a picnic and had recruited her mum to put it all together. They'd taken out a row boat and rowed across the man-made lake and found a deserted little inlet, with its own piece of beach.

It was as Bob exclaimed, "A perfect place for a picnic, no prying eyes."

Within minutes he'd moored the row boat on the small sandy beach. What did it matter if they arrived back at the boathouse three hours late, when there was the delights of everything the picnic had to offer?

After helping Becky out of the boat and laying down a blanket to lie on, Bob turned towards Becky and said, "You know I've been thinking, your old man's right, I should think about a trade."

"Where did that come from!" exclaimed Rebecca.

"I'm good at my job, but as Tom says, labouring is a young man's game."

"What's brought this on, it can't be my dad's influence?" she laughed.

"We've been going out solid for the last three weeks, I like you a lot and I really hope you like me."

"You ain't going to propose are you? I hope not," said a startled Rebecca.

"No! Fuck off," he laughed. You and me are okay as it is. At least I hope we are?

"Rebecca slumped back down, relief wafting over her. "Yeah Bob, we're good. I like you a lot, and maybe when we…if we see each other for long enough I might even fall in love with you."

"Don't do me any favours," he laughed and swung himself on top of her and stared into her green eyes. Her ripe red lips framing a row of perfectly white teeth demanded he kiss her passionately. Within moments they were devouring each other as if the world was going to explode.

After their lovemaking, they lay side by side staring into an almost perfect blue sky with only a few wispy clouds floating across their vision.

"These few weeks have changed me, a little over a month ago I was looking forward to the World Cup, to drinking beer and to maybe getting lucky."

"You did, you met me!"

"Yeah, but it's not just that. Me and my mates, we're close you know. But since the final, we seem to be going in different directions. Terry's already married, got a third kid on the way."

"Is that the future you want?"

"God no! One day maybe."

"Yeah," she cried softly.

"Then there's Jim, he's western mad, a bit of a dreamer, only the other week we thought he was going to chuck it all in and go see the world. He's a saver see, got a good job and not that long ago bought himself a four year old Vauxhall Cresta. Now it looks like he's buying a house. Which leaves me and Joe, he's down in the dumps at the moment and I'm over the moon."

Becky smiled. "I'm not daft enough to expect it to last, but your old man's words kept ringing in my ears. I've got to make something of myself."

*****

Joe sat in the Zodiac watching an office block in Alperton. He glanced at his watch, it was 12.20. His nerves were on edge as he waited for Grace to leave the office at lunchtime. While he waited, he replayed the moment his heart started to beat again.

*Terry had been standing at the bar talking to Eric. Minutes later both of them replenished their glasses and approach the table where Jim and Joe were sitting. It was Terry who spoke first.*

*"Joe, I had a word with Eric on your behalf. Tell me to mind my own, but I think you need to hear what Eric has to say."*

*"Terry asked me to put the feelers out about a certain detective sergeant."*

*Joe looked shell-shocked.*

*"As I told him, you're better off leaving things as they are."*

*"That's for me to decide! None of your business!" snapped Joe.*

*Eric snapped back, "Do you want to hear or not? I'm just giving you a friendly warning."*

*"Sorry Eric, yeah I want to know."*

*"This woman, is called Grace Fallon, from what I've heard she comes from a nice family in Elstree. Her husband is Detective Sergeant Sean Fallon. He my friend is one nasty bastard, he's as bent as they come. He has connections to some of the nastiest villains in London. He's also well connected within the Met. Which means if you fuck with him, you could end up in the canal. That cunt doesn't mess about."*

*"He's a copper, he wouldn'…"*

*"Wouldn't he! There are coppers and then there are the likes of DS Fallon. My advice, and I can see you won't take it, is stay away," warned Eric.*

*"Thanks Eric, and you Terry, thanks," said Joe.*

*"You ain't listening to me are you? This woman…"*

*"Grace," stated Joe.*

*"This Grace, knows the score, she did you a favour."*

*"I just need to see her."*

*"If you could and she told you to sling your hook, would you take the hint and fucking leave it alone?" Eric was losing his patience.*

*"Yeah, if she tells me to back off I will."*

*"Against my better nature, she works in some office block in the centre of Alperton."*

Joe looked at his watch it was 12.30. A small trickle of people began to emerge from the office block. His heart was beating nineteen to the dozen. He waited, his expectations depleting, then suddenly there she was; Grace. His heart skipped a beat as she turned and begun walking down the high street. Slipping the car into gear he drove past her and stopped about 50 yards in front. He waited with baited breath as she almost walked past.

"Hello Grace," he stammered.

"What! Oh my God, please go, please go before anyone sees." Grace looked panicked.

"Get in the car, I only want to talk to you. Please!"

Grace made a furtive look around then climbed into the car. Joe without taking his eyes off the road indicated and pulled into the opening in the traffic.

"You shouldn't be here! Someone might see."

Joe said nothing and concentrated on driving. Within minutes he found a half empty car park and drove into it. He parked, switched off the engine and turned and gazed into the distressed look upon her face.

"Tell me nothing happened when you saw me," He placed his hand across his chest. "I believe you did! If I'm wrong tell me, and you'll never see me again."

Grace sounded resigned, "Oh Joe, you don't realise what you're getting into. Of course I felt something. I've been miserable since we parted"

His heart leapt, "I know all about Detective Sergeant Sean Fallon. I know he's dangerous. I've done my homework, I also know that if you feel the same, even half as much as I feel towards you, then we've got a chance and we must take it."

The determination in Joe's voice took Grace aback. She'd known from the first moment she'd caught sight of him in the Starlight Ballroom; that's why she'd left so hurriedly.

'Perhaps,' she thought, 'no impossible!' she quickly corrected herself. She looked across at Joe and her heart lurched. 'Maybe, this is meant to be.' She looked out of the window at the parked cars, her eyes searching, 'for what? For someone to recognise me, for an excuse to end this madness?' "What the hell," she cried as she moved up close to Joe, "Kiss me."

Joe looked into those dark sparkling eyes and did what was asked. They shared a long lingering kiss, both not wanting the moment to end. As their lips parted she whispered, "This is madness."

"Agreed, but delicious madness."

"I don't know where this will lead us," cautioned Grace.

"Nor do I," replied Joe. "All I know is I can't stop thinking about you."

"Oh Joe, I only hope it'll be worth it. Sean was my first love. I never thought he'd hurt me. How could I have got it so wrong?"

"You were young, impressionable and slightly naïve."

"Young, like you?" she blurted, before she added a soft unspoken sorry.

"Yeah, I'm younger than you, but that's just a number. I ain't in this for the short haul. Whatever it takes, I'm here for you." He kissed her again and she responded. For the next thirty five minutes they talked, and they kissed, they laid plans; beginning with agreeing to meet on Friday night at their bus stop.

# Chapter 13

Getting the suitable property was more difficult than Jim had imagined. He and his dad had walked into the first estate agents that they came too. Jim had the mortgage which was music to the estate agent's ears. By the time they emerged they were a whole lot wiser.

"You know Dad, I thought second-hand car dealers were shifty, but that creep took the biscuit."

"Yeah, but we learned a lot, he at least told us that location was king, what to look out for, damp being a money spinner."

"Along with electrics and plumbing," added Jim.

"Freehold or leasehold. When you can pull out of a purchase and any number of other worrying things. Before you jump the gun, a bit of research would at least let these sharks know you're no mug."

"Agreed!"

Over dinner that night, Jim decided on a business plan. He'd find a suitable property, but for whom? There were questions on every aspect, I've no intention of saddling myself with a wife and kids, at least not in the short term. So buying as an investment might be the way to go. Renting, but on short term lets? There were more questions than answers. Jim decided he needed to consult either a bank manager or a firm of solicitors. Looking through the phone book he found a local law firm called Chandler and Lowe. He made an appointment for the following Friday afternoon at 1.30.

The appointment was far more enlightening than he could have imagined. Firstly he was shown into the office of a junior partner who listened to what Jim had to say. He listened intensely before explaining all the benefits and the pitfalls of taking on such a venture.

"It's not really my field of expertise, I think you would benefit from speaking to someone in our conveyancing department." He picked up the phone, "Are you free Georgia. I have a young man with an interesting venture, who I believe might need your guidance."

A brief handshake later and Jim was shown into another office. The young woman rose from her chair and held out her hand across the desk. Jim took it but it was only after he'd shook her hand and been offered a seat that he recognised the woman sitting opposite. That auburn pixie cut hair style he'd come to admire from afar was smiling back at him. It was Georgia, the girl of his dreams, the now 23 year old privately educated woman that he'd spoken too, oh so briefly over the last ten years.

"What is it I can help you with?" she asked.

'Plenty,' thought Jim, as his brain turned to mush. "I want to put my savings to work, I've obtained a mortgage and I want to invest in property."

Georgia smiled as Jim handed over his mortgage documents for her to peruse. "I know you, I use to see you on my way home from school," she said casually as she opened the folder.

"We spoke once, briefly at Harrow Tech."

There was no reaction to his remark as Georgia looked over his documents. He sat silent for what was just a brief moment but to Jim it felt like an eternity.

"Everything seems to be in order, I would be happy to represent you once you find a suitable property."

"Great!" he said, his mind telling him he wasn't going anywhere else. "What kind of property would you suggest?" Jim wanted their brief conversation to last a while longer.

"If you were to live in the property, I'd suggest spending as much as you can afford, without breaking the bank. If on the other hand you want renters, they will off set your mortgage, but you would have a number of legal requirements to take into consideration. These we could handle for you, no problem," she smiled. "That's what I'm here for."

Jim smiled back.

"The plus side to renters would mean you could increase the mortgage and buy a bigger, better property. If you had a short term lease of say two years, renewable as and when, you could see a substantial profit, increasing the rent pro rata of course. No point in you being out of pocket." She gave him a brief smile, before continuing. "The benefit of this, after a period of time, you could revisit your mortgage and invest in a second, possibly third property."

"I wish!"

"If you're serious, that should be your intention," Georgia said confidently.

"Yeah, you're right, I've a lot to learn."

"Is there anything else I could help you with," she said.

Jim saw no rings on her fingers, not even an engagement ring, "Well yeah, you could have dinner with me tonight?" 'Fuck no, why did I say that?' he thought. Jim hated rejection, if only he could put the genie back in the bottle.

"Okay, what time?"

"What! Whatever time's good for you," Jim was stunned. "Where would you like… to eat?"

"I'm easy, Chinese, Italian, or maybe a steak," Georgia volunteered, "You choose."

Jim had never been to an Italian restaurant, the only times he ate in a Chinese was late at night after eight pints. His safest bet was the Swan and Bottle."

Georgia could sense his indecision, "I could murder a steak," she suggested.

"What time shall I pick you up?" asked Jim

"Around seven would be nice. Let me give you my address."

"Don't worry I know where it is." He could have kicked himself.

Georgia rose from her seat, motioning that the meeting was at an end. Jim got up, took her extended hand, "Until seven."

"I'll look forward to it."

# Chapter 14

"Who am I, Billy no mates!" said Terry to Eric that Friday night. "Bob's seeing his tart, Joe's seeing that married sort, now Jim phones me and tells me he's been unavoidably detained. So I'm on me Todd!"

"You've only got yourself to blame for Joe. Doing favours can backfire," said Eric. "Anyway, have you anything for me."

"Yeah, I might have' just give me a couple of days, say Wednesday next week."

"I'm taking Gloria to Tenerife in a few weeks' time. Get some winter sun before Christmas. So that will come in handy. Don't let me down."

"No need to worry. This should be a doddle."

"Look Terry, I've some business up the Smoke, if you fancy tagging along you're welcome."

"Nothing worth staying here for, cheers Eric."

*****

"I've a mate that might take you on," said Becky's dad. "He's a plumber by trade, runs his own building company. If you're serious, I'll have a word."

"Never been more serious in my life," replied Bob.

"Good, now that's settled, can we go?" the impatience in Becky's voice clearly aimed at her dad.

"Yeah go, have a good time, just be careful."

Becky gave her father a withering look, then laughed. "Bye Mum, Dad."

Becky tugged at Bob's sleeve, "Come on, or else we'll miss the bus." They just made the bus stop as the double-decker was approaching. Becky climbed the narrow stairs to the top deck.

Bob hurried up behind her. "I see the moon," he joked.

Becky laughed, "You should have seen it last night, there was a man on it," she laughingly replied.

"There better not have?" said Bob half joking.

"Don't be daft," she said as they sat down. Bob seemed slightly quiet, so Becky snuggled up close and reassured him, "I'm wild and a little crazy, but one man at a time. You're all I want."

They gave each other a gentle kiss. Bob laughed, "I'd better be. I'll have you know there are women queuing up for me."

"Yeah, sure there are," she laughed.

Bob had kept Becky under wraps since that night at the Clay Pigeon, tonight he was hoping to introduce Becky to his best mates. Unfortunately Joe had informed him earlier that day that he was seeing his mystery woman, so that pleasure would have to wait. At least Terry and Jim should still be in the George when they got there.

"Terry can be a bit full on, thinks he's a ladies man. He's married, got two kids and another on the way. Bit too cocky for my liking, otherwise he's okay."

"Great! Can't wait to meet him," said Becky sarcastically.

"Then there's Jim, last I heard he was looking to buy a house. If you ask my opinion I think he has delusions of grandeur."

"Sounds like you might be a little envious," ventured Becky.

"No, not really. We are a happy go lucky bunch, having fun and relying on each other but suddenly life starts to change."

"Wow! That's a little profound coming from you," she laughs.

"I have my moments," 'God, how I love this woman,' the thought disturbed him.

"That's why you want to better yourself?"

"Yeah, I suppose. I've been thinking about it for some time. Labouring is hard graft, there's money in it, but the real money is in a trade. I should have thought about when I left school. But better late than never."

Becky kissed him on the cheek, "I'm proud of you."

"Our stop," said Bob. He walked in front of Becky, and started to descend the stairs, "A gentleman always goes first on the way down," he declared.

"Get you," laughed Becky.

Minutes later they entered the George saloon bar. Bob looked towards his usual seats and found a deserted table and four empty chairs. "I don't believe it. Hey Dave any of my crowd been in?"

"You just missed Terry, he left with that Eric bloke."

"Cheers, the usual and a vodka and lime, one for yourself."

"Cheers," replied the barman.

"Typical, the one day I bring you down to meet my mates, they've all pissed off."

"Another time," said Becky with a smile.

*****

Eric took Terry to a back street drinking club. Eric chuckled to himself, judging by the look upon Terry's face this wasn't what he'd have imagined. "I've a bit of business to discuss, so grab yourself a pint, sit down and soak up the atmosphere."

"Yeah real smart, like a palace," retorted Terry. With pint in hand he sat down in a corner while Eric along with a couple of shady looking characters went into a back room. The boys had always known Eric was a little dodgy, but until Terry stepped into the place he'd always thought Eric was just a small time villain, albeit with contacts. Terry looked at his watch, the meeting was going on longer than he expected. Knowing he couldn't sit there nursing an empty glass Terry stepped up to the bar and ordered another pint.

"Where you from pal?" Terry looked to the right of him. Judging from the man's appearance he was around his mid-thirties, looking every inch a builder straight from work. Without giving Terry the chance to answer he drew closer to his ear. "I asked you a question," he said menacingly.

"Sorry mate, I didn't know you were talking to me."

"Who the fuck do yah think I'm talking too."

Terry snapped back, "Hold it pal, not that it's any of your business, but I live near Uxbridge!"

"So what the fucking hell are you doing in my boozer?"

Terry could fight, though he would rather talk his way out if he could, 'where the fuck was Bob when you needed him,' he thought.

"I'm with someone."

"I don't see anyone."

'Oh fuck, here it comes,' he thought. "He's in the other room," said Terry, motioning with a nod of his head towards the door at the far end of the room.

"You're with Eric! Eric Sullivan."

"The very same," said Terry.

"I'll get that," he said, as he paid for Terry's pint. "Why didn't you say so?"

"You never asked!"

Next thing Terry knew he was drinking with Arthur, his new best mate. Terry was curious to ask if he knew what Eric and the two other men were talking about in that room, but thought it wiser to leave the subject alone.

Half an hour later, Eric walked back into the bar. Nodded to Arthur, and grinned at Terry. "What do you think of my boozer?"

Terry looked around and surprising felt safe to utter, "Nice, but I think it's seen better days."

"You can say that again Tel," said Arthur.

Arthur stayed and finished his pint, then got up, "Nice seeing you Eric, it's been awhile. You too Terry, see you around." He nodded to the barman then walked out.

"You really know how to pick em," laughed Eric.

"Why, what do you mean," asked Terry

"Arthur's okay, but he ain't the type to mess around with, he runs with some seriously dangerous company."

# Chapter 15

As they sat in the corner of the White Hart deep in the Chilterns, Joe looked at Grace, "Are you happy?"

"Happy yes, excited beyond reason, but a little apprehensive," sighed Grace.

"Why apprehensive?"

"Oh Joe, I know my husband, if he found out, Sean would smash this beautiful relationship of ours into a million pieces."

"We haven't done anything wrong, like I said I'm prepared to wait until you're ready."

"I might never be ready." She saw the hurt look in his eyes, "Not because I wouldn't want too. But because making love, true love, there might be no turning back"

Without warning he leaned across and kissed her gently. "One day, one day, you will be ready."

"I'd like to believe that, but until then, tell me about your friends, your brothers or sisters, what movies you like. Do you read, do you play sport, what team do you support?"

"Enough, enough, I get it!" he laughed.

They talked for hours, they laughed, they teased, they joked like star struck lovers on a first date. As their time together ebbed away Grace told him that she'd see him whenever she could. Sean's work load had increased considerably since the hunt for Harry Roberts, he was hardly ever home. Grace knew that when they caught him, things would change dramatically. Her time with Joe would become less frequent even non-existent. These few precious hours snatched from reality was what she lived for.

*****

Jim pulled up outside Georgia's parents' massive house. At least to Jim it was massive compared to the three bedroom semi he shared with his mum, dad and sister. He took a brief look at his reflection in the rear view mirror, checked his tie and got out of the car. He'd parked on the road outside, not daring to drive onto their double entrance driveway. 'Too presumptuous,' he thought.

He rang the bell. Georgia appear almost immediately, a bright cheery smile upon her face. "Come in," she cried, "I'll just be a sec." Then in one swift movement she turned and vaulted up the stairs.

Jim watched until she was out of sight, then still in some form of shock he looked around the extravagant hallway, *his front room at home would have fit in it*. To his left there were double doors, both open. "Come in young man, let me take a look at you."

Jim felt slightly intimidated, but then with a confidence he didn't feel, he stepped inside.

"How do you do, I'm Georgia's father," said a tall portly man in his mid-fifties.

"Hello sir, nice to meet you, I'm James." He looked back towards the hall, hoping Georgia would be flying down the stairs. No luck.

"Oh, she'll be down in a while, can I get you a small scotch?"

"No, I'm fine sir." To be honest Jim could have drunk the whole bottle, he was so nervous.

"Nonsense, just a little snifter." He poured it generously into a glass and handed it to Jim. "I understand you're taking Georgia to dinner, somewhere nice I hope."

Jim just nodded.

"Georgia told me you're investing in property."

"That's right sir, but only in a small way."

"You have to start somewhere. It's good to see Georgia's going out with someone with brains and ambition. You're not like the usual shower she tends to attract."

"Father!" cried Georgia.

Jim breathed a sigh of relief, before finishing his scotch, "Thanks for the drink Mr Chandler."

"It's George! Well, it was nice meeting you James." He held out his hand and Jim shook it.

As they walked across the driveway Georgia asked, "What time did you book the reservation for?"

'Oh shit,' thought Jim. "The table's booked for 8 o'clock. We should be there in time for a drink before dinner." 'A little white lie,' he thought. 'Hopefully we'll get a table close to 8 o'clock."

They pulled into the car park of the Swan and Bottle at 7.25. Jim raced around and opened her door, "Thank you," she responded as she emerged from his car. As Georgia walked passed the car she couldn't help noticing the wing mirrors on Jim's car, "They're different," she remarked.

"John Wayne fan!" he exclaimed, making a mental note to change them. Entering the restaurant all seemed to be going as planned. Jim found a small table in the bar, then he asked Georgia what she wanted to drink.

"I'll have a small glass of red."

Jim ordered the drinks brought them to the table and excused himself, "Bathroom." But instead of the loo he sought out the head waiter, "I'm in a bit of a bind, have you a table for two at 8 o'clock?"

"Sorry sir, we're fully booked."

"What, can't you just fit us in?"

"Sorry, nothing I can do."

How was Jim going to explain to Georgia; his date was over before it begun? Jim had seen it on the movies. He reached for his wallet, opened it and offered the waiter a pound. The waiter peered into the wallet." A blue one, guarantee's your table." Two minutes later Jim and Georgia were shown to that expensive table.

"Would you like a starter?" he said as he perused the menu.

"No thank you, I think I'll just have the rump," she giggled. It was clear to Georgia from the moment they walked into the restaurant that he felt out of his depth. It was time to put him out of his misery "Oh Jim, relax, I won't bite. When you walked into my office I was as surprised as you. Of course I had to act business-like, but you impressed me with your vision."

Jim was taken aback. Before he could say a word, Georgia continued.

"You wasn't some good-looking guy that I'd fancied as a fifteen year old school girl, you have drive and ambition. Believe me most of the type I mix with are so privileged or reliant on family money they wouldn't know what drive is."

Finding his voice, Jim said, "Wow! I wasn't expecting that."

Realising she was giving too much away she added, "I'd just like to qualify what I just said. I had a school girl crush on you, I also had a crush on James Dean and Paul Newman. I'm not that girl anymore, I'm a reasonably worldly young woman and I know what I want in life. Do you?"

"Again, wow. Build me up one moment, then knock me down the next. In answer to your question, yeah I know what I want. I intend to aim for the stars, but if that ain't possible I'll settle for the moon." He paused for a moment, knowing his next words could be burning bridges. "If anything I'm a realist, I never plucked up the courage to ask you out, because I believed I was out of your league. If tonight is anything to go on I guess nothing's changed."

Georgia looked slightly shaken, "I'm sorry if my words came out wrong, I'm a little too outspoken for my own good. I should have said, James Dean was a little rough around the edges and I guess Paul Newman was just a little too smooth. When you asked me out, I thought, wow! The best of both worlds." Gone was the slightly aloof Georgia, in her place a woman that like him was having to adjust to another world.

"Our first row, and we haven't had our first course. I'm sorry Georgia, I guess I over reacted."

"Well I guess I asked for it. Seriously I was only trying to put you at ease. I like you and I'd like to get to know you better; the real you."

"For a moment when I walked into your office I was completely thrown, but when you said yes to a date with me I was surprised."

"The men I've dated are to a certain extent sure of themselves, but that is mainly down to their upbringing. You on the other hand walked into my office, showed me your ideas and the fact you hadn't jumped in with both feet impressed me, so much so that when you asked me out I couldn't refuse."

"I hope it also had something to do with my rugged good looks and charming personality," he said roguishly.

"Yes, of course it was," she replied with a hint of good natured sarcasm.

They spent the evening talking about everything from politics, travel, education, music, the cinema and Jim's plans for his investment. Georgia was a mine of information about how to get the most from the project, ideas that Jim had never even considered. It was a pleasant evening which culminated outside Georgia's front door when she looked into his eyes and invited him to kiss her.

"We must do this again sometime," he said.

"I'd like that, call me."

# Chapter 16

As one week followed another, the boys began to see less of each other, meeting up on the odd occasions, but still managing Sunday lunch times, where they caught up on each other's news. Joe had been seeing Grace for close on three months. Their relationship had become very intense, but as yet they hadn't crossed the line.

"Christ-sake Joe, if you're taking the risk of seeing another man's wife, you could at least give her one," snapped Terry as he placed a tray of drinks on the table.

"You don't understand Terry, we'll do things in our own time."

"You'll kick yourself when it all ends in tears. You're risking more than you know and for what?"

"Leave it Terry, warned Bob, "We're all different, me I can't get enough of Becky."

"Yeah we've noticed. You're a changed man since you started seeing her," said Jim. He took a mouthful of his stout and cider, "Arrh, you can't beat it," he added referring to his favourite pint. "I never thought I'd say this but you being taken on as an apprentice plumber at your age, is a smart move."

"Hope he sticks too it," added Joe.

"So how's it going Rachman?" It was the usual banter that Terry revelled in.

Jim laughed, "We're hoping to have our first tenants in by Christmas."

"We?" said Terry, "You mean you and posh bird?"

"Yeah, what of it?" said Jim defensively.

"Nothing, just asking."

"How do those new tenancy agreements affect you?" asked Joe?"

"We're okay I think, we're renting it out as furnished."

"That's a bit of a lay out." said Terry. "I can maybe get you a carpet or two, at cost mind."

"I'll think about it, thanks." No way was Jim going to buy dodgy carpets, not with Georgia as partner.

Terry appeared to be doing well for himself, he was earning decent money at the airport. "It's the overtime, can't get enough of it since the baby."

"How's Heather doing?" asked Joe.

"Great, she's over the moon, after two boys she'd almost given up on getting a girl."

"Must be hard work, all those night feeds," grinned Bob.

"Yeah you'll soon find out pal, the way you're going," replied Terry. At which they all fell about laughing, except Bob.

"We're careful," he announced to anyone that would listen.

"You seen Eric lately?" asked Jim.

"Not since he and Gloria fucked off to Tenerife," said Terry, "If there's something you want, I've a few contacts of my own, legit mind. Well nothing traceable anyway," he added with a laugh."

"If you ain't careful," warned Joe.

"Nah I'm solid, always remember what Eric says. Don't get caught."

Joe looked at Terry and shook his head, "Same again," to which they all replied, "Yep"

Terry joined Joe at the bar, "I'll give you a hand," leaving Jim and Bob sitting at the table.

"So how's it going with Georgia?" asked Bob. "She okay?"

Jim ignored the innuendo.

*Since their first date he'd been seeing her quite regularly, some of it business and some pleasure. Georgia had put a proposition to him. She'd suggested buying a much larger house than he could afford and turning it into flats. Jim had baulked at the idea, until she said she'd match his deposit and they should go into partnership. She'd been talking with her father and he'd suggested the idea to her.*

*"You have to speculate to accumulate, you need to think big, however small the project is," said George Chandler, Georgia's father. It didn't take long for the penny to drop. Chandler and Lowe solicitors. It turned out he had offices in six locations dotted around the London area.*

*Jim had no illusions about their relationship, they were friends, albeit with a few concessions thrown in, but the partnership was strictly business. Jim had grown up in the last few months and was beginning to see what he wanted out of life. Finding the perfect property at the right price in a desirable area was their first job. Landing it was the second. Fortunately the solicitor's fees were at cost. Georgia did their conveyancing. Her father had a family friend do the surveying. Georgia haggled about the price, even walked away at one point, before they accepted Jim and Georgia's offer. Within six weeks it was a done deal. The conversion cost the most, but with Jim helping out with the electrics, Bob chipping in with a bit of labouring alongside Joe, they managed to come in a little over their budget.*

"You've seen her, she's something else, ain't she?"

"Yeah, I'll grant you, but hardly my type," said Bob. "Now Becky with those long legs and that mass of flowing red locks that's my kind of woman."

Joe had just finished his order when Terry said, "Seriously Joe, I don't mean any offence, but that woman's husband is bad news. You need to wet your whistle and get out while the going's good."

"I understand Terry, but I can't let go, I love her."

"Don't say I didn't warn you," added Terry as an afterthought.

\*\*\*\*\*

Two days later, with Terry's words still ringing in his ears, Joe heard the news that Harry Roberts had been captured. His heart sank. Since the beginning of the manhunt Sean and his police colleagues had been putting in more hours than seemed possible, allowing Grace to spend much needed time with Joe. Now the manhunt was over Grace's husband would have more free time, which could curtail most of their special time together.

Joe's biggest fear was, Grace in a vain attempt to protect him, might end their non-affair. He couldn't bring himself to call it an affair. The word held connotations of being sordid, but their love for each other was pure. He cursed himself for being soft. In the past Joe had had a number of girlfriends, and none of them would have called him soft. Yet Grace had turned his life upside down. Not being able to contact her was a torture, three agonising days of waiting until they could meet up.

His heart leapt as he saw the familiar silhouette of a windswept Grace waiting at the bus stop. He pulled up beside her and she got in. She smiled like nothing had happened. She kissed his cheek as he pulled away from the kerb. He knew things were different when Grace told him she didn't want to visit their special place. "Just drive Joe," she uttered. It seemed like he was driving for hours but in truth it was a little over thirty minutes. She snuggled up to him. Joe tried talking, "Don't speak Joe, not yet, just keep driving."

They were on the edge of the Chilterns when Joe pulled the car over. "If you're here to tell me it's over, just say it."

Grace was silent, she looked at Joe with a sad look in those deep brown tear stained eyes.

"We've had a magical time these three months and I didn't want it to end. You've been everything I could ever want. A lesser man would have taken advantage of the situation, but you didn't."

Joe was transfixed in time as he waited for those fateful words, 'It's over'.

"Joe, I love you, but with that murderer caught, Sean is going to be home more. We knew this couldn't last forever, but against all odds we've managed to keep our affair secret. Its been the most wonderful time of my life, but yes it's over."

"It doesn't have to be."

"Oh Joe, it does." She moved closer and brushed away a tear from Joe's cheek. "What we've got is now. We deserve to have these last precious moments together."

Joe understood what Grace was saying and he knew that whatever happened in his life, he so desperately needed this. Grace looked him in the eye and then pointed out of the windscreen to a country lane.

Minutes later they found a turning that terminated at a farmers gate. Joe turned off the lights and ignition and parked up. He reached beneath the bench seat and pulled a lever. The seat gently slipped back. Joe kissed Grace more passionately than he had before.

"I love you Grace, I'll always love you." Joe felt his eyes fill up with tears.

"Joe make love to me."

After it was over, laying in each other's arms Grace outlined how things could unfold if Sean found out about their affair.

He protested, he told her he was man enough to stand up to her husband.

"I don't doubt that, but he has friends, some very dangerous people. No Joe, our relationship has run its course. I love you and I always will, that's why I'm letting you go."

Joe knew their lovemaking was somehow symbolic. A line drawn, a line that neither could cross.

Grace had never felt so wretched in her life, she was letting the man she loved go. She'd finally persuaded Joe that whatever happened in his life their time together had been beyond special.

They drove back in silence, Joe studying the road though teary eyes, hoping Grace would throw caution to the wind.

She clung to him throughout the journey knowing that to weaken, their time together would be fraught with danger and uncertainty.

Joe kissed her lovingly at the corner of her street, knowing with a heavy heart that it would be their last kiss. He watched though tear stained eyes as she walked down the street and stopped and looked back as she found her key and went inside. He wept unashamedly on his journey home.

Later that night as Joe stared out of his bedroom window of his parents' house he reflected on their lovemaking on the front seat of his Zodiac. Not as he would have planned, a nice dinner at a swanky restaurant followed by a night in a hotel. But that front seat in the Zodiac down a country lane was perfect.

# Chapter 17

Becky finally met the boys on Christmas Eve when her and Bob popped into the George after having a bite to eat at the Wimpy.

"Thought we needed to wet our whistle, and maybe wish you reprobates a Merry Christmas, and of course for you to meet Becky."

Becky took off her coat and revealed a Mary Quant emerald green jersey dress, neat collar with a brass zip which was undone and revealed a hint of cleavage, whereas the bottom half was pleated and short, so short that Terry opened his gob. "Core!" he exclaimed, "Any shorter I'd have seen what you had for breakfast."

Heather gave him a dig.

She smiled at the backhanded compliment while Bob scowled. Becky's long dark red hair cascaded and fell almost to her waist, the emerald green of her dress accentuating her luscious locks. Her long legs looked even longer due to the miniscule second half of the dress.

Jim was the first to offer his hand, "It's a pleasure to meet you at last. Happy Christmas."

"Same to you Jim," replied Becky. "Where's your other half? Bob's told me all about you."

"Picking her up in about half hour, we're off to some club her parents belong too."

"Well you look very smart," she replied.

"Thank you," he said, surprised by just how personable Bob's girlfriend was

Apart from Terry's one liner, he was quieter than usual, having Heather on his arm so to speak. It wasn't often that Heather got to go out, babysitters were few and far between. But her sister had split from her boyfriend and she'd offered. Heather wasn't about to look a gift horse in the mouth, so she spent the best part of two hours getting ready.

"Blimey, you look a treat," said Terry when she'd finally emerged from upstairs.

Heather smiled appreciatively. Maybe it was just a night in the George but it was a welcome distraction from screaming kids and nappies.

"We're all standing around, shall we grab a table," suggested Bob.

"Why not," replied Heather.

"Where's Joe, surely he's coming out tonight of all nights?" asked Jim.

"I spoke to him yesterday, said I was bringing Becky to meet you all. He said he'd try to make it."

Since Joe and Grace had split up, the boys had made several attempts to get him to have a night on the town. Terry in his infinite style had fallen back on his old saying, "if you fall off a horse you need to get back on it." Needless to say Joe wasn't impressed. Bob worried about his oldest friend, knowing Joe the way he did, he knew it would take time, but eventually he'd get over her; he had too.

Terry and Heather sat down with Becky, Bob and Jim, and five minutes later in walked Eric and Gloria, both dressed to the nines. Eric was suited and booted, but not just any old suit, his came from Saville Row. As for Gloria, in her sable which she unbuttoned revealing an elegant black number, stylish but understated.

'Very classy,' thought Terry. "Come and join us Gloria, you can bring Eric if you have too.

Heather gave Terry another dig in the ribs. Jim grabbed another table and pushed the two together, while Bob brought over some extra chairs. "Where you off to Eric? You can't just be slumming it with us, or are you going somewhere fancy?"

"We've reservations at that new Italian place in Northwood. Thought we'd pop in for a swift one, and wish you guys the compliments of the season."

"A Merry Christmas to you too," cried the small gathering.

"Joe ain't around?" asked Eric.

"Nah, thought he might have showed, but maybe it's a bit too soon," said Bob apologetically.

"He don't know it yet, but finishing it with that woman was the best thing he could have done," declared Eric

"Maybe, but Joe don't think so," said Bob. "Sorry forgetting my manners, I'd like you both to meet Becky," he added.

"What manners," exclaimed Terry with a grin!

Bob gave Terry a withering look, then joined in with the lively conversation.

Jim made his excuses then upped and left after twenty minutes.

"Mustn't be late," mimicked Terry as Jim departed.

"I think he's going places," said Eric, "Talking about going places, we'd better get a move on."

"You can join us, if you'd like," said Gloria. "I'm sure they'll be able to fit you in."

"No ta," replied Bob, "we've just eaten."

Heather looked expectantly at Terry, "Well, it is Christmas."

"If you don't mind us tagging along," said Terry.

"If I minded I wouldn't have asked," replied Eric.

"You didn't! I did," said Gloria, with a mischievous grin.

And then there were two. "Just as well we ate," said Bob. "I'll get us another drink."

"Yeah, just as well," mimicked Becky playfully.

Bob stepped up to the bar ordered the drinks, collected them and placed them on the table. He smiled, "Just nipping to the loo," he informed Becky.

"Don't be long," she called after him as he disappeared into the gents.

Just at that moment a nervous looking bloke walked into the pub, he looked familiar but Becky couldn't be sure. He ordered a pint, took a sip; looked in her direction and locked eyes with Becky.

"Guess I ain't too late," he muttered to himself. He smiled over and she smiled back. He wasn't certain as he walked over, "It's Rebecca, either that or I'm in deep shit," he said in way of an introduction, "I'm Joe."

She smiled, "You're not in deep shit! I'm Becky, pleased to meet you Joe.

"You made it," cried Bob as he walked out of the loo. "You missed the boys, Terry and Heather went for a meal with Eric and Gloria, and Jim's round his bird's house, going to some fancy do, I suspect."

"Yeah probably. I thought, sod it! Christmas Eve, crap on the telly, what am I, a hermit!"

"I was beginning to wonder. I'm just so glad you could make it," said Bob with genuine warmth.

"Bob's told me all about you, and yes I won't pretend I don't know about your problem. I'm just sorry it didn't work out."

"Thanks Becky. Just one of those things I guess," he said unconvincingly

"Who knows, anything's possible in this world."

"I'm not that lucky. Anyway I heard you've got wheels Bobby," he'd seen the 1959 Thames van in the car park and guessed it was Bob's

"Yeah, not posh like your Zodiac, or Jim's Cresta."

A cheeky grin appeared across Joe's sorry face, "Oh, I've got to tell yah. You know those six-gun wing mirrors that Jim's so proud of. He's only gone and changed them for regular wing mirrors."

"You are joking, they were his pride and joy. When did that happen?"

"Oh, about three weeks ago. Said it didn't give a good impression."

They both burst into laughter, even Becky who'd just met Jim half hour or so earlier started to laugh. "He seems such a nice man, I hope this woman he's hooked up with is worth it," said Becky when she'd stopped laughing.

Bob saw Joe slid back for a second. His breakup was still very raw.

*****

Posh or what, thought Jim as he walked into the large hall of the 17th Century Mansion at Moor Park. "I shouldn't be here Georgia, how can I chat and mingle with these people."

"Don't be silly Jim, be yourself. You're an up and coming entrepreneur." "I'm a what?"

"Entrepreneur. Relax, most of these people are self-made men. Just like you."

The price of the tickets for the Christmas Eve Gala must have been expensive, thought Jim when he was approach by a waitress and offered canapes, and hors d'oeuvres. Georgia handed Jim a glass of champagne, "Just a little appetiser before the dinner. You're still not relaxed, go with the flow, I'm sure you'll enjoy it once you start to mingle."

"Okay," replied Jim, "just stay close." 'What the hell, Georgia's thrown me in the deep end, it's either sink or swim.' He caught the eye of a passing waiter and exchanged his empty glass for a full one. Then after taking a sip he smiled and said, "Let's mingle." Georgia did the introductions and before long he was swimming in the fast lane, well as fast as he could without breaking cover. He discovered to his surprise that most of the people Georgia introduced him too, thought his and Georgia's little venture was truly exciting. 'Praise from some of the stuff shirts, that's being unkind,' he thought. They all seemed genuinely interested in what Jim had to say.

Dinner was announce and Jim and Georgia sat down at a table of ten, with George Chandler, his wife Elizabeth, Georgia's sisters Pricilla and Jessica along with their husbands, and George's partner Johnathan Lowe and his wife. A sumptuous five course Christmas dinner, with a choice of turkey or goose for the main course.

Jim was on his fifth glass of champagne and was feeling a little light headed. Georgia pinched his thigh and whispered in his ear.

"Ease off with the champers, I want you fit for a little decadence after the meal." Her tone left Jim in no doubt that sometime during the dancing he was getting a Christmas present he wasn't prepared for. Needless to say Jim casually slid the glass of champagne to the centre of the table and began sampling the first course.

After the meal, a number of the men went into another room with their brandies and cigars. Jim watched the ritual with interest, before Georgia took his hand and they moved into a large room were a band was just beginning to play a few numbers. Surprisingly they weren't a stuffy Ted Heath and his Orchestra type, but a local group, complete with Fender guitars and Vox speakers. Not trendy like the Beatles more Cliff and the Shadows. 'But then you can't have it all,' thought Jim. Their music was versatile and the first few dances were for the elder generation. Jim had a smile on his face, possibly the promise he was on or most probable the two more glasses of champagne he'd drunk over dinner. Jim knew different.

The band began to play a Shadows number, Guitar Tango and Jim's eyes lit up. He took Georgia by the hand and led her onto the dance floor. "You can dance the tango can't you?" he asked with a confident air.

"Of course, but can you?"

The question was answered seconds later, "I'm a little rusty, but I'm sure I can manage."

They came off the dance floor to a rapturous applause. "Where the hell did you learn to dance like that?" asked Georgia.

"Just one of my many talents," he replied. "Between the ages of thirteen to sixteen I joined an amateur dramatics society. They taught us many diverse talents. I've forgotten most of them but somewhere in the back of my brain I learned to dance the tango. At least the basic steps."

"You realise it's going to be harder to slip away now. But trust me when we do, it will be worth it."

# Chapter 18

In Giovanni's Italian restaurant the seasonal cheer was very evident. Terry looked at Heather as they walked into the restaurant, it was clear to him that she was impressed: big time. Terry's knowledge of the finer things in life didn't extend much past a Chinese after the pubs had closed. Even then on an occasion he'd had it on his toes. 'Those days were over,' thought Terry. He liked the easy manner that Eric used so brilliantly when he told the head waiter that he'd specifically asked for a table for four people. Within a couple of minutes Eric had them eating out of his hand.

Eric knew his way around fancy restaurants and it showed. He was a man that knew what he wanted and how to get it. He was at home drinking with the lads, laughing, joking and telling tall stories, as he was gentlemanly when in the company of members of the opposite sex. The way he guided his guests around the menu and the masterful way he took charge of the orders resonated loud and clear with Heather. The conversation over dinner was light and full of laughter.Spending time with Gloria at close range was a revelation to both Terry and Heather. Her outward appearance suggested she was a little up herself, but around the table that night she was anything but. She chatted openly about how she met Eric, a revelation in itself. Gloria although very down to earth, was also very worldly. She knew the score, she even paraphrased Eric, "Whatever you do in life, 'don't get caught'. Heather took an instant liking to her.

The meal was superb; after an array of appetisers Heather played safe and chose Lasagne, while Terry decided on Bistecca Fiorentina cotta alla brace, once he knew it was barbecued T bone steak. Eric went for a fillet with porcini mushrooms and Gloria elected to stick to a traditional pasta dish that the waiter recommended.

"Italian isn't really my scene," said Gloria, "Don't get me wrong, I'm quite a cosmopolitan eater, but just as much at home with plain old fashioned home cooked meals."

Eric's stories of growing up in the East End were interesting and hilarious. Particularly his childhood and the escapades he and his friends got up to. He seemed to relish telling tales of some of the characters that crossed his path. "The East End's a melting pot of Jews, Maltese, Greeks and Turks and of course the Irish and Italians. As a kid you had bomb sites to play on and as you grew older, there was money to be had if you used your head, it helped if you had someone who looked out for you. Strange though it sounds there was a sense of community"

Heather asked why they chose to leave London and move to the suburbs. Eric looked at Gloria and they both smiled. "Living in the East End was great, but there comes a time when you need to branch out."

Terry tried to match Eric's stories but fell a little short. In truth his admiration of Eric went much further, he actually wanted to be just like him. Which if he'd thought about it, was dumb. Terry had a good looking wife, *who actually idolised him. Why, was anyone's guess?* He was tallish, fairly good looking, he could even be charming on an occasion. He had a good side-line going. Money in the bank; *but not serious money*, like Eric.

For two and a half hours he'd listened to Eric's exploits, but being a little out of his depth and plied with unfamiliar liquor it brought out the worst in him.

"I like you Eric, you're a great mate, but at times you're full of shit!" he snapped.

The laughter stopped. "He doesn't mean it! It's the drink, he's not use to liqueurs," gasped Heather in his defence.

"Yeah, I do," cried Terry.

Eric offered, "No need to apologies, Terry's right, sometimes I am full of it. It's nothing I haven't heard before," he laughed it off.

"He shouldn't have said it," said Heather. "Forget about it, it's Christmas."

Terry was now feeling the full weight of intoxication, he knew he'd fucked up, but little else, he was out of it. He could hardly put a sentence together. "Fuck it," he slurred before slumping back in his chair.

"Time to go!" exclaimed Heather as she reached into her handbag for her purse.

"Put your money away," Eric said softly, "The meal's on us."

"We couldn't possibly!" insisted Heather.

"No argument, our treat." He motioned for the bill and within five minutes they'd put on their coats and left via the back door, but not before Eric placed a wad of notes on the table.

Eric helped Heather with the inebriated Terry down the concrete stairs to the small car park. All the while Heather kept apologising.

"We all get like it sometime," cried Eric. He took his keys from his pocket and handed them to Gloria. "Cheers Glo."

"You can show me your appreciation when we get home," replied Gloria with a suggestive smile.

Terry slumped into Eric's Jag and fell asleep immediately. An embarrassed Heather climbed in beside him. The short journey home was punctuated with Terry's snoring and Heather giving Gloria directions. They pulled to the kerb and Eric got out to help Heather get Terry inside.

Once they'd settled him onto the couch, Heather walked Eric to the front door. "I'm sorry for the upset," adding, "Thanks for the meal, it was very nice," then spontaneously she reached up and kissed him. It was supposed to have been a kiss on the cheek, but Eric had turned suddenly, it brushed against his lips. "I'm sorry, I didn't mean that to happen!"

"That's a shame, it was nice." He paused unsure what to say next, "Merry Christmas Heather." Eric quickly turned around and opened the door before stepped out of the house. Heather clung to the door and watched him walk down the path and climb into the passenger side of the Jag. He waved as Gloria drove off. Heather waved back. *Lustful thoughts weren't exclusive to Georgia that Christmas Eve.*

\*\*\*\*\*

Earlier in the evening Becky had been working her magic with Joe. Down in the dumps on Christmas Eve wasn't something she could contemplate. Joe had poured out his heart to Becky, from the first moment his and Grace's eyes had met, to the bus ride, to the cosy pub in the Chilterns where Grace had told Joe her sorry tale, to the last time they met where they made love for the first time. It was a sad tale, but Becky had a solution to it.

"Don't say anything yet! I know it's been said before, but New Year's Eve's a fresh start; starting with you and Donna!"

"Who's Donna? Look I know you mean well, but I'm not in the mood for another relationship."

"Ha, that's where you're so wrong. Donna isn't looking for a relationship. Donna is a law unto herself, believe me, she's just the tonic you need. She loves a good time, a good laugh, a good drink and a good giggle. She is wild beyond wild!"

Bob looked straight at his friend, "It might be what you need, you never know."

"I'll think about it," replied Joe half-heartedly.

# Chapter 19

Jim didn't see Georgia until Boxing Day, mainly because of family commitments on both sides. The little matter of what happened as the clock struck midnight foremost in his mind as he set off that morning. Jim took stock of where his future was heading. His relationship with Georgia up until that night had been part girlfriend but mainly business partners. Mixing business and pleasure according to Georgia was a no, no. Reluctantly he'd agreed and apart from the odd grope and fumble it hadn't gone much further.

*With shouts of Merry Christmas at the stroke of twelve ringing in every ones ears, Georgia saw their chance to slip away quietly. She took Jim by the hand and led him out of the main hall. She said nothing, but her eyes spoke volumes. They walked down a long corridor. At the end they opened a door to the outside. A welcoming coolness greeted them as they moved into the shadows. Jim held her in his arms and kissed her. It was a long lingering kiss that suggested far more. As they broke away from their embrace Georgia took Jim by the hand and led him towards a small wooden shed. They found the door locked. Whether it was the champagne or the thought of what awaited him, Jim gave the door a swift kick and the flimsy lock shattered. Georgia let out a shriek of laughter, while Jim briefly looked towards the main building.*

*Georgia laughed again, "You're so naughty!" She grabbed his hand and pulled him inside, then she swung him around and kissed him as they leaned against the now closed door. Their kisses became more urgent as his hands began to slide up her dress. He was surprised to find Georgia had replaced her latest fashion tights and was wearing black stockings, a fact that registered when he felt the coolness of her thigh. He half expected to feel the firm grip of her hand, but there was no resistance. Her tongue explored the inside of his mouth and made him harder, if that was possible. She gasped as his fingers probed, seeking an entrance. Georgia grappling with his belt, the catch and the zip. He felt the coolness on his legs and buttocks as his trousers hit the floor. All thoughts of caution disappeared as her hand grasped his penis and guided him inside.*

'Was this the end,' thought Jim as he pulled up outside Georgia's house that Boxing Day morning. She must have seen him coming as she opened the door and ran up the driveway to greet him. She climbed in beside him, "Drive," she ordered. Jim didn't say anything, he just drove the Vauxhall around the corner and parked. 'Here it comes,' he thought, 'the brush off.'

Dignity was all he had left, "Okay Christmas Eve was a mistake. You want it to be over, I get it!"

Georgia looked slightly taken aback. "Do you want it to be over?"

"No, I..." stuttered Jim.

"Well shut up! I just want to know how you feel towards me, after what happened between us?"

Jim smiled, "So far, it's been the best Christmas ever; I don't want it to end."

Georgia leaned over and kissed him. "I don't want it to end either," she said with a grin, before planting another kiss on his lips reminiscing that of the other night in the wood shed. Before he could take it further she broke from their embrace, smiled cheekily and uttered, "We'd best be getting back, the family will be wondering where we are.

*****

Terry was in the dog house all over Christmas, along with a hangover that lasted until after the Queen's speech. "Was Eric upset? Was he narked?"

"No, as a matter of fact, he understood. He was a complete gentleman, not like someone else I could name."

"Now you're sounding like your old woman!"

"Don't bring my mother into this. You acted like a pig. You abused Eric and Gloria's generosity!"

"He can afford it, the business I put his way!"

"Terry, you're earning good money, don't try to be what you're not. We have a good life, we don't want for anything," cried Heather. "He's a little flash I'll grant you; but he is a gentleman with it."

"And I'm not I suppose?"

"Of course you are; when you're sober." "It was those fancy liqueurs."

"There's a couple of films on later, either Young at Heart, with Doris Day and Frank Sinatra on ITV, or a John Wayne film on the BBC."

"John Wayne!"

Heather ignored him, Young at Heart, was how she was feeling.

*****

Joe had a miserable Christmas, but he had no one to blame but himself. It had been over forty days since his world fell apart. He was twenty one, old enough to vote, old enough to fight for Queen and Country, but losing Grace had brought him to his knees. His friends had all been supportive, but even the boys were beginning to lose patience. Becky's offer of a blind date with her friend Donna on New Year's Eve was filling him with dread.

In the days between Christmas and New Year Joe did his best to take his mind off Grace with the return to work. As the build-up and anticipation of New Year's Eve drew ever closer Joe realised he needed to pull himself together. Terry's words began to ring loud and clear, 'if you fall off the horse you need to get back on.' Dating Donna wasn't the answer, 'but here goes,' he thought, 'she sounded fun.'

Bob was thrilled when Joe said he'd give it a go. "What's Donna like?"

"She's a dog!"

Bob laughed hysterically, "You should see your face. Actually she's nice. Blonde hair, blue eyes, stands around five one, maybe five two, seriously I'm not joking. You could do a whole lot worse."

"So where are we going?"

"The George!" said Bob straight-faced. "We're meeting Jim and posh bird. Terry's coming, with Heather if she can get a babysitter. Me and Becky and of course Donna. Couple of hours in the George, then we're off to a party."

\*\*\*\*\*

"You've met Joe, he's a little down in the dumps right now, woman trouble. Bob's the one that was knocking that wall down when you came on site. You haven't met Terry, he likes to think he's god's gift to women. He's okay really, but he can be a dick," said Jim, when he told Georgia she was meeting his friends down the George on New Year's Eve.

"Great, it's about time I met your friends formally, just remember Mum and Dad are out tonight and they won't be back until at least two," the implication in her voice spoke volumes.

"We'll stay for an hour or two, no more," said Jim.

"You're a bad boy," giggled Georgia.

\*\*\*\*\*

Joe was a little nervous when Bob and Becky walked into the George with Donna. He jumped up from his chair and greeted them at the bar. It was just after seven. He smiled at Donna, she was everything Bob had said she was, but she wasn't Grace.

"The usual Bob?" asked Joe, "and what will you ladies like?

"I'll have a vodka and lime, ta," said Becky.

Donna smiled.

"Can I get you a drink?" he asked.

"I'll have a gin and bitter lemon, thanks. I'm Donna, well you know that already," she laughed.

"Yeah sorry, I'm Joe," he said clumsily, before ordering her drink. He motioned them towards a small table where he'd been sitting. He glanced at the clock nervously.

"Don't worry you've plenty of time before the others arrive," said Bob. "Enough time for you two to get acquainted."

"Don't you just hate blind dates?" said Donna.

As an ice breaker, it wasn't bad, thought Joe, he grinned, "Not that I've ever been on one before, but I think you pass."

"I'll say I passed, having to sit in the back of that tatty wagon of Bob's. I think I need a medal," she cried a little loudly.

Judging the condition of Bob's van, Joe could only imagine how uncomfortable it must have been, but couldn't stop himself from laughing.

"I thought you said this bloke needed cheering up," cried Donna.

Joe felt a little guilty that on the surface he appeared to be enjoying himself, but deep down he felt he was cheating on Grace. Despite the company he couldn't get her off his mind. 'What the hell,' he thought as he resigned himself to enjoy the evening's revelry.

It didn't take long for the ice to melt. Donna seemed to be having Joe eating out of her hand. She was bright and bubbly and if the last half hour was anything to go by, a real tonic, thought Bob as he looked over at Becky and mouthed a silent thank you.

Jim and Georgia arrived just before eight, Terry followed ten minutes later. He apologised for the absence of Heather, babysitting problems he said.

Donna, the icebreaker was the first to introduce herself to Georgia, who seemed a little out of it. "Hi I'm Donna, I'm new to this crowd."

Georgia smiled and the awkwardness disappeared, "Me too, although I've met Joe and I think Bob on one occasion, but not to talk too."

Terry was his usual self, as he checked out the three girls. "I don't think we've met, I'm Terry, the good looking one."

The girls laughed, "Yeah sure you are," said Becky.

"You're Becky of course, I met you last week. I'd hazard a guess, you are Jim's bird Georgia. Which means you must be the delectable Donna."

"He's not daft," said Donna.

"What do you ladies see in these three gents when the real deal is standing here before you?"

Donna was the first to react, "Good looks, intelligence, great fashion sense, what more could we want!"

Terry could see he was on to a loser, "Okay girls, you got me. I shall quit while I'm ahead."

"Terry; you were never ahead, you wasn't even in the race," added Georgia with a smile.

"Don't worry ladies, you'll all love me by the end of the evening."

"Yeah sure," said Becky.

The girls giggled amongst themselves, then with the ice broken they began chatting about their jobs, makeup, hair, the latest fashions, the newest bands, the latest films, while the boys chewed the fat on the state of their football teams.

Jim being the exception, his game was rugby, due to the fact he went to a grammar school and their favoured sport was rugby union. Mainly because of his friends he followed Chelsea, but not with the same enthusiasm as the rest of the boys. Terry was an ardent Liverpool fan, and both Bob and Joe supported Arsenal.

"If you're talking football all night, us girls will go to the party without you!" interrupted Becky.

Jim looked at the time, caught Georgia's eye and used the interruption to make their excuses. "I'm afraid, we're going to love you and leave you, we've got somewhere we have to be," said Jim.

"You're not coming to the party," said Bob, "it should be fun."

"Nah," replied Jim. "You know how it is, places to go, people to see."

"Stay for one more round," said Joe, who actually seemed to be getting it together.

Georgia looked across to Jim, "We can stay for one more."

Okay, but just one, then we're off," added Jim.Bob got up to get the round.

"I'll give you a hand," cried Terry.

"Cheers."

Bob called up the order, while Terry gave his opinion on Donna and Georgia. "That Donna has a smart mouth, but she ain't bad in the looks department. Posh bird's okay, but I think she's a bit up herself."

"You would say that. She put you down, good and proper."

"Nah, she's just like the rest of them, playing hard to get," laughed Terry.

"Yeah sure," said Bob, then changing the subject he added, "I reckon it's working with Joe and Donna."

"Yeah maybe," replied Terry his thoughts elsewhere. "Check out the bird that just walked in. Looks like my luck's in!"

Bob was just about to pick up the drinks when he casually looked in the direction Terry had indicated. "Oh fuck!" he exclaimed.

"What?"

Bob looked towards the table, Joe had noticed her too.

"Grace!"

The woman looked bewildered as she looked around the bar. Joe had been in a deep conversation with Donna when he caught sight of her. Their eyes met, she looked sad, confused, upset.

'It's a mistake, I shouldn't have come.' thought Grace as she looked across at the happy crowd. Joe was shocked to see her, he started to rise. Swiftly Grace turned on her heels and rushed out of the bar. Joe looked at a bewildered Donna, "I'm sorry," then he grabbed his coat and raced out of the George. He looked left then right before catching sight of her just as she disappeared towards the High Street.

"Grace, stop!"

She stopped and turned, "I'm sorry I shouldn't have come. I should have realised."

"Realised what?"

"We're over, it's only natural for you to move on."

"Move on! Grace, I love you! That girl, I met only two hours ago. Bob set me up with her."

"Oh, I'm sorry," she said sadly.

"You're here, why? Has something happened?"

Grace hesitated, "I… I'm pregnant!"

# Chapter 20

"Well that was a turn up," said Terry, as he and Bob carried the drinks to the table. Jim looked at Bob, but no words passed between them. What the next few hours would reveal was any ones guess.

Bob and Becky had thought they'd cracked it. Then Becky turned to her friend Donna. "I'm so sorry, I didn't expect that."

"Don't worry about it, after being thrown from pillar to post in that van of Bob's, being dumped for another woman, the night's just got to get better," said Donna.

"Well looks like your luck is about to change," said Terry as he sat down next to Donna.

"Whoa boy, not so fast," warned Donna. "Joe's seat's still warm. He could come back in a few minutes and need consoling."

"Yeah Terry, back off," cried Bob. "Sorry Donna, since he's met this woman he's not been himself."

"Yeah, I could tell, just by the way our conversation was heading. We're still going to a party, right?"

"Of course we're still going, but give Joe a little time, he might be back," said Bob hopefully.

"Well like we said, we'll stay for this drink then we're off," stated Jim.

Twenty five minutes later, Jim and Georgia stood up, put their coats on and wished everyone a Happy New Year. "Give me a call late morning if there's any news," said Jim. "Just hope everything is okay."

"Yeah, let's hope so," replied Bob.

\*\*\*\*\*

Jim drove his Cresta onto the double driveway. A single light illuminated the front door. Jim got out slowly and looked at the dark imposing house as Georgia turned the key. Once inside Georgia threw off her coat and scarf, leaving them strewn across the parquet floor. Even before Jim could take his coat off she was helping him undress.

"Easy; this isn't a wood shed, I want this to be special."

Georgia took no notice as she continued to snog his face off while undoing his tie and unbuttoning his shirt. It was becoming too much for Jim as he responded in kind. A tell-tale trail of clothes discarded and abandoned upon the stairs of the winding staircase led all the way into Georgia's bedroom.

"It's not like we're kids," said Georgia breathlessly, "we're both consenting adults."

"It's still your parents' house," protested Jim very weakly as her lips pressed hard against his. He pushed her onto the bed. She laughed playfully as she felt his weight press upon her. Their passion for each other matched only by the sights and sounds of the numerous firework displays in the surrounding gardens.

\*\*\*\*\*

Georgia lay awake while Jim dozed beside her. Their lovemaking had been both passionate and somehow gentle at the same time. Not at all like the frenzied knee trembler in the wood shed on New Year's Eve. She reflected, that he was very masterful yet considerate in the bedroom department. She climbed out of bed and opened the curtains, allowing the moon's blue grey light to illuminate the room. Gazing up at the moon she wondered why she felt so uneasy. 'Could it be that I'm falling in love? It had been wonderful, no better than wonderful.' She looked down at the prone body of Jim as he broke into smile.

"You look wonderful, come back to bed."

She climbed in and sought the strong arms and warm body of her lover. Georgia had never been happier; how long this euphoria would last she could only guess.

"I wish this feeling could last forever, but something this good rarely lasts. It just makes me feel sad."

"Why sad and why so negative?"

"Oh, I don't know. In my experience nothing this good could last forever."

"Life's what you make it," said Jim. "Right now, I want to make love again, but slowly, savouring every moment."

"That's what I like to hear," purred Georgia.

As they lay in each other's arms exhausted from their lovemaking Georgia remarked, "So that woman was the famous Grace, well let's hope they patch it up whatever it was?" She kissed him playfully, "You know it's the other one I feel sorry for; Donna, she seemed real nice." She strained her eyes to make out the clock in her room, it was one thirty. She looked lustfully at Jim and kissed him passionately, "Happy New Year, you naughty boy."

*****

"I knew I'd end up with you," said Donna as Terry leaned down and kissed her. "You're a fucking married man, I should know better."

"But you don't, you're like me Donna, you take your pleasures where you can," said Terry as he lifted Donna onto the potting shed bench. The difference in their height made it impossible standing up. Donna eased herself forward just enough so Terry had easy access. Moments later he was inside her, a cry of sheer unadulterated lust emanated from Donna's lips, "Do me slowly, take your time," she purred. Terry felt her legs wrap around him, drawing him in. He kissed her passionately and thrust himself deeper. His movements became quicker as he raced towards his climax. Donna became more vocal as he thrust deeper and deeper, sending him over the edge. He was almost there when he felt Donna cum. Her legs held him in a grip of pure ecstasy, just as he was about to pull out. "Fuck no!" he cried as Donna's legs held firm. He gasped at the inevitable climax.

Clarity set in as Terry realised what had just happened. "You silly cow, you made me cum up you."

"You liked it though," said Donna smugly. "Now you've got an uncomfortable wait until I come on. Don't worry about it. I'll soon let you know if there's anything I might need."

"What's that supposed to mean?"

"At this precise moment nothing, I'm going back inside. Shagging you has given me a thirst," she said with a smile on her lips. "Happy New Year."

"Bitch," he muttered after her.

Becky and Bob saw the self-satisfied look on Donna's face as she walked back into the party.

"Well?" asked Becky.

Donna gave a cheeky smile, "I'd give him a seven, no a six plus." Then she laughed. "Silly arse thinks he might have got me pregnant, didn't tell him about the cap."

"You didn't tell him what?" cried Bob, as it slowly dawned on him.

"You're a bad girl Donna," giggled Becky.

"Yes I know, but he's a married man, he should know better. Let him sweat," she grinned. "Now Bob be a dear and get me a gin and bitter lemon, I'm parched."

Bob couldn't stop laughing, Terry had had it coming for more years than he could remember, "Like you said Becky, that Donna is one of a kind," then he walked off to get the girls their drinks.

# Chapter 21

Joe was stunned, "You're pregnant! How can that be?"

"I don't know," Grace shivered, the cold night air caused her breath to almost freeze. Joe could see she was close to tears; in desperation he flung his coat around her shoulders. Grace began to flounder, she struggled to speak. Realising he couldn't take her back into the pub, the place was filled to the rafters with his friends and other noisy revellers out for a good time so he led her back to the George car park. Without another word spoke he opened the passenger door of the Zodiac and helped Grace in. Moments later he was in the driver's seat with the ignition on and the heater at full blast.

Joe waited patiently while the car heated up and Grace had stopped shaking. In the space of a few minutes his life had been turned on its head. There was so much to say, so many questions to be answered, but they could wait. He needed to reassure Grace that he was there for her despite everything. "I haven't stopped thinking about you."

"I feel the same. I love you Joe."

Joe reached out and Grace flung her arms around him. They held each other tight for what seemed like an eternity, both afraid to let go; afraid to let reality rear its ugly head. It was Joe who eventual broke from their embrace. He was just beginning to understand the implications of the little Grace had told him. "Whatever it takes I'm there for you."

Grace smiled, and mouthed a silent 'Thank you'. "I guess I should start from the beginning. I missed my period two weeks after we broke up. I thought it was a reaction to the break up and didn't think to give it much thought at first, but a week or so later I came over very nauseous and dizzy. Then I was sick. I thought it was a bug, but it happened again the following morning, and subsequent mornings afterwards. I began to dream that something wonderful was happening."

"Something was," cried Joe.

"My whole body felt strange and when my next period didn't arrive I knew! But how could I be? I made an appointment with my doctor. Even when he confirmed I was pregnant, I was shocked."

"Have you told Sean?"

"Hell no!" She looked at him with a worried expression. "Joe, it's your baby. Sean hasn't been near me!"

"I just meant….."

"I know what you meant. I've slept with Sean on the few occasions that I couldn't avoid, it's true. But not in the time we've been together."

"I'm sorry, I didn't …."

"Yes you did, and you're right to think it. Being with you was like a breath of fresh air, I wouldn't want anything to spoil it. If you want to walk away, I'll understand."

"I love you, I wouldn't walk away." Joe was filled with emotion, the woman that he thought was lost to him was found. Tears streamed down his cheeks. She attempted to wipe them away and he kissed her.

Grace smiled the most enchanting smile he'd ever seen. "I love you Joe, more than anything. Daft as it may sound, I sensed there was something between us from the moment you took me in your arms and danced with me at the Starlight."

"I felt it too!" exclaimed Joe.

"That's why I left, I knew it was impossible. But you chased after me, you wouldn't take no for an answer. I should have been stronger. Sean's a monster, I believe he's capable of anything."

"Well it's too late now," cried Joe. "I've something to fight for!"

"Joe you are the sweetest man I've ever met, you're patient and kind and loving, but that doesn't hide the fact that when Sean finds out there will be hell to pay."

"Until then we need to think things through," said Joe. His world had been turned on its head. One minute he's footloose and fancy free, the next he's looking at a future of fatherhood with the woman of his dreams. 'If only it was that simple,' he thought. In that moment Joe began to see the reality of their situation. If he was to become a father he needed to cast aside childish dreams and start thinking like a man.

"How?"

"Firstly we seek advice."

"About what?"

"About grounds for divorce, a place to live, for a start. One thing's for sure, we need to find out why you were told you couldn't have kids! That's something we need to look into. Then when we know where we stand I'm going to ask you to marry me."

"Oh Joe!"

"Where's Sean now," he asked, fearing that Grace would be missed.

"He's at a Masonic function, a dinner dance. I told him I didn't feel well. He wasn't perturbed, I think he was quite relieved. Gives him the opportunity to take someone else."

"Short notice!" exclaimed Joe.

"Never bothered him before."

Joe put the car into gear switched his lights on and drove out of the car park. "Where are we going?" asked Grace.

Joe had a smile on his face, "We're going to Neverland!" Tomorrow could wait.

To be honest Joe didn't have a clue where he was going, he just drove, with Grace snuggled up next to him. For an hour they drove aimlessly chatting about their dreams and their future.

"We've got to figure out a plan. We need time to think things through." He glanced at his watch, it was nearing midnight, he didn't want to let her go but he knew things could get far worse if Sean found out before they were ready. Joe indicated then turned the car around and headed back towards Wembley. "I need to get you home, just in case Sean decides to come home early,"

"Not much chance of that. I don't want to go home, I'd love for us to keep driving." She paused as Joe's words sunk in. "I suppose you're right, we do need to think things through," said Grace.

"I hate it too," said Joe, "until we know what we're up against, it's best we keep things as normal as possible."

He dropped her off outside a three storied Victorian terrace, in a very affluent corner of Wembley. "It's the last one," said Grace. "I'll see you outside my work, Monday lunch time."

Joe pulled her too him and kissed her, "Happy New Year Grace."

He didn't want to let go, but the lateness of the hour left him no choice. Sadly he watched as she climbed out of the car and walked down the street. His heart ached for her, he didn't want their time together to end. He couldn't bring himself to leave until she climbed the steps of the house, only then when he knew she was safely inside did he start up the engine. He drove slowly by as a light appeared in the hallway.

*****

Only Jim and Joe made Sunday lunchtime. Neither of them the worse for drink. As Jim brought a couple of pints to the table he was already asking about last night. "Look tell me to mind my own business if you like, but what happened between you and that girl."

"I should tell you to keep your beak out of it, but funnily enough I need someone to bounce things off."

"I'm your man," said Jim as he took a large gulp of his stout and cider. "Sex three times in the night will do that to you" he added with a cheeky grin.

"Grace is pregnant! I don't want this to be general knowledge, not even to Bob and definitely not Terry."

"Oh fuck!" exclaimed Jim, the grin disappeared. "Okay before you go on, she's telling you it's yours? She's got a fucking husband for Christ-sake."

"Yeah, I knew I shouldn't have said anything."

"Well Joe, what did you expect me to say?" Jim took another gulp of his beer. "Okay, I'm listening. Bob's already filled me in about you not touching her until that last time. It does seem like a strange coincidence."

"I'll begin again, firstly I'm not a star-struck teenager. I've been around the block, more than a few times, I do know the score."

"I'll grant you that one" laughed Jim.

"When Grace and I met, I felt there was a chemistry between us. On our first date she told me it was a mistake to meet me. I persuaded her to get in the car and I took her for a drink in the Chilterns. She told me she was married, she told me it was a marriage that had gone sour, she told me her husband was a cop."

"The cop that Terry and Eric warned you about."

Joe nodded.

"Jesus, fuck! You do pick em," said Jim, shaking his head.

"We did nothing for three months, except talk, okay we kissed and cuddled, but nothing more. The reason being she didn't want to fall in love with me. On that last night, she told me it was over, but I should have something to remember her by. We made love in the front seat of the Zodiac."

"So here on New Year's Eve she comes to you and tells you she's pregnant." Jim shook his head. "It's the old, old story. I'm sorry Joe."

"No, that's where you're wrong. The reason her marriage turned sour, was she couldn't have kids. Her ovaries or something like that wasn't working. They tried for two years, during this time this Sean Fallon began to blame her."

"Maybe he was firing blanks," stated Jim.

"That's what I'd have thought except they visited a clinic just off Harley Street, where Grace and her husband had all the tests. It turned out he was okay, but Grace had to go back for further tests, then they received the report from the head obstetrician, that.... basically Grace couldn't have children."

"Well this fancy obstet... whatever, was wrong! Or this Grace is pulling your chain. Now don't go off on one, I'd suggest you get this Grace to seek a second opinion. You need to go with her. If she ain't pregnant, you need to get the fuck away from her."

"She ain't lying Jim," said Joe, a little agitated.

"All I'm saying is check it out before you commit yourself to a pile of grief."

*****

Later that afternoon Jim told Georgia about his conversation with Joe. "She's playing him for a mug."

"Not necessary," said Georgia, the trainee lawyer in her rising to the fore, "From what you've told me about Joe, he's not daft. This woman, Grace did you say her name was…"

Jim nodded.

"Firstly you have to listen to all the facts, you don't of course take them at face value, but you don't dismiss them either. So until you know the full facts; she's not playing him for a mug," she said with a satisfied grin upon her face.

"I stand corrected," he said with a wry grin. "I'd agree with you, but since he met this woman, he's a changed man."

"Maybe so, but her story seems so bizarre, it might possibly be true," continued Georgia. "Tell me all you know about Joe, and how he met Grace."

"You aren't going to let this rest are you?" said Jim.

"Let's just say I'm interested. I'm not sure what kind of law I intend to practice when I've finished my training but I'd like to speak to Joe and this woman. Detective Sergeant Fallon does appear to be a piece of work."

Later that night Jim phoned Joe, his mother answered. "Is Joe there, Mrs Dempsey?"

"Yes, its Jim isn't it. I'll get him for you."

A minute or so later Joe picked up the phone, "Yeah, what do you want," he said curtly.

"Listen Joe, I didn't mean to burst your bubble." "You didn't," snapped Joe.

"Tell me to mind my own business, but I've run what you told me past Georgia, and she thinks you may be right. As you know she's a trainee lawyer and up on these things. She's offered to listen to you both and if possible give you her honest opinion on what to do next."

"Yeah thanks Jim, but I think we can sort it."

"Maybe, but if everything you've told me is on the level, you'll need all the help you can get."

Joe thought about it, "I'll have a word with Grace tomorrow."

"Good, I'll let Georgia know you'll give her a call. Just call Chandler and Lowe and ask to speak to Georgia."

# Chapter 22

Terry fell into bed at 4 am, drunk as a skunk and smelling like a brewery. He'd been with plenty of girls but until that night he hadn't tackled anyone quite like Donna. The sex was good, well more than good, but her parting shot had sown the seeds of doubt in his brain. Hence the need to drink himself into oblivion. When he woke up on that first day of the New Year, his head was thumping, he felt sick as a dog, but above all that, doubt was taking pole position in his brain. 'What if that daft cow was pregnant? My marriage would be up the creek, Heather would kick me out, the kids, what about the kids! Child maintenance! Oh fuck!' These thoughts kept playing over and over throughout the day.

Over the next couple of days he reasoned it out, 'Heather would throw a fit, she'd make me sleep on the couch for a few days, but she wouldn't throw me out. She'd have too much to lose.' Satisfied he'd sorted his domestic problems out, he turned his attention to Donna. 'As for child support, she could go whistle, I don't even know the girl; she could have gone with loads of men.' He'd brazen it out. He even told Bob about his situation. "How well do you know Donna?" he asked.

"Not that well, but she seems a nice girl," said Bob, "She works in the same hair salon as Becky."

"I bet she puts it about!" stated Terry.

Bob wasn't going to give Terry the satisfaction that Donna was easy. He had intended putting his mate out of his misery, but listening to him slagging the girl off made Bob think otherwise. 'Fuck him, let him stew!'

"No I don't think so. In fact I remember Becky said something about Donna having broken up with some feller about six months ago. I believe she took it hard," he lied. "That's right," he added, "Becky said get Joe and Donna on a blind date; maybe it'll kill two birds with one stone."

How Bob managed a straight face when he looked at the worried expression on Terry's face he'd never know, but it was priceless. He told Becky about it the following day.

"Just wait until I tell Donna," laughed Becky. "You don't know what she's capable of. Just don't tell Terry just yet."

Bob laughed, "Terry is so cocksure of himself, I wouldn't dream of it."

"Don't mention it to Joe or Jim, keep it our secret for a while at least."

"You are such a bad girl Becky Marshall."

"Yeah, but you like me being a bad girl," she purred.

*****

In the hair salon that Monday morning the talk was all about the weekend's partying. "Why'd you go with Terry if you didn't like him?" asked Becky.

"Who said I didn't like him!"

"You did actually!" Then Becky told Donna what Terry had said about her.

Donna's face changed, "He's a cocky bastard; he needs knocking off his perch." "Just what are you planning Donna."

"Wait and see. I hope your Bob hasn't told him."

"Bob hasn't told a soul, in fact he thinks it's about time someone took Terry down a peg or two," said Becky.

"Good. Keep it that way. I'm not in a hurry to make his acquaintance but when I do, he's gonna get the shock of his life." Donna's mind was working overtime. She'd already started to form a plan of action. "Your bloke seems sound, do you think he's the one?"

"I don't know. We've been together for almost six months, he's a great shag and he's good to me. He takes me out quite a bit, doesn't mind spending money. On the other side he needs to dump that crappy van," she laughed.

"Didn't your dad set him up with a mate of his?"

"Yeah he did. Bob's taken to it like a duck to water. He's not earning as much, but my dad gives him a Saturday morning's, labouring. It boosts his money up. Dad says he's a really hard worker. Mum likes him too. Who knows, he might just be the one."

"If he is the one, don't make any mistakes, just be sure," advised Donna.

*****

Heather didn't notice the change in Terry's demeanour he was always a little grumpy when on late shift; her mind was still preoccupied with the events of Christmas Eve. The kids were all snuggled up in bed and Heather was just about to pour herself a nice whiskey mac, when the doorbell rang. She glanced at the clock, it was a little after 8.30. 'It'll be Carol from next door,' she thought as she opened the front door.

Eric Sullivan looking as cool as you like, smiled back at her. From behind his back he produced a gorgeous bunch of flowers.

"For you, a belated Happy New Year," he said with a smile. "I'm sorry I might have made you feel embarrassed at Christmas, please except these flowers from me," he noticed a small hesitancy on Heather's face; "it's just a token nothing more."

Heather gave a nervous smile, "Is Gloria with you?"

"No unfortunately she's laid up, caught a bug on New Year's Eve."

"I'm sorry, I hope she'll be better soon," said Heather.

"She's fine, just a little tired. I asked her if she minded me popping out for a couple of drinks. As long as you get me some cigarettes while you're out, she said. I popped into the corner shop to get them, saw these flowers and thought of you. Hope Terry doesn't mind?"

"Terry's at work," said Heather.

"Opps! Sorry, didn't realise."

Heather smiled, "I was just about to pour myself a whiskey mac, would you like one?"

"No, I'd best not, Terry might not like it?" he said.

"I won't bite," said Heather, "and besides I don't like drinking alone."

Eric smiled, "Well if you put it like that, how can I refuse."

Heather put some music on low and poured Eric a drink. Charming as ever Eric regaled her with places he'd been, his time in the army, "Conscript, nothing glamourous, spent most of my time square bashing before being shipped to Suez. A little action, but kept my head down."

Heather smiled, and took a sip of the warming liquid, then put a couple of logs on the fire. "Tell me about how you and Gloria met."

Eric rubbed his hands and warmed them on the welcoming flames. "Met Gloria in a casino in the West End about a couple of years after finishing my service. We hit it off right away, and before you could say 'Jack Robinson' we were married."

"Have you any kids? Only Terry's never said."

"No, unfortunately Gloria had several miscarriages from a previous marriage. She said she didn't want to go through it again."

"Oh I'm so sorry. Can I get you a refill," said Heather.

"That would be nice, but just a small one."

Heather refilled his glass, "Didn't you ever want kids?"

"It never bothered me one way or the other, but I guess the prospect of having kids wouldn't have fazed me."

"It must have been hard though," persisted Heather, the whiskey loosening her tongue.

"No not really, Glo's a fine looking woman, she'll be forty sixth next birthday," he said proudly.

"She's a really smart looking lady," said Heather. "Those clothes she wears must cost a fortune?"

"Yeah, tell me about it," laughed Eric.

Minutes later he finished his drink, stood up, "Must go; can't keep the lady waiting."

"Oh, you're going!" said Heather as she quickly jumped up and followed him into the hallway. She looked at him and joked about the last time at her front door. "I won't make the same mistake."

Eric looked at her and smiled, "No we won't." Suddenly his arms were around her and he kissed her full on the lips. It was an automatic reaction that Heather couldn't control as she kissed him in return. The kiss was passionate and sent out signals. Eric broke from the embrace, "I'm sorry I don't know what came over me!"

"Don't be sorry," cried Heather as she reached up and kissed him again. He responded and kissed her back. "It's just a kiss Eric. It's wrong, but it's only a kiss."

Eric smiled knowingly, a kiss maybe, but it promised so much more. "Good night Heather."

Before she could say another word, he was down her path and making for his car. She stood at the door and waved as he drove off. She should have felt a little guilty, a little embarrassed, but instead she felt strangely naughty. It was a nice feeling.

Heather was in bed when Terry came in from work. She pretended to be sleep when he opened the door and switched the light on. She let out a slight grunt and turned over. Terry mumbled, "Oh, you're asleep," then promptly switched off the light and went back down stairs. Heather breathed a sigh of relief. She couldn't face him right now, she was afraid he would see the guilty look on her face. She'd be up early with the baby and getting the kids their packed lunches. By the time Terry got up she'd be halfway through her day, enough time to lose that sense of guilt.

It was late in the afternoon, when Terry had gone off to work that the phone rang. It was Eric. Heather felt her heart racing, as he apologised. "Eric, there's nothing to apologise for; it was just a kiss. It shouldn't have happened but it did. Just forget it." She told herself it was nothing more than a mild flirtation, Eric was happily married….and so am I! As she walked back into the kitchen she couldn't help thinking there was chemistry between them.

# Chapter 23

Joe phoned Grace around 9.30, desperate to hear her voice. "Was everything okay when you got home?"

"It was fine, Sean staggered in around two thirty. I feigned sleep, and within a minute of climbing into bed, he was fast asleep. I laid there wide awake wondering if my actions would put you in grave danger. It must have been around four before I dropped off. Seeing you, brought it all back. I was worried I'd done the wrong thing."

"Grave danger, that's a bit of an exaggeration," laughed Joe. "You can stop that kind of thinking right away. We're in this together, so get used to it," he said, all masterfully. "Can you get this afternoon off?"

"I can try. Why?"

"We've an appointment with a solicitor. She might be able to advise us."

"You shouldn't be spend…"

Joe stopped her in mid-sentence. "She's a friend of a friend. It's a favour."

"I'll make it somehow."

\*\*\*\*\*

Joe looked at Grace, "Are you ready?

Grace nodded, then with a glance at the Chandler and Lowe sign in the window, they stepped inside. One reassuring smile later and they were addressing the receptionist. "We've a two o'clock appointment with Georgia," stated Joe.

"Who shall I say is calling?"

"Oh I'm sorry. Tell her Joe Dempsey"

"Take a seat, I'll see if she's free," said the receptionist with a smile and a flourish of her hand.

A couple of minutes later they were shown into Georgia's office. Dressed in a smart charcoal grey suit Georgia stood up and made her way around her desk, she smiled and held out her hand, "I'm Georgia." Joe having only met her very briefly felt slightly intimidated in the unfamiliar surroundings, shook Georgia's hand and then introduced Grace.

She offered them both a seat then sat down herself. "Can I get you something, tea, coffee or maybe a glass of water?"

"No we're fine," said Grace.

"Right before we start I must inform you that whatever's said in this office is strictly confidential."

Grace and Joe looked at each other and nodded.

"I'm going to ask some very intimate questions, some might not be to your liking, but they must be answered honestly. Do you understand?"

"Yes," replied Grace.

"Good, we understand each other. In your own time, tell me all about your relationship with your husband. Starting with his name."

"His name is Sean Fallon, Detective Sergeant Sean Fallon of the Flying Squad."

Grace began by how they met, their courtship, the engagement and finally the wedding. "There was nothing in our relationship to suggest Sean was a monster."

Joe sat awkwardly, finding it hard to take, but somehow managed to sit silently while Grace told her story.

"Once we were married, I started to notice little things, inconsequential things, like Sean would stay out late. The job, he'd say. I knew before we became serious that the job meant everything to him. Sean was ambitious, he wanted to climb all the way to the top."

"Who was it that suggested trying for a baby," asked Georgia. "Sorry I have to ask. I've been briefed, but I need to hear it from you."

Joe looked across the desk as Georgia made notes. He guessed she was using shorthand.

"I'd have been around twenty two, I had, or believed I had plenty of time before starting a family." Grace stopped for a moment; thinking. "Yes it was Sean, definitely! He said he didn't want to be the oldest father in the playground."

"So at twenty two you began trying for a baby?"

Grace nodded. "Sean was excited about us starting a family. I have to admit once I got around to the idea I was happy too. Sean was eager, too eager in my eyes, every month he'd ask me if I'd missed my period." Grace paused, she hadn't realised how painful reliving the memories could be. "Sorry, we'd been trying for three months when his attitude began to change. He would get angry rather than disappointed."

Joe could see the pain in her face as she relived every little detail. She asked for that glass of water, which she took a couple of sips from, then continued. She told Georgia about the nights he would come home drunk and demand sex, how after a year and a half, sex with Sean was becoming intolerable.

"Do you mean he indulged in rough sex," said a very serious looking Georgia.

Grace just looked down.

"I take it that's a yes!"

Grace gave a slight nod of her head.

"We'd tried and tried, life in our house was becoming intolerable. He's abuse me verbally for the slightest thing. Sean was like a man possessed, then he left me alone for three weeks. I knew he was seeing other women, and to be brutally honest I didn't care."

Georgia noted it down.

"Then it happened, he woke me from a deep sleep around three in the morning. He burst into our bedroom much drunker than usual, knocking into furniture and falling onto our bed. Then he climbed on top of me, "We're gonna make a fucking baby if it kills us," he slurred. I shouted for him to stop and began to struggle. He slapped me hard across the face, "You're my wife, you'll do what I fucking want! Then he forced himself inside me."

Georgia remained stone faced.

Joe could see it in Grace's face, she was reliving that night. She began to shake uncontrollably and tears streamed from her eyes. Joe held her in his arms and implored Georgia to stop, but Grace, wiping away the tears somehow managed to pull herself together. "I never thought it would be so painful to re-live that awful night; I need this," she added forcefully.

"What you are describing is rape. A man, whether he's your husband or not has no right to force himself upon you," said Georgia, her face betraying a sign of anger.

"He was sorry after it was over," said Grace.

"I bet he was!" exclaimed Georgia.

Grace retold how after that night, in the morning he showed what appeared to be genuine remorse, "He told me he was sorry and begged my forgiveness. I recoiled from him. I told him he was not the man I'd married and that my life with him was a living hell."

"How did he react?"

"He went silent and for about a week we hardly spoke. Until he came to me and said we should seek help. He had contacts with doctors at a nearby clinic close to Harley Street."

"A family planning clinic?" asked Georgia.

"Yes, I guess so. I was given a thorough examination and physical and they took all sorts of x-rays. We went back again a week later, something to do with checking out my ovaries. All this time Sean was the man I'd married, kind and attentive.

We were sharing a new experience together. I thought we'd turned a corner and somehow forcing himself on me had brought him to his senses." "So what changed," asked Georgia?

"It was a little over two weeks when the clinic sent us their report. The report basically said, my fallopian tubes were not functioning properly, which had caused the doctor some concern. They seemed to insinuate that it might have been caused by an untreated infection of some sort. The follow up examination had also found one of my ovaries had stopped working while the other was barely functioning. The chance of me becoming pregnant was close to zero. I was devastated."

Georgia had one question that she'd been putting off until she'd found the right moment, "Grace, I'm sorry to ask what might appear a dumb question, are you really pregnant?" "What the hell!" snapped Joe? He rose to his feet, "We're going!"

"No! Georgia's right to ask," cried Grace, as she grabbed his arm and motioned for him to sit down. "I've asked myself the same question again and again. How could I be pregnant? I've missed two periods, I've had morning sickness and my body feels different. Even I began to wonder if it was all in my mind. My doctor confirmed I was pregnant less than a week ago."

"Have you still got the report, the letter from the clinic?"

"I think so, it's probably amongst all our paperwork at home," said Grace.

"Okay, we'll deal with that later, please continue."

"Is this all necessary," said Joe.

"Yes, if I'm to build up a picture of events," said a rather haughty Georgia. "You were devastated."

"Devastated, more than devastated. My whole world had come crashing down around me. Sean was silent when we read the report, but instead of giving me the support I needed, he shut down until we got home, where he called me a dirty slut, saying I must have played around before I met him. That I must have caught something!"

"Pig" uttered Georgia.

"Worse was to follow. Our life hadn't been great, but with this devastating blow I believed things couldn't get any worse. How wrong I was! Sean received word that he was being passed over for promotion. He'd worked hard, passed the requisite exams and was a front runner, in fact he was the only runner. According to him two or three cases had folded partly because he'd dropped the ball. His future career in the Metropolitan Police was put on hold. In short he blamed me for everything."

"You couldn't be held responsible," uttered Georgia.

"I know, there was talk, rumours really about a death in custody, a low level thief and pill pusher. They said he fell and cracked his head on the corner of a table in the interview room. It was about the time Sean was passed over for promotion."

"You're saying…"

"I'm not saying anything. It just made me think, that's all."

"You think maybe…"

"I think nothing."

"Why didn't you leave him?"

Grace looked across at Joe, "I'm sorry Joe, I haven't told you everything!"

The blood drained from Joe's face.

"I told him I was leaving, that I'd seek a divorce, that I would take all the blame for the breakdown in our marriage. He grabbed me around the throat and slammed me against the door. His eyes bulged from their sockets, his face turned red, and in a quiet but blood curdling voice, he told me that would never happen."

"What were his actual words?" said an unmoved Georgia.

Grace looked straight at Georgia then Joe, then back again to Georgia. She took a breath, "I'd rather be a widower; it's much cleaner than a divorce!"

"The bastard! I'll kill him!" snapped Joe.

"Oh fuck!" exclaimed Georgia, "I wish you hadn't said that!"

"I'm sorry," replied Joe.

Grace looked startled.

Georgia shook her head; her eyes seething with anger. James was in for an earful when I see him, she thought.

"Continue," said Georgia rather more sharply than she intended.

"I believed he meant every word. I was trapped in a loveless marriage with no way out. In private he blamed me for everything, he treated me like dirt."

"The question I have to ask is, have you any proof, photographs, doctors, a witness?"

"No, I'm sorry. Now where is this all leading?" cried Grace sternly. "I thought you were going to give me some help or advice."

"I am, I will; just bear with me a little longer. What happened once you decided to stay put?"

"Sometimes Sean would play nice, which he did when he wanted us to buy the house we live in at the moment. He needed both our incomes to get the mortgage for the place. He needed my signature on the mortgage documents. I didn't realise until that moment that I had struck a deal with the devil. In return for him treating me with respect, I'd continue with the charade that was our marriage."

"What was so important that he needed you as the perfect wifey?"

The sarcasm wasn't lost on Grace. "The Met's social gatherings were very important to him, it's a place for him to mix with the top echelons of the force, networking he calls it. Having a sound marriage is important to the top brass and his chances of that promotion."

"You were very much afraid of him," said Georgia.

"For the last few years I've been living a lie!"

Georgia managed a faint smile. "I'm sorry if I sounded harsh and unemotional, it's just my way of dealing with these sort of things. Actually this isn't really my field of work. Perhaps in the future it will be, I've not quite decided. What I can give you is my professional opinion on what you've told me. I'm usually dealing with conveyancing, but I think I can give you some advice, whether you take it, is up to you."

Grace smiled, "I understand, go ahead."

Georgia took a sip of water, looked at Grace and then glanced at Joe, "Don't take this the wrong way, but is there anyway…?"

Grace stopped her before she could finish, "The answer to that question is no! I haven't had sex with Sean for months, certainly not in the timespan we're talking about."

"Sorry I had to ask," replied Georgia. "First thing, make an appointment with another doctor. Make one hundred percent certain you really are pregnant. Assuming you are, find that report from that clinic; that is most important. Then and only then make an appointment at that family planning clinic, ask them… No, fuck it! Make the appointment and I'll go with you."

Before Grace could re-act Georgia continued. "Don't ask. What you've told me, if you get as far as the appointment, could mean you have a case of malpractice against the clinic. In which case I'm sure Chandler and Lowe would be happy to represent you."

"Yes, but what about….."

"First things first," said Georgia. "My boyfriend Jim told me the story, he also told me that according to what they had learned, this detective sergeant Sean Fallon is a real piece of work. That I'm afraid is hearsay. What's needed is proof. We can deal with him, when the time comes. I knew I had to meet you, and for what it's worth, I believe every word."

# Chapter 24

Eric was troubled, it was just a kiss. It wasn't the first time that had happened; during his younger days women threw themselves at him, but once Gloria came on the scene he had eyes for nobody else. That was until Christmas Eve. It troubled him, he had no thought about taking it any further, so why did he call on Heather with a bunch of flowers? He guessed he liked her company, her lively inquisitive conversation, her down to earth attitude to life. The thought of being unfaithful had never crossed his mind, Gloria was everything to him.

Eric had prided himself on making the most out of any situation for the least risk. He had many contacts with the London underworld. Old lags that knew the score, old lags that wouldn't grass. They knew that working for Eric Sullivan wouldn't make them rich, but on balance the risks would be minimal. Eric's secret, *if there was one,* he wasn't a greedy man. He enjoyed a charmed and comfortable lifestyle. Gloria was his rock, more than that, she'd suggested the move and financed the antique shop. "It's the right move, you know it and I know it. Staying in the Smoke will either get you banged up or dead. It's my gift to you," she'd said, when she told him they were moving.

In her day Gloria Sullivan had been a formidable woman, she'd had a varied career. Firstly as a dancer at the Folies Bergere at the age of sixteen, where she lied about her age, an artist's model, both in Paris. *The stories Gloria could tell.* A hasty retreat back to Blighty, one step ahead of the Nazi's as they entered Paris. She tried her luck as a telephonist in a London hotel, before becoming, first a barmaid in a pub then a cocktail waitress in a club and finally a magician's assistant, where she met her first husband, Charles Benjamin a wealthy business man, twenty seven years her senior. They married on impulse on the 8th May, VE Day 1945. A marriage made in heaven, maybe not! But it lasted for twelve happy years until Charles succumbed to a heart attack and died at the age of sixty four.

Not blessed with children, Gloria returned to the lifestyle of her past. Still an attractive woman she frequented the best establishments that London had to offer. Her outgoing character and dynamic personality won her many friends, including several high profile flings with married men. Within a couple of years of reliving the highlife she was left feeling jaded and empty. Then on a night in a West End casino she saw Eric. He was youngish but carried himself with an air of confidence. He was around six feet tall, darkly handsome, good looking in a rugged way, her kind of man, she thought enviously. 'If only I was ten years younger.' Judging by the cut of his suit and what appeared to be handmade shoes he was a man of influence.

"Eric's a nice guy, always polite, well-mannered and a good tipper," said one croupier, "although the company he keeps…"

"Well, the company he keeps, are?" asked Gloria.

"Let's just say, not the kind you mess with."

"Oh, a bad boy, I love him already!" laughed Gloria.

Eric was a thief, pure and simple, where he differed from the rest was his ability to always stay at least one step ahead of the law. He was a thinker, if the job looked too good to be true, he left it alone. When he did get his hands dirty it was after meticulous planning. He was a known villain in the East End, albeit small time. Which is the way he liked it. He was able to go about his business under the radar of Jack Comer and Billy Hill. He watched as the old firms made way for the new and wanted no part in their plans. Violence was for mugs. Sooner or later things always go south. He liked a flutter, but knew his limits. Eric despite his outward appearance was a cautious man. Then he met Gloria.

He first caught sight of her across a roulette wheel. She was an older woman, quite a bit older than the usual women he dated, yet she had something about her that intrigued him. She wore expensive clothes, her blonde hair and immaculate makeup caused him to take a second look. He watched as she'd placed a small stake of chips on red. The tiny ivory ball bounced around the wheel and landed on red. She raked in her winnings then put a single chip on a corner bet. She lost, then she cashed in her chips before withdrawing to the bar. There was something about her that drew him to her. His first assumption was she'd be good in bed, but once he engaged her in conversation, he realised there was a whole lot more to this woman. An hour later they were in bed. Within a month they were touring the casinos and bars in Paris, taking in the Folies Bergere and other old haunts of Gloria's. She regaled him with tales of Paris before it was taken, how she'd barely escaped before the Germans got a foothold. Eric wasn't sure whether she was bullshitting him or if it was for real. She certainly knew her way around the back streets and bars, even bumping into some of her old friends. From the moment he first clapped eyes on Gloria, Eric had thought to seduce her. But somewhere in their whirlwind romance Gloria had turned the tables on him. Despite the difference in age, Eric asked her to marry him on their last night in Paris. Gloria eyed him with suspicion, and asked why a young man like him would be interested in a woman of her age.

"I could ask you the same, age difference shouldn't be a barrier. We haven't known each other long. I know you're not bad off, whereas I'm not much better than a thief, a rogue if you please. I've had my share of woman it's true, but until I met you I didn't know a real woman."

"Thank you, that makes me happy, I like to believe I'm still desirable."

"Believe me, desirable doesn't do you justice. I don't care about your money, that's a lie, of course money is important.

Agree to marry me, make all the safeguards you feel necessary and let's get on with the rest of our lives."

"It can work Eric, it did for me and Charles, I'll marry you on one condition, don't ever take me for a fool."

Over the next couple of years Gloria became his sounding board when he was thinking about getting involved in one scheme or another. He'd been approached on a number of occasions with get rich heists but turned them all down, including a certain train robbery. When the Krays and the Richardsons began to put a stranglehold on London, Gloria had suggested the move to Ruislip.

"Where? That's in the sticks ain't it! What will I do there?"

"Open an antique shop. You've always had a flare when it comes to a deal, beside it would be the perfect front for your extra curricula activities."

That was what Eric loved about Gloria. She was always one step ahead when it came to looking out for his welfare. No one had expected their marriage to last, but almost six years later they were still going strong. Despite his attraction for Heather, an attraction that appeared to be reciprocated, Eric knew he would never cheat on Gloria. Yet somehow Heather had gotten under his skin, probably because of the way Terry cheated on her with other women. She deserved to be treated better. Eric hoped his feelings for Heather would pass, so despite the lucrative business he did with Terry, he decided to end the arrangement. He liked Terry, in fact he'd thought that in the future he could be a good earner, but the man was a loose cannon, sooner or later he would screw up. Whether it was his feelings for Heather or good business sense, he couldn't say, but he intended cutting Terry loose.

*****

Becky emerged from the brightly lit salon into the wet and gloomy January night. She trudged along the wet pavement towards the bus stop, where she found several equally wet and miserable looking commuters. Though the teeming rain Becky could just make out the headlights of her bus as it turned around a bend in the road.

"About bloody time!" she muttered to herself.

"Becky!" She looked down at the car that had just pulled up to the kerb. "Becky, climb in, I'll give you a lift."

"No thanks, my bus is here now!" 'Shit,' she thought, it was Andy, her old boyfriend.

"Climb in, I'm passing your place."

Becky hesitated for a second as the headlights of her bus beamed down on Andy's car. "Just a lift!"

"Just a lift," echoed Andy.

Becky was strong willed and nothing fazed her; except Andy. For the best part of a year they'd been together, until out of the blue he dumped her. She'd never expected their relationship to last, but for it to end so suddenly had hurt her deeply, more deeply than she knew. It had taken her months to get over him, months full of heartache. When she finally thought she was over him, she started going out with the girls again. She vowed she was over men for good, *unrealistic maybe.* Then on her third Friday night with the girls she met Bob. 'Okay,' she thought, 'on the rebound maybe, but he looked fit, what the hell!'

"So how have you been?" asked Andy.

"How do you think I've been!" she snapped at him.

"Whoa… Easy… Yeah, I'm sorry about that."

"You should be, anyway I've met someone else. Someone that treats me right."

Becky was feeling uneasy. Andy had been the centre of her universe. She was in his car, it would be so easy, except there was Bob. The man who'd dragged her back from that whirlpool of despair. The man that had breathed life back into her. The man that made her heart race.

It was ten minutes of listening to Andy prattle on about his life, his ambitions and his new car, before he turned into Becky's road. Stopping seven doors down from her house he turned off the ignition and lights. He'd been mulling over Becky's words.

"Yeah, but I bet he doesn't turn you on the way I do."

"Past tense Andy!"

"Look I'm sorry about the way I treated you. Let's go for a drink and talk about. Who knows we might get back together," said Andy.

"You hurt me, more than you could imagine. My Bob's a good bloke, I wouldn't do that to him."

"Yeah okay, Bob's a good bloke, but he ain't me. Let's meet up, have that drink and maybe you'll change your mind."

It was in that moment when the streetlights illuminated Andy's confident smiling face that she saw him for the man that he really was. Becky laughed.

"Thanks for the lift. Thanks for showing me I was wrong!" Becky opened the passenger door and climbed out. She leant on the door and smiled back at Andy. "My Bob is worth ten of you! Bye Andy, have a nice life!"

She slammed the door shut and started walking the short distance to her house. She'd expected to shed a tear, but instead she felt a great weight had been lifted from her shoulders.

She remembered Donna asking her a question, "Your bloke seems sound; could he be the one?" 'A good question,' thought Becky, 'only time will tell.'

# Chapter 25

"I know she's Jim's girlfriend, but I felt like you'd just been interrogated by the Gestapo!" exclaimed Joe.

"Yeah, it did feel a bit like that," sighed Grace. "She did seem a little abrupt at times, but you have to remember she doesn't know me from Adam. Mind you, she did say she believed me."

"That was big of her," said Joe.

"No Joe, don't judge her! She's not one to suffer fools gladly I'll grant you, but I like her. She's looking at our problem from outside the box, whereas I've been looking at it from a different angle."

Grace took Georgia at her word and on a pretext of visiting her parents in Elstree, booked an appointment with the family doctor. In the years since she'd married she'd not notified her doctor that she'd moved. It was an oversight on Grace's part. She felt funny when she told the doctor that had known her since childhood that she'd missed two periods and wondered if she might be pregnant. Within ten minutes he confirmed what she already knew.

She phoned Joe at his place of work and told him about her visit to the doctor.

"Despite what Georgia said, you didn't need to convince me."

"Maybe not Joe, but even though I knew I was pregnant some part of me didn't believe it. I'm glad I went. Now all I've got to do is find that report."

"Yeah, I'm sorry if it feels like I'm a bit edgy, it's this hiding away that's getting me down. I just want us to be free of Sean, to live a normal life."

"It won't be like this forever," said Grace.

"I know; every minute we're apart feels like a lifetime."

The following day Grace searched through all their paperwork, their marriage certificate, both their birth certificates, their mortgage documents, their passports, reams of invoices, paid gas and electric bills, the water rates, old photographs, more bills until finally she came across an envelope addressed to Detective Sergeant Sean Fallon. She opened the envelope and there it was in all its gory glory; the report that put the final nail in the coffin of their marriage.

Grace phoned Joe, "I've found the report. Reading it for the first time in years brought back a lot of bad memories."

"You need to arrange a meeting with Georgia," said Joe. "Whatever day it's convenient, I'll just throw another sickie."

"Joe, I don't want you getting into trouble for my sake."

"I'm not, I'm doing it for us, the three of us."

They met Georgia in a pub in Harrow on the following Wednesday lunchtime. She smiled as they both walked in. "What can I get you?" she asked.

"I'll get them," protested Joe.

"No, you two sit down, I'm getting them."

"See," said Grace as they sat down at a table and waited for Georgia to bring the drinks over. "I told you she was nice."

Georgia placed the drinks down on the table, "Look I haven't much time, so we'd better get on with it."

Grace handed her the report.

Georgia took particular interest in the envelope, before even looking at the report, "Why was this report sent to Sean's place of work?"

"Because he didn't want me to open it when he wasn't there, in case the contents upset me," replied Grace.

"Funny that! From what you've told me, Sean wasn't really the caring type. My question, did he have prior knowledge of the report before he asked for it to be re-directed to his office?"

"No, I don't think so, he'd have told me."

"Hmm. Was the envelope open or was it still sealed when you saw it for the first time?"

"It was sealed, I remember him handing it to me," said Grace. "What are you driving at?"

"Nothing," replied Georgia, "Just checking all the possibilities. Are you sure you want to go on?"

"More than ever," said Grace.

"Good! Let me arrange the meeting on your behave. They are more likely to respond to me acting as your solicitor."

Outside the clinic a week later, Georgia tells Grace in no uncertain terms, "I stuck my neck out pretending to be your solicitor, so unless they speak to you directly let me do the talking. If this turns out to be a case of malpractice, I'm just a friend helping you out, not a solicitor. I don't want to jeopardise my future career, do you understand."

"Yes I understand."

"Okay, here goes," said Georgia with a non to convincing smile.

A receptionist showed them into a small magnolia painted non-descript office. The room consisted of a large desk, a comfortable chair and a couple of less comfortable chairs.

"I bet they don't use this room for private patients," said Georgia, with a wry grin. They sat there for what could only have been a few minutes but felt like hours to both of them. The door opened and a man in a well-tailored suit smiled, offered his hand and sat down in the comfortable chair.

"I'm Brian Bennett, co-partner of this clinic. I understand from your phone call that you believe there might have been a misdiagnoses. I can assure you that this clinic prides itself on the work we do here. Let me also assure you we take every complaint very seriously."

"My friend, received this report from this clinic four years ago."

All pleasantries on the man's face disappeared, as he took the envelope and opened the report. He sat there reading and digesting every detail of the report.

"What is your point?

"The report clearly states that my friend can't have children, is that correct?" asked Georgia.

"The report goes into great detail to explain this woman's condition. So yes. I ask again, what is your point?"

"The point is, this woman, this barren woman is now two months pregnant! Explain that!" demanded Georgia.

The man lost all his arrogance, sat down and studied the report again. After what could be described as a calculation of what this report would cost the clinic, the man got up, excused himself and said he needed to speak with someone.

Five minutes passed, before the man and another man walked back into the office. "This is my legal adviser, Gregory Slater."

Georgia had warned Grace this might happen, now both of them looked decidedly uncomfortable. It was Grace who spoke first, "I don't want any trouble. I just want answers. Nothing more."

Georgia gave Grace a withering look. She understood what Grace was trying to do, but she'd just relinquished the upper hand.

"This does indeed look like a genuine report of ours, but in light of your condition I suspect it is a fake!"

It was a bold statement, but Georgia, now completely composed said. "You must have a copy of this report in your archives! Can we see it?"

"That's rather irregular," stated Bennett.

"Look, this matter can be cleared up in record time if you produce your copy. Either that or we take this matter further!" Georgia was going out on a limb

Grace looked fearfully at Georgia, the woman, the woman she'd known for barely a few weeks was risking her future career in law.

Slater could see the determination on Georgia's face and with a knowing look at his colleague, picked up the phone. "Miss Green could you come in here please."

Within a few minutes the young woman was sent out to retrieve Grace's file.

"You understand in the circumstance we can't show you the copy of the report at this stage, but I will take a look at it in your presence. Hopefully we can solve this matter without taking it further," said Bennett.

"Hold it a moment! Is it usual to send out a report without speaking to the parties in question first?" asked Slater.

"That's correct but until we look at the file I wouldn't know who would have spoken to Mr and Mrs Fallon," replied Bennett.

"No one spoke to me!" snapped Grace

"It'll be on the file," said Bennett.

Grace looked panic stricken, "We weren't spoken too, you have to believe me!" she stared right into Georgia's eyes, imploring her friend to believe her.

Moments later Miss Green returned and handed the file to Bennett. He read through the file carefully, a serious studious look upon his face. Georgia studied the man as he read and re-read the report. She noticed the colour come back into his cheeks.

"I believe we have a serious breach of our confidential records. Mrs Fallon I believe you have somehow been given an altered report."

"Are you saying this report didn't originate from here?" asked Grace.

"That's exactly what I'm saying. We did indeed send as requested the report to Mr Fallon's place of work. Due to the unusual circumstances of this case I will allow you to read the report we have on file. He handed her a copy of the letter. It clearly stated that Grace Fallon was in perfect health and that there were no abnormalities. "As you can see, the address on your envelope and report is a slightly different type face to the one we use. Our secretary as was our practice at the time, typed out your report and also a copy for our files. That report of yours is clearly a fake!"

Grace was staggered, but Georgia was in full flow. "We need a copy of that report!"

"I'm afraid, I'm unable to give that to you," said Bennett.

Gregory Slater intervened. "I will be starting our own investigation into what happened, so on balance I would need your report. The one we have on file is an exact copy of the one sent to your husband, the one you received is fake. The copy you have does have Mr Bennett's signature, which as you can see quite clearly is nothing like his real signature. I'm afraid we've come to an impasse, unless we dispense with protocol and allow Miss Green to photo copy both sets of reports."

"Agreed!" said Georgia. "Provided you keep me appraised of your findings, I will likewise keep you informed of any progress on our part. All I ask is that you don't inform detective sergeant Sean Fallon until you have consulted with me." Georgia paused, then continued, "Criminal proceedings are at an early stage and any contact could jeopardise our investigation," she lied.

"Of course, we won't proceed until you contact us. Miss Green will you do the honours."

Miss Green swept up the letters and swiftly exited the office. For the next few minutes Slater indulged in small talk with Grace as to when the baby was due, did she want a boy or a girl. Thankfully Miss Green was super-efficient and returned with the copies that were required. Gregory Slater checked over the reports, before handing them over to Georgia.

Georgia thanked him, then chanced her luck. "Just one more question, was Fallon tested?"

"I can't answer that." he gave Georgia a knowing look. Then he spoke to Bennett, "I need a word outside."

Georgia's pushy attitude had paid off as the two men left the office leaving Grace and Georgia alone with the open file. Georgia took a look at the file. There was the second visit that Grace had told her about, it clearly showed that Grace had her ovaries looked at and that it was suggested that Sean Fallon should be tested.

"The bastard!" shrieked Georgia. "I'll bet he's the one firing blanks!"

Grace shook her head in disbelief, as she read more of the file. Her eyes almost popped out of her head, "Look at this Georgia!"

Georgia still fuming from the revelations looked at the last paragraph. It stated that Sean and Grace attended a meeting with consultants at the clinic who informed them of their results. Mrs Fallon was overjoyed at hearing her results while Mr Fallon was taken into a separate room. It was at Mr Fallon's request that copies of both sets of results should be posted to his work office.

"Of course, they wouldn't have sent out copies of their reports until they had spoken to both of you and explained the opinions that were left."

Grace looked at Georgia, "Under no circumstances did I visit this clinic for a third time. Whoever this Mrs Fallon was, it wasn't me."

"I believe you, I must admit they had me going for a minute."

Minutes later Grace and Georgia walked down the steps of the clinic and made their way to the tube station. "This changes everything," snapped Grace. "I can't go back to that house. I'd always believed that I was to blame, but knowing the truth has given me the strength to confront Sean."

"I understand your anger, but I'd advise that you think on it for a few days," said Georgia.

"No! I'm going to ask Sean for a divorce!"

Georgia could see the transformation in Grace's attitude, but knew she needed to tread carefully.

"So you're going to go home, tell him what you've discovered and then what? Before you could mention divorce, he'd be on the phone to his solicitor and turn the tables on you. Joe would be cited in his divorce petition and all hell would break loose. No Grace you need to think this through before you act."

"I suppose you're right. It's just that I've never really stood up to him since he threatened me. I wanted to see his face, confronted with the evidence."

"That's exactly why you should hold off until you've got everything in place. You need to tell Joe, but you also need to tell your parents. Do they know how unhappy you've been?"

"No, I've always kept it from them."

"Right, do me a favour, give me the paperwork, I'll put it in our safe and I'll also make copies. Then go home as if nothing has happened. Tell Sean your mother's unwell, that you're going to spend a few days looking after her."

"What about Joe?"

"Do you love him?"

"What kind of questions that? Of course I love him, I love him with all my heart."

"Good, then tell him everything, tell him what I've advised you to do, but most importantly impress on him not to over re-act. It could spoil everything. I'm going to speak to my father when I get home, he'll know exactly what needs to be done. Trust me!" implored Georgia.

# Chapter 26

Grace left the train at Wembley Park leaving Georgia with the two reports. "I'll phone you," she promised. As she stood at the bus stop she wondered how she was going to face Sean, it was beyond her. Firstly she needed to get home to gather her thoughts, then phone Joe.

"I really need to speak to you, can you meet me at the entrance to Barham Park in an hour?" asked Grace.

"Can't you tell me over the phone? I'm still at work. I can meet you later, say six o'clock."

"It'll be dark then and Sean is likely to be home."

Joe glance back to his workplace and stared straight into the angry stare of his foreman. "I can't talk right now. Can you meet me tomorrow, same place; ten o'clock." He could almost feel the hurt in her voice, "I love you."

"I love you too, so very much, until tomorrow," said Grace.

Joe reluctantly sulked back to his workplace under the watchful eye of the foreman. He knew his job was on the line, but he didn't care. He'd taken several days off without a certificate, been given a written warning and was very close to telling the bosses to stick their job up their collective arses. Phoning in sick the following morning, might be the last nail in the coffin, 'but what the hell, in for a penny,' he thought. As he drove home from work he couldn't help thinking he should have chosen a trade rather than following advice from his metalwork teacher at school.

***** 

He sat in the Zodiac with the engine running outside the entrance to the park, his brain was fried wondering just what had happened at the clinic. He'd tossed and turned and probably only had a couple of hours sleep. It had been an agonising wait and then his heart skipped a beat as Grace emerged from the park's entrance. She looked around then opened the door and climbed in beside Joe. She kissed him gently on the cheek, Joe smiled at her, put the car into gear and moved away from the kerb. Within a few minutes he saw a small parade of shops. He indicated then turned onto a single track that led to a small car park at the back of the shops. He turned off the ignition and turned towards Grace expectantly.

"Before I start, you must promise me you won't do anything hasty, said Grace."

Fearing the news wasn't good, Joe spoke sharply, "Like what?"

"Promise me!" insisted Grace.

"Okay, I promise," his voice had lowered.

Grace then told him chapter and verse about the meeting with Bennett and Slater. Joe slumped back against the bench seat, stunned by the revelations. It was better than he'd hoped for. He remained silent for a minute or two, mulling over what to say.

"Am I right in guessing you have Sean over a barrel?"

"I'd say so," said Grace smugly. "Depending on what Georgia has to tell us, yes, over a very large barrel."

"You know I never thought smugness would suit you," he joked. "I can't wait to see the look on his face when we show him the reports."

"Joe, I'm sorry, but I've had a long chat with Georgia and she believes I should confront Sean at our home with her by my side," she stated firmly.

"What! I should be with you. We should face Sean together," he said, feeling a little left out.

"Georgia thinks…"

"Georgia thinks this…" snapped Joe.

"Enough Joe! I know you mean well, but you have to let me do what I think is right. Georgia believes we should tell Sean as little as possible. That's why I'm not going to tell him I'm pregnant and I'm not mentioning you. All he needs to know is that I want a divorce and that if he contests it I'll use the evidence from the clinic to ruin him."

"Sorry, I just thought we'd do this together."

"So did I, but Georgia thinks otherwise."

"What if he turns ugly?" said Joe.

"Sean's too smart to do anything with a solicitor at my side."

"Yeah, I understand that, but I still don't like it."

Grace smiled, "I think you'll like this, I'm moving out of that house and moving back in with my parents in Elstree. We can see each other whenever we like."

"Now that I like," replied Joe, now fully recovered from his little outburst.

"I received a phone call from Georgia just over an hour ago. She's spoken with her father and he'd like to speak with us this afternoon."

"Sounds ominous," said Joe.


Three hours later Joe and Grace were shown into George Chandler office. He stood up to greet them, "I'm George Chandler, which is pretty obviously as it's my name on the door," he joked. "Georgia is dealing with a client at the moment, but will join us shortly. Tea, coffee, a glass of water perhaps."

"Thank you, I'll take a glass of water," replied Grace.

Joe declined.

"Right, I'll begin," said George. My daughter has filled me in on your situation. I can't say I'm happy with her getting involved. But my youngest has always been head strong. That said, at great risk to her chosen profession her instincts appear to have been right on this occasion. If this was just a straightforward case of deception on your husband's part I'd say you have a pretty good chance of winning, but according to Georgia this isn't straight forward."

At that moment Georgia knocked and entered the room, she glanced at Joe and Grace and smiled reassuringly.

"You want a divorce under the grounds of cruelty, grounds that until this week you didn't have. Your condition proves a point, but it also allows your husband to claim that it is you that has committed adultery. Do you see where I'm going with this?"

Grace felt her face flush, but nodded.

"What Georgia is proposing is not ethical and possibly a case of collusion. We can iron out the legalities at a later stage. I'll let Georgia explain."

"What Detective Sergeant Sean Fallon has done is illegal; fact. But time is not on your side, also fact. If you file for divorce because of the criminal act of fraud and deception, he would have to be made aware of the case you have against him. Criminal charges would most likely be filed. Great if you aren't pregnant, but being pregnant suggests that you could have committed the deception yourself. Giving you a motive to discredit him. Knowing what this man is capable of, the case could drag on for months, even years. He's falsified evidence before, think what he could do if his back is to the wall."

"All I want is a painless divorce," Grace was feeling increasingly disconsolate.

"Right here goes, firstly you obtain a divorce lawyer," said Georgia.

"Preferably not from Chandler and Lowe," stated George Chandler.

"Yeah, okay dad, we get the picture." She gave her father a withering look. "You state that you wish to divorce on the grounds of unreasonable behaviour. You say nothing to the divorce lawyer about the fraud and deception angle. We get the lawyer to draw up the petition and then you and I confront Sean at your house. We'll tell him you are moving out and that he will be hearing from your solicitor. You'll tell him you are divorcing him and you would like him to sign the divorce unopposed. He'll probably laugh, that's when we tell him an uncontested divorce is better than him facing criminal charges arising from his deception at the clinic."

"Won't that alert Sean to how we discovered his deception?"

"Good point. If that happens I'll tell him we've a dossier on him a mile high. I'll tell him we've been building this case, leaving no stone unturned."

"But what if he refuses, what if he says go ahead," piped in Joe.

"We cross that bridge when and if we come to it," stated Georgia. "The chances are Sean would favour an uncomplicated divorce."

"I don't want anything from the marriage," said Grace.

"Ah, it isn't that simply. Your lawyer if he's worth his salt is going to go after Sean for everything. If you don't, he's going to smell a rat. It'll be up to you and Sean to work out a reasonable settlement."

"How long will it take?" asked Grace.

"How long's a piece of string," said Georgia, "If it's not contested, it gets put on the court's list, where it can take six weeks to three months to get a hearing. Provided you both agree the terms of the divorce settlement, as there are no kids the judge should find the case proven and issue you with a decree nisi. Which means the final decree, called a decree absolute can be obtained three months' later."

"Why so long?" asked Grace.

"Here's the worrying part, this delay allows any irregularities to be discovered before the marriage is dissolved. Which hopefully won't happen. As you can see my dear, divorce is a long winded affair, striking a bargain with your spouse, in effect moral blackmail, will make for a smoother transition, but once he finds out about your pregnancy, well that could be an entirely different ball game," warned George Chandler.

# Chapter 27

Joe found Terry in the George that Saturday lunchtime. What's your poison," he cried.

"I'll have the usual," said Terry.

"Sit down I'll bring them over."

Terry scratched his head, he guessed that Joe had something on his mind.

"Okay," said Terry, as Joe placed the two pints on the table. "What gives?"

"You're aware I'm back with Grace and that she's pregnant."

"Fuck me! No one tells me anything these days. How do you know it's yours?"

"It's a long story, but believe me it's all true."

"So you've got this bird up the duff. Jesus, you don't do anything by halves!" cried Terry. "Do you know what you're getting yourself into?"

"Probably not," replied Joe.

"The first sensible thing you've said in a while."

"I'm on a final warning at work. I've been throwing too many sick days."

"That'll do it," chipped in Terry.

"The point is I need a job, preferably with plenty of overtime. I figured you could put a word in at BOAC."

"Oh, you do have it bad. Let me tell you, it ain't all married bliss. Shitty nappies, snotty noses, midnight feeds, believe me, you'd be better off joining the Merchant Navy."

"Yeah, yeah! All I want is an interview."

"You're serious! Its shift work mind," said Terry. "I'll see what I can do."

*****

"So how did it go," asked Jim?

"What that poor girl's been through, it beggars belief!" cried Georgia.

"You believe her story?"

"Every word," replied a determined Georgia.

"I guess you're going to go through with it? Isn't it a bit risky, I mean for your career," asked Jim.

"Not really, I like Grace, we've become quite close over the last week. She deserves a break, I'm only going to give her moral support. The divorce lawyer knows only that Grace and her husband are seeking a divorce on the basis of the irretrievable breakdown of the marriage, so it's all legal."

"So when are you and Grace going to break the news to Sean Fallon that life can sometimes kick you up the arse?" said Jim.

"Middle of next week. Grace is spending the time she's got left, moving her clothes and personal effects to her parents in Elstree."

"So they know all about it?"

"As much as they need to know," replied Georgia.

"What about the…"

"Baby," finished Georgia. "One step at a time."

"To be honest I've only seen her once and that was for the briefest of moments," said Jim. So what's she really like? What I actually mean, is she worth Joe throwing his life down the drain for."

"I think I'm a good judge of character, so I'd say if Joe's really in love with her, then yes, she's worth it. She's smart, articulate and charming, not only that, she's a raven haired beautiful looking woman. Her sense of style, the expensive clothes; the circles she moves in, suggest she's totally unsuited for Joe, except she's seen the flipside to that life and it's brought her nothing but heartbreak. She loves Joe, that's plain to see, she's excited about the baby and I think she could be the making of him."

"Wow, that was some endorsement!" exclaimed Jim.

"Oh I've some news, our first tenants are moving in next Friday," said Georgia.

"That's great, I was beginning to wonder," replied Jim.

"Oh ye of little faith," laughed Georgia. "We've got a couple for a viewing on the 20th, they seem keen."

"Okay, two down, two to go," said an apprehensive Jim.

"I never said it would be easy, but by springtime they'll be crawling all over us to rent," added Georgia. "Then the real fun begins."

"That sounds ominous," said Jim.

"Speculate to accumulate."

*****

Becky was troubled, she'd given Andy his marching orders, yet he hadn't taken the hint. Twice in the following week he'd turned up outside the hair salon. And twice Becky had told him to sling his hook.

"Won't he take no for an answer?" asked Donna.

"I guess not," said Becky. "I thought he was after a quick leg over, that's why I told him to get lost."

"Well he ain't taking the hint," said Donna, "You ain't thinking what I think you're thinking!"

"I don't know."

"You've got to be joking. Bob's a smashing bloke you've said it yourself."

"Yeah, I know I have, but if Andy's really changed…."

"A leopard comes to mind." Donna looked at her friend, she could tell she was wavering. "I think you're an idiot, but the easiest way to find out if the sparks still there, is to… you know what I mean."

It was cold and dark when Becky left work. She'd half expected Andy to pull up to the salon as he'd done on those two occasions. When he didn't arrive she didn't know whether she was relieved or disappointed. She'd thought about telling Bob that her old boyfriend had given her a lift and had wanted to go out with her again. But thought it better to say nothing, as she'd sent him packing, but then he'd re-appeared twice in one week. Her head was in a spin when Bob's Thames van pulled up beside her.

"Hop in the heaters lovely and warm, well it's warmish," said a very cheery Bob. She climbed in beside Bob and kissed him. "What was that for?" he cried.

"For being you."

"That's nice," he said as he crunched the lever into first gear. The van hopped and spluttered as he forced it into second. "Soon as I can I'll get me some proper wheels," he apologised.

Becky struggled with her emotions, should she tell Bob about Andy, should she say nothing and hope Andy didn't pester her again, but what if he did? Should she just go for it and to hell with the consequences? What if she went with Andy and the spark wasn't there. Could she keep it from Bob?

"You're quiet," said Bob.

"I need to tell you something," uttered Becky.

"What, you're not...."

"No," she laughed, 'if only it was that simple,' she thought. "Pull over into that slip road," she said with determination in her voice.

Bob pulled into the slip road and looked nervously at Becky. "You're finishing it with me!"

"No, not exactly. Last week I was given a lift home by my old boyfriend Andy. He asked me to go out with him again. I said no, I even told him where to go. But then he showed up at the hair salon twice this week. I told him I wasn't interested, that I had a boyfriend."

"So you're telling me now because..."

"Because I think I still have feelings for him."

Bob felt sick to the pit of his stomach, "You think you still have feelings for him! Have you been with him?"

"No of course not!"

"You told me you weren't the kind of girl that cheats."

"I haven't cheated, that's why I'm telling you now."

"I thought we had something special."

"We have…" said Becky. I just don't know what to do."

"You don't know what to do. What's that supposed to mean?"

"It's complicated."

"I love you, I should be angry but I'm sad, sadder than you could imagine. I thought we had it all, I know I've never said it and maybe that's my fault." Bob paused for a moment then added, "But, you've feeling for some other guy."

"It's not like that..."

"I knew it, I fucking knew it. I knew it couldn't last. You were the best thing that ever happened to me. I can't handle it! You've feelings for someone else. I think it's best that we end it."

"No Bob, I don't want us to end!" cried Becky. "I just couldn't keep it from you. I don't want to lose you."

Bob fell silent as he drove her home. When they reached her house Bob looked at Becky, his eyes filled with tears. "I don't know what else to say, I thought we had it all, I guess I was wrong." Then he kissed her gently upon the lips, "Goodbye Becky."

# Chapter 28

Sean wasn't anything like Georgia had imagined. He was tallish, around five eleven, dark haired with a few wisps of grey at the temples, clean shaven and immaculately dressed. She could see why Grace would have fallen for him.

Grace looked uneasy and nervous as she introduced Georgia. Sean's eyes seemed to undress Georgia as he smiled and took her hand.

"It's nice to meet you Georgia, it's quite unusual to meet one of Grace's friends. One that is such a sophisticated young woman."

"Not so unusual; your wife for example, they don't come more sophisticated." the tone of her voice left Sean with no illusion as too what she thought of his compliment. "I'm here to offer you a deal a very generous deal."

"I'll take it from here Georgia." Grace looked defiantly at Sean, "Our marriage is a sham and I want a divorce!"

Sean stared at Grace. "You're joking right" His brain went into overdrive. "You remember our little discussions."

"Our little discussions, you mean when you grabbed me around the throat and threw me against the wall and warned me how easily accidents could happen!"

Sean kept his head, at that moment he'd have willingly thrown her under a bus. "What are you talking about?"

'Smooth bastard, if I hadn't seen with my own eyes,' thought Georgia.

Grace smirked, "In the next few days you should receive a petition for divorce. Hopefully you will sign it uncontested."

"Like hell I'll sign!"

Georgia took her cue and handed Sean a manila envelope.

Sean looked puzzled as he snatched it from her hands and tore it open.

It was clear to Georgia that Sean understood what the contents contained. The façade of coolness deserted him. "Where did you get these?"

"I think that's obvious," stated Grace.

"What do you want?" he snapped.

"I want an uncontested divorce. A reasonable settlement and you out of my life for good. If you're not prepared to give me what I want, I'm making that report public." She let her words sink in, "At the very least, you'd lose your precious job, you might even go to prison."

"So you think you can blackmail me?" he snarled.

"No not blackmail! All I want is you out of my life," she could feel the tears begin to well up, but Grace quickly brushed them away.

"It's a once in a lifetime offer, take it or leave it. Either way you're out of her life," added Georgia.

"Who are you? Her fucking solicitor!"

Georgia remained silent apart from a smug smile.

Sean was caught on the back foot, "I'll need to think on it!" he said.

"You've until Wednesday of next week, after that I go public with the report!" stated Grace.

Sean was shocked, but wouldn't show it as both women turned on their heels and walked out. Neither of them spoke a word as they negotiated the steps and walked purposefully down the road. It was only as they rounded the corner that Georgia let out a yell and laughed. "Where did all that come from, you was so masterful! I couldn't believe my ears. You really gave him what for."

"Maybe, but I was shaking inside."

"But it felt good though?"

Grace thought about it for a few seconds, "Yeah. It felt real good." Then they both laughed.

Sean seethed with anger as he watched as the two women walked along the pavement, then slowly he closed the door. Inside he lashed out at the nearest thing he could get his hands on, sending an antique vase flying across the hall. He had a problem, the bitch couldn't have chosen a worst time to ask for a divorce, the promotion board was meeting next week. If they got wind of his pending divorce it could affect his chances.

"I should have killed that bitch when I had the chance."

Sean was ambitious, ambitious enough to kill. He'd been a sergeant for almost a decade, started out as a plod in the Met fifteen years earlier. It was during those days on the beat that he felt the power that his uniform afforded him. It wasn't long before the top brass began to take notice. Encouraged by the support of these senior officers, he studied hard, was eager to learn all the new innovations that were coming into the force. Eventually he worked his way up to detective, and then sergeant. He gained a reputation as a brilliant thief taker and the prospects of becoming a detective inspector looked certain. But after an ugly incident involving a death in custody of a beatnik pill pusher, Sean's prospects took a downward turn. Now after years of hard work, he was finally about to get the promotion he deserved.

"That fucking cow has to decide now of all fucking times to destroy me!" he shouted. 'That bitch is going to get hers, maybe not this year but sometime when she least expects it,' were his last thoughts before he shut his eyes at the end of a totally fucked up day.

*****

"You owe me," said Terry when Joe walked into the George on Saturday morning. "Job interview this Tuesday at 11.30."

"Wow! That was quick. Thanks Terry, you don't know what this means to me. I'm supposed to be working out my notice, starting Monday."

"Well, you can start by buying me a pint," laughed Terry.

"Yeah, an interview's great, but getting the job might not be so easy," said Joe.

"Don't be so hard on yourself, you'll walk it," said Terry, "Besides I put in a good word."

"That's fucked it then," said Joe. "No, seriously, thanks again mate, I really appreciate it."

"Think nothing of it. Big things are happening, B.O.A.C and B.E.A are in talks about a merger. Being in at the start; well the prospects for anyone with aptitude and a brain could be endless." Terry looked at Joe and laughed, "Best you don't apply."

*****

When Grace told her parents that she was seeking a divorce, they were shocked.

"But why?" asked Mum, "Sean seemed such a nice young man, I know we didn't see much of him once you were married, but we put that down to his job."

"Yes, Sean was quite the charmer in the early years," said Grace, "but all that changed when we couldn't have children. He'd expected me to fall right away. I told him it didn't always happen straight away. Which was fine for the first six months, then he became agitated and blamed me for everything."

"I'm not defending him dear, but it must have been a disappointment to him," replied Mum.

"It was a disappointment to me too!" exclaimed Grace.

"Of course it was, I didn't mean it the way it sounds."

"I know you didn't Mum," said Grace sympathetically. "With Sean, if things don't go as planned he flies off the handle. I slowly began to see the real man I'd married. For years I have been living a lie. Sure, he looks after me, I'm his showpiece of a wife, along with the smart car, the five bedroom house in Wembley with all the trimmings, but he treats me like dirt. He's hit me, where it doesn't show, he's slammed me up against the door, he's held me by the throat and he's threatened me."

"Just let me get my hands on him," snapped Grace's dad. He'd sat back and listened in silence, his blood pressure going through the roof

"No Dad! You don't know what he's capable of. Once I'm divorced I'll be free of him."

"We would never have thought he could be such a monster," said Mum and Dad together.

'Here goes,' thought Grace. "Believe me, he is. Do you remember us going to that clinic in London?"

"Where they told you that you couldn't have children," said mum.

"My life was just about bearable until then. After we got the results life became unbearable. He blamed me for everything. He said I wasn't a woman, how could I be. He said some terrible things."

"Why didn't you leave him?" asked Dad.

"Sean had the knack of taking things just so far, then he'd show some remorse, whisk me off to some fancy hotel, shower me with gifts and treat me special. It worked the first couple of times."

"After that?"

"I accepted he wasn't going to change, so I went along with it, playing the dutiful wife, even getting myself a job. Which caused an almighty row. Sean didn't want a wife of his working, that's when I finally plucked up the courage to tell him I was leaving him."

"How did he take that?"

"He flew into a blinding rage, that's when he threw me against the door and threatened me."

"I don't care who he thinks he is, you should have told me." Dad's face was turning beetroot in colour.

"Dad it's okay. Calm down. He isn't worth it." Grace didn't know if she should carry on. "I'm going to tell you something, don't fly off the deep end. Just listen," she looked anxiously towards her mum. "Sean falsified the report, it's him that can't have children," Grace judged the shock upon their faces. "I found this out when I visited the clinic a few weeks ago."

"Why would Sean falsify the report?"

"I can only surmise that not being able to father children was a blow to his manhood. Sean always prided himself on his masculinity," said Grace.

"There's nothing masculine about hitting a woman," said Dad.

"After six years of being treated like a doormat, I've met someone. Someone that has given me the strength to divorce Sean."

"Who?"

"No one that you know. Joe is a lovely caring, kind and gentle man. We fell in love almost immediately. Before you say anything, this isn't a fling, this is a warm and tender relationship. The reason I visited the clinic was because I'm pregnant!"

Mum looked for the tell-tale bulge.

"I'm just two and a half months," said Grace proudly, "You're both going to be grandparents."

Grace looked at her dad and saw tears in his eyes.

"We couldn't be happier for you," he said, as he wiped his face. Grace's mum's beaming face was a joy to see.

"Does Sean know about you being pregnant?" said Mum.

"No, and we want to keep it that way. I've threatened Sean with exposure. He's committed fraud and deception. He could deny it, but the damage would be done to his future prospects. That's why he's agreed not to contest the divorce."

"But surely he'll see you're pregnant!" said Mum.

"We've got a hearing in six weeks if we're lucky, three months if we're not. If Sean doesn't contest, the judge will grant us a decree nisi. Then provided there isn't anything to upset the apple cart I'll get my decree absolute."

*****

Joe's interview went like a breeze. A couple of days later he received a call from B.O.A.C.'s personnel department saying he was to report at nine o'clock on the following Monday morning. Joe was relieved and excited, especially as Grace had phoned him to say that Sean had signed the divorce papers. He'd been dreading telling her that he'd been sacked, but now he could tell her about the change in a more positive light. He'd told himself even before Grace had reappeared on the scene he'd considered leaving the factory.

He was starting as a warehouseman much like Terry had done some four years earlier. Terry was now a team leader, with his eye on moving up the proverbial ladder, so as far as Joe was concerned anything was possible. A new career beckoned, his life with Grace was falling into place, Sean had signed the divorce papers, and a baby was on the way, life had never looked so perfect. 'What could possibly go wrong,' thought Joe as he called on Grace at her parents' house in Elstree.

"Mum, Dad, meet Joe!" said Grace proudly.

Joe held out his hand and Grace's dad shook it. "Nice to meet you Joe."

Grace's mum's face dropped slightly, "You're so young!" she exclaimed.

"I'm twenty two," he said. "It's a pleasure to meet you both."

"I'm sorry, it's just that we were used to Sean, I suppose he'd be almost twice your age," said mum.

"Mum, you're forgetting I'm ten years younger than Sean, there's only six years between Joe and I."

"So Joe, what are you and Grace's plans for the future?" asked Grace's dad.

"Joe's a tool maker at a local factory," interrupted Grace.

Joe very wisely decided to say nothing about his new job until after he'd spoken to Grace, "Firstly we need to get the divorce finalised before we can move on. I believe Grace has informed you of the peculiar situation we find ourselves in. Provided we get the hearing early enough, Sean will still be unaware that Grace is pregnant. It only becomes awkward if he finds out, but even then a messy divorce isn't in Sean's best interest."

"It's the three months until the decree absolute where we need to be careful about. Sean mustn't know about my pregnancy until after we're divorced," added Grace.

"That's why we're looking for a place to live."

"Grace can live with us until then," said Mum.

"No Mum, I'll stay with you both until my decree nisi, then we're disappearing until the decree absolute. Sean mustn't find out about Joe or my pregnancy."

"I'm not sure your mother approves of me," said Joe when he managed to get Grace alone.

"I'm sure she'll come around when she gets to know you. It's been a lot to take in. Dad seems to like you though," said Grace.

"Ah! There's something I need to tell you."

"Sounds ominous!"

"I lost my job," said Joe.

"You what!" exclaimed Grace.

"I was fed up with it anyhow. Tomorrow I start work at B.O.A.C. It's more money and according to Terry there's chances for advancement."

"Are you sure?" cried Grace.

"Surer than anything in my life, except for loving you."

"Oh Joe."

# Chapter 29

Terry had told Joe during his interview to say he was familiar with forklift trucks, he'd even coached him in a little of the jargon. "Blind them with science, they wouldn't know one end of a forklift from another."

It was down to luck that first morning when Joe arrived, Terry was working alongside his crew and he was able to take him under his wing. "It's a piece of piss, you'll pick it up in no time."

In the three weeks Joe had been there he'd mastered the forklifts, learned the difference between imports and exports, learned all there was to know about airway bills, airline codes and city codes. It was a different environment to the closeness of a warm factory. As Joe was to find out, with the cold wind whipping through the open shutter doors of a warehouse in the middle of a February night during a blizzard.

He was pleased to note on his roster that a full week of nights only came around every fifth week. The early and late shifts were split equally, allowing Joe more free time than he'd have believed. Sometimes he'd be working alongside Terry, then other times it could be one of half a dozen other team leaders, each with their own characteristics. There was Sparky, not because he'd once been an electrician, it was mostly because his mouth looked like a burnt out fuse box, then the Wing Commander, he'd greet his men with a hearty "Good afternoon chaps." as he strolled across the warehouse floor smoking a fine cigar.

"Was he a Wing Commander?" asked Joe.

"Fuck no! He used to work in a tyre and exhaust place before he worked here. Didn't even do his military service," said Gary.

"He's a knob," cried Dickie.

"Sugar Ray's okay," remarked Gary. "He used to be an amateur boxer in his day. Once the works done he won't hustle you to do more. But take the piss, he'll be on you quicker than a dose of salts."

On the whole Joe liked the blokes he had to work alongside. If he was honest he'd have to say the work wasn't hard, uncomfortable maybe and cold at times. The worst job in Joe's opinion was tying down cargo to aircraft pallets with freezing cold and wet aircraft nets. The export door on a Friday night was probably the busiest job. You counted off pallets of air freight and using the forklift you either took the cargo to the loading bays where warehousemen were busy building aircraft pallets or you assigned it to the export racks, for later flights. Other times you'd work imports, where everything was done in reverse. You broke down pallets straight off the aircraft and assigned the individual consignments to allocated racking. Where it would stay until the freight agency drivers called for the respective goods and handed you a collection note. You'd locate and deliver the freight from the racks to the driver, who'd sign the release note.

It was on one busy night shift that Terry handed Joe a collection note, "Get this out of the racks, it's a special collection. Time sensitive consignment, the guys waiting on door two over in exports."

"Why exports?

"Driver's just dropped off a load around exports, saves him queuing up again on imports. Load it, I'll take care of the release note once we've hurried it through customs."

"Okay, will do," cried Joe.

Joe eager to please located the consignment on the third rung of row G and brought it down. He thought nothing of it as he drove the forklift and its load containing a consignment of expensive SLR cameras into exports where he deposited it at the loading bay of door two.

"Terry's just sorting out the paperwork, he'll be along in a few minutes."

"Cheers mate, I'll count them on while I wait," said the driver.

"Okay, see you later," said Joe. He turned the forklift around in one swift movement and hurried back to imports, where he and another warehouseman were tackling the queue. It had been an unusually busy night around imports. Hopefully the queue of drivers would thin out soon so Joe could get back to the book he was reading in the cosy shed/office next to the import doors.

It was a week later down the George when Terry handed him a fat envelope.

"What's this?" he exclaimed.

"You earned it," said Terry.

Opening up the envelope he found a hundred pounds in used notes. Joe gave Terry a bewildered look.

"Imports last week," said Terry.

The penny dropped, Joe realised he'd been duped into the theft of a consignment of expensive cameras and equipment. He handed it back to Terry. "I don't want your money!" Apart from feeling a fool, a fucking patsy, he could have been caught and his life would be down the pan. He stewed on it for an hour before confronting Terry in the car park of the George.

"You're a bastard Terry. I should grass you up!"

"Yeah, but you won't," said Terry, "It wasn't so long ago that you didn't care about getting your hands dirty."

"We were kids then," replied Joe. "I've responsibilities now."

"Yeah and you'd turn down a windfall. Take the money, you earned it."

Joe looked at the wad of cash, he knew that he and Grace could use it to put down key money for a place for them and the baby. "I can't say it won't come in handy, but don't try that on me again, understand."

"Joe, it's like taking candy from a baby. They're in talks about a merger and a brand new cargo terminal, those so called security cameras are nothing but a bluff. They're fake and even if they weren't, security wouldn't be able to see anything anyway."

\*\*\*\*\*

After Bob split with Becky he was having second thoughts about becoming a plumber. Turning up for a Saturday morning's labouring for Becky's dad filled him with dread. He didn't know how he could face him. What could he say, he dumped her, but Becky was the one that was at fault.

Tom was okay with it, "You're both young, it happens. Perhaps a break will do you both some good. I'm just glad you didn't chuck in this chance at learning a trade."

"I'm glad you see it that way Tom. I'm sorry that Becky and I broke up, I really care about her. I did think about going back on the hod, but thought better of it."

"Good man. Girlfriends come and go, but a trade stays with you. Becky's a good girl really, it's just a pity. That's all I'm gonna say on the matter," said Tom.

It was the weekend before Valentine's Day, almost four weeks to the day that Bob split up with Becky. Bob turned up for work on that Saturday morning, then without thinking his thoughts turned into words, "I guess Becky's going out somewhere nice with that Andy this coming Tuesday?"

"You gotta be kidding, that waste of space, he showed up to take her out a couple of weeks back, they'd only been out a couple of hours when she came back home crying her heart out. I guess he let her down again. God, she's been murder to live with ever since."

Becky's dad's words made his heart skip a beat. For a month he'd been as miserable as sin, there was no need to end the relationship, she'd been honest about her feelings. It was his pride that had kept him and Becky apart. Yet he was old enough to realise that feelings can't be ignored. Even if she never acted on them he knew it would always be there between them.

As he was finished up that Saturday morning, it was as if Becky's dad had been reading his mind.

"Me and the missus are off to the flicks in Rayners Lane this Tuesday. I told her it was a Valentine treat. She said, we've been going to the cinema on a Tuesday for years, so I guess I'd better throw in a couple of drinks before we go."

Bob laughed. "See you next Saturday."

When the phone rang later that Saturday, Becky was in no hurry to pick it up. It rang persistently for at least a dozen rings. "Hello," said Becky.

"Hi Becky, its Bob. I wondered if you'd fancy coming out with me this Valentine's Day." The phone went silent. "If you're busy I'll understand."

There was a moment when he thought she'd hung up. "Becky! Becky, are you still there?"

"Yes, I didn't expect you to ring. You wouldn't want to take me out I'm a mess. I fucked up our relationship. Find someone else, someone better than me."

"I've been miserable without you," he volunteered, "At the very least let's talk about it."

"I'm so fucked up," she sobbed, "I've ruined everything."

"It doesn't have to be this way. I'm sure we can work it out."

"I'm not so sure, but mum and dad are out Tuesday, come around then. We can talk honestly."

As she put the phone down a flicker of hope stirred inside her. *She remembered how her nightmare had begun, she had been standing at the bus stop a couple of days after her and Bob had split. She was feeling hurt and forlorn, angry and tired from a long boring day in the salon. Andy's car pulled up to the kerb in full view of the queue of commuters, "Hi Becky." It was the cocky way he said it*

*"Fuck off!" screeched Becky, leaving Andy no choice as the bus was beaming down on him.*

*It was a week later when he showed up again, this time outside the hair salon waiting for her to leave.*

*"You don't take no for an answer, do you!"*

*"If something as good as you comes along, you don't take no for an answer. Besides I know how much you love my charming personality"*

*"And bullshit!" Becky added.*

*It had been two weeks since Bob split from her. Two weeks of feeling miserable. She'd hoped Bob would have got back in touch, she'd even quizzed her dad. So what the hell she thought, maybe Andy and I are meant to be.She arranged to see him that coming Friday. He picked her up, running the gauntlet of Becky's parents. They found a pub close to home where they chatted, laughed and remembered old times. After a couple of drinks Andy suggested going somewhere quiet. "It's a bit early," cried Becky.*

*"Yeah I know, but I've got an early start tomorrow." He gave her that little boy lost look.*

*"Oh, okay, if we must," she said.*

*He drove down a dark secluded lane and parked up. "I thought you said, you had to be at work early?"*

*Becky felt strangely guilty, almost as if she was cheating on Bob as she leaned into Andy and kissed him. She kept remembering Bob's words "Its best we end it." They were over, it had been a fun time nothing more, she kept telling herself. She responded to Andy's passionate embrace and felt herself falling back under his spell. His right hand was quickly trying to undoing his belt and trousers. Once free of his garments he slowly began to run his hand up her inner thigh. She groaned as he slipped his fingers insider her knickers.*

*"It's not safe!" she cried in alarm. She knew he kept a packet of Durex in the glove compartment. She pressed the catch and a light illuminated the small compartment. Predictable as ever there on the shelf was a packet of three. She reached in and a shining object caught her eye. A wedding ring, lying by the side of the packet of Durex. Becky pushed herself up to a sitting position, holding the offending ring of gold in her hand.*

*"You're married, you're fucking married!" she screamed. "Oh I've really fucked up good this time. I let a good man slip from my grasp for a slimy letch like you. Take me home now!"*

*Andy came out with every lie that he could think of before admitting he'd been seeing this other woman when they were originally together. "That's why I ended it with you. I was getting married."*

*That cut right through her heart.*

*"Just take me home."*

*She sat in silence as Andy reversed the car and drove back towards Becky's home. He pulled up to the kerb outside her house and looked at Becky; there was nothing. She just climbed out of Andy's car without a single word spoken. She felt ashamed, foolish, cheap and angry that she'd let herself be taken in.*

Becky slumped down in her chair and thought about the last time she'd been with Bob. He'd told her he was angry, fucking angry to be exact, but he'd also said he loved her. She remembered their time at Ruislip Lido where she thought for one moment that he was going to propose, he'd told her in no uncertain terms to fuck off. It was a wonderful day, the sun shone, they made love and Becky remembered thinking she was well and truly over Andy. She owed Bob the truth. If, and she knew it was a big if, they did get back together she'd never leave out anything about her past life.

# Chapter 30

Georgia had an idea, hopefully Jim would take the hint. "We've three of our flats on a two year contract, the last one is only a matter of time."

"What about offering it to Joe and Grace!" said Jim? "I'm sure they're desperate to move in together"

"It's an idea, but can they afford it?"

"As far as I know Grace is still working in Alperton and Joe's doing okay at the airport," replied Jim.

Georgia saw her chance to broach what was on her mind, "It's a possibility: with all four flats let, we should be looking around for another suitable property."

"Isn't that a bit soon? We don't want to over extend ourselves," replied Jim.

"That's where you're wrong," cried Georgia. "Now is the perfect time. You live at home with mum and dad, likewise myself. We're both earning. Where's the risk. We've proved it can work."

"Yeah, I suppose if you put it like that, but what about us?"

"Us?" stated Georgia.

"Yeah, us," repeated Jim. "I thought we had something."

"We do have something, and I really care for you, but I'm not ready to settle down to married bliss. I've a career to sort out, I've yet to decide what path to take."

"Wow! Married bliss. What I've seen of it, marriage is for the birds!" exclaimed Jim.

"Thank God," said Georgia. "We're both in our early twenties there's plenty of time to think along those lines. To be honest Jim, I was hoping we could build a portfolio of properties with you taking the reins full time. Landlord, property management etc."

"Easy tiger! That's some ambition you have for me. When were you thinking about consulting me about it?" snapped Jim.

"I'm sorry, it's just me being impulsive, remember."

"Yeah I remember," he said, a twinkle appeared in his eye. How could he forget their impulsive lovemaking in the woodshed at Moor Park. It was true, the investment was taking off. That Georgia wanted to pursue their partnership pleased him no end. He just wished he'd had the initiative to have thought of it himself. Georgia was good for him in more ways than one. She was quick witted, intelligent, ambitious and confident. More than that she was classy, sophisticated, good looking and very sexy when the mood took her. Jim knew that if he was to keep her, he'd need to stay ahead of the game.

*Georgia had opened up an entirely different lifestyle to Jim. A lifestyle he felt he could get use too. Georgia's passions included playing tennis at her local club and horse riding when she could find the time. At first Jim found it quite daunting meeting Georgia's friends at the tennis club, they all appeared a little up themselves. He was asked if he played, to which he replied his sport was rugby, that tennis had never entered the equation.*

*"You should try it?" said Fiona, one of Georgia's friends. "Once you get started, you'll love it."*

*"I'll give it a try sometime. Perhaps Georgia can teach me?"*

*"You don't have to try anything you don't want," said Georgia when they were on their own.*

*"I know I don't, but it was really good watching you play. And besides, I could do with the exercise."*

*"You get plenty of exercise," laughed Georgia.*

*"Perhaps, but I believe I could be really good at it, given the right teacher. So teach me the basics."*

*"Really! You really want to learn to play tennis," exclaimed Georgia.*

*"If I'm to move in these circles, I need to be good at everything, so teach me."*

*When George Chandler heard Jim was taking up tennis and possibly horse-riding he said, "If the novelty hasn't worn off maybe you could try grouse shooting this August.*

*"I might take you up on that George," replied Jim.*

*"You don't have to agree to everything my father suggests," said Georgia.*

Jim was excited about where his ambition had led him and he now had the motivation to succeed. His background was so clearly different from Georgia's but his time at grammar school had moulded him into the person he wanted to become. Georgia was just the artist that was applying the finishing touch. But one thing his parents had taught him was to stay grounded. His friends, the kids he'd grown up with were important to him, but they weren't everything. Even now he could see the friendships, though strong, were beginning to go in different directions.

"Georgia, I love meeting new people, I love going to exciting new places, trying new things, but I don't intend to forget where I came from."

"And, nor should you," said Georgia. "We're building up a small business, how far it takes us, who knows. Friends are the ones that stand by you when the world is crashing down around you."

"You never cease to amaze." said Jim

"I never cease to amaze myself," she added, "So let's have a word with Joe and Grace, I dare say the idea might appeal to them. Believe it or not, I really like your friends, even Terry."

\*\*\*\*\*

Terry had a nice little earner going, one that didn't include Eric. For some unfathomable reason his side-line with Eric seemed to have dried up. At first Terry thought it was something to do with Christmas Eve, but since then he'd seen Eric and he'd seemed friendly enough. Terry wasn't worried, he'd found a new contact, Arthur the guy he'd been drinking with when he went to London with Eric. It transpired that Arthur had a cousin that had worked at B.O.A.C for a few years but he'd been sacked about a year ago.

"Yeah, we had something sweet going on back then," said Arthur.

Terry asked why he'd got sacked.

"Nuffin to do with our business, he got caught shagging one of the cleaners." They both had a good laugh at that, with Arthur giving Terry the club phone number, "Don't want to tread on anyone's toes, but if you're interested bell me. If I ain't there leave a message, I'll get back to you."

Well Terry was interested and so far it had worked out pretty lucrative for all concerned. Things weren't so good on the home front, Heather had turned a bit cold towards him, stating it wasn't him, but the baby. He accepted her excuses and believed normal service would recommence after a month or so.

*****

Since the beginning of the New Year all Heather could think about was Eric. She knew there could be nothing in it for her, just the dream. Gloria was still a stunning looking woman and by Eric's own admittance, the sole woman in his life. Yet, thought Heather, he'd shown her more interest than was healthy. She didn't agree with affairs. She'd always believed they ended in disaster, but of late her moral compass was shifting slightly.

Heather had just put the kids to bed and had made a pot of tea. She was about to put her feet up and watch the latest episode of Peyton Place when the doorbell rang. It was still dark so Heather peeked through the curtain. Her heart almost stopped at the sight of Eric. She paused for a moment, wondering, then she went into the hallway and opened the door. The first thing she noted was, no flowers, the second, Eric looked downcast.

"What's wrong?" she cried.

"Is Terry here?" asked Eric.

"No, he's on late shift, he won't be back until eleven."

"I'm sorry I shouldn't have come, it's a bad idea."

"What's a bad idea?" asked Heather.

"I need to speak to someone."

"I'm all ears, come in. Would you like a cup of tea, it's just brewed?"

"No that's very kind of you," said Eric.

Heather showed Eric into the front room and switched off the television.

"No need for that," protested Eric.

"I was getting bored with it anyway," she said.

"I'm sorry to bother you with my problems but I couldn't think of anyone more understanding."

"Are you sure you don't want tea, maybe something stronger?"

"No, Heather. I'll come straight to the point. Gloria has a drink problem!"

"What! How? I don't know what to say. Gloria seemed the most together person I'd ever met," exclaimed Heather.

"I know, on the surface she appears fine, she usually can hold her liquor. A lifetime of being in the limelight has finally come home to roost. Alcohol has been a big part of her life since the age of fourteen. She understands it, she even believes she can control it, but it's slowly taking over," said Eric, with a slight tremor of his lip.

Heather grasped his hand, and squeezed it gently. Eric seemed oblivious to her as he looked vacantly at the blank TV screen.

"I'm sorry, I shouldn't be burdening you with my problems."

"Nonsense. If you need to talk it out, I'm a great listener"

"If you're sure."

Heather smiled reassuringly.

"Gloria was a star almost from a very young age. It wasn't just her looks, it was her character, the easy way she looked at life. Everyone loved Gloria."

"I can understand why," said Heather.

"Of late Gloria has become obsessed with her looks, said Eric.

"She's only forty six, she's years ahead of her."

"That's what I keep saying," said Eric. "She found her soul mate in her first marriage, albeit he was a much older man, but she loved him right to the end. When he died she tried to capture some of her youth, but despite still being glamourous and popular she felt a deep sinking feeling inside.

"I remember Gloria saying something about that at Christmas," said Heather.

"She met me and I was captivated by her wit, her charm, her sexy looks, in fact the whole package. But for the last year she's begun to change. She's on forty plus cigarettes a day and knocks back at least a bottle of booze daily. That's when she starts feeling sorry for herself and starts accusing me of having affairs."

Heather felt herself blush.

"I've given up so much for this woman, I've loved her to bits. I've had offers, but I've remained faithful. I could have had an ordinary life, a young wife, kids like you and Terry, but I chose her above all else. I've took it because the following day life goes back to normal. But since Christmas, things have taken a downward spiral, she thinks I'm see another woman."

"Coming around here can't help. Does she know where you are right now?"

"That's just the point, her obsession and her drunken fits of rage are driving me into the arms of a woman I barely know."

The sudden realisation that Eric was talking about her, shocked and excited her in equal measures. For a few moments

Heather was silent. Slowly she gathered her thoughts. Her heart was telling her to throw herself into his arms, but her head said otherwise. He leaned towards her and kissed her softly, unhurried and tenderly. She kissed him back with a long forgotten passion; then the baby cried. The spell was broken, she pulled away from him, apologising as she left him on the sofa and raced upstairs. It was a full five minutes before the baby settled, enough time for Heather to gather her thoughts.

Eric looked at her as she walked back into the room. "She's gone off," she said, more to herself than Eric.

"Perhaps I'd better go," said Eric.

"No stay, little Maggie just gave me a stay of execution."

Eric sat back down. "I'm sorry I shouldn't have brought my troubles to your door."

"I think we need to talk about that kiss and what it means."

"I think it's plainly obvious what it means," said Eric. "I might be wrong, but I don't think Terry treats you the way he should."

"Terry's a good man, he provides for me and the kids. We want for nothing, newish car, television, Hi Fi, the best washing machine that money can buy."

"Those things ain't everything, what about shows of love and affection?"

"I know he loves me, he adores our kids, but what he doesn't give me is respect. I'm always known he had an eye for the ladies, I just wish he wasn't so blatant about it."

"I'm sorry, I didn't mean to open old wounds. I came here because I needed a shoulder to cry on. I shouldn't have brought my troubles on you, I didn't realise things between you and Terry were that bad."

"They aren't," she said defensively. "We've known each other from school, neither of us had much experience with members of the opposite sex. Getting saddled with kids at a young age wasn't how we planned it. Terry could just have walked away. In a bizarre way I know where he's coming from. What he doesn't seem to understand is my needs?"

"Maybe I best go," said Eric.

"No, please don't. What I think we both need, is for someone to tell our troubles too. If Maggie hadn't woken up I believe we might just have added to them."

"Maybe, maybe not," said Eric.

"Eric, you love Gloria, that's plain to see, yeah you're going through a rocky patch, but I'm sure you'll both get through it. As for me and Terry, we're destined to be together, that's how it's always been. We love each other of that I'm sure." She smiled at the thought. "But I can't see any reason why you can't come by once in a while, remember a trouble shared is a trouble halved."

Somehow the tension between them seemed to evaporate. Heather asked Eric if he wanted tea.

"I wouldn't mind a large scotch."

"You got it!"

They talked for nearly two hours, before Eric said he'd better be going. "It was good to talk," he said as he leaned down and kissed her cheek, "Until next time."

# Chapter 31

The knock on the door caused Becky to break from her thoughts. Bob had asked her out and she'd refused, agreeing instead to sit down and talk it through. The more she thought about it, the more it felt right. If they were to have a relationship there had to be honesty between them.

She opened the door and smiled sheepishly.

"Hi Bob, come in."

Bob smiled back and grabbed Becky around the waist. He looked into her eyes and said, "I must have been mad to let you go!"

Becky was shocked at how quickly he'd pulled her into his arms. "Oh Bob, it was me, I was the fool." She looked sad and nervous. "I told you I still had feelings for Andy, how did I expect you to act?"

"I'm here now, that's all that matters!" He held her tightly, afraid to let go.

"I made a promise to myself, I'd tell you everything. I just hope you still want me after I've said what I have too."

Bob held her tightly. "What happened is in the past, it's the future that matters."

The harsh reality of what Becky was about to say kicked in. "When you left me I was distraught with grief, I felt like my right arm was gone. Then a few days later Andy came by and pestered me until I agreed to go out with him. We went for a drink, we chatted and then he suggested we go somewhere quiet..."

"I don't want to hear anymore," protested Bob. "You don't owe me anything."

"Oh but I do, we started to kiss, but it felt wrong. You were out of my life but I felt like I was cheating on you. He didn't like it when I told him to stop. He called me a prick teaser." She knew she was going off script but couldn't help herself. "We struggled for a bit, but I pushed him away and slapped his face. He finally got the message."

She'd intended telling him the whole sordid truth but realised she'd been a willing partner until she learned that Andy was married and was only using her. It was an omission not a lie, she told herself.

"So it's over with this bloke? He ain't gonna come out of the woodwork any time in the future. I couldn't handle that!"

"Yes, it's over, he's a creep, I don't know why I didn't see it. Bob, I want it back the way it was."

"It can't be like before, things have moved on. I'm afraid of what you might say after I tell you what I want."

Becky stiffened, she was still being held tightly, "I want you Bob."

"Do you remember what you said to me in the summer at the Lido? *You ain't going to propose, I hope not?* Well I ain't going that far, at least at the moment, but Becky, I love you, and I'll do what it takes to keep you."

"I love you too, and yes I'll hold you to that," said Becky as she pressed her lips against his.

*****

Terry was on the prowl, his sex life at home since the birth of the baby had been slim to non-existent. It was Sunday lunchtime and the boys were all there. A catch up was in order, and Terry was of a mind to go out Friday night. "Top Rank in Watford seems to be heaving with crumpet from what I've heard, so I reckon we're due for a boys' night out. Who's up for it?"

"Count me out," said Jim. "I'm taking Georgia to a restaurant up the West End, then we're going to a show."

"Get you! With your new found friends, I take it," said Terry.

"No, actually, just Georgia and me, it's her birthday."

"Okay, so posh boy here can't make it, what about you two?"

"We're staying at Grace's parents' house this weekend," said Joe. "They're away visiting relatives in Dorset."

"Well at least Bobby's available," said Terry, looking hopefully towards Bob.

"Sorry to disappoint, me and Becky are back on."

"Oh, fuck you lot I'm off!" said Terry angrily.

"Looks like poor old Terry will have to settle for domestic life. Talking about domestic life, you've got Grace all to yourself this weekend?" said Jim.

"Yeah, it's a pity Grace's mum and dad don't go out too often," said Joe.

"Have you two thought about a place of your own?" enquired Jim.

"It's early days, Grace hasn't got the date for the hearing, so until the decree nisi we can't really make a commitment, that's why I'm keeping a low profile. Even then we've got to keep our heads down for three months."

"Why's that?" asked Bob.

"The decree absolute. The judge has to allow a period of three months just in case there's a complication in Grace's divorce."

"I guess, that complication might be Grace's pregnancy?" said Jim.

"In a nut shell," replied Joe.

"Will Grace's condition show at the hearing?" asked Bob.

"Hopefully not, if we get an early date then we should be able to get away with it."

"If you don't?" asked Bob.

"Then we'd better pray it's a cold spring and Grace can keep herself buttoned up."

"Georgia's going with her so Grace stands a good chance of getting the decree nisi," added Jim. "Actually while we're on the subject, it's only an idea mind, Georgia and I have one last flat to rent. I know it's not ideal, but if I can persuade Georgia to agree a short lease of say six months, would you and Grace be interested?"

"I'd say yes in a heartbeat, but I'd have to run it passed Grace first."

"There is a hidden benefit, said Jim. "If Grace registered her parents' home as her permanent address and lives in the flat with you, then until the divorce is absolute that copper won't know where she is."

"Yeah, you've got a point.

"What about her work," chipped in Bob?

'Stays the same, nothing's changed," replied Joe.


"A six month lease!" exclaimed Georgia, "We agreed a two year lease."

"Yeah, I know, but I had to sell it to Joe first," said Jim. "He's my friend and if I can help him, why not!"

"If Grace agrees to it, we'll let them know they could extend the lease if they wanted too." Secretly Georgia admired Jim's stand, loyalty wasn't something that comes around too often.

"Yeah, if all goes well. Grace should end up with a fair settlement, so I think they'd be able to afford it," said Jim hopefully.

"So where are you taking me on my birthday?"

"That's a secret, but it means you've got to ask your dad to let you have Friday afternoon off."

"Wow, sounds exciting!"


A late afternoon meal in a good West End restaurant then an evening performance of Fiddler on the Roof at Her Majesty's Theatre. To Jim it still seemed a little extravagant but Georgia was worth it. He reflected how far he'd come in such a short time, from a steak meal at the Swan and Bottle to a fancy restaurant in the West End. Not bad for a joint owner of four properties with a view to expand, all thanks to his beautiful girlfriend Georgia. He acknowledged that he'd always planned to broaden his horizons, but with her help he'd gone much farther than he'd have imagined in such a short space of time.

He smiled to himself on the way home from London at the show stopping musical number, "If I was a Rich Man." It was early days and he guessed there would be pitfalls on the way, but he felt confident that he would succeed.

# Chapter 32

Terry never made it to the Top Rank in Watford. Frustrated and angry that his mates had turn down a good time in Watford, he phoned his partner in crime Arthur.

"You free this Friday."

"Why, what have you got for us?" said Arthur.

"Nah, nothing like that, thought you might fancy a night out at the Top Rank in Watford, plenty of pussy!"

"Top Rank's not really our style, if you fancy a trip up the Smoke we can show you a really good time. We can take you to a couple of night clubs, have a flutter on the tables; chat to some of the prettiest girls in London. Who knows you might get lucky."

"Sounds great, but expensive."

"It can be, but a ton should do it," said Arthur.

"A hundred quid! It's a bit rich for me," exclaimed Terry. "Top Rank would at best cost me a pony!"

"Yeah, maybe, but you won't be rubbing shoulders with the likes of Judy Garland and Sammy Davis Jr or catching a glimpse of local celebrities like Barbara Windsor and the Kray twins."

"Well if you put it that way, how can I refuse?"

"Just wear a good suit and tie," said Arthur.

Terry met up with Arthur who introduced him to his cousin Roy. A couple of drinks in a Shepherd's Bush boozer then before he knew it the pair took him on a whirlwind tour of casinos. Terry's experience with gambling had been playing brag or pontoon with ten bob notes and the occasional pound in a local boozer, that and an each way bet on the horses once a week. He felt like a fish out of water when Arthur encouraged him to try his hand at Blackjack. Being familiar with pontoon Terry soon got the idea. Within twenty minutes he was up thirty quid and was about to give it all away when Arthur stepped in and took him away from the table. "Quit while you're ahead" he advised.

"You're playing with the house's money, a win win," added Roy.

"Isn't that…" cried Terry, who could have sworn he'd almost rubbed shoulders with a very well-known gangster.

"Yeah, now let's move on."

They passed a couple of familiar faces from television, one of them looking worse for wear. Terry was in his element, he couldn't wait to tell the boys who he'd seen. He was feeling that gentle buzz brought about by the effects of alcohol, when you're on your way, but still sober enough to understand what's happening.

"Jesus fuck!" exclaimed Roy. "Did you see that guy you nearly bumped into? You really are one lucky fucker."

"No, who was it?"

"None other than Tommy Drayton, freelance enforcer. Does the occasional work for the likes of the Krays."

"If Roy hadn't have pushed you out of his way, you could be waking up in a ditch or worse," said Arthur.

Minutes later, Terry now fortified with another drink, tried his hand at roulette. He placed his bets, won a couple of spins then was about to put all his chips on black, when a female hand stroked his crotch. "Hi Terry, it's nice to meet you."

Terry looked into the deepest green eyes he'd ever seen, framed by a mass of blonde locks and a sensual mouth to die for. "How do… you….know my…" He looked past her at the beaming faces of Arthur and Roy.

"Just thought you might want some company," said Roy. "Meet Jennifer, she'd going to turn your world upside down."

Terry looked back at Jennifer, and grinned. "Why so nice fellers?"

"Let's just say we want you to experience the finer things in life. There's a proposition we'd like to put to you," replied Arthur. "Jennifer is going to take you to her place, then when your head's clear she's going to put you in a taxi and we'll meet you at the club in a couple of hours."

Terry looked at Arthur for re-assurance, then said," Seriously." "Seriously," repeated Roy.

"Cash my chips in."

Terry couldn't believe his luck, he'd won at the tables, ate and drank to his heart's content, now he was being treated to an hour or so with the pleasures of the flesh. He wasn't that drunk that he didn't know Jennifer was bought and paid for, but what the hell, having a brass was something he'd never tried before.

The dingy flat above a neon signed club left a lot to be desired, but Terry wasn't interested in the décor. Jennifer pushed her key into the lock and opened the door. He followed like a dog on heat. He was focussed on her arse and legs as she threw off her coat and opened the door to a bedroom. The room was illuminated by a single red light bulb minus a shade. The opening scene from the film 'Peeping Tom' sprang to mind. Terry had barely taken off his jacket when she pushed him backwards onto the bed.

"We'll soon have these off," she said as she expertly undid his belt and zipper. One tug and a wiggle from him and his trousers decorated the floor. "You're a big boy," purred Jennifer as her hand grasped his erect cock. He could feel her hot breath as her red lips teased, then kissed, then teased again, before her lips opened fully. He gasped as her warm mouth engulfed his manhood.

"Oh, that feels so good," he stammered. Realising given time this could get messy, there was no way that he wanted to explain the lipstick stains on his white shirt. He quickly undid his cufflinks and tie. With his right hand he undid his shirt buttons. Free of his white garments he placed his hand back on Jennifer's head and gasped with excitement. Slowly and gently he released the pressure on her head, allowing her generous mouth to leave a trail of bright red up the centre of his torso until it finally reached his lips. He kissed her passionately before pushing her head back down to his awaiting cock. He gasped again as she took him fully in her mouth. The sight of her blonde locks and that sensuous mouth bobbing up and down nearly brought him off. Not wanting this part of his evening to end prematurely he asked her to stand up.

"Let me look at you," he commanded.

Slowly with a wicked smile she climbed off the bed and looked down at him. He gasped as he feasted his eyes upon her She looked so much taller as he looked her up and down. She was still wearing her high stiletto heels, fishnet stockings and suspender belt. Her knickers had been discarded revealing she wasn't a real blonde. Barely able to take his eyes off her hairy snatch he gazed up at her generous breasts which were bursting out from her black and red bra.

"How do you like these big boys," she purred seductively. "Now get down on your knees and pleasure me!" she commanded.

Terry groaned in anticipation, he thought he'd gone to heaven or perhaps that other place.

"You're a naughty boy, by the time I'm finished with you, you'll wish you were back in school!"

He looked up at her waiting snatch and was lost in a world of forbidden pleasure.

Jennifer then fell to her knees and positioned herself over his erect cock. She smiled wickedly as slowly she lowered herself on to him. He gasps...............

It all felt like a blur as Jennifer saw him into a taxi. She gave the cabby instructions on where to go. Terry was feeling relaxed as he glances at his watch. It was one thirty in the morning, going to a meeting didn't seem like a good idea, especially as he didn't know what time he was going to get home. Hopefully the meeting wouldn't take long, he thought.

Fifteen minutes later Terry now feeling soberer that he'd felt all evening arrived at the drinking club. It looked deserted but Terry knocked on the door, the boys had his winnings anyway.

"Who is it?"

"It's me Terry."

A couple of bolts make the only sound as the door opens and Terry was led into a back room, the same one Eric visited.

"What's all the cloak and dagger?" said Terry.

"Enjoy yourself, did yah," Roy's tone appeared to be one of agitation.

"Yeah, why the aggression?"

"You should have been here an hour ago," said Arthur.

"Yeah, sorry about that, Jennifer couldn't get enough of me," he said jokingly.

"Well it was your money," laughed Roy.

"What do you mean my money?"

"You didn't think we were paying for it, did yah," said Arthur. "Look when we tell you what we've got planned, you're think what it cost you is small potatoes."

"Sit down Terry. I'll fill you in on what we want you to do," said Roy. "As you're aware I used to be you. Not exactly you, I got caught shagging the cleaner. So all our plans went up in smoke, then you came into our lives."

"Let's face it Terry until you met me you was just a petty criminal, I'm giving you the chance to break into the big time," said Arthur. We've something big planned and you're a part of it."

Terry thought about it, "What if I don't want to break into the big time?"

"You ain't got a choice!" said Roy. "Tommy Drayton's already financing it."

"Tommy Drayton, that bloke in the club!"

"The very same," said Roy.

Terry looked to Arthur for support and found none. Suddenly the room seemed cold and hostile. The menacing looks from the two men left Terry in no doubt he'd stepped into a room of rattlesnakes. He weighed up his chances of making a swift exit. Roy was standing by the door. He was in their manor, he had nowhere to turn; his only chance was to agree to what they had planned. Once he was safely home he'd phone Arthur and tell him the deal was off.

"Tell me about the big time." He said, with bravado in his voice that he didn't feel.

"I knew he'd agree," stated Arthur.

Roy said, "When I worked for B.O.A.C I figured out a fool proof plan to get away with three million." He caught the look on Terry's face. "You're thinking the train robbers, well don't. They would have got away with their heist if they'd followed their plans carefully. Doing the business is the easy part, getting away with it; well that's something else entirely."

"We've a small plane that's going to fly to Belgium. From there we're taking a road trip to Paris, where we board a plane to Malaga. We've contacts there. Once we arrive we'll live like kings," added Arthur.

"They'll know it's an inside job," cried Terry.

"We won't do it when you're at work. You can meet us at the airfield."

"What about my family, I can't just uproot them!"

"They can join you when the heat dies down, or you just leave em," said Roy in a matter of fact way.

"Yeah Terry, with your share of the money, you'll be able to start a new life with them. There's no extradition from Spain," said Arthur.

Terry had to think on his feet, he was dealing with nutters. Hadn't these guy thought about Interpol? Firstly he had to convince the two men in the room, which was easier said than done. He pretended to let it all sink in, then feigning excitement he said, "There's no reason I can't send the wife and kids there a week earlier."

"Good idea Tel," said Arthur, "I told you he was smart!"

"Okay, I'm in. Now what's my part in this job?"

# Chapter 33

It was mid-April when Grace and Georgia turned up for the hearing. Fortunately it was a grey wet and miserable day when they appeared at the court steps. "You don't have to attend, but it will allay any suspicions if you do," said Georgia. "You look good for five months pregnant. Bundled up in that oversized raincoat works a treat. Just answer firmly if the judge speaks to you." Grace's divorce lawyer was there, dotting I's and crossing T's, it was all so formal and routine. Sean didn't attend, he was represented by his solicitor, more importantly he'd agreed to all Grace's demands, which on the face of it were very reasonable. With nothing to contest, the divorce proceedings went off without a hitch.

"One down, one to go," said Georgia as they left the court.

"As easy as that!" exclaimed Grace. "I'd have thought there would have been more too it."

"Believe me, there would have been, had you not agreed a mutual settlement. It's lucky Sean didn't know about your pregnancy."

"But would he risk disrupting the divorce proceeding with what we have on him?"

"You can never tell how people will act, just count yourself lucky. Remember you're not out of the woods yet!" exclaimed Georgia.

"I know; I can't tell you how grateful we are to you. I don't know how I'd have gone on. The flat was a great idea, it allows me to hide from prying eyes and relax. It's a great flat!"

"That was Jim's idea," said Georgia.

"I'm so relieved to have got this far. You know what? I'd like you and Jim to come to the flat tonight. Allow me to cook dinner.

It would be my way of saying thank you for all you've done. Just a little celebration to mark the occasion."

"I'll run it passed Jim, I'm sure he'd jump at the chance of a free meal."

"Don't be too sure, wait until he tastes it," laughed Grace.

"We'll see you around seven, if that's okay?"

"Wow! I'm stuffed," exclaimed Jim.

"Yeah I know the feeling, Grace cook's up a mean spaghetti Bolognese," agreed Joe.

"I'm glad you liked it," said Grace.

"You know what, cooking like that makes me feel inadequate," cried Georgia.

"Don't be daft, spag-bol is easy, even Joe could do it," joked Grace.

Joe laughed, and felt warm inside, he'd never seen Grace so relaxed.

They leaned back on their chairs sipping the wine that Georgia had brought and chatted about everything and nothing.

"We've just had our offer for another property accepted," said Georgia. "That's great. It won't be long before you're both property tycoons," said Joe.

"A bit optimistic, but maybe by our mid-thirties," chipped in Jim, " but the important news as far as I'm concerned is there's a new western, a different type of western starring that Rowdy Yates from Rawhide."

"You mean Clint Eastwood," said Joe.

"Yeah Clint," agreed Jim.

"He's still a big kid at heart," added Georgia.

"Yeah I've heard of it, it's an Italian western, personally I wouldn't get my hopes up; it'll probably be badly dubbed. Having said that, it couldn't be any worse than 'Gunfighters of Casa Grande," said Joe.

"It's got to be better than all the Elvis films they keep churned out," said Jim in defence.

"I like Elvis," said Grace.

"Yeah, he's still cool, but his first films before he went into the army were much better," added Joe.

"Talking about the army, Vietnam is never off the news. Things ain't going the way Johnson expected," said Jim.

"Don't get Joe started," cried Grace. "We have enough problems dodging my soon to be ex."

"Yeah, but fair play to Harold Wilson, for keeping us out of the war," piped up Joe.

"I guess we must be the lucky generation, conscription ended just in time, otherwise I reckon we'd have been shipped off to Vietnam," added Jim.

"It's still a bit worrying with this Vietnam thing, our government could change its policies if the war escalates," said Joe.

"I don't think it will," said Grace, "there are demonstrations and marches against the war in the US."

Joe had a stupid grin on his face, something to do with the wine, when he blurted out, "Oh, I meant to tell you, last Friday, I was having a drink with Terry, when in walked Bob and Becky. Guess who was with them?"

"Just tell us!" exclaimed Jim.

"Donna, large as life and four months pregnant. Terry's face was a picture. Hello Terry, she said and then smiled cheekily, before adding, I told you I'd let you know if I needed anything."

"So Donna's pregnant?" asked a shocked Georgia.

"No, it was a wind up. But before anyone could tell him, he flipped and stormed out of the pub. Bob raced after him and said, it's a joke. Terry stopped in his tracks and said, I don't fucking need this! Bob then told him it was a wind up that Donna had a cushion under her coat, for a laugh."

"What did he say to that?" asked Georgia.

"That's the point, instead of feeling relieved, he mouthed off about some scrubber taking the piss. He just couldn't see the funny side. Which isn't like Terry, he's usually the first one to take the rise out of people."

"Well you know what people say, 'if you can't take it, don't give it," said Georgia. "He was in a right funny mood. But I guess he'll get over it," said Joe.

*****

Terry wished he could get over it, but things had taken a sinister turn since he managed to talk himself out of the room at the drinking club. He'd phoned Arthur the following day and told him he was out.

"You backed me into a corner, what did you expect me to say. I'm out and as far as our other arrangement, well that's over as well," said Terry forcefully.

"I'm sorry you feel that way Terry, but it's not that simple. When Tommy sets his mind to something, it gets done. You enjoyed yourself last night didn't you? Yeah of course you did, judging by the photos I'm looking at right now," said Arthur smugly.

"Sorry Arthur, I ain't falling for that one."

"Yeah, I'm sorry about that, but Tommy always insists on a backup. So one day soon your missus is going to open a letter and find her whole world crumbling around her, unless you agree to the plan."

"You're bluffing," cried Terry. His mind began to race, images of that night flashed before him.

"Try me. Agree to our terms, or watch your wife take you to the cleaners. Your choice."

"I need proof you've got photos, I ain't taking your word for it," snapped Terry.

"A bit of an inconvenience, but I suppose I could take the tube to Ruislip. Say lunchtime tomorrow at the station."

Arthur grinned as he saw Terry waiting at the entrance to Ruislip station.

"Here you go, a souvenir of Friday night," said Arthur as he handed Terry a manila envelope. "They're pretty good aren't they, especially the ones where she's whipping your arse, almost gave me a hard-on."

"Shit," cried Terry, one look was enough. "Look all joking aside, the plan's madness. You'll never be able to come back to this country. That's if you get away with it."

Arthur's face darkened, "You don't get it do yah! It's happening!"

Terry's mind was racing, he was caught between the proverbial rock and a hard place. There was no way he could face Heather with those incriminating photos. The things he'd done with that woman, Heather would never forgive him. She'd walk out of his life and wouldn't look back, and who could blame her. He could agree to the heist, but that involved fleeing the country and never returning. Neither option appealed, he was fucked either way. He needed time to think of a way out.

"When do I get the negatives and the rest of the photos?

"Once we get the name, the address, the family, any animals, any visiting friends or relatives, the mugs shift pattern and the payload, then and only then."

"That's a fucking shopping list!"

"Yeah it is," said Arthur as he turned and walked back towards the station. "Call me."

Despite his philandering ways Terry deep down loved Heather with all his heart. They had been together since secondary school, and he couldn't face life without her. Add the kids into the equation and there was no contest. He examined every detail of the heist. The plan was simple, but effective. It had been done before, but emphasise this time was loaded towards a clean getaway, hence the light aircraft, the contact in Belgium, and the contacts in Spain. It could possibly work.

Terry wasn't as daft as they thought he was, he knew he would be left behind to take the consequences. He knew Arthur by first name only, Roy might have worked for B.O.A.C but that might not be his real name. Even being sacked for shagging a cleaner was probably a smokescreen. Arthur's phone number was the drinking club, and as for Tommy Drayton, that name was probably an invention too. He was being played as a patsy. Unfortunately the compromising photos left him no choice. He'd just have to work out a shopping list of his own.

# Chapter 34

It had been a turbulent two months since Eric had reached an understanding with Heather. Two months in which they'd talked out their respective problems. From his point of view those stolen hours with Heather had become a lifeline. Talking to Gloria was like talking to a brick wall. Drink was the only thing that bolstered her ego and confidence, adversely it was drink that caused her to neglect her fortnightly manicures, facials and her frequent visits to the hairstylist. Consequently the mirror was becoming her bitter enemy as she mistakenly began to see the ravages of time.

"Look at me Eric, I'm old! How could you bear to look at me?"

"Glo, you're beautiful, you still turn heads! You need to slow down your drinking, that's what. Pull yourself together, for too long you've neglected your appearance."

"I know I drink too much, but that's because of you. I know….."

"You know what!" he snapped.

"Those young women, I've seen how they look at you."

Eric was tired of the ceaseless arguments about his infidelity, which apart from the odd peck on the cheek with Heather hadn't evolved into anything more serious. Gloria unknowingly was driving him into the arms of a very vulnerable woman. That she loved Terry was unquestionable, but his apparent lack of consideration and respect could cause her to commit to the unthinkable.

Eric was a rogue and in his time he'd done more of his fair share of wheeling and dealing. He was an opportunist, but deep down he was a man of principles. His needs were simple, he could take Heather in his arms and for a time their problems would go away, but he wasn't the type to take advantage of her vulnerability. Besides he still loved Gloria, despite her drinking. Some days she was the old Gloria, oh how he wished they'd return, but alas those days were becoming very infrequent.

When he received a phone call from Heather at the antique shop on that Friday morning, he was concerned. She wouldn't go into any details, only asking him if he could come around to hers that evening at 8.30. Eric didn't know what to make of it as she'd never phoned the shop before.

Heather smiled when she opened the door, "Come in, I'll get you a drink." It was the curt way she invited him in that caused him to think Terry had found out about their liaisons.

"Is it Terry? Does he know about us?" he asked as Heather handed him a double scotch.

"No, Terry doesn't know."

"Then what is it," asked Eric.

"Remember I told you that since New Year I'd become unresponsive towards Terry, cold in fact. You advised me to make an effort with him. Well I took your advice, but he turned me down flat, which isn't like Terry. I think he's seeing someone."

"I doubt that, Terry might be lots of things but he ain't a fool."

"Maybe, but I've been a fool. I should never have stopped you." She looked into Eric's eyes, the intent in her voice left no doubt in what she wanted.

Eric rested his scotch on the coffee table and leaned over and gently kissed her. All the months of Gloria's obsession about her age, the drinking and the arguments had led to this. He wanted to talk it through with Heather, he wanted her to tell him to try one more time; that it would be all right. But deep down he knew; it was already too late!

Heather took the initiative and stood up, she took hold of Eric's hand and led him upstairs. She peeked into the boys' bedroom, and checked they were sound asleep. She looked in on Maggie, asleep in her cot, beside Heather's bed, then pulled Eric into the spare bedroom, and locked the door.

They lay in each other's arms and were quiet for a few moments digesting what had just happened.

"You'd better go!" cried Heather, as the ardour of their love making evaporated. "I'm sorry, it's not you............" she trailed off as she gathered her clothes around herself. That she was racked with guilt was understandable.

Eric swiftly dressed himself, "We'll talk soon."

Heather gave a weak nod of her head. He leaned down and gave her a gentle kiss.

Heather called the following day, "I want to apologise, I shouldn't have treated you so mean. Can you meet me at the park near my place this afternoon around one o'clock."

"I'll be there," said Eric.

Heather was sitting on a park bench with the baby in her Silver Cross pram beside her. She glanced up just as Eric's car came into view and involuntarily her heart skipped a beat. She watched as it slowed down and pulled up to the side of the road near the entrance. He climbed out of the Jaguar and slowly walked into the park. She turned as he approached her.

"Eric, it was my fault, I shouldn't have pressed you."

"It takes two."

"I said I was sorry on the phone, but to be honest, I'm not. I wanted it, probably more than you. But it doesn't take away this feeling of guilt."

Eric sat down next to her, his hand resting on hers. She didn't move it away. "I know you love Terry, admittedly he's been a bastard towards you, but what happened between us is not your fault. These things happen."

"I'm confused, I wanted to tell you what we did mustn't happen again, but my heart tells me that I have feelings for you," she cried.

"I'm glad you feel that way. I wouldn't want you to think it meant nothing to me, because it did. It meant a lot. I don't want to come between you and Terry, and I also don't want Gloria to know what happened, but my feelings for you......." His words trailed away.

There were tears in Heather's eyes, she wiped them away with a handkerchief, "So what are you saying?"

"I don't really know what I'm saying except I care for you. If you don't feel the same I'll understand and I'll back off."

"Oh Eric, if only... I owe it to myself to make a go of it with Terry. I need to confront him. For years he's rode roughshod over my feelings, I believe making love to you has given me the strength to face him."

"Let me have a word with Terry, I'll try to find out what's bugging him. I doubt if a woman is behind it."

"That's kind of you, but you don't have too. I wasn't going to tell him about us."

"Oh, I didn't mean it like that," replied Eric. "What happened with us was special."

No more words were exchanged between them as Eric slowly walked away, but the unspoken look in their eyes spoke volumes.

Eric didn't need to seek Terry out, he was sitting in the George contemplating whether to buy himself another double when in walked the man himself.

"Same again Eric," said Terry as he approached the bar.

Eric nodded his acceptance.

A minute later Terry put the drinks on the table and sat down. "I'm glad I've seen you, I've got myself a little problem, well two problems to be precise. I'd like your advice." Terry ran through his night out, winning at the casino, the blonde and his late night confrontation with Arthur, Roy and the fact this

Tommy Drayton was financing it. "They've got photos. It was a fucking set up!"

Eric was more than a little agitated, "What have I always told you Terry, don't get caught! So what do you want from me?"

"What should I do?" said Terry. "Are these dangerous people?"

"Well firstly Arthur, as I told you, runs with some serious people, his cousin Roy, never knew Arthur to speak of him, but there is a number of his family up there; as for this Tommy Drayton, never heard of him either. That's not to say he ain't muscle. If he's financing it the chances are he's big league."

"The plan, does it hold water?" asked Terry.

Eric seemed surprised, "You're going through with it?"

"What choice do I have? Heather means the world to me, her and the kids. I can't lose them. Despite what you might think, I love the pants off her."

Eric felt his heart plummet, but resisted telling him he should have thought about it before he let his cock do the talking. "You don't know you'll lose her, surely coming clean to Heather is better than getting banged up."

"There is another fly in the ointment; I think I caught a dose!"

"Oh for fuck sake," cried Eric, "Have you had sex with Heather since!"

"No! Thank God."

Eric's heart rate started to tumble as he realised what a lucky escape he'd had. "Good, at least you haven't got that to deal with. Get yourself to the quack first thing, get tested. If you're positive take the treatment, but keep away from sex with Heather until you're clear."

"Yeah, I'll do that tomorrow. How long before I know whether I'm infected and if I am, how long after being treated before I can have sex again?"

"How long's a piece of string? I don't know, but you'll know when you get your arse down to the doc's tomorrow. I'd say probably a month, six weeks, but I don't really know," said Eric, "You are a total fuck up, you know that."

"Yeah, I know. I've no choice, I'll have to go through with it; there isn't time to wait. The heist is going down in a few weeks' time."

"You asked me for advice, I know these kind of people, well here it is, don't get involved. Okay, so Heather gets to see you in action. She loves you Terry, it might piss her off, but she won't leave you." Eric knew that despite all the shit that was thrown at her Heather would stand by her man.

Terry shook his head, "Those photos, oh fuck! They were hard-core. I can't do that to her."

"That bad!" exclaimed Eric.

"That bad and worse."

"So what are you going to do?"

"Assuming their cockeyed plan works I know there won't be a seat for me on that plane, so I've got to brazen it out and hope I don't slip up, so I'm demanding all the photos and negatives, and asking for ten grand in cash, upfront."

"What if they don't come up with the money?"

"Then I've no choice, I'll have to go to the cops. Tell them everything!"

"Not something I'd recommend, but who knows?"

"Ten grand, will to some extent help Heather if I get put away."

"If they get away with it, you've just got to deny everything. Without evidence they won't be able to pin it on you. Make sure you stash the ten grand somewhere safe. Stick it in a plastic bag, seal it, make sure it's watertight and bury it somewhere away from your house. Bury it in a field, the woods, anywhere that doesn't implicate you."

"What if they get caught?"

"Well then you're fucked if they grass you up, which undoubtedly they will." stated Eric.

190

# Chapter 35

Bob was over the moon that he was back with Becky. He'd seen how his friends were drifting. He guessed it was what happened to most groups of friends when they reached a certain age. He was twenty one, old enough to vote and old enough to think about what he wanted from his future. Having lost Becky once, he wasn't going to risk losing her again. It was a gamble and he knew he could fall flat on his face.

"What's the occasion?" asked Becky, when they parked the van close to a Chinese restaurant. Not just an ordinary bog standard Chinese, but the most upmarket restaurant in the area.

"We never celebrated Valentine's Day properly, just thought it would be nice," said Bob, hoping to allay any suspicions she might have.

"I thought we celebrated it properly enough; if I remember correctly," laughed Becky.

"Wow! This looks a bit posh," she exclaimed as they walked in. Bob gave his name and within a few minutes a smiling a young Chinese woman respectfully led them to their table. Bob had failed to notice these simple courtesies when he use to frequent the Chinese with his mates after a few beers when the pubs had closed.They ordered drinks, then perused the vast menu. Within a few minutes their drinks were served to them. Again, Bob noticed how graciously the serving staff treated them; a far cry from the days of screaming waiters with choppers and other kitchen utensils in hand chasing after him and his friends as they raced up the deserted streets.

After their meal, while they sat back and sipped their glasses of wine, the waiter brought fortune cookies to their table.

"Great, I love fortune cookies!" exclaimed Becky. She proceeded to break open the cookie. Inside was a small message written in Chinese. "Oh, that's a disappointment, I wanted to know what the future holds for me."

"It probably means this," said Bob, as he handed her an open ring box with a small diamond ring inside. "You don't have to say anything now, just think on it," he said nervously.

"Oh my God! What can I say: yes of course I'll marry you; but not until you get a decent car. Then we can save up for a house."

Becky's mum and dad were still up when they arrived back home. "Bob's asked me to marry him and I've said yes! It's not what you're thinking. We won't be rushing it. We want to save up for a house, before we start a family."

*****

Terry steeled himself for the phone call he was making. "Is that Arthur?"

"Yeah," came the abrupt reply.

"You set me up, my own fault I guess, but I know I won't see any of that money," said Terry.

"Course you'll get your money," said Arthur."

"We both know that won't happen. Right here's the deal. I want paying up front. I'll get you the information you want, in exchange for the photos, the negatives and ten grand in used notes. Otherwise I go to the cops and take my chances."

"Coming on strong ain't yeah. You ain't in a position to bargain"

"That's where you're wrong. I've got nothing to lose."

"Don't even think about it," the hesitation in Arthur's voice spoke volumes. "I'll run it past Roy. If he agrees I'll be in touch," then he rang off.

Terry half hoped that would be the end of the matter. Perhaps they would see the flaws in their plan, in which case the only thing he'd have to worry about was the photos.

For the next two days at a prearranged time Terry waited outside the phone box at the end of his road. On the second day, just as he was hoping it wouldn't ring, it rang.

"Hello," said Terry.

"You ain't gone to the cops!" snapped Arthur.

"No! Of course I haven't," said Terry.

"Tommy and Roy weren't happy, but they've agreed to your demands. We need the name and address of the key holder to the strong room on Sunday morning 7th of May, his address and the occupancy," said Arthur.

"The money, you've got it, and the negatives?" stammered Terry.

"Yeah, I'll call you on Friday the 5th, same time."

Terry waited outside Ruislip station with the information the gang needed. It had nearly gone tits up, when the guy that was the key holder on that particular Sunday swopped his shift. Terry had to chase around to find the address of Daniel Torrance, the replacement key holder.

He explained this change of plan to Arthur, stating that the new key holder had a wife and a ten year old daughter.

"This works better for you," stated Arthur, as he handed Terry a small sports bag, "It's all there!"

"What do you mean it works better for me?" asked Terry.

"First person they're going to suspect is the man that swopped shifts."

Terry bent down and unzipped the bag, he gazed at more money than he'd seen in his life, then he looked at the folder with the negatives. He had no way of knowing if they were all there, but he had to trust that once they got away with the heist, they wouldn't even remember his name. He took another look at the cash, zipped up the bag, then reached into his pocket and handed Arthur an envelope containing type written information on the key holders address and the names of his wife and daughter.

"Can't say it's been a pleasure, just don't hurt anyone." Terry turned around and walked away. As he walked to his car he remembered what Eric had said about the money. "Bury the fucking stuff, don't even thing about the money for at least a year," it was good advice.

He drove straight home, knowing Heather was out getting their weekly shop. In their bedroom he was able to count the money, stack it neatly into a Tupperware box, and seal it with industrial tape. Then he checked the negatives, all thirty six of them. Once satisfied they hadn't pulled a fast one on him, he went into the back garden and burned the incriminating photos and negatives. Then he got back in his car and drove to the entrance to his local woods, where he parked and got out.

Luck was on his side, it had started to rain and the area was deserted. He walked swiftly along the path for a few minutes until he came to an oak tree. He stopped, then he paced twenty steps to the right. Hidden in the bracken was a freshly dug hole approximately a foot square and a foot deep. He dropped the sealed package into the hole and then using the spade he'd left hidden, covered the money. Once he was satisfied the hole was undetectable he picked up the spade and left. Near the entrance he threw the old spade into the undergrowth.

It was a strange feeling for Terry when he drove home. He'd just buried enough money for him to buy a three bedroom house in the best part of Ruislip and still have change. The wheel of fate had begun to turn, his fate rested on three villains getting away with a huge cache of currency, gold and jewellery. There was nothing he could do to stop it. As he wasn't due to work until Monday's late shift, he intended to spend time with Heather and the kids, maybe treat them to a day at Regents Park zoo.

Who knew what the next weeks would bring. Burning those photos had brought Terry a little piece of mind, that and the latest test results, which had proven negative. A jab on the arse and a follow up of antibiotics seemed to have done the trick.

# Chapter 36

Joe turned up for work on Sunday morning to find several police cars dotted around the B.O.A.C warehouse. "What's going on?" he asked one of his work mates.

"Don't actually know, but it seems there was an attempted robbery, that's all I know."

"Was any one hurt?"

"Don't know that either?" replied Gerry.

In the rest room the talk was all about the attempted robbery. All kinds of speculations and rumours were being bandied about.

"Okay! Enough talk, we'll find out soon enough," said the team leader as he dished out the various job assignments.

During the course of the morning, little snippets of information filtered through. A gang had turned up at Daniel Torrance's house at 5.30 in the morning, knocked on the door, only to be greeted by night turning into bright daylight and a command of "Armed police! Drop your weapons and get down on your knees!"

"Daniel's the key holder to the strong room," said a couple of warehousemen.

"I heard they were gonna kidnap his wife and kid."

"Bastards!" said Gerry.

"Sounds like an inside job," said Stan, another warehouseman.

"Well you know what that means!" said another.

"What does it mean?" asked Joe.

"It means that we are all under suspicion," said Gerry.

"Which means we'll all be given the third degree," said Stan.

"I heard Daniel had swopped shifts with Barry Turner," said Frank, one of the export clerks.

"Turner ain't the type," said Gerry. "He ain't got the bottle."

"Maybe, maybe not, but one thing's guaranteed, Barry Turner is going to get some grilling," cried Stan.

*****

Detective sergeant John Armstrong was feeling pleased with himself, he'd been handed this case by his mentor and superior officer Detective Inspector Sean Fallon. It had gone like clockwork. Only days before the attempt, his superior officer had pulled him to one side and told him the op was on.

"It's a pretty routine case of knowing who and when to turn a known villain. I leaned on an Arthur Briggs, small time, but I had him for a couple of thefts from warehouses at the airport. It seems he was moving up and was involved with planning an assault and possible abduction of a B.O.A.C. employee's wife and kiddie," said Fallon.

"Inside job boss," said Armstrong.

"You got it sunshine, just concentrate on nicking the villains in the act. I believe the inside man is the brains behind this heist, so give him a few days to sweat, I'll let you know when to nick him."

"What about this Arthur Briggs?"

"Nick him, then charge him, but put him in a cell away from the other two. I'll see to Briggs."

*****

When Joe got home from his early shift, he dropped in on Terry and gave him the news of the attempted robbery.

"Bloody hell!" exclaimed Terry, "Did anyone get hurt?"

"I don't think so, from the little we heard Daniel Torrance was sitting down with his wife and daughter on Saturday night when there was a knock on his door. He opened the door to be confronted by two plain clothes coppers. Within a few minutes of explanation the family were whisked off to a local airport hotel for their own safety, then two armed police officers spent the night watching television and preparing for the long wait."

"So they got them all," asked Terry, trying desperately to keep the panic out of his voice?

"It would appear so, although the boys at work reckon we'll all be interviewed in the next few days."

"Why? Do they think it's an inside job?"

"I dunno, but I wouldn't want to be in their shoes," cried Joe.

"Me neither," added Terry. "Thanks for the heads up, I'll catch you on shift change tomorrow."

What was not known until the following day was the copper leading the case, a Detective sergeant John Armstrong had positioned armed officers to stake out the home of Daniel Torrance. At around 5.27 a maroon mark 3 Zodiac pulled up fifty yards from the Torrance house. Quietly two villains stepped out of the vehicle and approached the front door. They knocked lightly on the door. A light from the front bedroom came on and within a minute a voice from upstairs shouted out, "Just a minute," then as the door opened the floodlights lit up the small close, and Armstrong's voice bellowed out from a bullhorn. "Armed police, drop your weapons and get on your knees." It was all over in a matter of minutes. The police recovered a small 38 calibre revolver and a sawn off shotgun. The two villains were Donald Fuller a well-known enforcer for a number of criminal underworld faces, aka Tommy Drayton and Keith Porter. Arthur Briggs, who coincidently waited in the Zodiac hadn't been arrested. The moment the floodlights went on Arthur slipped from the Zodiac and disappeared.

Arthur Briggs then handed himself over to Detective Inspector Sean Fallon. He'd given up two heavyweight villains and the name of the inside man. He could have been given a long stretch with all that Fallon had on him, but was assured he'd walk away scot free.

"So what now," asked Arthur? When he next spoke to Fallon.

"Nothing Arthur, over the next week or so you'll be asked by my colleague Detective Sergeant Armstrong who masterminded the heist. You will tell them nothing until I tell you differently. Understand, because if you fuck up you will be facing ten years minimum."

"I understand Mr Fallon."

"Remember this, until I speak to you again, you say nothing."

During the next few days Detective Sergeant John Armstrong conducted a series of interviews with the warehouse staff, and import and export clerks. It was a long and laborious task. There were over one hundred and fifty men to interview and John Armstrong thought it would have been much simpler to lean heavily on Arthur Briggs.

Fallon said, "I need time to complete my investigation, you're buying me that time. Believe me once we've caught the man behind this robbery, you'll be nailed on as the next Detective Inspector.

"Why are you giving me this collar?" asked Armstrong suspiciously.

"Because John, you'll have earned it, and besides I need someone I trust. In this job as you already know there's always someone that wouldn't think twice about stabbing you in the back." The truth was that Detective Inspector Fallon had chosen Armstrong because he was ambitious and more importantly he would cut corners.

It was on Wednesday that Terry's nightmare took a very twisted path. Heather was taking their eldest to school when the phone rang.

"Terry Richards, we need to meet. I have the answer to your problem."

"Who is this? What problem?" snapped Terry?

"I think you know what problem. Meet me on the far side of Ruislip Lido, I'll be waiting at one o'clock this afternoon, if you value your freedom."

The caller rang off.

"If you value your freedom," the caller had said. Terry realised he had no choice. Making an excuse to Heather that he had been called into work early. "Must be these interrogations," he'd said and left it at that.

Terry saw the man at a distance, he was tallish, well-built, dark and carried himself with a confidence that Terry didn't feel.

"Okay, what's this all about?" snapped Terry.

"Good, a man that comes to the point! I know you were blackmailed into this Terry. You're nothing but a small time crook, but if you don't do as I say you'll cope for the lot, which could cost you fifteen maybe twenty years inside."

"I don't know what you're talking about," said Terry.

"I can make this all go away, or you can take the rap for planning the whole thing."

"I still don't know what you're talking about?"

"Okay, it's your choice. Terry Richards, I'm arresting you for planning and setting up the B.O.A.C. heist."

Terry stood his ground. "You can do what you like, but you've no proof."

"There's no point in denying it, Arthur Briggs has told me everything, including the whore, the photos and the small matter of ten grand. How would you like to keep the ten grand and more importantly your freedom?" Detective Inspector Fallon couldn't resist a smile, he loved to see small time crooks squirm.

"Let's suppose I know what you're talking about, what is it you want?"

"Joe Dempsey to be exact. He's a work colleague of yours."

"He's more than that, he's a good friend." Terry's heart was racing, the penny finally dropped. The smug bastard in front of him was Grace's soon to be divorced husband. "Now I get it, you're Grace's ex!"

"Okay, I can see this might be difficult for you, so let me spell this out. I have a little job for you." He reached in to his coat pocket and brought out an envelope containing several pieces of paper. Terry recognised one as the type written information he'd given to Arthur Briggs. The other had dates and times, while the last piece of paper written on some kind of graph paper seemed to be a map of sorts. "All I want you to do is take these pieces of paper and Brigg's phone number and put them in Joe's locker at work. Making sure you secret them under clothes, a book maybe, but slightly concealed. Keep your mouth shut, deny everything. That's it, oh and you can keep the ten grand as a bonus."

"My thirty pieces of silver," said Terry angrily.

"I'll make this easy for you, I know Joe was involved with your earlier dealings with Arthur Briggs, so he's going down whether you like it or not."

"I'll say you fit Joe up, because of your wife, you'll lose your job at the very least."

If Terry thought that would throw him; he was wrong.

"You don't think I haven't thought of that. Apart from the fact I'm not involved in this case, there's a little matter of proof. Arthur will sing whatever tune I want, like the fucking canary he really is. So take your best shot. Just remember you've a wife and three kids, whereas Joe's got a heavily pregnant girl friend that's too old for him. Think about it as doing him a favour. He's going down with or without you. Now take these pieces of paper, stick it in Joe's locker and forget this ever happened." He held out the pieces of paper for Terry to take.

Terry looked at the three incriminating pieces of paper, "What's to say I won't destroy them and deny everything?"

"The second set of very pornographic photos I have in my possession," said Fallon smugly. "Here have this as a souvenir," He reached inside his jacket pocket and handed Terry a photograph. "Personally I don't give a rat's arse whether you cooperate or not. Either way I win."

Terry hesitated for a while, staring Fallon fully in the face. He'd never hated anyone more than the smug looking copper in front of him, but he took the photo and papers.

"Good," said Fallon. "Now trot along, we don't want to be late for shift do we!"

Terry glared at Fallon with pure hate in his heart, then he turned and walked away.

Fallon felt pleased with himself. He couldn't help wondering how Grace thought she'd got one over on him. She must have known that he was devious and cunning, a man that would stop at nothing to get what he wanted. He'd often recite the mantra, "I'm a detective for Christ-sake. A fucking good one at that!"

When Grace had confronted him about a divorce and had the gall to blackmail him if he didn't agree to an uncontested divorce, he was taken aback. She'd caught him off balance, partly because until then he'd always believed he was infallible. He'd never expected her to find out about the falsified clinic documents. Which meant only one thing, Grace had been unfaithful and as a result fallen pregnant. Knowing that his nailed on promotion to inspector was just weeks away and that a charge of fraud would scupper any promotion and quite likely dismissal from the force, left him no choice but to accept her terms.

But if Grace had thought he'd take it lying down, she was mistaken. Fallon asked an ex colleague, now head of a private security firm for his services. The security firm compiled a detailed report on Grace Fallon. A report that confirmed his suspicions. Grace had been seeing a much younger man, a man with low expectations of giving Grace the kind of life she'd become used too. The report made angry reading and Sean Fallon began to plan his revenge on Grace well before the ink was dry on the degree nisi. He had his lawyers agree to an uncontested divorce with a reasonable settlement on the condition that any and all documents pertaining to the fertility clinic be returned to him on the day of the decree absolute. Grace so desperate for her divorce willingly signed the agreement, despite being advised not to by her solicitor.

And now by pure chance fate had given him the tools to destroy everything that Grace held dear.

*Sean had been prepared to wait until the divorce was settled and he had all the incriminating documents in his hands before he exacted revenge. But destiny took a different course, when in the space of a few weeks two unrelated sources of information fell into his lap. The private security firm noted on their report that Joe Dempsey the main man in Grace's life, had recently been sacked from his job as a tool maker. Only to gain employment as a warehouseman at B.O.A.C. Sean had smiled at that insignificant information, and shelved it for the foreseeable future. But it was during a routine takedown of a small time crook that really set the ball rolling. Arthur Briggs was being interrogated by Detective Sergeant John Armstrong when his superior officer entered the room.*

*"Carry on John, I thought I recognised the name. Do you mind me sitting in?"*

*"No problem inspector, not really in your league, smash and grab."*

*Detective Inspector Fallon smirked. "Looks like you've done it this time Arthur. With your record I'd say you're going away for a long time."*

*"Have a heart Mr Fallon, what if I can put you onto something big?"*

*"Not me Arthur, detective sergeant John Armstrong."*

*Armstrong gave his Inspector an appreciative look.*

*"Go ahead, I'm listening," said Fallon, slightly disinterested.*

*"Three, maybe five million quid in an airport strong room," spluttered Arthur.*

*"You'll have plenty of time to dream where you're going."*
*Fallon stood up, put his hand on John Armstrong's shoulder, "I'll leave you too it John." He gave Arthur Briggs a pitying look and walked to the door.*

*"Which airline?" snapped John Armstrong, "If you're fucking with me, I'll personally put you away for ten years!"*

*"B.O.A.C.!"*

*Sean halted in his tracks as he felt a tingle run up his spine. "We'd want more than that!" said Fallon as he turned around and sat back down. "It might be worth a listen," he said to Armstrong.*

*Detective Sergeant Armstrong looked a little put out. "Give me a break!" exclaimed Armstrong. He was fed up with superior officers nicking his collars.*

*"I'll only talk to you Mr Fallon," said Arthur, realising his chance at a deal was possibly on the table.*

*Newly promoted Detective Inspector Sean Fallon motioned for the junior officer to leave the room. "I'll fill you in, if this comes to anything. Don't worry, the collars yours!" He waited until the disgruntled Armstrong left the room. 'This might be nothing, but who knows,' thought Fallon. "Okay Arthur spill your guts."*

*"I ain't writing anything down and I'll deny everything, so I'll want your assurance that this goes away."*

*"If what you tell me is kosher, I'll personally see it disappears," said Fallon.*

*"You've always been fair with me Mr Fallon. I'm involved with a couple of big time villains."*

*"How big?"*

*"Keith Porter and Donald Fuller!"*

*"Fuller! Fuck me, I've wanted to put him away for years!" exclaimed Fallon. "Okay Arthur start from the beginning."*

*"I met a bloke in a drinking club in the Bush. Small time crook, did a bit of business with him. He works at B.O.A.C...."*

*"Name!" interrupted Sean Fallon.*

*"Terry Richards!"*

*"Go on," demanded Fallon.*

*"When I told Porter about my contact at B.O.A.C. I also told him about a plan that my mate Roy had milling around in his head for a couple of years since he'd been sacked by the airline. Porter seemed interested, but said he'd run it by Fuller. A day later he got back to me, Fuller approved it, and said he needed an inside man, one that wasn't too smart, one that could get him names, addresses, and shift patterns, basically someone that could finger a particular key holder of their strong room when there was a big haul inside." "So this Terry, ain't that smart?"*

*"No, that's just the point, this bloke ain't daft, he knows the finger could point straight back to him. I told Keith it was a non-starter. He said he'd get Donald to lean on him."*

*"Well has Fuller leaned on him?"*

*"Well, no, not yet."*

*"Oh, for fuck-sake, you're wasting my time!" He stood up and left.*

*"Keep him on ice!" exclaimed Fallon.*

*"What about the other charges?" asked Armstrong?*

*"I'll see how he is in the morning. If it doesn't pan out he's all yours." "What if it does? It is my collar," said the detective sternly.*

*"John, don't worry about it. Depending what I can find out, this could be a feather in your cap."*

*The name Terry Richards, he was sure he'd seen it somewhere before, it was a common enough name, but where? He searched through his files, nothing showed up. He had an itch that needed scratching, it was an instinct that had brought him many arrests in the past. On the way home he scratched that itch, he was sure he'd seen the name Terry Richards on the report on Grace, or was that wishful thinking? Immediately he walked into the house he went to his office and found the report. Under the name Joe Dempsey was a small list of his known friends, James Newton, Robert Walker and a certain Terry Richards. Listed alongside of their names were their occupations, Joe was listed as tool maker, terminated, and warehouseman, James was listed as Electrical Engineer, Robert was an apprentice plumber and the jewel in the crown was Terry Richards, warehouse supervisor at B.O.A.C.*

*The following day Arthur was brought up from the cells and shown into the interview room. He sat and stewed for ten minutes before Detective Inspector Sean Fallon entered the room.*

*"How'd you sleep Arthur?"*

*"Well as can be expected."*

*"You could be sleeping in your own bed, if you play ball. I don't care how you do it, get something on this Terry, something that will make him sit up and take notice."*

*"Like what Mr Fallon?"*

*"He's a drinker, right. Does he gamble, does he like the ladies? Does he reckon himself a player?"*

*"I'd say you got him to a tee," said Arthur.*

*"Get him into debt big time that seems to work, threaten him, or better still compromising photos, that usually presses all the right buttons," said Fallon. "I'm letting you go, but before you leave, remember I want a step by step report on hooking this fish. It's either him or you." The threat was said in a friendly way but Arthur knew his freedom depended on getting that fish landed.*

*Fallon was growing tired of waiting, he'd been in contact with Arthur once a week for the past three Fridays, and nothing. He'd decided to cut his losses, when Arthur came up with the photos.*

*"Good man, you just saved yourself." He took a look at the photos, "How the fuck did you get such artistic photos, that Terry must be some kind of acrobat. I want a copy of these."*

*Arthur looked nervous.*

*"What is it?" snapped Fallon.*

*"I told you he weren't daft enough to go through with it; well the photos made him sit up. He said he knows he's going to be left holding the baby, reckons with as many as a hundred and fifty suspects he has more than a fifty, fifty chance of getting away with it, but he'd demanding the photos, negatives and ten grand. If he gets that, it's a go," said Arthur.*

*"Our boy's a lot smarter than we thought." Fallon's mood darkened, there was no way he could get permission for that kind of money. I don't care where you get it, rob some old lady of her life savings. If you don't Armstrong's gonna put you away for a fucking long time."*

Sean Fallon looked after the retreating Terry Richards with a smile on his face. As he turned away and found the hole in the chain-link fencing he climbed through and walked back through the woodland to his car parked at the side of the road near the entrance to the woods. 'So far everything had gone like clockwork,' thought Fallon. 'If Terry Richards does the Judas drop, the rest should fall into place and Grace's hopes of a perfect future would be in tatters. Joe Dempsey would be in custody.' He chuckled to himself as he walked through the tranquil woodland, life for this detective inspector was getting better and better, 'Even if things don't fall into place, then Terry Richards goes down alongside Donald Fuller and Keith Porter. As for Detective Sergeant John Armstrong he'll learn one of life's lessons and could wait in line like all the other suckers.

# Chapter 37

It was just another ordinary day when Grace struggled into work. The long kept secret of her pregnancy was now old news. Someone had made a chance remark about her glowing complexion and Grace had coloured up. Her obvious discomfort at the remark left no one in any doubt she was expecting a baby.

"Okay. You're right, I'm having a baby."

"When's it due?"

"Around August sometime, not sure yet," said Grace.

Which led one work colleague to say, "That's wonderful, but I thought you said you couldn't have children?"

"That's what I thought, but miracles do happen." Her secret was out, and Grace did all she could to keep it low key. Much to her embarrassment and excitement she was showered with baby gifts. Now openly she wore her pregnancy with pride, she only hoped the decree absolute would come though before the baby was born.

The phone rang on Grace's desk. She picked it up and her world began to crumble. It was Georgia, "I've some disturbing news. I'm sure it's a mistake, but Joe's been arrested! I didn't think you'd want to stay at work so I took the liberty of borrowing a car. I'm outside your office by the telephone box."

Grace went white as a sheet, her heart began to flutter and she felt a little dizzy. Unsteadily she walked into her boss and told him she was feeling unwell. Within a couple of minutes she had left the office and was walking towards Georgia waiting in her father's car.

"Wha... what happened?"

"Joe phoned me because he didn't want you distressed. Dumb I know, but he also asked if there was anyone that could represent him. To be honest I'm as much in the dark as you," said Georgia.

"I think it's to do with a robbery at Joe's place of work. But it's nothing to do with him, he wouldn't do something as stupid as that. It's a mistake."

"Of course it's a mistake. Dad's sent one of his solicitors to Shepherd's Bush Police Station, he'll soon have Joe out. Don't worry, it's just a hiccup."

But as Grace was to learn, it was a little bit more than a hiccup. Joe was remanded in custody, interviewed with his solicitor present and charged. "That can't be! My Joe is innocent, he wouldn't do such a thing."

Georgia stayed with Grace that night, and for several days after. Over those days Grace learned that according to the solicitor, two or three men had conspired with Joe to abduct a B.O.A.C employer's family and force the man to steal the contents of the strong-room, which on that particular day contained valuables to the tune of a possible eight million pounds.

"That's ridiculous. Joe's not the type. He wouldn't harm a fly!"

"They're saying it was Joe that masterminded the crime," said a hesitant Georgia.

"That's beyond ridiculous, he's been set up!" exclaimed Grace. A dark cloud descended upon Grace. "This has got Sean's handiwork over it. I'm sure of it."

"According to our solicitor, the man in charge of this case is a Detective Sergeant John Armstrong. I can ask him to make enquires but you already know these people always close ranks," said Georgia.

"I know Sean's behind it."

*****

For a few days after Joe was arrested and charged with the planned robbery of the B.O.A.C warehouse, Terry had kept a low profile. It wasn't until Sunday when he stuck his head around the saloon bar door and walked in.

"What the fuck is going on?" asked Bob angrily.

"Can't I get myself a pint first," snapped Terry.

"Get Terry a pint will yer Jim," said Bob.

"Usual Terry," asked Jim.

Terry nodded and sat down next to Bob. "Believe me Bob, I'm as much in the dark as you are. All I know is...." Jim appeared with Terry's pint and placed it down on the table. "Cheers Jim." He took a sip, "All I know is we were all brought in and interviewed, interrogation more like..."

"Yeah, yeah," said Bob impatiently. "We know all that, what we can't understand is Joe. Why the fuck was Joe arrested? You; we could understand."

"Cheers for that!" exclaimed Terry. He took a sip of his beer, then steadied himself, "I think it's all my fault."

"What!" exclaimed Jim?

"Joe hadn't been working at B.O.A.C. for more than three or four weeks when he found himself working on my shift. I asked him to drop a pallet of freight at a certain door, which he did, without question. What Joe didn't realise was this driver and I had an arrangement. A week later I handed Joe a ton and told him he'd earned it. Stupid I know, and Joe wasn't happy about it. But he took the money," said Terry.

"Yeah, but that don't explain how and why Joe would get mixed up in something like that," said Bob.

"You don't know the set up at the airport. Drivers come and go all the time, it's easy to strike up a relationship with warehousemen. It's all very friendly and relaxed. That's how I got mixed up with the odd pallet or two. It's easy money, no real risk. Security cameras don't work. The temptation to steal is enormous."

"And you'd know!" said Bob.

"Yeah, I'd know!" snapped Terry. "I know enough to keep away from the big boys. This might be hard to believe but I can only assume Joe got himself involved somehow. Either that or someone set him up!"

"Who the fuck would do that?" said Jim.

"Any number of people. There's some really nasty people that work at the airport," replied Terry, "I'm not saying that's what happened, but these things do happen."

"I still can't see Joe risking it," added Jim. "He's not the type."

"To be honest, I've been shitting myself. I thought when they interviewed Joe he might have dropped me in it with my little arrangements."

"Joe ain't the sort to grass," said Bob.

"Yeah, I know. I got pulled in, all because I recommended Joe for the job. Twice I got asked to go over my statement. They accused me of being involved."

"Yeah, but they let you go," said Jim.

"I think they're clutching at straws."

"Let's hope so," said Bob.

*****

Facing his friends had been an ordeal, one that he hadn't been looking forward too. Yet somehow they'd bought his story. Since Joe's arrest, Terry had been going over his story until he almost believed it himself. What gnarled the most was the fact Terry had betrayed his friend; an unforgivable crime. *It was on the late shift after meeting with the copper that he opened Joe's locker and slid the incriminating notes into the pages of a paperback, then he re-locked it. He began to retch, he felt nauseous and nearly re-opened the locker but for a work colleague who happened to walk into the locker room, just at that moment. Throughout the rest of the shift he fought with his conscience but the thought of losing his wife and kids held him back. When Joe was initially arrested, he felt compelled to confess but chickened out at the last minute. He reasoned that despite that bastard Fallon having it in for Joe the police would realise he was just a patsy. Joe hadn't a criminal record so there was the possibility he'd only get a couple of years, but deep down Terry knew he was only kidding himself.*

Terry knew there was one person he couldn't lie too; Eric Sullivan. With trepidation Terry walked into Eric's antique shop first thing Monday morning.

"Morning Eric."

Eric looked up from what he was doing, "You've got a fucking nerve, coming here!" he exclaimed.

"I need your advice. I don't have to spell it out to you what happened," said Terry ignoring the tirade of abuse.

"Well Terry, you fucking do! If you were to put someone in the frame, you don't do it to mates, friends that you've grown up with. In my book, framing a friend, is worse than grassing on someone. Where I come from, what you've done could amount to a death sentence."

"I had no choice! It was that fucking copper!" shouted Terry.

"What copper?"

"Joe's bird's soon to be ex."

"The Detective Sergeant?"

"The very same, only he's now an inspector. Detective Inspector Sean fucking Fallon."

"Are you sure? According to what I've read in the papers, it's a Detective Sergeant Armstrong that's leading the investigation."

"Sure I'm sure. I fucking met him. He phoned me after it went down, told me he knew everything. Arranged for me to meet him at Ruislip Lido. He stood there against a backdrop of woodland and virtually told me he'd set the whole thing up to trap me."

"You should have told him to fuck off. You should have walked away."

"I did! Then he showed me copies of the photos. It stopped me in my tracks. Why me? I cried."

"Yeah, why you," snapped Eric.

"He told me it was Joe he wanted, that's when the penny dropped. It was that bastard Fallon. He said it didn't matter to him either way, I was going down and Joe was coming with me, unless I put some things in Joe's locker."

"You didn't, tell me you didn't!" cried Eric.

Terry lowered his head.

"You cunt, you fucking stupid cunt!" Eric tempered his anger, as self-preservation rose to the fore. Guilt by association sprang to mind. '*If Terry was facing charges, he might implicate me in our previous transactions.*' Eric needed to distance himself.

"Well that sheds some light on it, but it don't change the outcome. Fallon has fucked you up the arse son! Done you up like a kipper! What about the ten grand?"

"It's gone! Took your advice."

"It's a pity you didn't follow my other piece of advice and faced up to Heather."

Eric was angry, not that he'd shown Terry. The man had a woman that loved the pants off him, a woman that would run through fire, yet the dumb fuck couldn't see further than his nose. He felt like breaking the man's trust and telling Heather everything, yet despite how he felt, he knew it would break Heather's heart, so he kept his anger hidden.

"Terry I gave you a piece of advice, don't get caught, well you didn't heed it. I'll give you one more piece of advice, you've chosen your path, now you've just got to live with it. Either that or own up!"

# Chapter 38

Grace rushed out of Shepherds Bush police station with Georgia close behind. It had been a brief and disturbing visit.

"I don't believe it, Joe wouldn't do that to me," snapped Grace. "I'm going to see Sean!" she exclaimed. "I have to do something! Joe's locked up with all sorts. He's dying inside. I could see it in his face.

"I wouldn't advise that," said Georgia.

"I'm past worrying about the divorce! I just want my Joe back!"

Georgia had been trying to change Grace's mind for over an hour, but to no avail. "Okay, you win. I'll get our solicitor to set up a meeting, but I'm going too!"

They arrived at the imposing Victorian terraced house, walked up the concrete steps and knocked on the door. Grace waited nervously until the door opened.

"What the hell!" exclaimed Fallon? "Yo…you're pregnant!" He looked past Grace to her friend and a man that was obviously her solicitor.

"Cut the crap Sean!" spat Grace.

"Wow that kind of language doesn't become you."

Grace could see him laughing at her behind those dark evil eyes.

"What is it that you want? Your phone call was a little vague, I thought the settlement was fair." He looked at her swollen stomach with distain. "But I can see there might be more to discuss."

"I'm not here to talk about the divorce. I'm here to ask you about why you're trying to frame my boyfriend for something he didn't do!"

"Hold it, this has gone far enough. I took the liberty of bringing my solicitor to discuss whatever you wanted discussing pertaining to the divorce. But in the circumstances I'm sure he will bear witness to such an accusation."

Grace's solicitor Peter Atkins intervened, "My client withdraws that remark on the grounds of her pregnancy and the distressing incarceration of her friend for a crime he didn't commit." Sean's solicitor looked over at Fallon, who more or less dismissed the accusation.

"So I take it your boyfriend has been a naughty boy. What's he done, stolen a car?" asked Fallon.

"You know exactly what he's been accused of, he's Joe Dempsey. You've got him locked up at Shepherd's Bush police station," said Grace.

"Dempsey, hmm... Nothing to do with me, never heard the name."

"You must have! He's been accused of involvement in a robbery from B.O.A.C." stuttered Grace.

"Oh, that case, big time villain from what I've heard. No that's Detective Sergeant John Armstrong's case. I wish I was assigned to it, Armstrong's likely for promotion if he gets the convictions."

"You're a heartless bastard!" exclaimed Georgia.

"Sorry I can't help; now is there anything we need to discuss as far as our divorce. Perhaps the little matter of your pregnancy. That's something we could discuss. Possibly a tweak of the settlement, but then I'm not that heartless. You'll need that settlement for your baby as it looks like your man won't have the means to provide for you both."

Within minutes they were in the solicitors' car and heading homeward. "The smug bastard, he's behind it. He's doing this to punish me for having the front to stand up to him," said Grace angrily.

"You could force his hand and threaten him with the fraudulent documents we have on him," said Georgia hopefully.

Grace's solicitor piped up, "That wouldn't help and it could make matters worse. You have inadvertently agreed to conceal a criminal act. You have omitted in court certain details that could see you in the dock. At the very least apart from being tied up in litigation for years, it certainly wouldn't help Joe. The best way for you to help him is to have the baby, get your divorce absolute and use the settlement to fight for his freedom," said the solicitor.

"I feel so frustrated!" snapped Georgia. "I should have insisted you didn't confront him, we could have made it worse. Now Fallon knows how you discovered his deception. For pure spite he could contest the settlement."

"He could, but he won't. I lived with him long enough to know how his mind works," said Grace.

A few days later Grace, Georgia and Jim watched as Joe along with his co-defendants were remanded in custody. Joe was assigned a category B status and was sent to Wandsworth Prison, whereas Keith Porter and Donald Fuller were sent to a category A prison.

Grace wasn't allowed to speak to him after he was remanded, which upset her enormously. Georgia looked to the solicitor. "You need to get her visiting rights as soon as possible!"

On the following Monday Grace received her visiting order and the following day she arrived at Wandsworth prison.

Joe professed his innocence the moment Grace walked in.

"I know darling, I know. Don't torture yourself, I know you wouldn't be so stupid," said Grace, "He's behind this, I just know it."

"You don't know that."

"I'm sure he's got a hand in it somewhere," repeated Grace.

"Someone's covering their arse. Whoever it is put something incriminating inside my locker."

"What was it!" cried Grace impatiently.

"I don't know, they won't say."

"But what, who? You've only been there three, four months at the most. Have you upset anybody?" asked Grace.

"I doubt it, I've always kept my nose clean. There's around a hundred or so warehousemen, some are okay, most are friendly enough, but there is a small element of blokes that are at it," said Joe.

"You've got to tell your solicitor, give him a list of names, anything!"

"Those men that raided Daniel's house kept insisting I set the whole thing up, but I'd never seen them in my life. Why me? Why pick on me, I ain't done anything to them.

"It's Sean, I know it's him. Who else!" said Grace?

"You may be right, but would he risk it?"

Grace paused, there was something needling away inside, "I know you're not going to like this but have you thought about anyone closer to home?"

Joe glared at Grace, "Like who? Terry you mean? Forget it, Terry's solid, he's a friend for Christ-sake! Believe me Grace, I wouldn't put this past some of the blokes I've worked with."

"Yeah, I know, but you've got to look at everyone. Terry is the least likely, the guys you've been talking about are a possibility, but whoever it is, my bet is Sean's behind it."

"It's possible, but according to Peter, when he accompanied you to Sean's house, it seemed to take him by surprise when he saw the bump. Besides you told me Sean was ambitious, ruthless yes, but above all careful. It wouldn't be worth it to risk his career and freedom for revenge."

"You don't know Sean like I do," said Grace. I wanted to expose Sean for fraud, but Peter advised against it."

"Peter was right, with the baby due soon, you'll need that settlement for you and our child." Tears began forming in his eyes.

The buzzer sounded like an alarm clock from hell.

"Oh Joe, I love you. We'll get through this somehow."

# Chapter 39

It was two weeks after Joe had been put on remand that Heather received a phone call from Eric, his voice sounding high and hysterical with grief.

"What is it? What's wrong?"

"It's Glo, she's dead!" Eric's voice sounding like a lifeless monotone. "Sh.. She's been … Her car crashed into a lamppost, she's dead Heather, she's dead and it's all my fault!"

"Oh my God! I'm so sorry Eric. What happened?"

Eric was distraught and wracked with grief, "It's my fault. We'd had a flaming row and I'd threatened to leave her."

"Had she been drinking?" asked Heather.

Eric's silence spoke volumes.

"You shouldn't be alone. Have you got anyone to call?" asked Heather.

"No, no one."

"Do you want to come round," she asked.

"What about Terry?"

"Don't worry about him, we're friends," emphasised Heather.

Fifteen minutes later a cab pulled up outside. Heather peeked out the window as Eric paid the driver. Seconds later he knocked on her door. "Come in," she said and held out her arms to comfort him. Eric fell into her arms and wept.

"I can't believe it happened, we'd had rows before, but not one that was so charged with rage. She'd downed three quarters of a bottle of scotch by the time I came home from work!"

"Oh Eric!"

"We were supposed to have been going out to dinner, but I told her I wouldn't take her out in that condition. I'd had it with her! If only I'd kept my cool."

"Don't do that!" exclaimed Heather, "Don't blame yourself!"

"She was like a woman possessed, screaming all kinds of abuse. Then she threw the bottle of scotch at me. In that moment I lost it bigtime and said I'd had enough, that I was leaving. It halted her in her tracks, her shocked expression, her crest fallen face. That look was the last I saw of her. Before I could act she'd snatched up the car keys and raced out the front door." Eric went silent.

"Oh Eric!"

"Ye… yeah," he spluttered. "I should have stopped her, but at that moment I couldn't have cared less. She'd worn me down Heather, I was done. I should have gone after her. The truth of it is, I still loved her, probably more than when we'd first met. She was such a vibrant woman, so alive, so full of fun. That look will haunt me for the rest of my days," sobbed Eric.

"Enough of that, you did your best for Gloria. She couldn't have wished for anyone better. Now come and sit down," said Heather.

She offered him a scotch but Eric declined. "I'll have tea."

"When did it happen?" asked Heather.

"Yesterday."

"Why didn't you call!" exclaimed Heather.

"I suppose I was in shock. I guessed that once she'd run out of steam she would come home sooner or later. When the police knocked I thought it was Gloria, why she'd knock I don't know. I just knew that she was dead by the look on the young copper's face." Eric looked vacantly into the fire, gathering his thoughts. "They told me there was no rush to identify Gloria's body. Something inside me didn't believe what he was saying, I just needed to see for myself. I had to see her. The other cop was more obliging and drove me to the mortuary where I identified her."

"I'm so sorry for you, I'd have been there for you if you'd asked," said Heather.

"I know you would, but you've got Terry to think about. How's he doing? I hope he's not involved in the business that Joe's mixed up in?"

"No, of course not, Terry's no angel but there are limits. He feels really bad about what's happened, blames himself," said Heather.

Eric didn't ask why.

"I imagine you've got a lot to sort out, the death certificate, Gloria's things and you'll need to make arrangements with the funeral parlour."

"Yeah, but it hasn't sunk in yet. We can't do anything until they've done the autopsy, which I'm not looking forward too. Then I guess they'll hold an inquest."

"If you need any help with anything, I'm only too willing to help," volunteered Heather.

Just at that moment they heard Terry's key in the front door.

"Eric!" exclaimed Terry eyeing him suspiciously when he walked into the front room. "This looks cosy," he said when he spotted the teapot and tea cups. "Biscuits too."

"It's Gloria! She's dead!" exclaimed Heather.

"She was killed in a car accident last night. I didn't know who to turn too. You're the closest I've got to friends around here," said Eric.

"My God, what happened?"

"I'll explain it all to you later, Eric doesn't need to go through it again," said Heather forcefully.

"I'd better be going," said Eric. "Thanks for the tea."

"You don't need to go," cried Heather.

"It's best I do," said Eric.

"Remember, I'm here for you, whatever you need," she added.

"I'll see you out," said Terry.

Eric stepped into the hall, with Terry a step behind. "I don't really know what to say mate, I'm just so sorry for your loss."

"Thanks."

"How are you getting home?"

"I'll walk it," replied Eric.

"I can give you a lift if you'd rather," added Terry.

"No, I'm good, just look after your wife, you never know when misfortune can hit," said Eric.

"Yeah, I'll do that."

\*\*\*\*\*

It was two weeks before the autopsy was performed and a further couple of days before the inquest was held. Nearly three weeks since the shock of Gloria's death, before another shock hit him. When the autopsy report was read out Eric slumped down in his seat as the true reason for Gloria's drinking became apparent.

Gloria had been suffering from early stage Scleroderma. For the last year of her life she had experienced a hardening and tightening of patches of skin alongside digestive symptoms. When she was diagnosed a couple of days after Christmas with systemic sclerosis she was devastated. She knew that over a period of time she could expect skin changes over the whole of her body, it most likely would also affect her internal organs, along with joint pain and stiffness. She was told that with new medicines coming on the market within a few years, her prognosis wasn't as bad as they'd feared, but to someone like Gloria, Scleroderma was a death sentence. Eric's heart broke in two.

After the funeral, Eric couldn't face going through all Gloria's things, so it was inevitable he'd asked Heather if she'd help him go through all her personal effects. It was while going through her drawers that Heather found an envelope addressed to Eric. She handed it to him and left him alone to read it.

*Dear Eric,*

*If you're reading this then you probably know the truth. I love you more than you'll ever know. You're kind, patient and loving towards me, even though at times I let drink take a hold. It's my vanity that gets the better of me, I know that a man as handsome as you, with the charm and wit of a God will one day look at much younger women and feel the temptation. I pray that I never have to watch as you slowly turn away from me. We fight, yet I bear you no malice, I know that you truly love me, that you want the best for me. Those years before my diagnosis have been the happiest of my entire life, even happier than my time in Paris. Our life together has been brief but hopefully as the years pass you'll remember our good times and raise a glass to me.*

*Goodbye My Love,*

*Glo*

Eric, slumped down on the bed and re-read Gloria's letter his eyes filled with tears, blinding him momentarily. He wiped them away, and stared at the written word. "If only," he uttered over and over. He began to sob and was glad of the privacy Heather had allowed him. Finally after wiping away the tears, he asked Heather to come back into the room. He handed Heather the note to read. She took it from him and read it, then re-read it. A lump formed in her throat, as she handed the note back. That he loved Gloria more than anyone could ever know was apparent and heart wrenching. She thought of her brief encounter with Eric and knew that it couldn't compare to his life with Gloria.

# Chapter 40

Sunday lunchtimes changed during those turbulent weeks of summer. Joe was on remand with a possible trial date of mid-October. He, like Grace and his friends hoped the nightmare of the year would be over by Christmas. Regular visits by Grace and his mates kept Joe buoyant. His lawyer reckoned the case was too flimsy to get a conviction, as Joe had kept stating he'd never met them before he was remanded. It was his word against two known villains. As for the alleged incriminating evidence in Joe's locker, anyone could have planted it. With the hope that Joe's conviction would be quashed before Christmas, Bob suggested they should all stop feeling guilty about enjoying themselves and meet up at least twice a month on Sundays. It was Becky who suggested that as they all had the same goal which was for their friend to be set free, that wives and girlfriends should be invited.

Terry was the first to agree, which raised eyebrows all around. "I'd have thought you'd have been the last one to agree," stated Jim.

"Since Eric's loss of Gloria, it's made me rethink my life," he said with a serious tone. Like the rest of them Terry believed there was a strong chance of acquittal. In which case his and Joe's nightmare would be over. No way would Fallon be able to implicate him, without implicating himself.

"How is Eric holding up?" asked Georgia.

"He's coming to terms with it slowly. Heather's been a great comfort to him over the last six weeks. So yeah, I think it would be a good idea. I'm a changed man," he said tongue in cheek, before adding, "Heather deserves my support."

"Fuck me!" exclaimed Bob, "Whoops! Sorry Georgia, I can't get my head around this man. I think the rest of the male race are doomed," he laughed.

"Don't mind me," laughed Georgia. "I can mix it with the boys and I dare say Becky can too."

"Heather's had to put up with Terry for years, so I'm sure she's conditioned," said Becky, giving Terry a sarcastic grin.

"What about Grace? I'm sure now there's some optimistic news she might enjoy a little light relief. She's got a couple of months before she's due. Georgia and me can bring her along if she wants," said Jim.

"It's Georgia and I," corrected Georgia.

"See it's begun!" exclaimed Bob.

The first Sunday, Grace wasn't up to it, but Terry brought along Heather. Bob and Becky were there sitting on their usual table deep in discussion.

"You know Becky, I still can't get my head around them thinking Joe was involved with something like kidnapping. It just ain't him."

"You're right Bobby. I didn't know Joe long, but in the short time I've known him, I couldn't see him getting mixed up with serious criminals."

"Hi" cried Heather as Terry pulled out a chair for her.

"Your usual?" asked Terry.

"We're okay at the moment," relied Bob.

Ten minutes later in walked Georgia and Jim. "Do you mind if we join you," laughed Georgia as she squeezed between Bob and Becky.

"We were just talking about Joe not being the type to get involved in kidnapping," said Becky.

"Sometimes people aren't what they seem," said Georgia. "Easy money can turn some people." Quickly she added, "I'm not saying Joe was involved, it's just a fact. Sorry, it's just the lawyer in me."

Becky gave her a little smile of understanding. "Georgia's right, if someone waved a wad of cash in your face and only wanted names and dates it would be hard to resist."

"Nah, that ain't right Becks! Joe might nick something that fell off the back of a lorry, but not this. He's too smart to get himself involved. He's been fitted up. Once it goes to trial the judge will see through the whole dirty business," said Bob.

"Yeah, Bob's right. Joe wasn't the type to get involved," added Jim.

"If I could get my hands on the bastard that fit him up, I'd tear him limb from limb," said Bob.

"Steady on tiger! I don't want you ending up inside. If you want my opinion I think Grace's right, that arsehole husband of hers must be behind it."

"It's possible but unless those bastards change their story, it will be up to the judge and jurors to see though it," added Georgia.

"How's Joe taking it?" asked Becky.

"When I went up to see him, he's still very optimistic. He reckoned his brief thinks there's a very strong chance the Judge might throw the case against him out."

"Right let's talk about something else. Like what are we planning for Joe's homecoming?" said Terry.

"Us girls will put our heads together, we'll figure something out. If we leave it to you boys it'll turn into a glorified piss up," said Becky.

As the drinks flowed the conversation moved on to when the new football season was starting, who was going to win the league,"Never mind the football, have you heard 'A Whiter Shade of Pale,' by Procul Harem?" stated Georgia. "It's really groovy!"

"I told you, you'd have trouble with her, she's turning into a hippy!" laughed Bob.

"Yeah, she is that," agreed Jim. "Actually when I first heard it, I didn't give it much thought, but over the weeks I've gotta say it's psychedelic man!" then he laughed.

'It was good to hear laughter, there hadn't been much of it lately,' thought Heather. Her mind had been preoccupied with worrying about Eric's mental condition. On the surface he seemed okay, but Heather sensed he was not coping. She felt a little guilty not because of their brief dalliance but more to do with Terry's caring offensive. Nice as it was she found it a little too much.

"Did you see 'the Eamonn Andrews Show' on the telly the other night?" asked Jim, trying to get everyone's attention. "He had Clint Eastwood on."

"You mean Clint Walker, don't yah," interrupted Terry.

"No! Clint Eastwood, you know, Rowdy Yates from Rawhide. I told you about it a month or so ago. They showed a clip. It looks pretty cool," said Jim.

"There he goes again, the hippy!" laughed Bob.

Heather took it upon herself to pop into Eric's shop the following Tuesday. She felt nervous as she entered, and a little startled as the bell attached to the door clanged announcing her entrance. Eric appeared from the back, "Heather!"

Heather smiled awkwardly, "I was in the area, thought I'd pop by, see how you're coping."

"You know you can call in anytime. What's on your mind?"

"Nothing really! We was in the George yesterday, and they all asked how you were keeping."

Eric looked sad and forlorn, Heather's heart went out to him.

"I'm getting by, day by day. I miss her so much."

"I'm sure you do Eric. Just remember I'm there if you ever need to talk about anything."

"I'd appreciate that," said Eric, a weak smile upon his lips.

226

"We're down the George every other Sunday, so don't be a stranger. Everyone would love you to join us."

"I'll bear that in mind."


Two weeks later Jim and Georgia managed to coax Grace into joining them for a drink.

"Are you sure? I feel bad about Joe, if it wasn't for me he'd be here."

"Joe will be out soon. How do you think he'd feel if we abandoned you?" said Jim.

Grace waddled to the car and remarked, "To think less than a year ago I'd never have dreamed I'd be such a fat lump."

"Waddling like a duck maybe, but fat lump, never," said Georgia playfully as she helped Grace into the car.

Grace was greeted by Bob and Becky as she walked through the door. Jim asked Grace what she wanted, "An orange juice or lemonade, not fussed, thanks."

Heather and Terry arrived ten minutes later, "Sorry we're late, had to wait for my neighbour to sit in with the kids," said Heather apologetically.

Any news on Eric?" asked Bob.

"Yeah, he said he might pop in for a swift one, later," said Terry.

"That's not what Eric said." Heather contradicted, "I'll see how I'm feeling is what he actually said."

Georgia caught the edge of impatience creeping into Heather's voice. It was only slight, but it was there nonetheless.

Jim took command of the conversation, "Are you going to see it this afternoon?"

"See what," asked Terry.

"He means, this Italian western, Fistful of Dollars. He saw the trailer last week," said Bob.

"Yeah it looks great," said Jim, then he paraphrases it, "This is the first motion picture of its kind. It won't be the last. We're going to see it this afternoon."

"Is that right Georgia?"

Georgia gave a resigned pout, "If we must."

The conversation continued in much the same vein, very light hearted, but inevitably Gloria's drinking was touched on.

"I didn't know Gloria that well but she always looked immaculate. Her hair, her makeup and those clothes, you'd never think she had a drink problem," said Georgia.

"Yeah," replied Becky, "I hope I look as good as she did when I'm her age."

"I only saw her once or twice but, maybe it's me, she did look a little on edge during unguarded moments," observed Grace. "I should know."

"No one knows what inner demons lurk behind a perfect façade," added Heather. Eric had confided in her, adding Gloria wouldn't want anyone to know about her condition.

"Yeah you and Terry knew them slightly more, did you know there was something up?" asked Georgia.

"No! Of course not," replied Heather. "We had dinner with them on Christmas Eve and Gloria seemed really relaxed. In fact apart from a drink of wine over dinner she hardly drank at all. Not like Terry! But that's another story," she laughed. Hopefully no one noticed how quickly she replied to Georgia's loaded question.

Then as if on cue, Eric Sullivan walked in and stepped up to the bar. Terry rushed over, "I'll get that Eric."

"That's okay Terry, I'm only staying for one."

Eric insisted, then with a double scotch in hand he walked over and sat down. "I see the crowd have grown some," he remarked.

"Yeah, my fault, I weakened," joked Bob. Promptly he received a dig in the ribs from Becky. "Ooh."

"It's good to see you Eric," said Jim.

"We were all sorry for your loss," said Grace, amidst muttering of muted cries of sympathy.

"You're all really kind. I really loved her you know. Despite the difference in our ages I loved Glo with all my heart.

Georgia couldn't help noticing the angst in Heather's eyes.

# Chapter 41

On the 11th of August Grace gave birth to a healthy 7lb 9oz baby girl. Grace's mum and dad gazed down proudly at their first Grandchild. "She's beautiful!" exclaimed Grace's parents.

"She's everything I thought she'd be," said Grace, "I just wish Joe was here with me," she added sadly.

"He'll be home soon," said Grace's dad encouragingly.

"Well until Joe's acquitted you and the baby are coming to stay with us," said Grace's mum.

"We'll see," said Grace, not wanting to give up her independence just yet.

"She's gorgeous!" exclaimed Georgia when she entered the maternity ward with a bunch of red roses. Jim took a disinterested peek at the baby, in his eyes babies were still a few years away.

"How long before they'll let you leave hospital," asked Grace's mum, feeling a little put out by the intrusion of Georgia.

"I'm not sure, but a week, less if I can help it," said Grace.

"We'll leave you now Grace," said Mum. "You'll need your rest."

Grace waited until her doting mother left the room then pleadingly she looked at Georgia, "Will you take us to see Joe; he must see his daughter."

"It's all in hand," replied Georgia, having already anticipated Grace's first thoughts.

On the drive home Jim said, "I'll be damn glad when the trial is over, then we can get back to normal."

Georgia laughed, "Things won't be normal for Joe, apart from a new mouth to feed, he's got to find himself a job."

"Won't B.O.A.C. take him back? If they throw out the case against him, surely they must give him his job back at least."

"That isn't going to happen. Just because the case is thrown out, doesn't mean he's not guilty," said Georgia.

"Still, the settlement should tide them over," said Jim hopefully.

"To be quite honest, I'll be glad when it's all over, then we can get on with our lives," replied Georgia. "Eight properties isn't four, but it's certainly not sixteen."

"Aren't we over-stretching a bit," cautioned Jim.

"On the contrary, we need another two, maybe four places before Christmas. The secret of this business, is not to let the grass grow under our feet."

Jim bit his tongue, Georgia had been the spark that had seen them build up a portfolio of properties and so far things had worked out well. Not counting Joe and Grace's flat they now had income from six others with one still vacant. Until that was filled and contracts signed he wasn't moving on anymore before the year was out.

"Any news on the let?" he asked.

"Yes, we've a couple coming to view it this weekend," replied Georgia.

"Good, then we can think about a week away somewhere," said Jim. "All work and no play makes Jill a dull girl.

"Who are you calling dull, you don't say that when we're in bed together."

"Ah, but that's different," said Jim with a glint in his eye.

"Yeah! But you're right, perhaps a week in Bournemouth, mid-September, or we could be a bit daring and try Rimini," suggested Georgia.

"Rimini! Where's Rimini?"

"Italy, silly," she replied.

"Bournemouth sounds great," I don't fancy all that foreign stuff."

"You liked it well enough at Joe and Grace's. Besides it's part of your re-education, culinary dishes of the world."

"Yeah but that's different. Do you know where I'd really fancy going?" said Jim.

"Where?"

"America!" exclaimed Jim. "Trouble is it's a bit too expensive."

"Exactly! That's why we need to keep going with purchasing more houses."

*****

"My mother's like a woman possessed!" remarked Grace when Georgia came to pick her up from the hospital. "She wants me to go straight to her house, but I told her that I must see Joe."

"Don't worry we're going straight there, I got the visiting order here," said Georgia. "Then I'm afraid it's straight back to Elstree. You're mum's right about that, at least for a week or so."

"You know Georgia, I don't know how to thank you. You've been so kind and caring. I don't know how I'd have coped without your help," said Grace.

"I think you would have managed, and besides I'm a sucker for a lame duck!" she grinned at Grace, "Now I'd suggest you and the duckling sit in the back seat, it'll be safer." Grace looked at her and laughed as Georgia opened the rear door for her and the baby. As they left the car park at the hospital Georgia asked, "Have you and Joe settled on a name for her?"

"Not yet, I want Joe to see the baby before we name her," replied Grace.

*****

Joe stood up the moment Grace carrying the baby walked into the visiting room. His face lit up despite looking tired and gaunt. As Joe had said on other visits when they mentioned his weight,

"The food's shit!" He so desperately wanted to hold her but unfortunately all the guards were jobsworths.

"Don't worry Joe, when they let you out you can cuddle her to your hearts content," said Grace.

"What have you called her?" he asked.

"You know me better than that Joe Dempsey. We'll decide together."

"Wow, this is difficult," laughed Joe. "We could call her Josephine! Nah, they'd call her Joe for short."

"What's the name of your favourite actress?" suggested Grace.

"Well, that's obvious, Grace Kelly of course," he laughed.

Grace felt warm inside, Joe was feeling more relaxed. Even he was beginning to believe the nightmare would soon be over. "We are not calling our little girl Grace, that's as bad as Josephine," she giggled.

"Well, you're not going to like it, but my real favourite actress is Billie Whitelaw."

"Billie," mused Grace, "Billie, hmm… Billie Dempsey! I like it!" said Grace firmly.

"I'm not sure she's gonna like it," said Joe, "It's kinda tomboyish."

"Believe it or not, I was a tomboy, I loved climbing trees, making camps, swinging across rivers."

"Rivers?" questioned Joe.

"Well, more like brooks," added Grace.

"So Billie Dempsey it shall be," stated Joe, "Only one problem, your last name's Fallon."

"Not for long. Once the divorce comes through I'll change it back to Delaney."

"Grace Delaney, I'd never have thought you was of Irish descent," said Joe.

"Yes, way back. My great grandfather on my dad's side."

"Billie Delaney, it has a nice ring about it, but I think Billie Dempsey sounds a shade better," said Joe, "Which leaves me to ask you Grace Delaney, will you marry me?"

Grace looked shocked, then surprised, she'd not expected Joe to propose and despite the unromantic surroundings she cried out, "Yes Joe, I'll marry you!"

\*\*\*\*\*

Georgia spotted the stunned look upon Grace's face as she left the visiting room. "What's up?" she asked with concern in her voice.

"Nothing's up, quite the opposite. Joe just asked me to marry him," she cried.

"He what?" said a startled Georgia.

"He asked me to marry him and I said yes!"

"But… But I thought you were going to show Joe the baby. Maybe even select a name."

"Yes that's right, meet Billie!"

Who?

Joe's favourite actress, Billie Whitelaw.

# Chapter 42

A little over two weeks later Grace received her copy of the decree absolute. She read it and re-read it, she couldn't believe her eyes. She was a free woman! Free to live the life she'd always believed she was destined for; free to marry the man that she loved; free to have his child and free of the monster Detective Inspector Sean Fallon. She phoned Georgia with the news.

"I can't believe it!" she exclaimed. "It's almost like an anti-climax. I can't wait to give Joe the good news."

"Anti-climax, I've heard that many times before, but importantly you're free of that monster. Now all we've got to do is make sure Joe has the charges dropped," said Georgia; ever the lawyer.

"I'm going up to the prison to give him the good news," said Grace excitedly.

Not having taken her driving test; mainly due to Sean's controlling influence over her, Grace had either to use public transport or rely on the good will of others. Living back with her parents did have many benefits, access to transport being one. Her dad insisted on driving her to the prison, "It's the least I can do," he'd said.

Her mother looked on disapprovingly; though supporting Grace, she wasn't so sure about Joe. "Can't you wait until your next scheduled visit," she uttered, then adding, "Are you sure he's the one."

"I've never been surer," said Grace.

"You thought that about Sean. I'm only concerned for you and the baby."

Grace knew her mum meant well, but she'd stayed a week longer than she anticipated, so despite all her mum's help and advice she was going back to the flat after the weekend. She knew she had to get use to looking after Billie on her own. Besides, what with the trial looming she wanted to be prepared for Joe's home coming.

*****

Sean received the decree absolute with distain. Grace had been the one big failure in his life. He'd believed she was the perfect woman to decorate his arm. Someone that would bear him children, someone that would be the genial hostess when he was in a position to entertain guests. Prestige went hand in glove with ambition as far as Sean was concerned. Chief Inspector of Constabulary was his aim, all before he was fifty; then who knows. That had been the plan, but it faltered when she couldn't give him children. A fact he automatically dismissed as being her fault. When the clinic insisted on testing him, he'd quite expected them to come back with a clean bill of health. He was stunned when he received the report. He knew he couldn't face Grace with the truth after the abuse he'd given her over those years of trying for a baby. He knew she'd have been sympathetic, understanding, disappointed yes, but he knew she'd stand by him.It was the ugly truth and his vanity that drove him to corrupt the records. Over the years that followed when he looked at his wife, the wholesome woman that he'd fell in love with; his attitude to her changed. He despised her, even at times feeling hatred, knowing in time divorce would be inevitable, but Grace had found the truth, thanks to the boy/man that had impregnated her.

The trial as far as he could tell wasn't going quite the way he'd planned. There were rumours that the case against Joseph Dempsey was close to being thrown out. He couldn't allow that to happen, but until he'd received the incriminating documents from Grace's solicitors, his hands were tied. He phoned his solicitor to make doubly sure the documents were in their possession. When the solicitor gave him the confirmation he needed, a malevolent smile spread across his face. Now he could act.

His ace in the pack was Arthur Briggs. For months he'd kept Arthur on ice, schooling him on what to say at the trial. At first Briggs had been frightened that Donald Fuller would think he was the one that grassed them up. "My life won't be worth a plugged nickel, if he thinks I gave him up," he'd moaned to Fallon.

"Well you did!" Fallon said unsympathetically. "Your choice, Fuller will find out either way."

"Whatcha mean?" snapped Briggs.

"My way you stay out of prison. On the other hand if you're prepared to do the time, I'm sure someone will drop a word in Fuller's shell-like."

"You wouldn't!"

"Try me!" snapped Fallon.

\*\*\*\*\*

Detective Sergeant John Armstrong had been a pain in Sean's arse for months. "When are you giving me Briggs, without his testimony my case against them starts to fall apart."

"Trust me John, by the time I've finished with Briggs he'll be your star witness."

"I don't know what your angle is, and I don't want to know. Just keep me out of it," said Armstrong.

"When I give you Briggs he's yours, has been since you nicked him on a lesser charge. He's your informant, you make the deal with Briggs but remember he stays out of prison.

\*\*\*\*\*

It was two weeks later when Joe's defence were told new evidence had come to light and the case against Joseph Dempsey was to go ahead. Joe and Grace were devastated. "What evidence?" snapped Joe to his solicitor?

"New evidence. From what I've heard, the prosecution have the third man in custody, a Mr Arthur Briggs."

"Never heard of him," snapped Joe. "It's a fit up!"

Grace phoned Georgia the moment she heard about the new evidence. "I tell you Georgia, my ex is behind this. I'm sure of it."

"Then we go after Fallon. There must be a connection. If we find even a slight connection we can build from it," said Georgia. "I'll have a word with my dad, he might have some ideas."

Later that night Georgia asked her dad's advice, "I know you don't want to hear this, but have you considered this Joe might be guilty."

"He's not guilty! I'm sure of it," snapped Georgia.

"I know you were all pinning your hopes on the case against him being thrown out, but it's not over. They have to prove in court that Joe's guilty. I'm afraid that's all I can say on the matter," said George Chandler.

"What about the bad feeling with Grace and her ex, surely we can go down that road?"

"What evidence have you got against him? Your friend Grace went against her solicitor's advice and agreed what incriminating evidence she held would be given up as part of the settlement. She was warned. It was good advice, but she didn't heed it."

*****

Not all the boys heard the news until Jim told them in the George that Sunday.

"What the fuck are we going to do about it," cried a stunned Bob. "They're fitting him up and we're sitting on our hands."

"In my experience when Old Bill get their teeth into something as big as this, they've usually got all their ducks in a row," said a serious Eric Sullivan. He gave Terry a meaningful stare. "What's your take on this Terry? You worked with Joe, you know the blokes he worked with, have anyone of them caused you to be suspicious?"

Terry looked uncomfortable. Eric hoped that in putting him on the spot he'd crack. Since Gloria's death he'd took his eye off the ball and things had moved on. Terry took a swig of his pint, masking the guilty look with a pint glass. Eric knew then, Terry didn't have the balls to come clean, to tell them he was being blackmailed, that Detective Inspector Sean Fallon was behind the conspiracy. He was too far down the road to stop.

"All I know as far as I'm concerned, Joe ain't guilty."

"Ain't that the truth," replied a steely eyed Eric Sullivan. He wanted so desperately to break the code he'd lived by and grass Terry up, but a number of factors stopped him. Firstly he'd never betrayed a confidence. Secondly it would be his word against Terry and where would that lead, considering his dealings with him. Thirdly it would break Heather's heart; and how would she feel towards him after he'd grassed Terry up.

"Georgia's in the thick of it at the moment. She's hell bent on proving that arsehole Fallon is behind it," added Jim. "But in answer to what you said Bob, there ain't really anything we can do, except don't give up hope."

"What about Grace, has anyone been around to see how she is?" cried Becky after finding her voice. She'd sat there in silence at hearing the news.

"Yeah," said Jim, Georgia's been with her since the news broke."

"What's everyone having," asked Eric.

Everyone spoke at once. With the order clear in his head Eric turned towards the bar. "Terry give me a hand with the drinks, will yah."

"Yeah sure."

Eric reeled off the drinks order, then looked Terry straight in the eye. "You know what I'm gonna say, don't yah."

"Yeah, I guess so."

"You could still fix this Terry. Expose Fallon!"

"Yeah, expose Fallon! To whom, the police, forget it. Turn on their own I don't think so. Besides, Fallon said even if I come clean, he'll make sure Joe goes down with me."

"Okay, I take your point, but you could still admit it was you. Fallon's bluffing about Joe. Take the responsibility! Joe doesn't deserve this, he's got a new born kid."

"What if I don't? Are you going to give me up?"

"Fuck you Terry, you know I won't. That's up to you," said Eric as he paid for the drinks. The exchange had become a bit heated as Eric turned his back on Terry and brought the tray of drinks over.

"What was that all about?" asked Bob.

"Nah, it was nothing. You know Terry, he's trying to fix be up with some bird, the prick don't understand." replied Eric.

# Chapter 43

It was a dull and rainy day at the beginning of November when Grace and Georgia stared up at the statue of Lady Justice at the top of the Old Bailey.

"I always thought she was blindfolded," stated Grace.

"That's a misconception, she has the scales of justice in her left hand and the sword in her right to depict justice. Why she doesn't have a blindfold is because her maidenly form is supposed to guarantee her impartiality," replied Georgia.

"I'm glad she doesn't wear a blindfold, she must be able to see that my Joe is completely innocent of the charges against him."

Georgia said nothing as they took the steps to the entrance. Inside they spotted Bob and Becky, who greeted them nervously when they walked over. To the side they spotted Terry chain smoking and stubbing out one cigarette after another. Bob tried making light of it, "You'd thing Terry was on trial, not Joe."

Within twenty minutes they were summoned to the public gallery of number one court. Within a few minutes they found their seats amidst a hubbub of conversations. In the public gallery sat Grace, Georgia and Joe's parents, behind them sat Bob, Becky and Terry. A sudden hush came over the court.

"All rise."

Grace felt nervous. This was the real deal. The hearing some three weeks earlier had been a formality. Joe pleaded "Not Guilty," to the charges that were brought against him and in a mere few minutes it was over. Her heart skipped a beat as Joe, along with Donald Fuller and Keith Porter appeared and stood in the dock. Grace looked at Joe and mouthed a silent "I love you." He half smiled, and Grace could tell he was extremely nervous.

She looked at his co-defendants, they even looked like hardened criminals. No way would Joe have gotten himself involved with the likes of them. For a moment she felt hope, 'surely the judge can see the difference. The prosecution began to lay out their case before the jury. Detective Sergeant John Armstrong took the stand and began his testimony.

"In the course of my duty I apprehended a Mr Arthur Briggs on an unrelated case. I was about to charge him, when he said he had valuable information that he wanted in exchange for a deal. A warehouse robbery at London airport, he said. I then listened to what Briggs had to offer. The information appeared sound and certain names of well-known villains came up. I asked him when this was going down. He said they (pointing to Keith Porter and Donald Fuller) were waiting until they received the right information."

"By right information, you mean the name and address of the key holder on a particular day."

"Yes sir, that and what consignments were in the strong room on that day. To be honest I thought Briggs was just spinning me a line. I lost all patience with him and said he was wasting my time. He started to panic and practically begged me to give him two weeks, adding; I'll deliver them on a plate."

"And you were prepared to let this Arthur Briggs walk, on the information he'd given you?"

"Yes sir. The charges I had on him could wait. If he didn't come up with the goods I'd nick him, there would be no second chance. I went on my instinct."

"So what you're saying is you used this Briggs as an 'Agent Provocateur," suggested the prosecuting barrister.

"That's about it sir," said Armstrong.

One after another the witnesses took the stand and slowly the case began to take shape.

On the third day of the trial the prosecution saw fit to introduce Arthur Briggs as the main prosecution witness.

"State your name and occupation," cried the court usher.

"Arthur Briggs, driver," he replied.

"Tell us in your own words how you first met Joseph Dempsey," said the prosecuting barrister.

Arthur Briggs looked around the court and locked on Donald Fuller. Briggs knew he was a dead man if he even stepped one foot inside prison. Fuller frightened him; Keith Porter might put him in hospital but he'd live to tell the tale; then his eyes rested on Joe Dempsey the poor sucker that was his pass to freedom. Then it dawned on him where he'd seen him before, he was the warehouseman that brought the pallet load of camera gear to his van.

"I first met Joe sometime in late January. I was collecting a consignment which Joe brought from the warehouse. It was a reasonably slack night and I got talking with him about how easy it would be for him to slip me the odd consignment along with the legit ones. He seemed interested, but was none committal. I thought nothing of it. You have to ask don'tcha. But the next time I was on the import door, he asked if I had room for more. I wasn't gonna say no, was I?"

"That's a lie! It's all lies!" shouted Joe.

"Silence, you'll get your chance to speak later," said the Judge sternly.

"So you had an arrangement, is that correct?"

"You could say that; a lucrative business arrangement. It wasn't long after when he asked if I knew anyone with the bottle to earn serious money. I said what kind of serious money. He said three maybe five million quid. I laughed at first, he was a young feller, trying to impress, acting the big man. He didn't get narked, said he understood, that he was dead serious. He laid out verbally his idea. It seemed a simple enough plan, so I said I'd run it passed a couple of people I knew. That's when I mentioned it to Don Fuller."

"One of the defendants. Point him out."

Briggs pointed straight at Fuller and was greeted with an ugly scowl. His testimony was damning and painted Joe as the man behind the attempted raid. Whether that was to appease Fuller or not, it didn't look good for Joe.

In a whispered tone his defence barrister reassured Joe, "We'll get our chance to discredit their witness; it's your word against his."

It was day five before Joe's barrister got the chance to blow Arthur Briggs out of the water. He'd asked a few routine questions, before asking Briggs his opinion on Joe's intellect.

"Yeah, I'd say he seemed far to qualified to be working in a warehouse."

Joe's barrister smiled. "Correct me if I'm wrong, the value of the contents of the strong room would be around three to six million pounds."

"Yeah I guess, I don't actually know," said Briggs.

"What would stop Fuller and Porter from taking the lot, leaving my client to take the rap while they sunned themselves on the Costa Brava? If he was so smart wouldn't he have realised the major flaw in that particular plan?" Joe's barrister casually looked across to judge the temperature of the jury. "I suggest you Mr Briggs have concocted this cock and bull story to save yourself from jail time."

Briggs looked defiantly at Joe's barrister. "I said he was smart, because he is smart. Fuller and Porter needed him to fly them out of the country!"

Joe's barrister looked physically shaken by this new information. He turned towards Joe, who looked back at his barrister nonplussed. The barrister looked back at Briggs having gathered his thoughts. "Is this another figment of your vivid imagination?"

"No sir. He said they were to drive straight to Denham Airfield after they'd done the job. He had access to a light aircraft to take them all to Belgium."

Joe's barrister smiled, "My client doesn't possess a pilot's licence."

Briggs braced himself as he delivered the killer line, "He didn't need one, he'd learned to fly light aircraft during his years in the Air Cadets."

An audible shock echoed around the courtroom. The barrister turned back to look at Joe for a denial. There was none.

"Your Honour, may I seek a recess to speak with my client?"

The judge allowed the recess. Joe's legal team were in total disarray as they marched out of the courtroom. Joe was white faced and bewildered as he was taken downstairs to talk with his barrister.

"Did you know Joe could fly a plane?" asked Georgia.

"No, he never mentioned it," said an anxious Grace.

*****

In the judge's chambers Joe's legal team asked him if he could fly a light aircraft. Joe replied, it was ridiculous. "Yes during my time as an Air Cadet I was allowed to take over the controls, and yes with a qualified pilot I was able to take off and land. But that was years ago, I'd have been sixteen, seventeen maybe, but not confident enough to fly to Belgium. I suppose I knew the theory, but my actually time in the cockpit was minimal. Besides I've probably forgotten most of what I knew. I most certainly wouldn't have the confidence to try it. I'm not suicidal!"

"I'm going to have to ask for a continuance," stated the barrister.

The case was adjourned to the following day, with Joe's barristers preparing his defence.

Day six day, Joe's defence lawyer put him on the stand. He asked him to state his name and occupation. When all the legal jargon was done with, the defence barrister began his questioning. "Have you ever flown a light aircraft?"

Joe explained that as an Air Cadet he had flown a light aircraft on several occasions. "Not enough to navigate or fly to Belgium," he insisted.

Then the prosecuting barrister tore into Joe with one question after another. Joe stuck to his story throughout, but the prosecution had managed to paint him in a bad light. Amongst paperwork found in Joe's locker was a flight plan to Belgium and a flight manual of a de Havilland Chipmunk. Joe acknowledged the manual but denied the flight plan and the other incriminating paperwork.

The prosecution and defence gave their summing up and the judge ordered the jury to retire to the jury room to consider their verdict. Grace was in tears, she knew it didn't look good, but Georgia tried to keep her spirits up. Although deep down Georgia was having her own doubts on Joe's innocence. If someone had framed Joe, how did they know about his Air Cadet history? Why did Joe have a de Havilland Chipmunk flight manual in his locker? As for the shift patterns and address of Mr Torrance; it was looking pretty bleak. The only thing that didn't ring true, after all they'd been through was Joe preparing to abandon Grace and the baby? That part didn't make sense.

It was three forty five when the jury returned. Grace looked fearfully at each member of the jury, but none gave anything away as they took their seats. The foreman of the jury stood up and was asked if the jury had reached a verdict. The reply was "Yes your honour."

"How do you find the defendants," asked the judge.

"We find the defendants Donald Fuller and Keith Porter guilty on the charge of attempted kidnapping. On the charge of being in possession of firearms we find both men guilty. On the charge of attempted robbery of B.O.A.C warehouse we find them both guilty."

For the briefest of seconds Grace thought Joe was off the hook.

"We find the defendant Joseph Dempsey guilty of planning the execution of the attempted kidnapping. Guilty of supplying Fuller and Porter with the information that was needed to commit the robbery. And lastly being in possession of flight plans for their escape from the country."

A cry from the public galley was greeted with a stiff reprimand, then the judge told the jury they were discharged before saying he would consider overnight the sentences he would pronounce the following day. The judge then looked towards the three men in the dock, "I should warn you that the sentence I pronounce on you will reflect the seriousness of the crime you attempted to commit. Take them down."

"Can't they see, Joe's no more guilty than I am!" snapped a very distraught Grace, as they left the courthouse.

When they returned the following day Grace, Georgia, Jim, Joe's parents all filed into the public gallery. They were joined by Terry, Heather, Bob and Becky who took the seats behind them, while Eric Sullivan stood at the back. The three defendants walked in and took their places in the dock. A hushed silence reigned for a minute before the court usher requested they all rise as the Judge entered the courtroom and took his seat.

"In the case of Donald Fuller, you have been found guilty and I sentence you to serve a minimum term of seventeen years. Keith Porter you have been found guilty and I sentence you to serve a minimum term of seventeen years." Grace held her breath, "Joseph Dempsey, because of the seriousness of the crime, I have no alternative but to sentence you to serve a minimum term of twenty years! Take them down!"

"No!" cried Grace, as Georgia threw her arms around her.

# 1977
# Chapter 44

As Heather turned into the exclusive estate that her and Terry had moved into just over a year ago, she couldn't help reflecting how well they'd done. Talk about rags to riches, one minute Terry was being treated for depression, which found him chewing Valium like sweets, to the lovely four bed detached house in Gerrards Cross. It wasn't long after Joe had been sent to prison that Terry had the nervous breakdown. Joe's imprisonment played on his mind, he blamed himself for getting his friend the job at B.O.A.C in the first place. It was a year before he was fully fit to return to work. In that time B.O.A.C. cargo had moved into a modern cargo terminal and amalgamated with B.E.A and had become British Airways

Heather drove down the tree lined avenue, remembering how Terry fought his way back to fitness. He was prepared to work whatever shifts were required of him. Slowly and surely he received recognition and was promoted back to team leader. About that time they moved from their three bed council house and bought a three bed semi in the best part of Uxbridge. As B.A. cargo grew, Terry took on more responsibilities and moved steadily up the ladder and was now an assistant manager, hence the recent move to Gerrards Cross. Heather laughed to herself, 'Terry would hate being called upwardly mobile!' At the end of the avenue of trees she turned right, her new house was the fifth on the left.

'That's funny Terry's car's still here, I thought by now he'd be at work.'

Unconcerned Heather parked her car next to Terry's, making sure she didn't scratch the paintwork on his Cortina Ghia. She remembered when she knocked the door of the Capri against the wall, he was furious. She climbed out of her car and opened the boot, then she put her door key in the lock and turned.

"Terry, I thought you was on late shift. Help me in with the shopping will you." There was no answer. "Terry!" she cried, "Where are you?" Receiving no response she carried the bags of shopping into the kitchen and put them down. She looked through the kitchen window expecting to see him in the garden. "That's funny. Terry!"

A sense of foreboding crept over Heather as she walked back into the hall, "Terry!" As she began to climb the stairs she looked up to the landing.

"Oh my God!" she screamed as she ran up the stairs. Terry's limb body was hanging from a rope attached to the rafters in the loft. She tried in vain to lift him, to keep his lifeless body alive, all the time screaming for help, for what seemed like an eternity. Two neighbours raced through the open door, but like Heather they were too late. One of them quickly brought Heather downstairs, trying her best to comfort her, while the other phoned the police.

Joan, her neighbour at number seven busied herself making tea, while they waited for the police to arrive. Paula from next door, sat opposite Heather stroking her arm when instinctively Heather thought of the kids, "The kids! The kids, they….. They'll be coming home from school soon."

"Don't worry, I'll take them to mine," said Joan, as she brought in the tea.

"This can't be happening," exclaimed Heather. The shock of what she'd seen kicked in.

"Is there anyone I should call?" said Paula.

Dazed and confused Heather gave Eric's number to ring. He had become a good friend to Heather and Terry over the years, especially during his nervous breakdown. "I should have seen this coming," she muttered.

Eric arrived just as the police drew up. A crowd of neighbours had begun gathering on the other side of the road. He rushed into the house, brushing passed one of the neighbours, not knowing what to expect. "What's happened!" he cried. Heather looked up from the couch than raced towards him, throwing herself into his arms.

"It's Terry! It's awful. He's hanged himself!" she cried, as tears gushed from her eyes.

"What?" cried Eric, not quite understanding? Two uniformed officers walked in, and spoke with the neighbour in the hallway. She pointed to the stairs.

Eric followed close behind the police and stared up at Terry's limp body, hanging through the square opening of the loft door. "Jesus, fuck!" he exclaimed. He knew, or at least believed he knew why Terry had done such a thing.

Minutes later a couple of plain clothes coppers along with a crime photographer walked in and took charge. A uniformed woman officer accompanied them. She sat down with Heather and the woman officer motioned for the neighbour to make another pot of tea.

While the police photographer climbed the stairs to photograph the scene, the officers milled about in the hallway. "Was there a note?" asked the shorter of the plain clothes coppers.

"Not what we've seen so far," said the first policeman on the scene.

"Have you called the undertaker?"

"The undertaker's on his way."

"Once the photographer's done his bit, we'll need to cut him down. It's too distressing for his wife'" he paused for a moment, "Has he got kids?" added the detective constable.

"Yeah, they're across the road with a neighbour."

"I fucking hate these suicides, especially when there's no note to be found. Makes for more paperwork. Did the deceased have a history of depression?" asked the detective sergeant.

"I'll find out," said the uniform.

"Maybe I can help!" said Eric.

"Who are you?"

"Eric Sullivan, I'm a close friend of the family."

"Do you know whether Mr Richards had any health issues?"

Eric glanced into the living room at Heather, then back to the detective, "He suffered a nervous breakdown some years back."

"Well that's something," said the detective sergeant in a matter of fact manner.

'Fucking unfeeling prick,' thought Eric, as he turned away and returned to Heather in the living room.

Once given the order to cut Terry down, the undertaker and his assistant went about their business quietly and professionally, transferring Terry from the landing to the waiting trolley in a dignified manner. Heather insisted on seeing Terry, Eric advised her to wait, but she wasn't having any of it. "Terry!" she screamed before collapsing, luckily Eric and an officer managed to stop her falling. Eric gently led her back to the sofa. She seemed in a daze, then suddenly she cried, "My kids!"

"I'll bring them over in a while," said the WPC. "Can anyone stay with her tonight?" she asked.

"I'll stay!" replied Eric.

The two detectives shuffled back into the room. "We're off now Mr Sullivan, we'll be in touch in due course if need be. Sorry about your friend," said the detective constable.

"Mrs Richards, I'm so sorry for your loss," said the detective sergeant as he went through the motions.

"I'll walk you out," said Eric. 'Fucking filth, all they're concerned about is paperwork. As for plod, they ain't worth a wank either,' he thought as he closed the door

Eric motioned Paula into the hall, "Does Heather have the same doctor? I think we should call him, just to be on the safe side."

"Yes, she's with Doctor Robinson. Would you like me to ring him?"

"Yeah, that would be kind of you," replied Eric.

The woman police officer looked at Eric as he walked back into the room, "I'm bringing the kids back over in a while, could you tidy up before they get here?"

"Yeah sure. Give me a few minutes," said Eric. "Are you alright to stay with Heather?" he asked Paula.

"Yeah we're okay," she replied.

Eric wearily climbed the stairs and gazed up at the loft opening. In the centre of the dark entrance hung the remnants of the turquoise coloured nylon rope which had been hurriedly cut by the undertaker. On the landing he picked up the discarded aluminium step ladder and proceeded to climb up to close the loft hatch. His original intention was to untie the rope from the rafters, but decided to leave it, in the unlikely event the police might wish to return. At the top of the ladder Eric peered into the darkness and couldn't imagine the torment that Terry must have been going through as he tied the noose around his neck.

In the darkness Eric fumbled for a light switch, that wasn't there. Then he remembered Terry hadn't got around to asking Jim to install the necessary lighting he required. As his eyes became accustomed to the darkness he followed the end of the rope up to the rafters. A shudder ran down his spine. Quickly he found the lost hatch cover and began to slide it over. He was just about to close it, when his peripheral vision noticed something white. Curious as to what it was, he pushed the lid back. Lying between the rafters and ceiling was a long white envelope. He reached his hand in and retrieved it. The envelope was sealed and addressed to Heather.

Eric slid the hatch cover over and quickly climbed off the step ladder. He gazed at the sealed envelope and felt it. Judging by the way it felt there must have been several pages. Not just a short sincere goodbye to loved ones, but something more substantial. Eric's intuition made him suspect it contained a full and detailed confession. The fallout from what it might reveal could be immense for a number of people including Eric himself.

By right he should have left well alone, but Eric being Eric carefully tore open the envelope, putting the discarded envelope in the inside pocket of his jacket. Then he began to read the letter.

# Chapter 45

Georgia had been out visiting a client and arrived home late to find Jim sitting in their front lounge with his head in his hands. He looked white as a sheet.

"What's up?" she asked, "What's wrong?"

Jim turned and looked at Georgia, "You'd better sit down," he said.

"It's not my dad! Is it?" The words tumbled out.

"No, George and Elizabeth are fine. It's Terry! He's dead! By all accounts he committed suicide."

"How! Why!" stuttered Georgia.

"According to Eric; Heather came home with the weekly shopping to find him. He hanged himself!" sobbed Jim.

"Oh my God, that's awful!" She sat down next to Jim and put her arm around him. "Why would he do such a thing? Did he leave a note?"

"I don't know. Eric's staying with her and the kids tonight. He said if he has any more news, he'll call. Also, if we want to go around, leave it until tomorrow evening. Eric's picking Heather's mum up from Euston around lunchtime."

"Does Becky and Bob know?" asked Georgia.

"Eric said he was going to call them after he'd spoken to me," said Jim.

*****

Eric was troubled, he'd thought to say nothing about the letter, let sleeping dogs lie, but in his heart he knew he couldn't live with himself. He couldn't spring the letter on Heather just yet, it would all be too much, and besides he needed time to think it through.

Firstly he'd phoned Heather's sister, who insisted on coming over, then he'd phoned her mother, before phoning Jim and Bob, and then he'd called home.

In the meantime, he had to look after Heather and see to the kids. Wayne was fourteen, a bit headstrong, but a good kid all the same, Jason almost a teenager was the quiet studious type, must take after his mother, thought Eric, and then there was Maggie, all grown up at ten years old. It was Wayne who took it worse, most probably because he was able to understand what had happened, even though nobody had told him anything.

Eric took him aside, "Wayne, you're now the man of the house. You have to look after your mother and your brother and sister. At the moment your mum needs you to stay strong."

Eric knew the boy would have to grow up fast, once the letter was read, things could look pretty bleak for Terry's family.

The phone rang. Eric automatically answered it. "Richards' residence."

"Is that you Eric? It's Georgia. What happened?"

"I told Jim all I knew, but there is something you might be able to help me with. I'm picking Heather's mum up from Euston tomorrow lunchtime. Could you meet me around three o'clock, I need your advice."

"Advice on what?"

"I'd rather not say, but it's important."

"I'll clear my desk. Where should I meet you?" said Georgia.

"In the park, by the gazebo."

"It's a bit cloak and dagger!" stated Georgia.

"It's delicate."

*****

"I'm going round there after I finish up," said Bob, the following morning. "I'll ring you when I know exactly what happened."

255

"Take care," said Becky more to herself as Bob drove off. The news of Terry's suicide had shocked him to the core. They'd been friends since their teens. Terry being the oldest, Bob had looked up to him as 'Jack the Lad,' until he decided to take on that title. A good mate, yet in his earlier years irritating sometimes. But since his nervous breakdown some nine years ago, Terry had become far mellower, more thoughtful, more caring, especially to Heather. He was like a Phoenix rising from the ashes. His devotion to Heather and the kids was almost matched by his rapid rise up the corporate ladder. His new house had to be seen to be believed. Suicide just didn't wash with Bob. Something must have triggered it, but what?

Becky continued to watch until Bob's van disappeared from view.

Despite Joe's shock verdict and sentence which Bob had a hard time getting his head around, life for him and Becky had gone from strength to strength. Since his proposal in the Chinese, he'd thrown himself into leaning his trade and continued working for Becky's dad on the weekends. Within no time he'd managed to save enough to buy Jim's Vauxhall Cresta. Becky had laughed when Bob had drawn up at her Mum and Dad's house.

"Looks like the countdown has begun," she said flashing her ring at him.

They married three years later and moved into a three bed terraced house. Bob laughed as he swept his new bride up and carried her through the threshold of their new home. "To think, no one gave us much of a chance when we first met. Look at us now, five years later, married, three bed house and no kids!"

Becky laughed, "No kids, don't bet on it!"

Seven and a half months later Becky gave birth to a seven pounds four ounce baby girl. A year later Bob started his own plumbing business and one pregnancy later they bought a large semi in Eastcote. It needed a lot of work on the property, but after a year of hard work and money it met Becky's approval.

"Good, I'm glad that's settled, I haven't enough energy for any more changes in our life," said Bob.

Bob's plumbing business had started slowly, but with word of mouth, mainly from his father-in-law, the work picked up. So much so, that Bob was handed the contracts for a number of house conversions from Manco Contractors, one of Jim's companies.

'What was it all about,' thought Bob, 'first Joe gets put away for something he didn't do, now Terry's suicide.' Bob had never doubted Joe's innocence. He'd visited him many times during that first year along with Grace; that was until he was transferred to Durham. *The move changed Joe physically and mentally. With no one to guide him he'd channelled his anger inward. The move to Durham had been the final straw, he'd told Grace it was time to forget about him, to start a new life. Watching his own daughter, not able to hold her, to give her a fatherly cuddle was like a knife through his heart. When Grace protested he flew into a rage, scaring little Billie. He flipped at the distress he'd caused and stormed out of the visiting area. He was hardening his heart to the outside world. Twenty years was a lifetime. It was then that he refused any and all visiting orders and returned Grace's mail unread. Bob wrote to him in Durham requesting a visit a few months later. To his surprise he received a visiting order, hoping he'd changed his mind. Bob drove up to the prison.*

*It wasn't a change of mind, it was a final goodbye. Joe explained to Bob that with just under nineteen years left on his sentence, he couldn't bear for Grace to continue serving the same sentence. "Bob, you're my best mate, you know how much I love Grace, if I didn't break off our relationship the years ahead of me would tear us apart. Better I end it now. I love her more than I've ever loved her. Just tell Grace to make a new life for her and Billie."*

*Bob tried reasoning with him.*

*"For fuck-sake Billie will be twenty, a young woman starting a life of her own."*

*"Who knows Joe, you might change your mind, don't give up."*

*"I have too. If I'm to survive in this shit-hole, I have to do it alone."*

The visiting hour passed very quickly and reluctantly he shook Joe's hand and wished him well. Leaving Durham jail Bob felt like his right arm had been pulled from its socket.

Grace had seen the visiting order as a sign that Joe realised he was wrong to push her and Billie away. How could Bob tell her she'd got it all wrong? He arrived home late that night, too late to give Grace the news she was hoping for.

In the cold light of day Bob told Grace, that Joe had given up. He tried to explain that the only way Joe could survive was to erase all memories of Grace. Not even the thought that one day he'd see his daughter could dissuade him.

*"This is a bad place Bob. I keep myself fit, I work out in my cell, I keep my nose clean, I only speak when I'm spoken too. I'm twenty two, fit and alert, what will I be like when I'm in my forties, if I live that long. I've had nearly eighteen months to come to terms with the rest of my life. I don't want Grace to waste more of her life than she has already. I want her to live it! I want my baby girl to know nothing but happiness. That's why you've got to make it perfectly clear. Tell Grace there is no us!"*

After that Grace reluctantly turned her back on Joe's friends and moved out of her parents' home in Elstree and bought a small cottage somewhere in the Chorley Wood area. Georgia felt it the most as she'd become extremely close to Grace during that turbulent year and the months that followed. The first anyone knew where she'd moved to, was when they received Christmas cards with her new address. Inside each card she'd written a small personal message explaining that to stay close to Joe's *friends had been too painful, that she needed to find her own independent way in the world.*

Throughout the day Bob kept returning to the day when Joe turned his back on the world. Now with the loss of Terry, his thoughts wandered...........

*****

Georgia approached the green gazebo close to the entrance of the park and spotted the lone figure of Eric waiting for her. Something told her that whatever he needed to speak to her about, it couldn't be good.

"What's so important we have to meet here?" asked Georgia.

"The police missed these," as he handed Georgia two letters. "Read the brief one first, then sit down and digest the other one."

Serious faced Georgia sat down and began reading.

*My darling Heather,*

*My life with you and the kids has been my biggest joy, despite what you're bound to find out I loved you with all my heart. So much so I chose my happiness with you and the kids over the life of my friend Joe. I threw him to the wolves, rather than face a life without you. I changed my ways after Joe was sent to prison, hoping I could right the wrong by giving you and the kids everything I possibly could. My love for you has never diminished. Farewell my love. Please forgive me.*

*Terry xxxx*

Georgia looked up from reading the letter, "Oh my God! Does this mean what I think it means? Terry couldn't have done that to Joe!"

"Read the other one," said a very sombre Eric.

Georgia put the letter down and unfolded the second.

*To whom it may concern,*

*I, Terry Richards wish to confess my part in the attempted B.O.A.C robbery and kidnapping of an employee and his wife. I shall tell this true account of the wrongful conviction of Joe Dempsey, leaving out nothing. My friend had a bum deal from the authorities and it has cost him ten years of his life. Some of what I'm writing was never disclosed to the public, only through this letter can the whole truth be told.*

*The one and only time Joe met Arthur Briggs was when I as team leader asked Joe to deliver a consignment of camera gear to a door in exports. Joe being new to the job unwittingly and unknowingly handed Briggs the gear. That was the only time he ever met Arthur Briggs. I had an arrangement with Briggs at that time, it was working out well for both of us. Then one night I was invited to join Arthur and his cousin for a night out in the West End. A few drinks, a few wins at the tables, I was having the time of my life, then Arthur introduce me to Jennifer, whether that's her name I'll leave that to you. Later I met up with Arthur and Roy. This cousin of Arthur's said he used to work at B.O.A.C cargo but got caught shagging a cleaner, he laid out a foolhardy plan of abducting the key holder's wife and family, and getting away with three or four million pounds in cash and bullion. I laughed, it was a dumb idea. They said it was fool proof because Tommy Drayton was financing it. That he had a plane that would take us all out of the country. It didn't take a rocket scientist to know if the robbery went as well as they expected I'd be left holding nothing but my cock in my hand. I was in a bind, these two men weren't the kind you mess with, and so I agreed to the dumb arse plan. These boys were getting a bit heavy and I wanted outta there.*

*Following morning I phoned Briggs told him I was out, that it was a fuck up of a plan. Tommy Drayton doesn't think so, said*

*Briggs. Not interested I said. So you're quite happy for us to send a set of photos of last night's escapade are you? I was shocked, yeah it all began to fall into place. I'd been set up. Idiot. I thought they were bluffing but it soon became clear to me they weren't. I decided my best course of action was to play hard ball and demand all the photos and negatives, in exchange I'd give them what they wanted. Which was the name of the key holder, his wife's name and his daughter's name, their address and the shipments that were being held in the strong room on the date of the robbery. I knew it was wrong but I really thought they might decide not to go through with it, hoped.*

*When they were caught I couldn't believe it. Two men I'd never heard of Donald Fuller and Keith Porter but no Arthur Briggs or his cousin. I thought if there was no Arthur Briggs I might have a chance of brazening it out.*

*Now this is where it starts to get interesting. It was a few days after the attempted robbery I received a phone call.*

*"Terry Richards, we need to meet. I have the answer to your problem."*

*"Who is this? What problem?" I snapped?*

*"I think you know what problem. Meet me on the far side of Ruislip Lido, I'll be waiting at one o'clock this afternoon, if you value your freedom." The caller rang off. I felt I had no choice so I went to the meeting. That was when I came face to face with Detective Inspector Sean Fallon.*

Georgia sat bolt upright at the name. Shock, anger, excitement passed briefly across her face. "Read on," encouraged Eric.

"This is fucking dynamite!" exclaimed Georgia.

"It gets worse!"

As Georgia continued to read, she noted that Terry was recording on paper every single detail, relevant or otherwise. He was covering all the bases. Despite the contempt she felt for him, she couldn't help but admire his forethought. This letter was truly dynamite.

*Before I go on, just a little information about detective inspector Sean Fallon that you might not be aware of. Detective Inspector Sean Fallon for your information had a connection to Joseph Dempsey. Joseph Dempsey was the lover of Grace Fallon, Sean Fallon's long suffering wife. She became pregnant by Joe, which was a miracle as a few years before Grace had been informed by the London Clinic that she was barren. This report was false, as Sean Fallon had falsified the medical report to cover up the fact he was firing blanks. This evidence was used to get an uncontested divorce with a reasonable settlement. The agreement stated that all evidence of the fraudulent medical report would be released to Sean Fallon on the day of the divorce absolute. Unfortunately I doubt that report still exists. What could exist would be a record of each of their visits at the said clinic. Another connection to this case, that wasn't explored.*

*Until my meeting with Fallon the above information was all I knew about the man. I'd been living on a knife edge, my nerves were shot, but I wasn't prepared for what Detective Inspector Sean Fallon had in mind. He wanted Joe put in the frame for what I'd done. I told him to go fuck himself, I told him I knew who he was, and that I'd grass him up to the police. He wasn't fazed in the least. He said if I didn't do what he wanted he'd fix it that Joe was involved alongside me, and with Arthur Briggs jumping to whatever tune he called, we'd go down anyway. I told him to do his worst, and started to walk away, that was when he told me he had a set of photos. It stopped me in my tracks. I know I should have walked away, but I couldn't bear the thought that Heather would see those photos. He then handed me three pieces of paper, the original type written names, address, dates and value of the goods in the strong room. A page of graph paper with some kind of route or map and another with Arthur Briggs's phone number. He wanted me to plant them in Joe's locker that night or Heather would receive the photos the following day. This is very important, when I planted the incriminating evidence I put them inside the cover of an aviation manual. This small detail wasn't known or reported at the trial.*

*I know I was a coward, no worse than that, I betrayed one of my best friends. Sean Fallon was blackmailing me into setting my friend up. I should have beaten him to a pulp, smashed his head in with a rock. But it's useless to say what I should have done, I did nothing and from that moment on I was damned. I genuinely believed Joe would probably get off with a lengthy suspended sentence. I know my friends, Bob and Jim must hate me for what I did, but their hatred is as nothing to the hatred I feel for myself ever since I put Joe away. Thankfully my pain will soon be over.*

*To Joe, I know you won't be able to forgive me, and why should you, I was a coward, I betrayed you. I deprived you of a family. I hope this letter helps you to rebuild your life. I hope also that it will see the end of that bastard Detective Inspector Sean Fallon.*

*Goodbye.*

*Terry Richards.*

Georgia looked at Eric, "We need a copy of this before we hand it over to the police. I'm not saying they'll lose it, but it does condemn one of their own!" stated Georgia. As a successful defence lawyer Georgia had seen all too often pieces of evidence conveniently lost. "Once we've got copies we must file an appeal and hopefully get Joe released. That has to be our main objective!" said Georgia.

"What about Fallon," asked Eric?

"Fallon will have to wait. This new evidence only starts the ball rolling. The appeal won't go unopposed, we've got to be prepared for a fight. Finding Arthur Briggs might help. Otherwise we might even have to concede Fallon, if it's the only way we get Joe released."

"So he could get away with what he's done!" exclaimed Eric.

"It could come to that, yes." Georgia looked at Eric, "This revelation will affect many people's lives, some more than others, she paused momentarily, and looked directly at Eric, "Have you told Grace yet?"

"No," he said forlornly.

"You know you could have destroyed the letters, said nothing to anyone!"

"Thought about it, that's why I brought them to you."

"You know we have to hand these in to the police," stated Georgia, "but not before we make copies."

"Let's get it done," said Eric. He knew there would be difficult questions of how he came by the letters, but 'fuck em' he thought. If those arseholes had done their jobs properly these letters might never have seen the light of day.

At Chandler and Lowe's Ruislip office they photocopied both letters and envelope, then just as they were putting the copies into the office safe, Georgia stopped herself. "No! We're just about to make a big mistake. We keep hold of the originals, at least for the time being. Let them see the copies first. We want to go as high up the chain of command as possible before they see the originals.

At the police station Eric asked for the detective that had attended Terry's house the day before. "Something you missed yesterday."

The detective looked surprised, angry even, then relieved. "Great, at least now we can pass this over to the coroner."

"I think you better read the letters first before you think about closing the file, this ain't over by a long shot."

The detective began reading the first letter, then he stopped in his tracks. "What the fuck's this? I think you need to come with me." He led them into an interview room, but stopped, "No need for you to come Miss."

"On the contrary, I'm Mr Sullivan's solicitor. I believe you'll need someone of a lot higher rank than you, to deal with this sergeant." The look on Georgia's face told him she was deathly serious.

"Wait in this room, while I get the inspector."

Georgia and Eric sat down and waited. "Good on you," cried Eric.

"Cocky little prick, we want the organ grinder, not the monkey."

A few minutes later a uniformed inspector entered the room flanked by the detective.

"Good afternoon, I'm Inspector Tomlinson. You are?"

"I'm Eric Sullivan and this is Georgia Chandler my solicitor."

"Right, these are copies, I take it you have the originals?"

Yes we do, they're in a safe place, once we're satisfied they won't mysteriously disappear you can have the letters," replied Georgia.

"You realise it's an offence to hold back evidence!"

"In light of the circumstances of the letter, it's a risk we are prepared to take," stated Georgia.

An angry silence filled the room, while the Inspector thought it over. "I've read the two letters and if true these accusations need to be taken very seriously. First question, how did you come by the letters?"

"After your men had finished with questioning those present, taken their notes, and photographed the incident they left. Leaving me to inspect the aftermath. I found the loft hatch wide open with a length of cord still hanging from the rafters. On the landing floor was an overturned step ladder. I think your boys were hungry for their tea," said Eric sarcastically.

Eric saw the angry exchange between the inspector and the detective.

"I'm sorry about that, it must have been distressing. The letters?"

"I climbed up into the loft space to untie the cord, then as I started to climb down I noticed them lying close at hand between the joists."

"Why didn't you bring them straight to the station last night?"

"In light of the content, I felt it would be safer if I got some legal eyes to give it the once over."

"What are you implying?"

"He's not implying anything. A man has spent the best part of ten years in prison for something he didn't do. At this moment in time we are more concerned about launching an appeal on behalf of Joseph Dempsey than starting a witch hunt!" said Georgia in a calm but forceful manner.

"I understand, but I can assure you the original letters would be kept safe."

"Good," said Georgia. "Once we have verified the letters we'll hand them over but in the meantime will you sign this form, acknowledging the receipt of said copies?"

The inspector paused for a moment, weighing up the pros and cons, he didn't much care to get embroiled in an argument with the female solicitor, so he signed the receipt. "What the hell," he said, "the top brass can look after themselves."

# Chapter 46

"I'll take it from here, you've done enough, said Georgia. "Heather needs to hear the truth, better from me than a copper or worse a reporter."

"Maybe I should…."

"No Eric, you need to talk to Grace, she needs to know, go home. I've a feeling you have a lot to talk about."

"I can't say I'm looking forward to it. I figured we had more time," said Eric solemnly.

"Good luck, I'm sure things will work out," said Georgia. "I'll start moving on the appeal first thing in the morning."

Eric pointed his car towards Ruislip. At this time of day, what with the traffic in Uxbridge it could take him twenty minutes to get home, barely enough time to gather his thoughts. As he drove it all came back to him.

*It was during the summer of 72 that Grace resurfaced. She cascaded out of a department store in Watford with bundles of shopping bags and five year old Billie at her side when she ran straight into Eric.*

*"Eric!" she exclaimed. "Sorry didn't see you there."*

*"Evidently," laughed Eric. "How are you? You're looking good."*

*Grace looked a little awkward, but smiled, "Yeah, we're fine. Actually better than fine, we've been shopping for school uniform. Billie starts primary school this September and she's looking forward to it. Aren't you Billie?"*

*Billie smiled up at the tall man, "Yes, I think so."*

*"You don't seem so sure," responded Eric, "You'll be fine, school's fun."*

*Grace laughed, "Billie's five going on fifteen."*

Eric noticed a distinct air of optimism in her voice. *"I don't suppose you'd fancy a coffee?"*

Grace hesitated for a moment before saying, *"Yes, why not."*

*"Perhaps an ice cream for the school girl,"* said Eric smiling. *"Here, let me take them,"* he added as he gathered up Grace's shopping bags and led them back inside the store

*"I like him mummy!"* said Billie

*"She likes anyone that buys her ice cream,"* added Grace with a smile.

They sat down at a table in the stores restaurant department and Eric ordered two coffees and an ice cream sundae. For the first few minutes the conversation was a little stilted and awkward, they danced around the elephant in the room until finally Grace asked if anyone had heard anything from Joe.

*"Nothing, I'm afraid! Although Georgia attempts to lodge an appeal each year. It comes to nothing. I believe Bob writes him once a year, but his mail keeps being returned. He says one day Joe will respond but until then he uses it as a form of therapy."*

*"That's sweet. They always were close. And Georgia, I so miss her,"* said Grace.

*"You know they'd love to see you, and Billie of course."*

*"I still feel it's a bit soon,"* replied Grace.

*"It's been nearly four years."*

Grace looked a little unsure, *"Can I tell you something?"*

*"You can tell me anything,"* replied Eric.

*"It's not that I don't want to see everyone, it's just...."*

*"Just..."* said Eric.

*"It worries me that they might blame me for what happened to Joe,"* she finished the sentence in almost a whisper.

*"That's nonsense, why would they blame you?"*

Grace looked down at her coffee cup, contemplating what to say. *"I still believe my ex-husband had something to do with Joe ending up in prison. I know it might sound daft, paranoid maybe."*

*"Not in the slightest,"* responded Eric.

"In my heart I believe Joe's not guilty, yet some of the evidence was compelling. Joe never mentioned anything about being able to fly, but then I counter that with the fact we'd only really known each other less than a year."

"That's true, none of us really know each other."

Grace looked straight into Eric's dark eyes and asked, "Do you believe Joe's innocent?"

It sent an icy cold shiver down Eric's spine. He'd hoped that Terry's nervous breakdown would have been the catalyst for him to come clean. "Yes, I do. I honestly believe his innocence."

"Thank you Eric, that means a lot. I think we'd better be going. Oh, and thanks for the coffee and ice cream. It's been nice catching up."

"You could take me up on my offer," said Eric. "They'd love to see you."

"I'll think about it. Do you still have the antique shop?"

"Yep, still open for business."

"I'll give you a ring sometime," said Grace as she gathered her shopping bundles.

"Bye Billie, you enjoy school."

"I will. Thanks for the ice cream Mr Sullivan."

Eric watched as Grace and her five year old daughter took the escalator down. He hadn't seen much of her during the brief time she'd spent with Joe, most of that she'd appeared stressed due to the arrest and subsequent trial. But as he took a last look before she disappeared from view he understood what Joe had seen in her. Eric was troubled, he couldn't get Grace out of his mind. He believed her love for Joe was still strong, yet he couldn't help thinking that maybe … …

It was a week later when Grace called the antique shop.

"Sullivan's Antiques,' Eric speaking."

"Hi Eric, about your offer," said Grace tentatively.

"Oh, hi Grace! That offer still stands, I'm sure everyone would be pleased to see you."

*"I've been giving it some thought. My biggest fear is will my presence open old wounds?" asked Grace.*

*"To be honest I can't say. I can tell you, no one blames you for what happened, but opening old wounds, that's something we'd all have to deal with," said Eric.*

*"I'd love to meet up. I've finally come to terms with my life, my life and Billie's that is. I just don't want anything to spoil what we have."*

*"Do you want to talk some more before you decide," suggested Eric.*

*"Yes, I think that would be nice," said Grace.*

*Eric took Grace out for dinner the following Friday. As the evening progressed Grace regaled Eric with Billie's first weeks at school. "Oh God, I must be boring you, Billie this, Billie that."*

*"Not in the slightest. I always wanted kids, but with Glo it didn't happen," he said sadly. "Perhaps if we'd had kids she'd still be here now. So no Grace, you're not boring me."*

*"Tell me how Georgia's doing? The last I knew she'd thrown herself into the property market with Jim."*

*"The business Georgia and Jim started really took off. She'd only got involved with the property business because of Jim. He had the ideas but he needed someone like her to get him started. Despite the success of their ventures together, it was always Georgia's intention to pursue a career in law. So after a while she cut herself free from the business and went straight back into law. She's now a successful criminal defence lawyer*

*"Oh! They're not together."*

*"Sorry, yeah they're still together, not married, but from what I can tell, still very close."*

*"That's good, I really like Georgia. What about Bob, is he still with Becky?"*

*"Still with Becky," Eric laughed. "I'll say. Still loved up, two kids, a mortgage and his own boss. If you exclude Becky."*

*"What about Terry? No setbacks from his breakdown I hope?"*

*"No, surprisingly once over the breakdown, he became a changed man. He's doing well at British Airways. I think deep down he still blames himself for getting Joe the job."*

*"And Heather, how's she doing. If I remember you and her were pretty close during Terry's breakdown," asked Grace. "To be quite honest I thought with the loss of Gloria and Terry's illness, you two might have got together." Grace felt her face flush. "I'm sorry I shouldn't have said that."*

*"Was I that obvious?" exclaimed Eric, a little too quickly.*

*"I'm sorry Eric, I didn't mean to pry," said Grace.*

*"No, I'm sorry, I've never told anyone, but those few months before Gloria died, we'd been having problems. She'd begun to doubt herself. For most of her life she'd a vivacious personality, but as the years flew by that diminished. She began to doubt herself, she began to doubt me. Being almost ten years younger she believed as her looks faded I'd leave her. She couldn't have been more wrong. I loved the bones off her," his words faltered.*

*"Eric, you don't have too...*

He cut her short, *"Despite my reassurances she began to drink heavily, we fought, or should I say she fought. At first I thought it was a one off, but as it became more frequent, anything could set her off. A trip to a clothing store, the changing room with all its mirrors. If I spoke to a woman, if I held the door open for someone. It was becoming unbearable."*

*"Oh Eric, I'm so sorry!"*

*"Don't get me wrong, there were good times. Our last Christmas springs to mind. We met up with Heather and Terry, and Gloria asked them if they'd like to join us for dinner. It was the happiest I'd seen her in weeks. During the course of the evening Gloria talked incessantly with Heather about her varied life when she was young. She seemed to come alive. Heather was enthralled with Glo's tales of Paris before the Germans. Don't get*

me wrong Gloria was a two way street. She asked Heather about how she met Terry, how old the kids were, and what it was like juggling three kids and a home. She soon realised Heather had a worse problem with Terry. As you're probably aware he wasn't the monogamous type."

"Yeah, from what Joe told me."

"I thought we'd turned a corner, but a week later Gloria was drinking heavily again. I couldn't take it much longer so I stormed out of the house. I'd thought to go to the pub, have a few drinks, but what would that solve. I needed someone to talk too. Before I knew it I was outside Heather's house. Why there? You may well ask? I thought maybe Heather could get through to Glo? I don't really know why. We got to talking and before you knew it we were confiding in each other about our problems. Believe it or not, it helped. We became close, maybe too close, but it came to nothing."

"Did you ever re-marry?" asked Grace.

"Since Gloria's death, I haven't had a serious relationship. I guess I never will. It wasn't until the inquest that I learned the truth of Gloria's behaviour. She'd been diagnosed with a debilitating illness and had kept it from me. If only she'd told me, things could have been so different. I just wish Gloria knew how I felt towards her. She was the love of my life," said Eric.

"Oh, I'm so sorry Eric. In a way, I feel a fraud!" exclaimed Grace.

"How so!"

"Compared to you and your loss, I don't think I compare. I thought Sean was the love of my life, but that dream shattered pretty early on. I should have left him years ago, but I hung on. Then I met Joe. He was so young, so vibrant; so innocent in his outlook. He made me feel young again. Six years married to Sean can age a girl. Then I found myself pregnant and the truth was revealed. I thought I knew what love was, that Sean was the man I'd spend my life with, then along comes my saviour in blue jeans.

*Was it love? It was only after I gave birth to Billie that I really knew what love was."*

*Eric felt his heart race, he should have been trying to persuade Grace to return to the fold, but instead he asked her out for the following Friday.*

*"I thought you were trying to persuade me to meet up with Georgia and the rest?" replied Grace.*

*"I was, I thought you might prefer to take it slower," he said.*

*"Slow is good," she replied. "Next Friday, I'll check with my mum. She should be able to babysit. I'll ring you."*

*It was six months before she returned to the George. Nervous about their reaction to the news that she'd been seeing Eric, she'd enlisted Georgia's help.*

*"Wow you're a dark horse!" exclaimed Georgia when she arranged to meet Grace after receiving a cryptic phone call from her.*

*"You're not shocked, or mad, disappointed even!" exclaimed Grace.*

*"Why would I be? You've been wearing widow's weeds, figuratively speaking for far too long!" exclaimed Georgia.*

*"How do you think the others will feel?" asked Grace.*

*"Jim will be no problem, trust me. Terry and Heather have been going through their own kind of hell, so I'm sure they'll understand. Bob and Becky, well that might be a little problematic, especially Bob."*

*On the day Eric and Grace decided to tell everyone about their relationship Georgia arranged to get everyone together at the George. It was a bit risky, but Georgia guessed any hostility would come from Bob and possibly Becky. "Jesus!" exclaimed Jim, when Georgia told him about Eric and Grace, later that evening.*

*"You're probably going to say a whole lot more. I'm arranging for all of us to meet at the George this Sunday."*

*"You really like dancing with the devil. Bob is going to freak," cried Jim.*

*"Never mind Bob, how do you feel about Eric and Grace?"*

*"Doesn't worry me either way. Joe's gone. He chose not to stay in touch, the man must know his own mind. Twenty years is a lifetime."*

*Eric drove into the George car park and noted Bob's car and Terry's Jag. He panicked for a second before spying Jim's in the overflow car park. He parked and looked at Grace. "You don't have to go through with this. We can turn around if you like."*

*"No, if we're going to have a life together we can't live in the shadows."*

*"Let me go in first," said Eric. "Once I see how the land lies, I'll come out and get you."*

*Eric braced himself as he pushed open the door of the saloon bar.*

*"Here he is!" exclaimed Bob. "What's with the cloak and dagger?"*

*Eric took a deep breath, before walking over to their table. "A few months ago I bumped into Grace and her daughter." He had a whole speech thought out, but in the end he came straight out with it. "We've been seeing each other."*

*"You mean, a relationship!" exclaimed Heather.*

*"Yes, Heather, we're in a relationship."*

*Bob stood up, his face told its own story. "You're a fucking back stabbing bastard! How could you? He's a mate, he's your friend," snapped Bob.*

*"I'm sorry you feel that way. Neither I nor Grace expected to feel the way we feel towards each other. Joe's gone, it's a fact. He even told Grace to forget him, your words Bob." replied Eric.*

*"Well fuck it! I'm not happy about it! If she'd met someone else, I could understand," his first reaction was to storm out, but Bob thought better of it as he slumped back into his chair.*

*"Agreed, but you can't help who you fall in love with," added Eric.*

*"It's too hard to swallow," muttered Bob.*

*"He'll come around, given time," said Becky with a weak smile.*

*"Pleased for you mate," said Terry.*

*"Well, bring my little mate in from the cold. I know she's waiting in the car," said Georgia.*

*A year later Eric and Grace married. Most of their friends attended the wedding, Bob had an urgent job that needed fixing, but him and Becky did make the reception. It was the closest to acceptance that Bob could live with.*

*****

As Eric pulled onto the driveway of his Ruislip home he wondered how Grace would take the news. They'd talked about this moment many times, neither of them had considered it would be ten years earlier than they expect.

# Chapter 47

As she feared, the wheels of justice moved slowly. Once Georgia began the appeal on behalf of Joe on the grounds of new evidence, she ran into a brick wall. The Court of Appeal were disinclined to accept Terry's written confession.

*Even if we accept this written statement, it in itself doesn't exonerate Joseph Dempsey from guilt. If it were to be used in evidence at a re-trial there is much to consider. The allegation of blackmail, intimidation and manipulation of justice by a senior member of Her Majesty's Constabulary is a serious and unsubstantiated charge that could damage a man's unblemished career and cause untold damage to the reputation of the Metropolitan Police.*

"They can't do this, a man's life is at stake. Where's the fucking justice!" cried Bob when Georgia showed them the reply from the Court of Appeal.

"I'm not surprised," stated Georgia, "This is round one; we'll appeal their decision and let them know we're not backing down. I've been in contact with a number of high ranking officers who are sympathetic to our cause and have been assured there are wheels in motion to address the alleged corruption in the Met's ranks. I've also petitioned our local Member of Parliament and am awaiting the findings of the inquest into Terry's death. All this takes time."

"Yeah, but in the meantime Joe's freedom is ebbing away," stated Bob. "It's about time we played dirty with the courts, we need to get the press involved, show them the fucking letter!"

"Not yet," cried Georgia, "We leave that for now."

"Why the fuck not!" snapped Bob angrily.

"What's the most important thing here!" cried Georgia.

"Getting Joe out," said Jim.

"Exactly, getting Joe out, might mean a little horse trading," replied Georgia.

"Are you saying what I think you're saying," said Bob, the anger welling up inside him.

"Unfortunately, yes. We might have to leave Fallon out of it. He's not a lowly DS or even a DI anymore he's a chief inspector. He's so well connected the top brass won't hang one of their own out to dry. We're talking funny handshake brigade. The only way that happens is if we find Arthur Briggs and get him to collaborate Terry's letter. Which I'd say would be almost impossible. The chances of putting Fallon in the dock is very unlikely. We go down that road at our peril. Getting Joe off has to be our immediate priority!"

"Okay, supposing we agree to your softly, softly, approach, what about compensation?" asked Bob sarcastically.

"I've told you, our first order is to negotiate an early release. Once we achieve that we can consider our options. I've contacts that can help with that. Believe it or not, there are some good coppers out there. Some with an axe to grind. Even if it takes a year, we'll get Joe out."

"Has anyone informed Joe about Terry's confession?" asked Becky.

"The short answer is no. I'm driving up to Durham first thing tomorrow morning. My father's managed to arrange a visiting order. I'm hoping to see Joe, to fill him in on Terry's confession," said Georgia.

"I'd like to come," said Bob.

"Sorry Bob, not this time. I'm taking Grace. Hopefully due to the circumstances, after I've told Joe about Terry's confession, they might allow Grace to visit. It's not a certainty."

"Is that wise?" stated Bob.

"Wise or not, we've discussed it, and feel Grace needs to speak with Joe," said Eric.

"Oh great! Joe gets told Terry confessed all, but he ain't getting out of prison just yet, and by the way Grace married one of your friends! That's fucking torture!"

"You're right Bob, but there isn't a better way of breaking it to him. Grace, hopefully will be able to speak to him. Its better it comes from her than anyone else," stated Georgia.

*****

Right from the moment Eric walked in Grace could see there was more to Terry's death than suicide. He gave her a hug and then asked her to sit down.

Once Eric had broken the news of Terry's suicide and confession Grace, erupted, "I knew it, that bastard! Does Joe know?"

"No," he'd replied. "Georgia is moving on Joe's appeal first thing in the morning. These things take time and we don't want to fill Joe up with false hopes."

"But you just said Terry's confession exonerates Joe completely."

"Yeah, I did say that, but Georgia did say there might be hoops to jump through before we're finished."

"Meaning?"

"Fallon might get away with it. But according to Georgia, there's enough doubt to re-open Joe's case."

"He will get out?"

"Yes, I'm sure of it. It might take a little while, but he will get out," said Eric reassuringly.

Grace looked pensive, "I need time to get my head around it, there's a lot to think about. Billie, we need to tell her when we're sure. I should visit Joe, I owe him that."

Eric felt his heart sink, he looked devastated, "Where does it leave us?" he asked.

"What do you mean?" asked Grace. "We knew that one day Joe would be released from prison. I didn't ask to fall in love with you, no more than you expected to fall in love with me. Joe being released early doesn't change anything. I love you!" She looked up into Eric's dark brooding eyes and repeated, "This doesn't change anything, I love you."

"And I love you, but the fact still remains, Joe is likely to be released a lot sooner than we expected."

"That's a good thing, right!" exclaimed Grace. "I owe Joe a debt. I need to be the one to tell him about us. As for Billie, it's as we agreed before we married. Billie knows Joe's her father and one day he might want to be a part of her life. If Joe wants to see her I've no objections, that's his right. My only stipulation is he abide by my rules until Billie is eighteen."

"What if you suddenly realise you still love him?"Grace looked straight into Eric's eyes and reached up and caressed his cheek, "Oh Eric, that girl died when Joe was transferred to Durham. I had a child, I was on my own; my life was changing rapidly. My life was Billie. Yes I did love Joe. It was a rush, it was exciting; it was everything that was missing in my life. I was given a second chance to find that heart thumping ecstasy of my lost youth."

"I love you Grace!"

"And I love you Eric Sullivan, that won't change."

*****

"Dempsey, you've a visitor!" cried the warder. "Report to the warden's office."

"I don't have visitors," snapped Joe.

"It's your brief! Now move it!"

Puzzled by the command Joe made his way to the warden's office. 'Strange,' he thought as he reached the door. He knocked and entered.

"You wanted to see me sir."

"Your defence lawyer has some news."

Joe looked to the left of the warden's desk. At first he wasn't sure who the person was, then recognition hit him. "Georgia! What the…"

"Sit down Dempsey, I'll leave you to it," said the warden. "Give a shout if you need anything," he added before closing the door.

Georgia noticed the physical appearance, the trim waistline and the muscled biceps. He seemed taller, a little gaunt and he carried a nasty scar across his right cheek. He was probably a little under nourished but on first glance he gave off an appearance of being fit.

"It's good to see you Joe….."

"What are you doing here?" an edge of impatience creeping into his voice.

Georgia looked him in the eye, "We have proof of your innocence. It might be weeks, most probably months but rest assured you are coming home."

"How? What's happened?" Joe's whole demeanour changed.

"Right, this isn't pretty and I dare say you're going to get mad, just remember where you are," warned Georgia.

"How could I forget?"

"Terry committed suicide and left two notes, one to Heather, the other a detailed report of how he fit you up for the attempted robbery."

"Fuck off Georgia!" The incredulity of what Georgia was saying suddenly hit home.

"The short version is Terry was being blackmailed by Arthur Briggs, the man that gave evidence against you in court."

Georgia could see the cogs working as Joe digested her words. "I remember," he said in a subdued tone.

"Arthur Briggs was being leaned on by Detective Inspector Sean Fallon to implicate you in the crime."

Joe's face turned a deathly pale. The jigsaw were beginning to fall into place. "Why would Terry… No Terry wouldn't; fit me up?" he asked, searching for that final piece of the jigsaw.

"Briggs had compromising photos of Terry and some unnamed prostitute. He'd got in deep with bad people; they threatened to show them to Heather unless he helped them in the robbery. That's when Detective Inspector Fallon stepped into the picture; Arthur Briggs was his snitch. It was Fallon's sick twisted way to get back at Grace.

Joe went quiet for a few moments, gathering his thoughts, "So Terry's fucking about with some brass, gets me twenty fucking years. If he weren't dead I'd fucking beat the bastard to a pulp. He's cost me ten years of my life." His anger had gone up a notch. "When do I get out?"

"That's the tricky part. Terry's detailed confession clearly states that Fallon was behind the frame up." Georgia looked uncharacteristically out of her depth. "The judges are hand in glove with the top brass in the Met. We will get you out! But I'm afraid the chances of Fallon paying for what he did looks bleak. My first priority is to get you released."

"How did Terry die?" asked Joe maliciously.

"He hanged himself from the rafters of his house," said Georgia.

"Well, that's something, I suppose. Went out like the fucking scum bag he really was. Good riddance!"

"Basically that's it in a nutshell. Here's a detailed report for you to digest," said Georgia, handing him a sealed envelope. "Rest assured we'll leave no stone unturned to get you released as soon as possible."

"Grace, Billie….." he uttered. His anger subsiding.

Georgia didn't envy her friend who was waiting in the other room. "Life's a bummer Joe, but at thirty three you've got the rest of your life ahead of you."

"What's that supposed to mean?"

Georgia remained closed mouth.

"Well answer me!"

Joe became fearful, he'd burnt his bridges ten years earlier. "Thirty three, with no prospects. What kind of life's that?"

"You've got your friends behind you. You'll survive." She stood up to go, while Joe sat staring at the table. "I'll see you soon." Just as she opened the door, she turned. "There's someone waiting to talk to you in the next room," she pointed towards a door.

Joe looked up, then followed her pointed finger at a door on the far side of the office. He looked puzzled, scared, worried… "Grace?"

# Chapter 48

*Georgia had smiled encouragingly as Grace looking stony faced emerged from the warden's office. She'd squeezed her hand and then purposefully walked back to the car park. Grace slumped down into her seat and sat in silence as Georgia started the car and drove away from the prison. She was physically and emotionally drained from her meeting with Joe and was grateful that Georgia hadn't bombarded her with questions.*

*She'd been shocked at his appearance, gone was the youthful exuberance and cheeky smile and his eyes had lost a little of their sparkle. She'd looked up from across the table and half-heartedly attempted a smile as he entered the room.*

*"I guessed it was you," he said in way of greeting.*

*"Oh Joe!" she exclaimed at seeing him for the first time in almost nine years. His hair was cropped short and he hadn't shaved for a few days. He sat down at the chair provided and looked across at her.*

*"You haven't changed," he said as she reached across the table and touched a circular scar which ran upwards across his right cheek and disappeared into his hairline.*

*"Oh Joe," she repeated.*

*"It's nothing, some guy tried taking my eye out with the lid of a baked bean tin."*

*It was the matter of fact way that he'd spoken that shocked her more than the scar itself. "I'm so sorry!" Tears began to run down her cheek. She retrieved a tissue from her coat and wiped her face.*

*"Don't be, it wasn't your fault! Anyway he came off worse, spent a week longer than I did in the prison hospital."*

Grace looked at the man she'd given her heart too, and didn't recognise him from the kind and loving young man she'd fallen in love with.

Joe glanced at her left hand, "You got married!" It shouldn't have shocked him, but it did. He felt an emptiness in the pit of his stomach. He stayed silent for a few moments, gathering himself together, "How's my little girl?"

"Oh Joe, if only you'd have let me visit, you could have seen her, as often as you liked. I've brought photos."

"Seeing you and my little girl would have broken my heart. Twenty years is a lifetime Grace. I dare say I'd have looked forward to your visits, knowing that once you'd gone the doubts would creep in. Doubts that would magnify after each visit. The subtle changes of your voice, the tone, the false smile, it would have driven me to suicide."

"Oh Joe, I would have remained faithful, I would never have abandoned you!"

"But you did!" he said cruelly, his eyes indicating the rings on her finger.

"I waited six years! Six years, hoping to receive a letter, a visiting order, anything to acknowledge I still meant something to you!" Without realising it she was almost shouting.

"Okay, okay. Feisty, that's something new!"

"Look Joe, I didn't come here to fight, I came because I care about you. Yes I'm married and I'm happy and Billie is happy too."

Those words cut him to the quick. "I suppose he's become the loving father, the ideal stepfather. I bet he adopted her?" he said maliciously.

"That's where you're wrong. From the moment Billie was old enough to understand I told her you were her father and you were in prison for something you didn't do. And no Eric didn't adopt Billie, she's your daughter."

"Eric? No not Eric Sullivan!"

Grace hadn't meant it to come out the way it did. Now there was no way to put the genie back in the bottle.

"Yes, Eric's my husband."

"I bet he was sniffing around once I was sent up here!"

"No, it wasn't like that. I hadn't seen Eric, Georgia or the others for years, until I bumped into him in Watford some years later. You cut me out of your life, I in turn cut your friends out of my life. We were both stupid for doing so. I regret it now!"

"Do you love him?"

Grace knew her words might open old wounds but realised Joe needed the truth, not a sanitized version of the truth.

"Yes, I love Eric. Hopefully you'll understand my feelings. Since the news broke with Terry's suicide, I've had time to think. I was seventeen when Sean came into my life. I was a young impressionable teenager. He killed my youth, I had to grow up fast living with Sean. It was a nightmare as you well know."

Joe was now listening intently.

"Then you came charging into my life on a grey and maroon stallion. My knight in shining armour. You bowled me off my feet, I became a teenager again. You know what that's like? I was given a second chance to recapture my youth."

Joe looked sad, beaten. "Did you love me?"

"Yes I loved you, I wanted to spend the rest of my life with you. But it wasn't to last. I ask myself would we have survived. The honest answer is I don't know the answer? What I do know, is I love Eric very much."

Joe fought back his emotions, prison did that to you, "Thank you for that. The truth is a rarity in places like this."

"Hopefully you'll soon be free of this place," said Grace. "I know Billie is excited to meet you, to get to know her dad. You don't deserve to be here. She's only ten going on twenty, she's smart and very switched on. I love her very much and as you get acquainted with your daughter you'll love her as much as I do. *My only words of caution are, whilst you have free and unfettered freedom to see her, there are rules."*

*Tears suddenly rolled down Joe's cheeks. Grace reached in her pocket and handed him a tissue. "Sorry, I didn't mean too…"* *He quickly wiped his face, smiled and said, "I'll see those photos now."*

*Grace handed him a folder of carefully selected photos of Billie, as a baby, a toddler, her first day at school, sports days, birthdays and Christmas. "They're yours," she added.*

*Grace waited patiently while he looked at the photos of Billie and her heart went out to him. He'd lost so much, his life had been torn from him in such a cruel way. For the briefest of seconds she felt that if Eric hadn't entered her life she'd have thrown herself into his arms. But sympathy wasn't love, it wasn't even a close second. The man she'd loved ten years ago died in that courthouse in London. Joe was damaged, probably more than she could imagine.*

*"When can I see her?" he said, as he looked up from the photographs.*

*"Once Georgia has been able to arrange your release, we'll set something up."*

*"Let's make it soon," he said.*

*She glanced at the clock, there was less than ten minutes before Joe would be taken back to his cell.*

*"We haven't much time. Joe, I just want you to know there will always be a piece of my heart that belongs to you. You have given me the greatest of gifts, our Billie."*

*****

Half an hour into their drive home Grace broke her silence. "It's all my fault," she sobbed. "If only I'd had the courage to leave Sean when I first saw the warning signs. It's my fault."

"Stop that! No way are you to blame for Joe's imprisonment," snapped Georgia as she pulled over to the kerb. "No one could have seen this coming!"

"Yeah, I'm sorry, you're right, it's just that the man's suffered far more than he's letting on. He's changed Georgia, he's not the Joe I fell in love with. He's harder, I can see it in his eyes, but there's a strange calmness about him that I didn't expect, yet underneath that calm I sense a deep anger. I hope I'm wrong."

"He's been in prison for ten years, he's a right to feel angry. The best thing we can do for Joe is to petition these so called judges. I'm going to light a fire under those that are sympathetic to our cause. I'm going to pile on the pressure," said Georgia as she pulled away from the kerbside.

"I loved him Georgia, I truly loved him."

"And now?" asked Georgia.

"Yes, in a way. I guess I'll always love him."

"And Eric?"

"Of course I love Eric, why wouldn't I?" replied Grace.

Georgia smiled and let the matter rest.

# Chapter 49

Fallon had been apprised of Terry Richards's suicide within days of Georgia filing an appeal on behalf of Joe. Within a few weeks he was asked to appear before the newly formed Police Complaints Board to explain why a member of the public had accused him of being behind the wrongful conviction of Joseph Dempsey.

"Good afternoon Chief Inspector Fallon."

"Good afternoon sir," he replied.

Once the preliminaries were over, Fallon cast his eyes over the Board. An officer of equal rank, but looking like he was on the eve of retirement, and two other officers of lesser ranks faced him.

"I believe you've been made aware of the allegations against you. We're here to assess whether there is anything inappropriate on your behalf. Do you understand Chief Inspector Fallon?"

"Yes fully. Firstly I'd like to state I had nothing to do with this case. Inspector Armstrong was the officer in charge, and from what I've been led to believe he did everything by the book."

"What we're concerned with is the allegation from the late Terry Richards of your involvement!" exclaimed the officer, trying his best to intimidate Fallon.

"I could give you my assumption of what I believe was his reasons to implicate me, but that's not for me to comment. So I'll deal with the facts only. I was married to Grace Fallon for six years, in what I believed was a happy marriage. Of course we had our rows, but doesn't everybody. Then out of the blue Grace stated that she wanted a divorce. To be honest I'd sensed something was amiss for some time."

"I'll stop you there chief inspector! What relevance has your divorce got to do with this investigation?"

Sean Fallon realised this old fart didn't know Jack-shit about the case. The lazy bastard hadn't even done his homework.

"If you'll let me continue, the relevance of things will become a lot clearer."

"Very well, but be brief."

It was clear to Fallon this Board didn't know its arse from its elbow. "Yes sir. I was able to find out she'd been having an affair with Mr Dempsey and had become pregnant by him!"

"Ah, Mr Dempsey, the man that was sent down?"

"That's correct sir. I challenged her and she admitted everything. It could have been a messy divorce. I was in line for promotion so chose not to contest the divorce. It was only after the arrest of Joseph Dempsey that it was brought to my attention that he was the man living with Grace and was the father of her new born baby."

"Thank you for being so precise, but what were your feelings towards Dempsey when you realised who he was?"

"Like any other villain, no more and no less. But having said that I've got to say I did get some satisfaction at knowing Grace really knew how to pick em! Other than that, I haven't given my ex-wife another thought."

"So you're saying Terry Richards's confession is unfounded?"

"That's exactly what I'm saying," replied Fallon defiantly.

They continued to question him for a further half-hour, before thanking him for his answers. Dressed in his uniform with his peaked cap tucked under his left arm, he saluted the board and walked out. A self-satisfied smile spread across his face. He knew that once Armstrong stuck to Fallon's side of the story he was home and dry. Inspector John Armstrong was old school, he knew when to keep his mouth shut. He knew he'd been manipulated by Fallon, but how, he never knew nor asked. He was grateful for the arrest, which had furthered his career prospects.

"Piece of cake," stated Fallon as he passed Inspector Armstrong in the corridor.

Armstrong was up next. "Take a seat Inspector Armstrong."

"Thank you sir," replied Armstrong as he sat down.

"I'm going to be blunt. Did Chief Inspector Fallon play any part in the arrest of Dempsey, Porter and Fuller?"

"No sir. I'd arrested a suspect on an unrelated charge, and was in the process of having him charged when he asked for a deal. It wasn't until he gave up the name of Fuller that I took interest."

"This suspect, he has a name?"

"Oh, yes sir. Arthur Briggs."

"Can this Briggs collaborate your account?"

"It's been ten years, he could be anywhere. He had informed on two very dangerous criminals, I'd imagine he's probably moved."

"Well thank you inspector, I think that concludes our investigation. You'll know our findings in due course."

"Thank you sir."

Chief Inspector Sean Fallon was just about to get in his car, when Armstrong called to him across the car park. "Wait up Sean, can I have a word?"

"What is it," said Sean when a breathless Armstrong finally caught up with him. "Jesus, you need to get down the gym."

Armstrong ignored the quip about his weight, "They asked about Arthur Briggs."

"Yeah, what about Briggs?" asked Sean.

"They asked for his whereabouts."

"What did you tell em?"

"What could I tell em, he's long gone, left the manor and scarpered?"

"Is that it?" asked Fallon.

"Yeah!"

"Last I heard he was living in Glasgow with the druggies and winos," said Fallon as he opened his car door and climbed in. He'd only driven a few yards before his temper got the better of him. "Arthur Briggs, that greedy cunt!" he cried as he accelerated away from the nick.

*The moment Sean Fallon heard the news of Terry Richards suicide he suspected Arthur Briggs was somehow involved. Within a couple of days he'd found him in a drinking club close to his manor.*

*"We need to meet," said Fallon, "but not here! Do you know that new office block that's going up near Paddington Station?"*

*"Yeah, I know it," said Briggs.*

*"I get off shift at ten, meet me there around ten thirty tonight."*

*"Why? What's it about?"*

*"You know only too well, just be there!" snapped Fallon.*

*Arthur Briggs hadn't been surprised he'd half expected a visit from Fallon. "There'd better be something in it for me," he responded.*

*"We'll see." replied Fallon.*

*Fallon left work at five o'clock and walked half a mile to the flat he rented for when he had to work late, where he grabbed himself a bite to eat and changed out of his uniform. He phoned Jackie his wife, to say he was working late and that he'd see her the following day. Then he waited until just after dusk before venturing out. It was a murky night, typical late spring weather. As he walked to the bus stop three streets from the flat it began to rain. Sean Fallon turned up the collar of his coat and waited for the bus.*

*At just after ten thirty Fallon spotted Arthur Briggs, or to be accurate the light from the end of his cigarette. "Over here," cried Fallon.*

Briggs looked into the darkness and could just make out Fallon. *"What the fuck do you want?"*

*"Why didn't you leave well alone? Do you know how much shit you've landed at my door? If you'd needed money you could have come to me,"* lied Fallon. *"I need to know everything, we need to cover our arses."*

*"Sorry Mr Fallon, I didn't know he'd top himself. I was in a spot of bother, I needed a stake. So I contacted him."*

*"How?"*

*"I called his work's phone and said we needed to meet. He seemed shaken at first, lost for words, then after a few seconds he asked where. We agreed a pub carpark in Harlington after his shift. I waited in the carpark until he arrived. All I wanted was five grand, he was good for it."*

*"What did he say?"*

*"It wasn't what he said, he fucking grabbed me by the collar and head butted me. Then he told me to fuck off, said he'd kill me if he ever saw me again. He was like a fucking mad man. I took off."*

*"Did anyone see him hit you?"*

*"I didn't notice, I was gone. It was nothing."*

*"Nothing to you maybe, but it mattered to him. How long was it before he topped himself?"*

*"You mean..."*

*"Of course I mean, after you got the shit kicked out of you."*

*"Three, maybe four weeks. I don't think it was down to me, if it had been he'd have done it that day."*

*"That's all the contact you had with him, are you sure? Did you tell anyone about it?"*

*"I did try calling a week later, but he put the phone down."*

*"Did you call him again?"*

*"Nah, nothing to tell."*

'The stupid prick doesn't even realise that phone call must have tipped him over the edge,' thought Fallon. *"You've caused* me and Inspector Armstrong a heap of trouble, but provided you stick to the original story we should be okay. Understand!"

"Yeah, but a sweetener wouldn't go a miss," said Briggs.

Fallon reached for his back pocket, as Briggs greedily anticipated a pay out, "Like I said Arthur, if you'd come to me I'd have straightened you out."

Arthur Briggs didn't feel the blade as it ripped through his stomach, only his eyes gave any recognition, before they too fade.

Fallon stepped back and let him fall, making sure no blood was on his clothes. He casually wiped the blade on the slumped body of Briggs. It had felt good, almost as good as that first time. She'd deserved it more, the fucking diseased whore.

Sean knew that Arthur Briggs's body showing up a month after Terry Richards's confession could mean the end for him. Anticipating what needed to be done Sean had arrived early and checked out the site. He'd walked by it several times in the last month and watched as they brought in Mixer Lorries' to fill the gigantic footings of the building with concrete.

Fallon dragged Briggs's body to a half filled footing, where he jumped down into the ditch leaving a foot print in the still not cured concrete. With a shovel he'd found earlier he began to dig out the still wet concrete. An hour later he'd buried Arthur Briggs under a shallow layer, smoothing it off ready for the next day's delivery. Once he was certain there were no tell-tale signs of Arthur Briggs he found a hose attached to a standpipe and hosed his shoes off. Again he checked his appearance until he was satisfied, then he walked a zig-zag path along several streets until he reached the bus stop. He was in luck as he caught the late bus home with two minutes to spare.

It was later the following morning that Detective Chief Inspector Sean Fallon on the way to a meeting in Paddington had a smug grin on his face as he drove by the new construction to see a mixer lorry pouring several tons of concrete on to the shallow *grave of the late Arthur Briggs. 'Fortuitous or what,' he thought and smiled wickedly.*

As Sean Fallon's car turned into his driveway he thought about the new Police Complaints Board and grinned. It had been unexpected, but Sean had learned at an early age, to expect the unexpected. Dealing with Briggs left no loose ends. If the new Police Complaints Board was all that was policing the police he could sleep well in his bed for many years to come.

*\*\*\*\*\**

Sean was now a chief inspector, with an eye to become a Superintendent within a few short years. *He'd come a long way since he joined the force as a green rookie just out of Hendon in the autumn of 1953. One important lesson that as a copper on the beat Sean learned, was to keep his eyes and ears open. Not just amongst the public he came in contact with, but his colleagues at the station. Sean wanted to be a good copper, the best of the best, but he wasn't averse to taking handouts; they were classed as perks of the job amongst a certain type*

*It didn't take him long to realise it wasn't just the bobby on the beat, the Met had its fair share of high ranking officers living the highlife with their swanky cars and posh houses. Sean was a quick learner and soon realised the keys to the kingdom were there for the taking. Being a plod meant what you picked up was chicken feed compared to what the big boys were earning. Of course not everyone was on the take, as Sean learned early on in his career. Some were straight arrows that would turn you in for the slightest indiscretion. Sean tended to keep himself well away from them.*

*His first introduction into the big time came when on a raid he spotted a certain detective constable pocketing a wad of cash. Sean was discreet and kept his mouth shut. It was duly noted when he found fifty quid in fivers tucked into his locker. It soon got around amongst certain individuals that Sean Fallon was a very discreet individual, someone that could be relied on to get his hands dirty from time to time.*

*Sean liked the feeling of power he felt when he wore the uniform and he wasn't opposed to wielding that power. He'd been on the beat six months, not exactly green behind the ears, but he'd become smitten by this young prostitute. Her name was Cynthia, she was a couple of years younger than Sean when he nicked her. She took him to a dinghy room in a doss house and told him she'd only been on the game a couple of weeks. The story she told was a familiar one, her father had interfered with her when she was young and as soon as she could she ran away. Something clicked in Sean's head, and the tough young bobby on the beat fell head over heels in love with her. For the next couple of months whenever he could see her, he'd pay her not to turn tricks and she paid him in kind. He found a flat for her to live in and even paid a month's rent, before he learned she'd played him. Incensed by her trickery he confronted her in the dinghy flop house and beat her senseless. It was over two years later that he discovered he had syphilis. He knew it could have been any number of prostitutes, but in his head he knew who'd given him the clap. He sought discreet treatment and after weeks of humiliation every time he visited the clinic he eventually was given the all clear.*

*A few years on the beat where Sean was feared and respected, then a stint in the detective squad where as a detective constable he became an integral part of the squad. During his years on the beat he'd cultivated a number of key snouts. Now in the flying squad he was becoming known as a really good thief taker. By the time he'd passed his sergeant's exam Sean had earned a hard reputation as someone you didn't want to cross. For the next couple of years he studied hard and after passing his inspector exam it looked as if he was being fast tracked. But during an over-zealous interview with a known pill pusher, who died in custody, it was deemed that the move to inspector should be put on the back burner for the time being.*

*Sean took it as a wakeup call, and decided to cultivate a new softer image. He was still the same flash detective sergeant, hard drinking, hard gambling, womaniser, but some of his sharp edges had been sanded down. Then he met and fell in love with the woman, in truth young naïve girl that would become his wife. Grace only just eighteen was swept off her feet. He wined and dined her, took her to the best London shows and paraded her as the future Mrs Fallon at posh parties. She was charming and sophisticated beyond her years and the top brass took a real shine to her. A year later he asked her to marry him. Sean knew that having a family was the next thing on his agenda. But when that part of his perfect plan didn't materialise the marriage began to go south. When he found out the truth about why Grace couldn't have kids, he covered it up and blamed her.*

*Then on the eve of his hard fought promotion Grace asks for a divorce on the grounds of physical and emotional abuse, citing the forged medical documents about Grace's infertility. Not wanting to prejudice his promotion he agreed a non-contested divorce. Then to add insult to injury he found out that she was pregnant with another man's child. His hands were tied, but his brain wasn't. That part of his plan had come unravelled was a little disconcerting but Sean had a way of dealing with loose ends, as Arthur Briggs's to his cost, couldn't contest.*

# Chapter 50

It was early autumn before Georgia, using every tool in her arsenal obtained Joe's release. It had been a hard slog. At first they wouldn't budge, but as leading members of the judiciary began to lend their support, the powers that be offered time served and license for the remaining years. Georgia was incensed, and turned the offer down. She asked for a complete pardon knowing it wasn't really on the cards, but after a month and a half of legal wrangling, where she threatened to take the campaign to the papers, they came back with what they described as their final offer. Joe would be released on the grounds that the conviction wasn't safe.

She so desperately wanted to push it farther, but was advised that the only other course of action would be a re-trial, where the odds of winning were vastly in the Met's favour. Georgia wasn't prepared to gamble with Joe's freedom. It would have been a David and Goliath situation with the full force of the Metropolitan Police Force's legal team up against her team. Joe would just be a mere pawn in a trial where the Metropolitan Police's reputation was at stake.

"It's the best offer you're going to get," said one high court judge.

"What about compensation? He's spent ten years in prison for a crime he didn't commit!"

"For that you'd need collaborating evidence to prove his innocence," advised the judge.

They needed to find Arthur Briggs and force him to testify, but since Terry's suicide, Briggs had disappeared. No one had seen him in months.

"So that slime ball Chief Inspector Sean Fallon walks away without a blemish on his record," snapped Georgia.

"That my dear, remains to be seen," replied the judge.

It was a very cryptic statement, one that Georgia drew some crumbs of comfort from. She'd heard though the rumour mill that a task force was being formed to investigate certain corruption claims against the City of London Police. There was also a strong possibility the Met was being looked at too.

*****

Bob and Jim drove up early that morning and were waiting outside Durham prison as the rain began to lash down. "Fucking typical, the last few days have been great. It takes today of all days to piss down," grumbled Bob.

"We were lucky on the way up," said Jim, "It's nearly time," he added nervously as he glanced at his watch. "Joe should be appearing any minute now."

On the dot, the door opened and Joe stepped out. It might have been raining but Joe didn't seem to notice as he raised his arms to the sky. The cold rain splattered his face as he took a deep breath of fresh air, it was over he thought as the daily routine of slopping out had finally ended.

Bob honked his horn and flashed his lights. "Over here Joe," he shouted excitedly.

Joe unperturbed by the rain smiled half-heartedly and walked at a leisurely pace and climbed into the back seat of Bob's Granada, "You'll catch your death," said Bob.

Jim swung round in his seat, he smiled and grabbed Joe's hand and gripped it tightly, "Good to see you mate, it's been a long time."

"Really," said Joe with a hint of sarcasm, "Sorry Jim, just need time to adjust."

"Think nothing of it."

"Before we start for home I noticed a pub a couple of miles back, any objections?" stated Bob. "One for the road!"

"Just the one," stated Joe.

"Understood," said Jim. Georgia had warned him that Joe might not be too talkative.

Bob pulled into the car park of the Fox and Pheasant, and the three friends got out. It was a little after eleven o'clock and the place seemed quiet. "We can find another pub if this ain't to your liking," said Bob.

"Look, let's get things clear, I ain't terminally ill, I ain't a cripple and I'm not that much older than you, so for fuck sake stop pussyfooting around me! Now get in there and buy me a pint"

Bob looked at his oldest mate, smiled warmly and laughed, "Today you don't put your hand in your pocket, come tomorrow it's your shout!"

"What you having Joe?" asked Jim.

"I'll have a light and bitter, cheers."

Bob looked at Jim, then back at Joe. "Seriously."

"Yeah seriously, light and bitter, why what are you two having?"

"I'm having a pint of Hofmeister," said Bob.

"Mine's Carlsberg," added Jim.

"And what the hell are they?"

"They're lagers!" exclaimed Bob. "No one drinks light and bitter anymore," he added.

"Well I do, I've often thought about this pint. You pair of pricks can drink your girly lager, mine's light and bitter."

Minutes later they took their pints and sat down at a table. "Where are you staying when you get home?"

"I'm staying with Mum and Dad for the time being. Mum is over the moon, but Dad's a bit miffed. Thinks I should have at least stayed in touch with them."

"Maybe you should have?" said Bob.

"What's that supposed to mean!" snapped Joe.

"Easy Joe, Bob doesn't mean anything by it!" exclaimed Jim.

"No Joe, for fuck-sake, lighten up will yah!"

Joe managed a wry smile, "Still the same old Bob, diplomacy isn't in your vocabulary."

"Damn right! It ain't," said Bob as a grin spread across his face.

"Look I'm sorry I keep snapping, it's just that fucking place." His eyes looked back down the road to the prison. "If I hadn't have had my wit's about me, I'd either be dead or permanently blinded. It's a fucking hell hole, they all are, but at least in London I had people looking out for me."

"Is that how you got that scar?"

"Joe, you don't need to answer, it's your business," said Jim.

"It's okay," replied Joe. "Bob always was a nosey bastard."

"Not so much of the nosey," laughed Bob.

"When I got sent down I was just a kid. I thought I could handle myself, but prison's a different ball game. I got tested two days into my sentence, and I mean tested. I got the crap kicked out of me. I spent my third and fourth day in the hospital wing. On the fifth day an old lag came up to me. When I say old I mean forty, built like Charles Atlas. He was in for a twenty year stretch, had fifteen more to do. Anyway he starts talking to me, says I've got a guardian angel on the outside. I thought fuck, he's after my arse! I couldn't have been so far wrong. It turned out he'd served in the army in Suez, with Sullivan."

Bob and Jim looked at each other. "Eric Sullivan."

"Yeah, Eric Sullivan, the man that's fucking Grace!"

For the briefest of moments Jim looked at Bob then back at Joe.

"It's a bummer," stated Jim.

"It is what it is," said Joe in a matter of fact manor.

"It's only natural you'd feel the way you do given the circumstances. We found it a little uncomfortable at first, but then you learn to live with it. The rest you know," said Jim.

"Yeah, the rest I know. I don't like it but there ain't anything I can do about it. My own fault. I never expected Grace to wait for me. That was the whole point of setting her free. What I didn't expect was being released early and finding out she'd married someone I knew."

"There ain't gonna be trouble with you and Eric, is there?" asked Bob.

"Nope, I owe him."

"You owe him!" said Bob

"Like I said, this old lag said I've a guardian angel. It seems Tommy Atkins got himself into a scrape with three French sailors and was about to be given his guts on a plate when Eric stepped in. Or should I say a lump of four by two connected with the back of the head of one of the sailors. I don't know what happened after that as Atkins clamed up. All I know is Eric asked him to look after me."

"That was handy," said Bob.

"You could say that. Needless to say this old lag took me under his wing. During my time in Wandsworth he taught be how to survive, how to fight, how to keep fit, how to stop going mad. Books! You wouldn't believe how many books I've read."

"What's books got to do with survival?" asked Bob.

"Stops you going off your rocker for one thing, passes the time for another and for a few hours a day you escape."

"So how did that scar come about?" Asked Jim.

"I'd been in Durham about a week when I noticed this big Jock giving me the eye. There was something familiar about him, but I couldn't quite put my finger on it. Then it came to me, that Scots bloke that Terry had a run in with at the Oldfield a few years back. I don't know if it was him, sandy coloured hair, they all look alike to me. My senses told me to watch my back. I didn't know anyone, so I stayed ready."

"He was a big fucker, if I remember," said Bob.

"Yeah, this one I think, lived off his reputation. It was during exercise, he came at me out of the blue. I saw it coming and moved but not before he'd opened my cheek. I spun around and found myself facing him. He looked stunned as he admired his handiwork. My face was a bloody mess. He still held the baked bean lid in his outstretched hand, wide of his body. I saw my chance and rushed at him, swinging a right hook at his chin, and I connected. He staggered back, a little off balance. A swift kick in the bollocks followed, but I knew if I was going to survive in Durham he had to go down and stay down. I needed to send a message."

Bob glanced at Jim and exchanged a knowing look.

"The poor fucker had gotten by with his physical strength and not much more. He came at me, I sidestepped and slammed a short jab just under the back of his ear. He went down in a heap. He was dazed as he started to get up. I kicked his right leg from under him and he landed in an awkward position. I stamped on his knee as hard as I could. I heard a tendon snap and he began to scream in agony. I was on him punching and head butting the fucker. I was like a wild animal. He was done but I kept punching away, I swear if the guards hadn't dragged me away I wouldn't have stopped."

"Fucking hell!" gasped Bob, "I remember when you couldn't fight!"

"It wasn't fighting Bob, it was survival. There's a big difference. After that no one came near me. They thought I was a nutter!"

# Chapter 51

"How was he?" asked Georgia when Jim arrived home.

"A little touchy, a little nervy, but Joe still has his own brand of humour, but he ain't the young naïve twenty two year old anymore."

"How did he react about Grace and Eric?"

"Well, he doesn't like it, that's for sure. But he appears philosophical about it, which is a good thing."

"Yeah it is. Did he say anything about Billie?"

"Yeah, he did. He's excited about meeting her, but nervous too. Doesn't want to make the wrong impression."

"Didn't you tell him to be himself," said Georgia.

"Yeah of course I did," answered Jim in a sarcastic manner. "What I know about kids you could put on a postage stamp."

"Yeah, sorry," replied Georgia.

Kids were a bone of contention between them. Once Jim's property development scheme was up and running Georgia returned to her career in law. They bought a large house in Northwood, with as Jim thought the intention of starting a family. But Georgia was hell bent on carving out a career as a defence lawyer. She worked hard to get where she was and hadn't found the time or inclination for starting a family, much to the chagrin of Jim. Georgia had kept promising him kids' but her biological clock was edging towards midnight.

Quickly Georgia changed the subject, "Was there any mention of Terry?"

"What do you think!" he exclaimed. "If Terry hadn't been cremated he's have dug him up and dismembered him!" said Jim. "Well not quite," he added.

"I can't say I blame him. On the subject of Terry I heard today that Heather's put the house on the market. She said she couldn't live with the shame of what he did, so they're moving up to the Manchester area, while the kids are still young enough to make new friends."

"Near her mum?" asked Jim.

"Not far, but a little more upmarket."

"Probably for the best," said Jim.

*****

In the Sullivan household the talk was of Joe meeting Billie on Saturday morning. Grace was pacing the floor nervously. "I told Joe he was free to see Billie whenever he liked. Was I wrong to say that? I keep doubting myself."

"No you wasn't wrong, but it's going to take Joe a few weeks, maybe months to settle. I guess a little leeway would be in order. But don't be afraid to let him know if he steps out of line," said Eric. "And remember I'm with you all the way," he added.

"Have no fear about that! Billie comes first."

*****

Joe had chosen to go straight home to his parents' house. "It's what they'd expect," he'd told Bob when he was dropped off.

He'd seen them a couple of times very briefly when they visited him once the news was out. In Joe's eyes his mum didn't look much different, whereas his father had grey thinning hair and a pallid complexion, making him appear much older than his sixty years. Like his wife he'd never believe that Joe was guilty, but the self-imposed isolation hadn't sat well with him.

Joe had just finished the meal his mother insisted he eat, "We need to fatten you up," she said.

"That was great mum, but I couldn't eat it all, my stomach won't take it," he said, as his mother gave him a mock look of displeasure. "At the moment," he added quickly.

"Let's take a walk," said Joe's dad gruffly. "Walk off those pounds your mother is intent on you putting on."

Joe looked puzzled his dad wasn't the one to one type of person, but he followed him outside, "We never really hit it off when you were a teenager. My fault I guess, possibly the war had something to do with it, I don't really know. Believe it or not, teenagers' were something new back then."

"Yeah okay Dad, forget it. It was a long time ago."

"Basically what I'm trying to say is me and your mum always believed in your innocence's and we're glad you're back. We love you son." Joe started to wonder where all this was leading as they turned the corner into the next street.

"Welcome home!"

There parked against the curb was his old Zodiac, all gleaming and shiny. "Dad!" The words wouldn't come out. He turned and hugged his father and the tears began to fall. "You kept it! You kept it all this time."

"You might not thank me when you see all the new cars out there."

"Dad, I couldn't give a shit about the other cars, this is the nicest thing anyone has ever done for me."

His dad handed him the keys, "It's taxed and insured and more importantly it's got a full tank, if you fancy taking it for a spin."

"Tomorrow maybe. I think I'd like to sit in it for a while, gather my thoughts."

"I understand," said Dad as he turned around and walked back the way he came.

Joe put the key in the lock and turned. He opened the door and slid onto the leather bench seat and closed the door. He stared in wonder at the large shiny black steering wheel and the column change, and beyond to the long dashboard with its optimistic 100 mph speedometer. His hand slid along the cool leather of the bench seat and the unobtrusive lever that caused the seat to slide back, and he was there. *Close to the four bar gate at the end of the lane, and it felt like yesterday as he remembered making love to Grace for the first time. The night Billie was conceived.*

He began to cry unashamedly. He'd paid a hard price, ten years of his freedom, the loss of the only woman he'd ever loved and the wonder years of his daughter's life. As he stared though the windscreen at the streetlights he couldn't help thinking about the one book that he'd read three times over. The Count of Monte Cristo.

# Chapter 52

"He's here!" cried Grace. A lump formed in her throat as the maroon and grey Zodiac pulled up outside the house. The memories came flooding back. Grace realised she wouldn't have been normal if she hadn't felt some emotion.

Eric watched as Joe emerged from his car. He knew that today was important in so many ways. For his part he knew he had to clear the air, so he walked outside to greet him. "Hello Joe," he said as he extended his hand.

Joe looked at the extended hand, "Not what I expected!" He half smiled and shook the offered hand.

"No hard feelings I hope," said Eric. It was a dumb thing to say, he'd intended saying something more appropriate.

"I was treated unfairly, but not by you or Grace. I'm here to see my daughter, and hopefully get my life back on track."

"We'll help in any way we can," said Eric.

"I don't want handouts, I only want what's mine."

Eric flinched slightly, surprising himself, he'd thought Grace's reassurance would be enough.

"Well, let's go in. Grace and Billie have been looking forward...." He stepped aside and indicated for Joe to enter. He showed Joe into the lounge where Grace was waiting nervously.

Joe's heart skipped a beat and suddenly he was taken back in time. The hair style was the same, only a little shorter, but those dusky brown eyes still held him transfixed.

"Hello Joe. I can't tell you how pleased we are to see you. Would you like tea or coffee? Maybe something stronger?"

"Why so formal Grace? I'm here to see Billie."

Grace found his words cutting, but realised it was just as difficult for Joe as it was for her. "Of course you are, and she'll be down in a while. There are things between us that need to be talked through. So tea or coffee, your choice."

Joe found himself smiling, Grace hadn't changed; she was ever the lady. One of many things about her that he loved. "Tea would be nice."

"Right, I'm off," said Eric, "Been meaning to drive over to Heather's, wish her good luck with her move. It'll give you two time to talk."

"Thanks Eric. Give her and the kids our love."

"Will do, I shouldn't be more than a couple of hours."

Grace smiled after Eric as he made a brisk exit, "Poor dear, he's just as nervous as we are."

Minutes later Grace was sitting opposite Joe with a coffee table between them. A far cry from the unfriendly warden's office at Durham. Joe with cup and saucer in hand looked around the room.

"This is a beautiful room," he said. "You've changed it somewhat, since Gloria's day."

Grace ignored the throwaway comment, "Yes, it is a beautiful room. But you're not here to discuss the décor. We had something special, but it was torn from our grasp. It took me five years to get over you, and as I said at Durham I'll always have a place in my heart for you."

"But not enough to give me a second chance?" And there it was the elephant in the room.

Grace had gone over it in her head a thousand times, trying to find the right words, and failing, "No Joe, you brought this on yourself. How do you think I felt when you refused to see me, you cut me out of your life."

"I thought I was being fair to you," he cried.

"Yes I understand your motive, but you never gave me a chance to prove my love for you."

"Twenty years Grace, a lifetime! What else could I do?"

308

"I waited, I waited for you to change your mind. If it hadn't been for Billie I'd have gone out of my mind. Then five years ago Eric rescued me from my malaise and gave me my life back. We fell in love and we've been very happy together, the three of us."

"I'm sorry I did that, but we've a daughter between us, that must mean something?"

"It does Joe, it does. We've never held anything back from Billie, she knows that you're her father, but she's grown accustomed to Eric as a father figure, hopefully that won't change as Billie and you get to know each other. It does frighten me a bit but it's only right that you develop a close bond."

"Okay, I get it! But you must understand, I feel cheated; not by you, but by life itself. I can't help how I feel towards you. I've never stopped loving you. I'm sorry it's not what you might have wanted to hear, I'm just being honest, I can't help it."

Grace reached across and laid her hand upon his, "I'm sorry, how could I not be."

Joe managed a slight smile, "It's been a little over twenty four hours since I was released. Hopefully I'll settle down and accept how things are. But at this moment looking at you, I doubt it very much."

"Joe, you have to try, if not for your sake or mine, try for Billie."

For the next twenty minutes or so Grace did her best to fill in details of Billie's life, until Joe said, "You know what, I wasn't nervous about meeting you and Eric, but I'm nervous now about meeting Billie. Will you stay for a while, give me support?"

"Of course I will," replied Grace, as she laid a hand upon his arm for reassurance.

Joe rose from his seat when Billie entered the room. From the moment he saw her he fell in love. She had Grace's dark almost black mop of hair, but it was her eyes he recognised, they were blue like his and carrying a hint of mischief.

"Hi Joe! Whoops, start again, hi Dad!"

"Hello Billie! There hasn't been a day that I didn't think of you. You're beautiful!"

Billie half laughed, "I wouldn't go that far," it was laden with false modesty. Billie knew only too well what she looked like. "If I'm half as good looking as mum when I'm her age, I'll be happy."

"Can't disagree!" responded Joe.

"Told you, ten going on thirty, just don't let her wind you around her little finger. I'll let you two get acquainted," said Grace.

They watched as Grace left the room, smiled at each other, laughed nervously and began to speak at the same time. "Where to begin," said Joe.

"Let's start with how you first met Mum." Billie saw the worried frown on his face. "Don't worry about putting your foot in it. I'm nearly eleven, I know all about the birds and the bees. I also know about that horrible man that Mum was married too."

Joe was shocked, but in a nice way at the maturity of his daughter, "Right, a little background of my childhood, then onto the good stuff, my teenage years."

"Steady on Dad, remember I'm only ten," she joked. "Is that your car out front, it's a bit ancient."

"It's a classic, I'll have you know."

Their conversation went from deep and meaningful to light and hilarious. Her likes and dislikes, the latest pop charts to her love of tennis and her great passion, horse riding.

"I go to a local riding stables, usually on Saturdays where I muck out the stables in exchange for a riding lesson. Mum made an arrangement with the stable owner, she said if riding was a real passion then I needed to show her how serious I was," said an enthusiastic Billie.

"Well, your mum's right. It'll teach you the value of your labour. Learning that lesson early enough will hold you in good stead as you get older," said Joe. "I'd like to see you ride sometime."

"That would be great, how about next Saturday?"

"Not so fast, I'll have to run it passed your mum first."

"She'll agree I'll give her my most disappointed look: she'll cave."

"I'll what young lady?" said Grace as she came back into the room.

"Joe, I mean Dad, wants to see me ride," replied Billie.

"Of course he can," said Grace. She looked straight at Joe, "You can see Billie whenever you want, you're her dad, but not during school days. School holidays are fine. My only stipulation is you phone first; just in case we're busy.

"Will do," replied Joe, before glancing at his watch. "Whoa, look at the time," he said. "I've a meeting with Georgia and I should have been there, like five minutes ago."

"I'll ring her, let her know you're coming," said Grace.

"Great, much appreciated."

After giving Billie a hug and a kiss on the cheek and then another hug, Joe reluctantly made his way back to the car. Grace walked out with him. "It still looks good," she said as she admired the Zodiac. "I heard you dad kept it in tip top condition. What a nice man."

"Yeah, he is," said Joe.

"Oh, before you go, Eric's business card it's got our home phone number on it. If you need to talk, ring me."


As Joe drove to his meeting with Georgia, an involuntary tear gave him away. Seeing Billie was everything he could have wished for and more. But seeing the only woman he'd ever loved heightened how he felt about her. He couldn't help it, the pain was real; he still loved her. The loss of Grace was so much harder to bear than his wasted years in prison.

# Chapter 53

Georgia was just about to leave when Grace phoned. "Joe's running ten minutes late. He's on his way," said Grace.

"That's fine, I'll hold on. How it go?" asked Georgia.

"It went fine, a little strained at first, but Billie was great with him."

"And you Grace, how was it?"

"Good, I think. He was so much more relaxed than when I saw him in Durham."

"That wasn't what I meant," said Georgia.

"I know what you meant," sighed Grace.

*****

Joe arrived at Chandler and Lowe to find the offices locked. He knocked and Georgia came out of a side office and let him in. She smiled, "Only a skeleton staff on Saturday mornings."

"Mornings! It's past two o'clock. I hope you haven't stayed late because of me?"

"I have actually, I knew you'd probably be later than we'd discussed, but no matter you're here now," stated Georgia. "This way." She walked ahead of him for several yards before standing at the side of an open door. She invited Joe in and offered him a seat. "Why so formal, you may well ask."

"Yeah, I kinda wondered."

"It was because of you and your case that I became a defence lawyer. I went totally against my principles, I'm really a throw away the key, kind of girl."

"I'm glad my case helped you in your choice of careers," he said flippantly.

"I'll give you that one," said Georgia, "The next one could cost you," she warned.

"Sorry, I guess I've still got a few rough edges."

Georgia gave the presence of a smile. "I don't know if you're aware, we, my legal team and I appealed your case, on several fronts, the word of a petty criminal and the circumstantial evidence found in your locker. As you're aware most of the case hung on the fact you hadn't disclosed your flying abilities."

"That's because there wasn't any!" exclaimed Joe.

"You and Terry were friends, correct?"

"Yeah, I met him when I was fifteen or sixteen."

"Did you at any time mention your interest in aircraft and that you'd been an air cadet?"

"I can't remember, maybe, too be honest we mostly talked cars, girls and booze."

"But it's possible?"

"I guess."

Georgia was making notes as she conducted the conversation.

"Reason I ask; we didn't have the benefit of hindsight when we first appealed your case. You went to prison allegedly on charges brought by detective sergeant, now Inspector John Armstrong, who used the allegations of your guilt from a known criminal; Arthur Briggs, who incidentally has dropped off the map. I suspect even with your disclosure we'd still have had a tough hill to climb."

"So why ask?"

"Basically I'm trying to leave no stone unturned."

"Why? I'm out!"

"We now know from Terry's detailed confession that Chief Inspector Sean Fallon was allegedly behind the whole conspiracy. But proving it, is another matter. I won't lie to you Joe, as far as the judiciary are concerned you've been let out on time served. Not the satisfactory outcome we wanted, but better than motioning for a re-trial which would at best have taken a year or so to prepare, with your chances of being found not guilty no more certain than the first trial."

"Yeah, I understand, I've been briefed."

"How does it feel to be a free man, no pardon, no compensation, no criminal charges against Armstrong and Fallon and no justice?"

"Where's the punch-line Georgia?" The younger Joe would have been shouting from the rooftops, whereas the man sitting across from her wasn't rising to the bait, he had his own agenda and he didn't need any interference. "You didn't bring me here to tell me what I already know."

"We all know what was done to you and it isn't right. I'm asking you to be patient for a while longer. If you're willing I'll take on your case pro-bono?"

"Yeah, sure. Why?"

"I think that's plainly obvious, I was there at the start. I believed like Grace that you were innocent; we all got played. Sean Fallon shouldn't be able to ruin people's lives and get away with it."

"So what can you do about it?"

"Things are changing in this country of ours. It might seem that the whole of the Met is corrupt in one way or another, but there are quite a number of high ranking officers working to rout out the corruption once and for all. Your case is just the tip of the iceberg. In the not too distant future I strongly believe we'll bring these corrupt officers to book."

Joe softened in his approach, "I appreciate what you're doing for me, and I understand what you're trying to say. Keep my nose clean, no taking the law into my own hands! Much as I'd like too, I've lost ten years of my freedom, I don't intend going back."

"Thank you Joe. I promise I'll do my level best," said Georgia.

Joe managed a wry smile, "Well good luck with that."

Seeing Grace had thrown into perspective what he'd lost. Their first meeting in the warden's rooms at Durham had become a blur. Terry's suicide and confession, the possibility of his early release, Grace's ex-husband's role and finally seeing Grace. It had all happened in a rush. It was only later in his cell that he began to make sense of everything. Yet this morning had turned his life upside down. Grace at thirty eight was even lovelier than the first time they'd met, *if that was possible.* She looked happy in her life-style, comfortable in her surrounding and from what he could tell she was extremely devoted to Eric. The pain was excruciating.

The entrance of Billie was like a soothing balm as she bounced into his life. She was young and old, naïve yet worldly. Billie was full of life and lit up the room, and when she took him by the hand and led him into the garden his heart felt like it was about to burst. She chatted incessantly about her hobbies, her school and her ambitions for the future. As they walked under the apple and pear trees of the mini orchard the autumn sun cast its broken rays of sunlight through the red and gold leaves, the air was heavy with the pungent smell of windfalls. Being with Billie gave him a sense of hope.

Georgia had been a revelation, business like and honest, offering her services free of charge. Yet warning him off. Telling him to be patient. Basically offering him everything and nothing. Well Georgia didn't need to worry, at least in the short term.

# Chapter 54

He'd promised to meet up with Bob for a drink in the George later that Saturday night. Joe was surprised to see Becky when he walked in. She was sitting with Bob in their favourite spot. Bob jumped up and asked what Joe was having.

"You know that already," said Joe with a wry grin.

"Two light and bitters please!"

Joe enjoyed the gesture. "Cheers."

Both men joined Becky at their table. "Becky wanted to say hi!" exclaimed Bob as they sat down.

Becky smiled, "Mum's offered to baby sit, so I couldn't say no!"

"No need to explain, I unde….." he stopped mid-sentence as Donna walked out of the ladies.

"It's not what you think! I knew Bob would probably monopolise you for most of the evening so when Donna phoned I asked her to join me," stated Becky.

Joe looked at Bob. "It's the truth!" cried Bob.

"Okay," said Joe unconvinced.

Seeing Donna brought back memories from New Year's Eve at the tail end of 1966. 'If Grace hadn't burst into the George that night I might have …………'

"We hadn't seen each other for about six weeks. We needed a catch up. I'm Donna by the way, we met once."

"Yeah, I recall…" replied Joe.

"I'm so glad you're out, it must have been dreadful?"

"Yeah it was, but that's behind me now."

Bob snapped him out of his melancholy thoughts. "I know I'm jumping the gun and I know it's too soon, but I'd like you to come and work for me. It's only labouring but it's a start."

"Bob, you're my best friend, I don't need charity; I'll get by."

"This ain't charity, believe me you'll work for your money!" responded Bob. "Give yourself a week or two to get your bearings, then come work for me."

Joe smiled, "You know, I never in my wildest dreams believed I'd be working for you."

"So you'll accept?"

"Yeah maybe, I'll think about it. Give me a week."

"A week Monday it is then."

"I didn't say I would!" exclaimed Joe, "But thanks!"

"Oh, no need to thank me, you'll earn every penny."

Both men stood up and shook and hugged each other. "It's really good to see you mate. Right, it's my round what you all having?" asked Joe as he turned around and made his way over to the bar. He brought the girls drinks over first, then swiftly he returned with his and Bob's "I need a catch up with you guys. So fill me in? "You finally married him. I thought you'd have had more sense Becky"

"No I was always dumb," she laughed. "It's really good to see you. I understand you've seen Billie."

Bob looked slightly awkward.

"Yeah, wow! She's great. She's so confident for someone her age. We hit it off straight away."

"We've two of our own. A boy and a girl. I don't know if Bob told you, but we live on the Eastcote Park Estate."

"Oh, very posh," quipped Joe.

"Nah, not really, better than Northolt," giggled Becky.

"What's wrong with Northolt!" blurted out Donna. "I still live there!"

"Only because you went back to your mum's," added Becky.

"Yeah but it's only temporary."

"So you done okay Bob," said Joe.

"Yeah, you could say that. Thanks to Becky's dad. If you remember it was him that advised me to get a trade. That, and an in with a top builder in Northolt."

"See, what did I say, Northolt's the business," chipped in Donna.

"Of course I ain't in Jim's league, once that property business took off he couldn't fail, he was always going places, that one."

"Grammar school boy, likes rugby more that football. Something wrong there!" laughed Joe.

"Nah!" cried Bob. Jim's okay, he ain't flash, he's still one of the lads, he talks better than us, but he hasn't forgotten where he comes from."

"I was surprised he was still with Georgia. I thought when the novelty wore off she'd have been long gone. But fair play to her, she's been fighting my corner. Why I can't understand, I wasn't the friendliest to her before I got sent down."

"She's alright once you get to know her," added Bob.

The evening was full of interesting chat, a bit of gossip between Becky and Donna, more piss taking and a bit of soul searching by Joe.

As last orders were called Bob jumped up and asked the bartender to call him a cab.

"What's wrong with your car?"

"Nothing! You must have heard of the breathalyser when you was inside," said Bob.

"Vaguely, just didn't give it a thought," said Joe. "I'll drive you home. I don't feel a bit drunk."

"No Joe, you shouldn't either considering...."

"Considering what Becky," asked Joe?

"You're only just out of nick, and the Zodiac does attract attention," said Donna. "Leave your car in the car park, I'll drive you home."

'Full marks Donna, diffusing what could have been an ugly situation,' thought Bob.

Joe was caught on the hop, "You set this up Bob!"

"You wish!" exclaimed Donna.

"Believe me Joe, that was not my intention."

Whatever it was, something deep inside of him knew Bob was telling the truth.

"Now do you want a lift home?" asked Donna.

"Bossy ain't she," said Joe, "but you've been drinking."

"Shows how much you know. Two shorts, the rest orange juice."

"My, my, how did we get so civilised?"

"Do you want that lift or not?"

"Yeah, why not."

Donna pulled up outside Joe's house, pulled on the brake and switched off the ignition.

"Answer me one thing," she asked. "What did you mean when you said Bob had set you up?"

Joe looked at a loss.

Donna turned in her seat and looked Joe in the eye. "What gave you the right to think I was the same girl that I was ten years ago. People change, you've changed. You're not the only one that's had a fucked up life. We had a nice evening together, why did you presume I was out to screw you?"

"Whoa, I get you're point. I'm sorry if I presumed so much. It just seemed a set up. I'm truly sorry," said Joe. "And you're right we did have a good evening, I should have read the signs, it's just I'm a little out of practice with females, especially the new kind. Again, I'm sorry!"

"Enough, enough! One sorry was sufficient. I didn't mean to give you a hard time. I phoned Becky to pour out my troubles when she asked me to join her and Bob for a drink. When she told me you were meeting up with them I turned down the invitation, but Becky snapped at me, I ain't asking you to jump into bed with him. Just keep me company, Bob really wanted to feel Joe out about a job."

Joe didn't really know what to say. Since coming out of prison, his friends his mum and dad and everyone he'd come into contact with had all been pussyfooting around him; this was something new. Struggling with his words he blurted out, "So what kind of troubles were you pouring out to Becky?"

"Just the usual, nothing very important. You on the other hand have a lot to deal with, considering ten or eleven years ago you ditched me when she walked in. Judging the look on your face I'd say the years haven't diminished the love you still feel for her."

Joe risked a smile, "I must admit it did feel a little déjà vu. Almost as though the past ten years was just a dream."

"And you wished it was? Do you want to talk about it?"

Joe thought about it, but then shook his head. "Maybe another time."

"Give me a call, if you change your mind." Donna tore off a scrap of paper from out of her handbag and scribbled down her phone number.

# Chapter 55

Joe woke early, sluiced handfuls of cold water over his face and hair, towel dried himself, then cleaned his teeth. It was Sunday morning and the house was quiet, too quiet for Joe's liking. He'd grown use to the early morning activity in prison, so it was going to take time. He threw a pair of jeans on and grabbed a tee shirt from the wardrobe. Picking up his wallet and keys he hurried down the stairs.

"Is that you Joe?" cried his mum from her bedroom.

"Yeah, I'm going for a walk, getting a paper and collecting my car. See you later mum, won't be long."

Joe breathed in the cool morning air and began to collect his thoughts. His world had changed in ten years. "We've joined the common market, whatever the fuck that was!" Those were Bob's exact words. Our money had recently changed to decimalisation, and more and more people were taking overseas holidays. It was a lot for Joe to get his head around. The thing that Joe had to come to terms with, was his friends. They had all moved on during his time in prison; while he was still stuck in the late nineteen sixties. 'If only,' he muttered. He smiled to himself, there was a lot to catch up on, and Sunday lunchtime seemed the ideal place to start.

His parting words to Bob on Saturday night were, "See you here tomorrow, twelve noon; don't be late!" Joe started to doubt himself, 'Sunday lunchtime it's a tradition; yeah he'll be there.' He thought about ringing him, but realised apart from Eric's business card with Grace's home number printed on it, he didn't have anyone else's number. His mood darkened, the thought of Grace with Eric soured his feelings.

He picked up a copy of the News of the World at a local newsagents then after giving the headlines a cursory look, he tucked it under his arm and walked back towards the George car park. Apart from the odd person the high street was deserted, thinking about it Joe realised in his younger days he'd never seen seven thirty on a Sunday morning.

Despite the breathalyser Joe drove to the pub arriving two minutes early. He was relieved to see Bob sitting on the wall adjacent to the pub doors. "You made it then!" he said.

"Of course I made it. 98b runs past my estate, if you remember," responded Bob. "Jim said he hopes to make it by half past."

Joe sensed Bob seemed a little nervous. "Is something up?"

"Sorry mate, Eric asked if you'd mind him joining us. I told him it might be a bit soon. He said he understood, but looked a bit down so I said Joe seems friendly enough, but it's your funeral. So he might turn up. Just preparing you, if he shows."

"It is what it is. I expect I'll see a lot more of him than I'd like too. But I've got to live my life. Just one thing, don't mention Donna took me home last night!"

A glint appeared in Bob's eye, "You did! Didn't yah!"

"No, as a matter of fact I spent ten minutes sitting outside my house apologising for thinking bad of her," said Joe as he walked into the saloon bar of the George. "What you having?"

"My usual," replied Bob.

Joe brought them over and sat down. "The reason I don't want anyone to know is they might get the wrong idea. Donna gave me her phone number on a scrap of paper, said if I needed to talk about it, she'd be prepared to listen."

"Actually Donna's had a bad time herself recently. She'd been living with some bloke for about three or four years, then they split and she went back to her mum's."

"I didn't know that. I'm not looking to get involved with anyone." He paused for a few seconds then added, "But in the meantime if I do see Donna I don't want anyone to know."

"Ah ha!" cried Bob.

"All I'm really concerned with is getting to know my daughter."

Bob gave him a quizzical look. "You ain't over her, are yah?" When it came to his best mate he could read between the lines.

"No! I'm not actually. Maybe I never will be."

"You need to forget about Grace, I know you won't take my advice, but that ship's sailed," said Bob.

"Right, change the subject here comes Jim," warned Joe.

"Back in your rightful place I see, what can I get you?"

"Light and bitter please Jim," said Joe, as he handed him an empty glass.

Bob gave Joe a worried look.

"What's up," asked Joe.

"Nothing! Forget it."

Jim brought the drinks over and sat down, "How goes it?"

"A lot to take in. Getting my head around this new money for a start. Amazing ain't it, they only know how to round things up, never down."

"Way of the world Joe."

"I was just about to fill him in about the job," said Bob.

"What's that to do with Jim?" asked Joe.

"I'll answer that," said Jim. "Bob has a contract with my company Manco Contractors for the plumbing work on all my properties. He's taken on a massive project, in charge of hiring and firing all the sub-contractors we're likely to need over the next five years. Manco prides itself on its standard of workmanship, hence Bob."

"So this job?"

"When we knew you were getting out Bob suggested you come and work for us," replied a very business-like Jim.

"Let me get this straight, you own Manco, Bob basically works for you and I would work for Bob. Sounds more like a John Cleese sketch to me." Joe shook his head, in mock despondency.

They all laughed.

"The truth of it is, Jim's handed me a lucrative contract, I'm offering you a chance to learn, an apprenticeship, where you'll have one day a week at a college, learning all there is to know about our trade. In five years you'd be able to branch out on your own or possibly become my partner," said Bob. "Unless we're sick of the sight of each other!"

"Like I said before, I don't want charity. I know you mean well Bob, but ain't you going a little too far?"

"I'm paying you for the days you work. Jim's making up the rest including your college fees."

"Neither of you owe me anything!" protested Joe.

Bob looked towards Jim to answer.

"We were mates all four of us, we looked out for each other. Then Terry fucked up and you paid the price. There wasn't anything we could do to help. We were powerless. My Georgia did her best, but she could only do so much. I've done alright in my life, so has Bob, that's why we both want to give something back. Take the fucking job, it ain't charity!"

Joe could feel himself welling up, kindness like this had been absent for far too long. "I'm sorry, it just gets to me. Give me a minute." For the briefest of moment Jim and Bob looked at each other. "Okay, thanks I appreciate it."

"Don't thank us, just get the next round in!" said Jim.

Joe stepped up to the bar, and was just ordering when in walked Eric. He stiffened momentarily, but recovered in an instant.

Eric looked a little awkward, smiled at Joe and walked up beside him. "I'll get these," he said.

"Nah, I'm here now, I'll get them. Double scotch one cube of ice," said Joe.

"Good memory, I'll help you with these," said Eric as he grabbed a hold of two of the drinks and walked over to Jim and Bob.

"Cheers," said Jim.

"How's it going," inquired Eric.

"Slowly but we're getting there," said Bob.

Joe brought his and Eric's drinks over, smiled and said, "How's the antiques business?" It was as good a line as any, and it took the tension in the air down a notch.

"Yeah, not bad, well good actually, but then of course it's seasonal. Drops off about now, picks up a couple of weeks before Christmas, then it dies down until spring," replied Eric.

"I see Man U have been expelled from the European Cup," said Jim. "Fan trouble I understand. We don't get that at rugby matches."

Joe laughed, "Some things haven't changed!"

"You're not wrong there," cried Bob. "Jim tell him about your visit to Wimbledon. Likes tennis now, would you believe. Belongs to a tennis club."

"Of course I play tennis. In my job now I don't get the exercise I use too. Believe me a good workout on the court twice maybe three times a week does help. Going to Wimbledon for the first time was quite an experience. We were lucky, we got tickets for the men's semi-finals. Saw Jimmy Connors, Bjorn Borg and Vita Gerulaitus and some mouthy qualifier. Great entertainment," said Jim.

"See what I mean," laughed Bob. Whatever you do, don't ask him about the Glorious Twelfth. He's part of the Hooray Henry brigade now, loves his grouse shooting."

"Take no notice Joe, a lot of my activities involve meeting important clients, most of its for show," cried Jim.

"Ask him about the origin of his company name,"

"Manco?"

"You won't have seen them but take my advice, once they start rerunning them at the cinema, go see the Dollar westerns," said Jim enthusiastically.

Joe laughed, "Durham prison wasn't Devil's Island: we did get some television. Clint Eastwood, the man with no name, but what's that to do with Manco?"

"Ah ha, Clint might be known as the man with no name, but in each of his films he's called Joe in Fistful, Manco in the second and Blondie in the third."

Bob in an effort to get Jim off his pet subject tried changing the subject, "Shame about Elvis last month!"

"Yeah, it was," said Joe. "Very sad."

Despite the small talk, the chatter and the laughter emanating from their table the undertone of tension between Eric and Joe was building. Eric who'd sat there listening to Jim and Bob doing their best to keep the conversation going, decided it was time to break the tension. "Joe I think we need to have a talk outside, man to man."

Joe didn't seem surprised. "Yeah let's take it to the garden."

"Hold it you two, there's no need for a scrap," cried Bob.

Without taking his eyes off Eric, Joe said, "There's no need to worry. We need to clear the air. We've things that need saying privately!"

"Get us two large scotches," said Eric, as he handed Bob a fiver. "We'll probably need them when we come back in."

Bob stepped up to the bar, his eyes nervously watching as two of his close friends casually walked into the pub garden. "Fuck it!" he said to himself. "Give me four double scotches!"

Joe and Eric walked over to the farthest table and chairs and sat facing each other. Eric was the first to speak. "I don't know about you, but I needed this chat to explain how I feel towards Grace. Believe me none of us saw this coming."

"I'll give you that."

"I hadn't seen Grace for years, when I bumped into her in Watford."

"Yeah, she told me."

"Did she tell you she'd had a hard time after you got sent down? You were gone and she was on her own with a baby. She stayed with her parents, but although they meant well she found it a bit suffocating. When the divorce settlement came through she bought a small cottage near Chorley Wood."

Joe cut in, "What's this got to do with your relationship with Grace?"

"I'm coming to that Joe, just bear with me. No offence. She was grieving, she was grieving for you, as if you'd died. She cut herself off, because she believed she was somehow to blame. She'd always believed her ex-husband was behind it. To see your friends, knowing how she felt, would have driven her insane."

"Do you think I don't know that! I was going insane myself, that's why I cut all ties. I wanted Grace to forget about what we had."

"Her life changed almost as much as yours. An abusive husband, a pregnancy, a divorce and then seeing you go down for a crime you didn't commit, all these were as nothing compared to you abandoning her. She felt empty inside. She loved you Joe, she loved you until she didn't." It was a cutting remark, but Eric wasn't pulling any punches.

"What's that supposed to mean? Until she didn't?"

"I think you know, Grace's entire life had been turned upside down, Billie was the only constant in her live. Your daughter was her way back. By all accounts it took years for Grace to become whole again."

"And then she met you!" The venom in Joe's voice was unmistakeable.

"When I met Grace, she was an entirely different woman to the one I'd last seen coming out of Wandsworth like a woman bereaved! She'd eventually got her life back. She was surprised to see me and eager for news of everyone. The first person she asked about was you. There was nothing I could tell her."

"But you were there to lend her a shoulder to cry on!"

"No Joe it wasn't anything like that. She wasn't interested in me. Grace expressed a desire to get back in contact with everyone, especially Georgia."

"And you gave her a nudge in that direction," spat Joe.

"Grace wanted to get in touch but it took her several months before she felt ready."

Eric could feel the tension rising, but knew this might be his only chance to tell Joe his side of it.

"Believe me, it was friendship I offered. Yes I found her attractive, I won't lie to you, but something inside of me told me it was wrong to feel that way. Guilt I suppose."

"Guilt, why guilt?"

Eric ignored the question, "I have to admit I fell under her spell. I didn't dare tell her how I felt, I believed it would frighten her off."

"Why are you telling me all this?"

"Because Joe I feel I owe it to you. I need you to hear it from me. As the weeks flew by we became close. Then one day she asked why I hadn't made a play. I said I believed she still had strong feelings for you. She smiled sweetly and said there would always be a place in her heart for you, but she wasn't giving up on life. I told her then and there that I had very strong feeling for her. She looked up at me and told me those feelings were mutual. We took it slowly, then married just over three years ago. The rest you know."

"The rest I know…" Anger and rage seemed to emanate from every pore in Joe's body as he fought for control.

"Two things you need to know," said Eric, "from as early as Billie could understand, Grace had told her who her father was, and where he was. She was preparing Billie for the day that she'd finally meet her father. It was made quite clear, that as much as I loved Billie, you would always be her father."

Joe's anger slowed down a notch or two at the mention of Billie.

Eric paused for a few seconds, bracing himself before adding, "I love Grace and nothing will ever change that. She's my wife, I love her and she loves me. You're free to see Billie anytime, but don't use her as a weapon to come between Grace and me."

"I can't promise that!" said Joe coldly. "I've taken on board everything that you've said. And yes, I cut Grace and Billie out of my life because I loved them. I was facing twenty years in prison, I couldn't bear the torture of prison visits. I wasn't prepared to see her waste her life."

"Then you understand!"

"Twenty years Eric, the thought of twenty fucking years. I knew that I needed to let her go. I didn't come to that decision lightly. I knew that one day she'd find happiness, but I never thought it would be with someone I knew. My mistake. I know you love Grace but so do I. She probably thinks she loves you, but somehow I will win her back."

"I can't help how you feel, but you're wasting your time. Hopefully you'll find someone and the pain that you're feeling will disappear," said Eric.

"I've a rage boiling inside, it's tearing me apart!"

"Hit, hit me if it'll make you feel better!"

"Hit you, I'd love too, but it wouldn't help me get Grace back."

"You're not getting her back," replied Eric.

"Two things puzzle me about you. Tommy Atkins! Without his help I might not have made it, so thanks for intervening on my behalf and lastly, this surprised me the most, according to

Georgia it was you who found Terry's confession. You could have easily binned it, but you didn't. Why?"

"You were set up, you wouldn't have lasted five minutes without Tommy Atkins support. It was the least I could do, he owed me. As for Terry's confession, yeah I could easily have burned it. It would've saved me a pile of grief, but despite not having always been an honest man, I am an honourable one."

"You may well be an honourable man, but you're not my friend!"

# Chapter 56

"How'd it go?" asked Georgia.

"It was going alright until Eric walked in. Before that Bob had outlined to Joe the plans we'd discussed. As predicted he said he didn't need handouts. Once I explained the advantages to our plan, plus the little matter of us wanting to help a mate he came around. In fact he became a little emotional. Then Eric joined us; the atmosphere around the table became slightly chilly. Bob and I did our best with small talk, trivia, the usual stuff, but you could cut the tension with a knife. In fact I was slightly relieved when Eric asked Joe outside to talk."

"They had a fight?"

"No, quite civilised really, but from what Bob and I could see through the windows, it wasn't a friendly chat."

"Did they part as friends?"

"Not really, Joe walked in looked at the two double whiskies on the table, picked one up and swallowed it down in one go. Then without a by your leave he walked out."

"What about Eric?"

"He walked back in, sat down, apologised for the tension and sipped his scotch slowly. I asked if they'd settled anything. "No," he said, "I believe we just drew the battle lines.""

"Oh I was afraid of that," said Georgia. "Will this make it difficult for Joe to work with Bob and yourself?"

"It won't on my part. I know that over the last couple of years Grace and Eric have become very close with us; so no way will we jeopardise our relationship with them," replied Jim. "What Joe does outside of work is his own business, we aren't getting involved and we aren't taking sides." He gave Georgia a long lingering look.

"It's early days for Joe at the moment but there is movement in high places, slow movement I'll grant you, but believe me things will get better for him, I'm sure of it," said Georgia.

"Hopefully it'll come sooner rather than later," said Jim. "Compensation might go some way to easing the hurt Joe must be feeling right now," added Jim.

*****

Becky looked at the clock in the front room, it was close to three o'clock. If the bus was on time Bob should be almost home. She glanced out of the window and within a minute he came into view. "Right kids, get sat down, your dad's here."

Bob walked in, took his coat off and walked into the dining room. The welcoming smell of the Sunday roast permeating the air. The excited cries from his kids as Becky put their dinners on the table made him feel grateful to be alive. He couldn't help reflecting how his friend had sunk the scotch and walked out without a word.

"Well! How was it?" asked Becky as she sat down.

"You obviously know how last night went, I bet you was on the phone to Donna the moment I left."

Becky gave him a knowing smile, "Yeah, Donna said he was quite sweet really, kept apologising. Did Eric show?"

"In spades. Joe's going to start next Monday I think, I hope. We were doing okay until Eric walked in. Then everything changed. Eric asked Joe to go outside for a private chat to thrash out their differences. I thought they might have come to blows, but it was all civilised, too civilised for my liking. I just hope when Joe settles down things might work out. One interesting point, Joe didn't rule out seeing Donna, but doesn't want anyone to know, said she wrote down her phone number."

"She's vulnerable you know. He better not use her," said Becky.

"They're both vulnerable. Perhaps they'll be good for each other."

*****

"Where's Billie?" asked Eric, the moment he walked through the front door.

"She's next door, playing with Susan. How did it go?" asked Grace nervously.

"Let's say I don't think I'm on his Christmas card list. He seemed okay when I walked in, but it soon became clear we needed to have a man to man talk. We went outside and as politely as I could, I told him how difficult it was for you to come to terms with him cutting you out of his life."

"What did he say," she asked fretfully.

"More or less what he told you yesterday, said it was his only way to cope. I can understand that, if I'd been in his shoes I might have done the same."

"You don't have to defend him, you're not like him," sighed Grace.

"I'm more like him than you think. He's still in love with you, and I can't blame him. He said he knows how much I love you, but somehow he intends winning you back. I said he's free to try, but not to use Billie as a weapon. He said he couldn't promise that. I told him you loved him, and that you loved him until you didn't! I'm sorry Grace, I wanted to hurt him."

Grace held Eric and pushed her face up to his, "We knew what lay ahead of us when you asked me to marry you. We knew then that this day would come and that somehow we'd deal with it. What we hadn't expected was Joe to get out ten years early. I'm not saying it would have been easier if he hadn't been released, I'm glad he's out, I'm glad that maybe one day Sean will get his just desserts, but mostly I'm glad I'm married to you."

Eric looked into Grace's dusky smouldering eyes that smiled up at him and knew he was the luckiest man alive. He kissed her gently and she responded in the only way she knew.

*****

Joe regretted storming out the moment he was outside. He walked unsteadily to his car, angry and probably a little tipsy. He'd no intention of going home, but he had nowhere else to go. His friends were going home to their families while he was stuck in a time warp inside a thirty three year old body, with the prospects of a man barely out of his teens. His friends had given him the chance to rebuild his life, but without Grace it felt meaningless. He put the key in the ignition, but stopped. He sat back against the seat, then reached inside his jacket pocket and pulled out his old address book. "A relic from the sixties like me," he cried out.

He'd looked at it fondly that very morning, but now it felt like a symbol of his plight. The car, the address book, his choice of light and bitter, he was living in the past. He started up the Zodiac, stuck it into reverse, turned the wheel, put his foot down on the clutch and slammed the car into first gear. He pulled out of the George car park and turned right, then left up Bury Street. With tears streaming down his face he drove aimlessly, increasing his speed as he drove towards Ducks Hill. In an instant it became clear, he wanted to end it.

Slipping the column change into third gear he accelerated up the hill, putting his foot down as far as it would go. He remembered a solitary oak just past the brow of the hill on the downward slope. It made perfect sense. As the car touched eighty, he reached the top, ahead no more than two hundred yards in front stood the large oak. As his foot pushed even harder on the accelerator suddenly he thought about how his father had lovingly looked after the Zodiac. His dear old dad! He couldn't do that to him. As he hurtled towards the tree he slammed on the brakes, causing the car to whip from one side to the other, clipping the curb and spinning towards the middle of the road. Gripping the steering wheel tightly with his foot hard on the brakes *in what appeared like an eternity* he brought the Zodiac to a halt at the far side of the road. Sweat poured down from every pore, his heart was racing, his nerves shattered as his brain struggled to come to terms with what he'd nearly done.

The now stationary Zodiac had spun in a half circle and was facing back towards Ruislip. Somehow or other he managed to pull himself together, as his instinct for survival kicked in. He was lucky there had been no oncoming traffic, although he recalled two cars passing as he remained stationary. Realising that at any moment a police car could pull up, he checked the road was clear then drove slowly, turning right into the car park at the woods. He'd wanted to do it, he'd seen no way out; he parked the car, turned off the ignition and cried.

He sat there gazing out at the autumn colours, not seeing their beauty, only the misery of his existence. He sat like that for almost an hour, slowly coming down from the alcohol he'd consumed and brought his thoughts under control. His near brush with death and the realisation that he was drowning in self-pity made him feel ashamed.

He turned on the ignition and was about to stick the car into gear when he noticed a scrap of paper sticking out of his discarded old address book. He picked it up and saw it was the scrap of paper that Donna had scribbled her phone number on. "Do you want to talk about it?"

Joe drove until he saw the familiar red phone box of his youth. "At least that hasn't changed," he mumbled as he rummaged around in his pockets for change. "Jesus Christ!" he exclaimed as he saw the price of a phone call. 'No button A or B,' he thought as he read the simply instructions. He dialled Donna's number, but nearly put the phone down. He was doubting himself.

"Hello?"

"Is that you Donna?"

"Who's that? Is that Joe?"

"Yes, it's Joe. I was wondering if we could talk."

"What, right now! Over the phone."

"No, tonight."

"I normally wash my hair Sunday night, but as it's you," she said sensing a desperation in his voice.

"Great, I'll pick you up at seven, okay."

"Hold it, don't you want my address?"

"Yeah, that would help. I'm a little out of practice," replied Joe.

"We'll see about that!" exclaimed Donna as she recited her address. "Don't be late."

# Chapter 57

While Joe was struggling to come to terms with his life, Sean Fallon was contemplating his future career in the Met. At forty nine closing in on his fiftieth birthday he'd hoped to spend the last decade of his illustrious career in relative comfort as a Superintendent, but Arthur Brigg's greedy but fatal mistake seemed to have scuppered any such plans.

Chief Inspector Sean Fallon was tipped the wink by his superiors at a masonic lodge meeting that a number of complaints against the Metropolitan Police were gaining traction. One such complaint was the alleged wrongful conviction of Joseph Dempsey for his part in the attempted kidnapping and robbery of the then B.O.A.C cargo warehouse at London Airport.

"In light of the gathering storm which maybe on us sooner than we'd hoped, you might consider it more prudent on your part to accept retirement as opposed to seeking promotion," said Jock Ballantine, a friend and well-informed Chief Superintendent. "I'm not saying right away, but you might want to consider your options."

"Thanks for the heads up JB," responded Sean. "I'll take that under advisement." Sean knew that Ballantine had his finger on the pulse of the Met. There had been rumblings of police corruption in the Met almost from the inception in 1829. It wasn't a new thing. But JB made sense, the chance of promotion to Superintendent would bring his whole career under the spotlight. Not something he'd have bothered about in the past, but the accusation of a frame up, would at the very least scupper his chances of promotion.

Sean prided himself on always being one step ahead, so begrudgingly he made his decision. He would continue as usual with is eye on leaving the Force on his fiftieth birthday in March. Enough time for him to settle scores, Grace would be at the top of the list, followed closely by that meddling she-cat solicitor; Georgia Chandler.

Using the arsenal of tools at his disposal, Sean started a dossier on both of them, starting with Grace. Her husband an antiques dealer with a very colourful past interested Fallon. Eric Sullivan was a bit of an enigma, born and bred in the East End, a mystery man, on account he ran with the hare and hunted with the hounds. There was no doubt in Fallon's mind that Eric Sullivan was at it like most of his ilk, but strangely was never charged, not even in his youth. "Clever cunt!" said Sean out loud as he continued reading the report. Flash dresser, frequented casinos, gambled only what he could afford, drank scotch but never seemed to lose control. "Flash bastard," snapped Fallon. Married an older woman, moved out of London and settled in the leafy suburb of Ruislip, where his first wife died in a car crash leaving him her entire estate. "Interesting," he mused. After her death he maintained an orderly lifestyle up until he met and married Grace "Mister squeaky clean, somehow I don't think so," muttered Sean.

Sean Fallon arranged to meet an old friend Bernie Abrahams, a known face amongst London's criminal underworld for the last thirty years. If anyone could shed any light on Eric Sullivan, then Bernie was your man.

Sean met Bernie in a pub in Stoke Newington where they greeted each other as long lost pals. Appearances can be deceptive, *Bernie had run a string of girls in the fifties and hadn't taken kindly to a young copper beating up one of his flock. When a week later whilst checking doorways as he patrolled his beat the young Sean was accosted by two heavies and bundled into a van. On the ride over Sean had been relieved of his handcuffs and was wearing them with his hands behind his back. Ten minutes later he was sitting across from a short but stocky muscular man of Jewish appearance, dressed in a white shirt with the sleeves rolled up, who looked at Sean and asked in a chilling way, "How are you going to recompense me?"*

*"Recompense you, for what?" snapped Sean, still green behind the ears, he thought his uniform was a suit of armour. When Bernie Abrahams reached into his waistcoat pocket and whipped out a pearl handled cut throat razor and slammed it onto the table between them, the young constable lost his swagger.*

*"Yo..you... wouldn't!"*

*"That's not for you to say. I decide what happens next. It has come to my attention that one of my girls, Cynthia was badly beaten up by a young copper."*

*"It wasn't me!"*

*"Shut it," snapped Abrahams as he flicked open the blade. "Don't insult my intelligence, police constable Sean Fallon. I know everything about you, I know where you live, I also know where your parents live. But we're not here to talk about your life story we're here for my recompense. You owe me for loss of earnings, poor Cynthia couldn't work for two weeks. You owe me two hundred nicker."*

*"How am I going to get my hands on that sort of money?"*

*"You 'ave a choice, you feed me information as and when, and pay off what you owe by instalments. Maybe if you're smart you'll make a little on the side."*

*"The other choice?"*

*"I kill you right now."*

*Sean stared at the open razor and felt his bladder loosen, any thoughts of toughing it out evaporated as he pissed his pants. "Okay, I'll do what you ask."*

*"That was quick, maybe too quick. For your sake don't misjudge me. Grass me up, you'll be dead within a week and so will your parents."*

*Abrahams snapped shut the razor and returned it to his waistcoat pocket, whilst retrieving the key to the handcuff, which he threw onto the table. He stood up put on his jacket, then overcoat and with his cohorts left Sean sitting by himself. At the door he turned around, "I'll be in touch, I expect a score a week from today."*

*Sean sat there frozen to the spot until he heard the van move off. Then he stood up and found himself shaking uncontrollably. Once he had his nerves under control he turned his back to the chair and with his handcuffed hands fumbled for the key. Once free he picked up his helmet which had been thrown on the floor when he arrived. Thankful to be alive Sean weighed up his options, he guessed he'd been off his beat for a little under an hour. He was surprised to find he was only minutes away from where he'd been taken. Acting as if nothing had happened, he returned to the police box near his beat, and weighed up his options. If he phoned in, it would be all round the station in no time, so Sean decided to sleep on it until he found out what he was up against.*

*Over the course of a couple of days he asked around about his abductor. By process of elimination he discovered he'd been threatened by a notorious night club owner, Bernie Abrahams, an associate of Jack Comer and Billy Hill. The word on the street was that Abrahams had grown up a founder member of a notorious razor gang during the war. Bernie Abrahams was in some quarters regarded as untouchable.*

*Over the course of that week Sean extracted a tax off the public, namely pimps, prostitutes and petty criminals. By the time of his second meeting Sean was well aware who he was dealing with.*

*"There's a score Mr Abrahams. I'm sorry about the inconvenience I might have caused you."*

*"That'll do for starters, you're a smart young man Sean. I could really use a man of your talents."*

*"Can I be so bold as to say, you didn't need to put the frighteners on me, I'd have come on board willingly. I've ambition*

*Mr Abrahams, I mean to progress in the Met. I believe I will become very valuable to you in the future."*

*"Sean, I'm glad you see it my way. If you're loyal to me, there might come a time when I could be of service to you."*

*An arrangement between them saw Sean watching Abrahams back on many occasions, which in turn were reciprocated with the odd bundles of cash. But it was one particular service which really cemented their partnership.*

*Little did Sean know that two years later Bernie Abrahams would be of service to him? "You're a silly boy Sean, you need to control that temper of yours. You were seen leaving a certain house in Whitechapel. Who do you think you are Jack the fucking Ripper?"*

*"Fuck! Who?"*

*"It's taken care off, but there's something you can do for me." So began a relationship with Bernie Abrahams that grew over the years until Abrahams decided to retire some three years ago.*

"It's been a while Bernie, retirement suits you; you're looking good," said Sean.

"Enough of the flattery, just get me a double Glenfiddich while you're at it," stated Bernie Abrahams. Life had been kind to Bernie, at sixty nine he still had his hair, albeit his raven locks had more than a touch of silver.

Over the years Sean Fallon and Bernie Abrahams had formed a mutual respect for each other. Not friends in the true sense, but sharing a bond that had lasted more than a quarter of a century. Sean brought the drinks over to the table and sat down. "Looks like I might be joining you in the retirement stakes early next year."

"Retiring at fifty, I must have been in the wrong game!" laughed Bernie

"They do say crime doesn't pay," laughed Sean as they chinked glasses.

"Right you ain't arranged to meet me for my scintillating wit. What do you want?"

"A little information. Eric Sullivan, antique shop in Ruislip. Approximately thirty nine, forty. Lived in the East End, until the early sixties, married a Gloria Benjamin. Then dropped out of the London scene. Married a second time to a woman called Grace. Never had a criminal record, but no one is that squeaky clean."

"I knew Gloria, back in the day. She was a sight to behold. I remember a time during…" Bernie stopped himself, no point in thinking about what could have been. "Eric Sullivan… How important is he to you?"

"Just some loose ends…" said Sean.

"Not that important then. My advice, and you would do well to listen. You've had a good run, you're leaving the force clean, don't fuck it up; leave things lie," he said casually.

"Now you've tweaked my curiosity."

"Forget about Sullivan, he's nothing to you. You've more important things to consider, you're months away from retirement!"

When asked what he meant by it Abrahams said, "Hopefully you didn't have your sticky fingers into a large payroll robbery at the offices of a certain daily newspaper last year?"

"I don't know what you're talking about?"

"Well if you did, I'd be making certain nothing traces back to you."

Sean kept his face straight, he hadn't been involved with that particular investigation, not directly anyhow, but he'd been advised to lose certain key evidence in the case. Routine really, money for nothing.

Yet another indicator, this time from the criminal fraternity. The storm clouds were indeed gathering. Taking Bernie's advice Sean knew the best use of his time left, would be served making sure nothing came back to haunt him. Covering his tracks should be simple enough, he'd always been careful.

With an eye to his future Sean had put the word out to a world renowned security company that he might be on the verge of retirement and he would be interested in a position they'd outlined. Leaving the Force without a blemish would almost guarantee him that position.

Sean had become wealthy over the last few years, he'd held off selling the Victorian house in Wembley after paying Grace off in the divorce settlement. He'd since married a forty year old divorcee having met her at a friend's party at a country retreat, seven years ago, she fit his profile. Almost at once she took a dislike to the Victorian Terrace and eventually after a couple of years persuaded Sean to put it on the market. He made a killing on the house in Wembley and bought a small estate in the Surrey countryside, which befit a Metropolitan Police officer of his station and rank. Over the years with insider knowledge he'd made a few shrewd investments, all legal. Jackie, his new wife also owned a villa in Spain, as part of her divorce settlement.

Sean reflected on the warning Bernie Abrahams had given him about an investigation into corruption in the force. It was good that Abrahams had marked his card, but what puzzled Sean was the old Jew was too quick to dismiss any talk about Sullivan, which posed the question. Why?

# Chapter 58

"Where do you want to go?" asked Joe, the moment Donna closed the door of the Zodiac.

"Anywhere, but not around here," she replied. "If it's just a bunk up, say so. Then we can get on with it and I can go home and wash my hair."

Joe's face glazed with shock.

"You should see your face!" laughed Donna, "It's a picture. I was only joking, I'd need at least six gin and tonics!"

Joe laughed nervously, he couldn't make her out. Fifteen minutes later they pulled into a quiet pub on the outskirts of Harefield. On entering they notice two or three locals sitting at the bar while the rest of the pub was almost empty. Donna found a secluded corner while Joe ordered their drinks. He looked pleased with himself as he approached their table.

"Got myself a pint of lager, instead of my usual." He plonked his pint down on the table and handed Donna her gin and tonic. "Only five more to go!" he joked nervously.

"You wish!" Donna smiled back at him. "What's the big deal about changing your drink?" It wasn't the best line she could have used but it might make him open up.

"Glad you asked, something happened, something I didn't really want to talk about, but I feel I have to let it out to someone," cried Joe.

"Go on, I'm a good listener."

"Maybe this isn't a good idea," he hesitated.

"You don't have to say anything, but if you feel like telling me, it will remain confidential. I'll keep it to myself. I won't even tell Becky."

Joe remained silent for a few moments, unsure of what to say, then suddenly the words began to flow. "What the fuck! I had a few words with Eric at lunchtime over Grace. Well, to be honest, I told him how much I still loved her and that I'd do anything in my power to win her back!"

"Not the smartest idea!" exclaimed Donna.

"I just lost it. Eric to his credit, did his best to explain how they got together, how if I hadn't have cut Grace out of my life we might not be having this conversation now. I thought I could handle it, but seeing Grace with him yesterday hurt like fuck. He was a friend, if only she'd moved away it wouldn't have hurt so much. We were getting nowhere, so I upped and left."

"Probably for the best," said Donna.

"I sat in my car and tried sorting the pluses from the minus. It was then I realised everyone had moved on but me. Hence my change from light and bitter to lager." Joe took a sip, "Tastes like shit!" he exclaimed and smiled weakly.

Donna let out a faint giggle.

"It wasn't just that, my car, my clothes, my out dated address book, together they screamed at me, you've lost your identity! On the plus side, I met my daughter, I'd been offered a job from Bob, which I'm taking by the way. I've my freedom, which believe me shouldn't be taken for granted along with the slight possibility of some compensation, although I won't hold my breath. I've a chance to rebuild my life."

"Then take it," said Donna imploringly.

"You'd think so, wouldn't you? But all that meant nothing to me without Grace. I contemplated ending it all."

"For fuck-sake, listen to yourself. You've got what most people in your position haven't. Get over yourself! If you can't have Grace, so what! Live your life, if not for you, live it for your daughter, your friends that love you. Live it for Grace! How do you think she'd feel if you killed yourself?"

Joe sat there in stunned silence. He'd needed someone to straighten him out, but he hadn't expected it to be so brutally honest.

"Stop playing dumb, now get up to that bar and get me another drink. Make it a double!"

It was as if he was seeing the real Donna for the first time. In mid-afternoon he'd so nearly ended it. He got up and took the glasses back to the bar and then as if on automatic pilot he turned to look at Donna and said, "A double! That counts as three in my book."

Donna smiled, "Don't worry I always stop at five on a Sunday."

When Joe brought their drinks to the table he looked straight at Donna and said, "Thank you."

"For what?"

"I think you know. Anyway enough about me, tell me all there is to know about the little dynamo called Donna?"

"She's cute, she's cuddly, a live wire at parties and she's compassionate. What else is there to tell?"

"I'd suggest there's a whole lot more than you're telling."

"Okay. Despite what you might have heard, I'm not easy; yes I've been around, but it's been of my choosing, not there's; mine. Blokes love sex, it's a given, right!"

Shocked by her mini outburst he could only say, "Yeah."

"Well us girls like it just as much as you blokes, the only difference is the way we distribute it."

"Whoa! Has all this happened whilst I've been away?" asked Joe.

"No, we've always been that way, but I guess to a certain extent the advent of the pill has set us free."

"Has there been anyone special in your life?" asked Joe.

"You mean the bloke I just broke up with?"

"You don't have to tell me."

"I lived with Chris for three years on and off. He wasn't the love of my life but it was better than living with my parents, until he fucked me about once too often."

"So he wasn't the big deal?"

"Nah, on the bedroom Richter scale he barely made a rumble."

Joe found himself laughing, a surprise in itself.

Donna continued, "The only one that ever came close to breaking my heart was when I was fifteen, in my first job. He was eighteen, absolutely gorgeous, he was a hod carrier on a building site opposite where I worked. It was love at first sight, at least that's what I thought. We went to the pictures once or twice a week, the pub on occasion, but mostly it was the flicks, didn't matter what was showing, as long as it was dark and warm. Then one day he met me from work, told me I was the greatest thing since sliced bread and that I was too good for him. I never saw him again after that."

"How long did it take you to get over him" asked Joe?

"I never did, but it didn't stop me from living my life," sighed Donna. "Now tell me about life in prison."

"What! You never seem to stop surprising me," laughed Joe. "Apart from explaining how I got my scar, no one had asked about my time inside. Probably because they thought it was a touchy subject, but you just steam on in there."

"If it's touchy forget I asked."

"No, it's refreshing, I can't stand it when people feel like they're treading on egg shells.

"Good, then get on with it," she said, as she gave him a cheeky grin.

"I can't speak for others, but boredom was the worst. Same routine day after day. My escape was though books. I must have read every book in the prison library. My favourite was 'The Count of Monte Cristo,' by Alexander Dumas."

"I've heard of it, they made a film of it didn't they?"

"They made several over the years, like they've done with 'The Three Musketeers' but nothing compares you for reading the book."

"What's it about?" asked Donna.

"You don't have to humour me," said Joe.

"I'm not! I'm actually interested."

"Okay then. It's about a French sailor whose accused of a crime he didn't commit. He gets sent to a horrific prison called the Chateau D'if which is located on an island. He's there for years and years until he escapes by taking the place of a dead man. The man had told him before he died of a treasure buried on an unhabituated island called Monte Cristo. When the man died they wrapped him in sacks, stitching him up ready for burial at sea."

Joe took a sip of his lager, "it's a bit gassy," he remarks.

"Go on with your story."

"Are you really that interested?"

"Get on with it."

"The corpse was left in his cell awaiting men to carry him out before throwing him into the sea. Working quickly the sailor exchanges places with the dead man, sows himself into the sacking and awaits his fate. He's dumped into the sea and escapes his watery tomb and eventually over a course of months manages to sail to this island Monte Cristo."

"So I would imagine you saw parallels between you and this sailor."

"Sort of. But I must be boring you. Let me get you another gin and tonic."

"Okay, but make it another double," she said it with a sparkle in her eye.

"That'll be five," he said. "I guess we'll be going home after that."

"That depends on you finishing your story."

Joe ordered their drinks and glanced at the clock behind the bar, it was twenty to ten, and he remembered last orders was at ten thirty.

"You don't really want to know how the story ends," said Joe. "It's a bit long and drawn out."

"I'll be the judge of that!" stated Donna.

Joe had switched lager for light and bitter. Taking a sip he declared, "Ah that's better."

"Carry on with the story," said Donna eagerly.

"The short version, the sailor finds the treasure, becomes very rich, buys the island and becomes the Count of Monte Cristo. Now unrecognisable he returns to his home town to find his fiancée had married one of the men that had conspired to have him condemned to the Chateau D'if. Another was a banker that had profited from his misfortune, whilst the other was the magistrate who passed the harshest sentence on him. The Count decides to extract his revenge on all three of them."

"And he lives happily ever after," said Donna.

"Well, not quite. Do you want another," he asked.

"Nah, I've got to get up for work in the morning," replied Donna, as she gauged the disappointment in his eyes.

Donna sat quietly in the car as Joe drove out of the car park and turned onto the narrow country road. She was facing a dilemma, she knew she wanted him; but would it be too fast, too soon. The look in his eyes could just be wishful thinking. She had no doubt that he liked her; that he enjoyed her company, but he'd made it quite clear the only woman he really wanted was Grace. She was torn between doing the right thing, but where would that get her. He might ask her out again, then again he might not. She hadn't felt this way about a man since God knows when. Her head was in torment as the Zodiac cruised along the dark country road. As they climbed a hill the lights from the nearest town twinkled as they drew nearer. It was now or never, thought Donna.

"Can you pull over, I'm feeling a little sick," not her best line. "It might have been one gin to many."

Joe saw a layby just ahead and pulled the car into it. He stopped the car, "Do you want to get out?"

"No, I want you!" she said as she pushed her face up close to his, her lips inviting him to kiss her.

The smell of her perfume mingled with a feeling of animal lust tore through him as his lips pressed against hers. He was lost in her arms and he felt himself surrendering to her. Then as quickly as it started he pulled away. "I can't do this, it wouldn't be right. At this very moment I want you, I want you bad, but my heart belongs to Grace, it always will belong to her."

"I'll take my chances," cried Donna as she pressed her mouth against his, resistance was futile.

# Chapter 59

The moment Bob walked through the front door after a tiring day at work his kids rushed to greet him. Bob smiled, picked the youngest one up and tousled his older ones hair as he entered the hallway, "Give me a second to get my coat off at least," he said as the kids unravelled from him and returned to the television in the front room. He took his work boots off and walked into the kitchen.

"Don't get excited, guess who Donna was out with last night?" cried Becky the moment Bob stepped into the kitchen.

"James Bond!"

"Stop it, you know very well who I'm talking about!"

"That was on the cards, but sooner than I'd have expected," said Bob.

"Its early days, but who knows."

"Don't get ahead of yourself, Becks. Donna ain't bad looking but she ain't really Joe's sort."

"How do you know what Joe's sort is? Ten years in prison can change people's perception of others"

"So Donna's been blabbing her mouth off to you, go on then, give me the gory details!"

"That's just it, there were no gory details, as you so eloquently put it. It's what she didn't say. I tell you Bob, that girl's fallen for him."

"It won't last, she's the opposite of Grace. For a start, Donna's blonde, blue eyed and wild, with a capital W."

"Wild! I'd say that's a bit extreme, she's calmed down a hell of a lot over the last few years."

"Okay I'll give you that. What I was trying to say was she's the complete opposite. But if it takes his mind off Grace that won't be a bad thing."

"Yeah I can see your point, but you're not getting mine. Donna's my friend and I don't want to see her get hurt!" exclaimed Becky.

"I get it, but it's none of our business. Donna's a big girl now, she knows the score. We've just got to let nature take its course."

"God! Donna, you look rough!" exclaimed Sarah when Donna rolled in to work on that Monday morning.

"So would you be, if you'd got to bed at two this morning!"

At lunch four hours later Donna reflected on the night before. She'd taken a gamble, she liked Joe; a lot. She'd acted on instinct and put him in an impossible position. Now after a few hours of a very disturbed sleep she hoped she hadn't frightened him off.

*He'd responded to her tongue down his throat and didn't seem to mind as her hand felt the bulge in his jeans. Expertly she loosened his belt and slowly she undid the zip on his fly. Her hand groped around until she managed to get his cock free. Resisted the temptation of going down on him, she concentrated her efforts at freeing him from his jeans. His hand began fondling her breast making her nibbles hard as his mouth devoured their erectness. She felt his right hand as it found its way onto her knee and she shuddered in anticipation as it slid upwards before stopping for one nervy moment.*

*Suddenly Donna understood. "They're tights, no one wears stocking anymore," she uttered. She arched her back and allowed him free access to the waistband of her tights. In a brief struggle she was free. Joe manoeuvred himself between her legs and she gasped as the tip of his cock began to enter her. She kissed him passionately as he buried himself deep inside. She held him tightly knowing his excitement couldn't last before she felt the tell-tale signs that he was about to cum. He thrust faster and faster and Donna gasped as she felt herself coming. Joe began to moan pleasurably as the pent up release of pure joy reached him. In the throes of their joint ecstasy Donna snatched a glimpse at Joe as a slither of moonlight illuminated his face. A silver river of tears trickled across his cheek. In that moment she fell in love. They lay in each other's arms, neither uttering a word. Each lost in their own private thoughts.*

*Making love had freed the mind and guarded conversation was lost as both of them shared their inner thoughts. Some sad, some hopeful, some frightening. They spoke of their pasts, their childhoods and their futures. Donna dropped the façade of always being a fun loving girl without a care in the world. She told him she'd been hurt many times on her journey through life searching for the one thing that had eluded her, she wanted what others had, someone that truly, unconditionally loved her for who she was. Joe hugged her close and kissed her softly, but inevitably he brought up Grace and how life had cheated them both. Donna snuggled up to Joe, safe in his arms, but afraid to let go. They were alone in the darkness with just a brief glimpse of moonlight as the clouds drifted by. She didn't want the night to end, but eventually Joe broke from their embrace, "It's late, we'd better make a start for home."*

*As they sat in his car outside her mum's house, Joe kissed her and said, "I'll give you a call."*

Donna had given Joe her works number, just in case he couldn't reach her at home. Dumb move, she thought, 'I was too eager, he'll never ring.' Despite her misgivings she froze every time the phone in the salon rang. Her heart leapt, then plunged to the depths as one appointment booking after another increased her worry that she'd blown it.

After an evening staring at the family phone, willing it to ring, Donna cried herself to sleep. By the morning she was red eyed and swollen, she had a lot of repair work to do before she could go to work. A long shower, which did its best to revive her, followed by an hour at the mirror. Satisfied she looked presentable she set off to work.

"That's more like it," said Sarah, "You look a million dollars."

"Thanks Sarah, I might look it, but I sure don't feel it."

Sarah sensing it was man trouble tried giving her advice. "Donna, no bloke's worth it. Just get yourself back out there!"

"Yeah, you're probably right, but this bloke was special."

"Take it from me, they're all the same!"

Donna bit her tongue, she wanted to say Joe's different, he's not like that! But chose not to. She looked back over the past few days and wondered how her world had been turned on its head so fast. The week-end had started slow, then one phone call to Becky and it started to take-off. She'd known half way though that Saturday evening that she really liked Joe. There was an inner anger which she could sense, an edge of danger, a wildness in him which acted like an aphrodisiac to Donna. She'd seen a glimpse of the gentler, softer side when she driven him home. She'd hoped he'd phone, not expecting it to be so soon. She thought she'd struck a chord with him on Sunday night, but she'd let her heart rule her head. Sadly she glanced at the salon phone, as it began to ring.

"Sarah's Hair Studio."

# Chapter 60

"This job you and Bob have lined up for Joe, do you think he'll stick it," asked Georgia. "Is it maybe too soon?"

"No, I don't think so. I've known Joe since he was nine, not bosom pals like him and Bob, but I feel I know him as much," stated Jim. "Once he gets Grace out of his system, he'll realise where his bread is buttered."

"Yes, but how long is that going to take. I don't want you wasting your money on a lost cause."

"I ain't," snapped Jim. "Once he realises that he can't do anything without money he'll buckle down to it. Besides, if he wants any chance with Grace, he needs to get his act together."

"Like I keep telling you, that ship has sailed. Grace loves Eric and that's all there is too it," snapped Georgia."

"How can you be so sure? You don't seem convinced to me," cried Jim.

"I'm convinced alright! You forget, I spent a time or two in Joe's company. He's head strong, quick tempered and liable to do something daft. Even after ten years in prison, he's still a boy. I can see it in his eyes. He's going to fuck up," cried Georgia.

"I thought you'd quit swearing."

"I have, it just slipped out."

"He ain't a boy," said Jim irritably. "That's Joe's he's always been that way."

"Maybe so, just look at Grace and Eric. Smart, successful, good looking; the ideal couple, and Billie idolises Eric."

"You always said we were the ideal couple, but your fucking career put pay to that!" snapped Jim.

"What's that supposed to mean?" Georgia snapped back.

"You know very well. You say you love me, yet you won't marry me, you say we'll have kids, but nothing happens."

"I meant it Jim! But it wasn't the right time."

"How many times have you said, it's not the right time. I'm sick of your excuses. Fuck it Georgia I've about had enough!"

Georgia looked shocked, "You can't mean it. You want to break up! You want us to go separate ways? Well you picked a fine time to tell me, now I'm pregnant!" she cried.

Georgia's words stopped Jim in his tracks. "You what!"

"I'm pregnant, we're having a baby!"

'The irritability, the mood swings, it all made sense now,' thought Jim. He stared at Georgia, mere words couldn't express how he felt. His eyes misted over and a few tears began to form, "Come here," he said, "I love you Georgia Chandler!"

"And I love you, you bully!" she cried as she fell into his arms. They kissed tenderly before Georgia let out a final plea, "It'd better not fucking hurt!"

Joe was the topic of conversation in another household that evening, "I talked to Donna again today. She said Joe hadn't phoned. He told her he'd call, but he hasn't."

"Give him a chance Becks, it's only been a couple of days," replied Bob.

"Yeah I know, but Donna's broken up about it. She's really got it bad, I've never seen her like this. I just knew this would happen."

"So what do you want me to do about it?"

"Talk to him, ask him what his game is!"

"The man's not been out of prison a week, I can't ask him that." He looked at the disapproval on Becky's face, "If he ain't called by Friday I'll have a word in his shell like."

Becky knew she could twist Bob around her little finger; that was one of the reasons why she loved him so much. She felt he deserved an explanation, "Look, I ain't supposed to say anything, and if you breathe a word about what I'm going to tell you, I'll cut you off until Christmas."

"You wouldn't!"

"Try me!" The look meant everything. "When Donna started work at the hair salon she was fifteen, naïve, if you could believe and impressionable. She'd only been working at the salon for a couple of weeks when she met a boy who worked on the building site, that's that block of flats opposite her work. They began dating and she fell in love as teenagers do. Then after going out for three or four months he chucks her. That wouldn't be a big deal but a week or two later she finds out she's pregnant. She tried contacting the boy but he'd left the site and the last anyone heard he'd joined the Merchant Navy. It was a little over three months later that Donna miscarried, it was a horrendous time for her as she'd kept the baby a secret from her family. I was the only one there for her, I did what I could but what did I know I was only sixteen myself, but eventually after a few months she bounced back."

"And you've been keeping an eye on her ever since," said Bob.

Donna was numb by the time she arrived home. She'd convinced herself that if Joe was going to call he'd probably leave it until nearer the week-end. But it still didn't stop her heart from leaping every time the salon's phone rang.

"How was your day luv," asked her mum.

"The usual, phone didn't stop ringing and my legs are aching."

"Oh, that reminds me, some bloke rang; he said he'll call you tonight."

"What time!" shrieked Donna?

"He didn't say. Now what do you fancy for dinner, liver and bacon, or fish pie."

"Not really hungry, I'll get something out of the fridge later. Are you sure he didn't give a time."

"You've got it bad, who is he; Prince Charles?"

Donna ignored her, and started her vigil.

It was around seven thirty when the phone rang, Donna snatched it up immediately and cursed herself for being so eager.

"Hello."

"It's Joe, I wondered, can we talk."

"You mean now, right now."

"No, I mean face to face talking. I could pick you up in fifteen minutes if that's okay?"

"Okay, see you then."

Donna raced into her bedroom, then the bathroom, back to the bedroom, then a quick look at herself in the mirror, all before Joe's car pulled up.

Self-doubt crept in as she walked towards the Zodiac, 'Is this the soft brush off.' She climbed in beside him and she could feel her heart racing, it was fit to burst. Joe gave her a smile and without a word pulled into the traffic.

"How have you been?" asked Donna.

"Yeah, okay," he replied.

Within a few hundred yards he turned left and entered a side road, stopped the car and switched off the ignition. He turned to face her in the dim light as dusk crept upon them.

"Sunday night was magical, I didn't want the evening to end," said Joe.

"Me too," replied Donna, her heart lifting.

"I'm confused, you made me see there is a future. When I'm with you, the pain of not being with Grace disappears. It's not fair to use you that way."

Donna could feel the gentle let down coming, but she wasn't giving in so easily. She told herself she wouldn't beg him; that was beneath her dignity. "Sunday night you wanted to talk, and I was willing to listen. It surprised me how well we got on. It felt like a real date, albeit there was three of us on that date, but I'd like to think I got through to you somehow."

"You did," replied Joe.

"What happened later, I instigated it. It wasn't your fault it was all mine. So don't feel guilty on my account."

"I don't feel guilty in the slightest. I want you, not just because you take the pain away, I want you, because you're funny, you're kind and you're loving. You stimulate me in more ways than you could imagine."

"So what's wrong?"

"It isn't right to use you, while wanting another woman. A woman that is so far out of my reach, that it hurts," cried Joe.

"No its not!" said Donna, "But I'm willing to take the chance. I knew I wanted you last Saturday night, I didn't know how much, until Sunday. If I can soothe that pain, perhaps in time it might disappear altogether."

What then?"

"I'm willing to cross that bridge when I come to it," stated Donna. "One stipulation, you don't use me as a weapon to win her back."

# Chapter 61

Joe arrived early Saturday morning at the riding stables, feeling less nervous and more relaxed than he did the previous week. His heart lurched as he spotted Grace's car as it pulled onto the dusty driveway and came to a halt no more than twenty feet from where he was standing. Grace had barely turned off the ignition before Billie clambered out of the car and came running towards him.

"You came! You came! I wasn't sure you'd come," she cried as she flung her arms around him.

Joe's heart filled up, "I said I would, I've a lot of catching up to do." With his arms engulfing Billie he watched as Grace stepped out of the BMW 320 and walked gracefully towards him; a smile on her lips.

"I'm so pleased you could make it Joe. Billie would have been disappointed if you hadn't showed," she said.

"Watch me and Abbie on the jumps Dad!" interrupted Billie excitedly. "I'm off to the tack room, see you in a few minutes."

Joe couldn't take his eyes off Billie in her riding hat and jodhpurs as she walked across the dusty courtyard. "Every bit the lady, just like her mother."

Grace gave Joe an old fashioned look and smiled, "Her mother never had riding lessons at eight years old."

Briefly Joe imagined they were a family, before reality took a bite out of his dreams.

"How's it been?"

"I'm getting there," he found himself saying. It all felt so strange, so false

"I understand you're starting a job on Monday?"

"Yeah, it looks like it. Although it feels like a handout to me," he replied.

"From what I've been told, it won't feel like it! Bob's a hard taskmaster" said Grace. "Oh look, here she comes!"

"She...She isn't going to do those jumps," he cried in a concerned voice.

"No, not yet, she's only on the baby jumps at the moment, although she'll be on them soon enough." said Grace as she pointed to the far side of the arena. "Don't look so concerned, Billie is a natural."

Joe was finding it a struggle, the small talk was excruciatingly difficult, he found himself wanting to take Grace in his arms and tell her how much he still loved her.

At the end of Billie's lesson she rode over to her mum and Joe. "I wasn't as good today as I usually am, but if you come next week, I'll be better."

"I'll do my best," he found himself saying.

As Billie led Abbie to the stables Grace turned towards Joe and couldn't help noticing the pain on his face. "I'm sorry Joe, I know it's hard. It's downright cruel the way life has treated you, but she's your daughter, so make her proud."

"Nothing would make me happier, except maybe…" He didn't finish, but then he didn't need too.

*****

"How was it?" said Donna nervously.

Joe had promised Donna he'd be straight with her, and he meant it, but he could see, almost feel the tension in her. "It was good, Billie threw herself into my arms, and called me Dad. God, it tore at my heartstrings. I watched her riding around this arena: she worried me at first, but I soon realised she's a very competent rider."

"What I meant was, how was it with Grace?"

"I know what you meant," he said softly. "She was polite, very pleasant, very Grace. I'd be lying if I said I didn't feel something. What hit me the most, despite how friendly everyone was, I felt like I didn't belong. I needed your support!"

"Really," cried Donna.

"Yes really. I thought when I was released from prison, everything would fall into place. I'd see Grace, the old feelings would come flooding back and it would be goodbye Eric. But I was wrong."

"It's never as simple as you imagine," said Donna.

"Everyone has become so civilised while I've been away. Eric had spoken to me man to man, and despite the things I said, he'd remained polite. Then today with Grace, she was friendly, but I felt she was keeping me at a distance."

"So you're coming to terms with it?" suggested Donna.

"I didn't say that!" he exclaimed. "But I can't compete. She says she loves Eric, I can't change that! We have a daughter together, that's the only bond between us. Life is so uncertain, and moping over something I can't change is pointless. Especially when I've someone like you waiting for me. If I'm not careful and don't treat you right I might even lose you."

"Not if you treat me right," purred Donna. "Let's forget about going for a drink, I've a much better idea."

\*\*\*\*\*

Bob watched as Joe's Zodiac pulled into the George car park and hoped there wasn't going to be a repeat of the previous Sunday. He smiled to himself as Joe walked towards him looking far more relaxed than he should have been. 'Amazing how pussy changes some people,' he laughingly thought. "How goes it Joe."

"Yeah, mustn't grumble."

"Definably pussy," muttered Bob as he stepped up to the bar.

"What's that?"

"Nothing," replied Bob, "Just need you fit for tomorrow."

Joe laughed as he ordered their drinks. Bob grabbed a seat and contemplated the change in his friend.

"Is Jim coming," asked Joe as he brought the drinks over and handed Bob his pint.

"Well I thought he wasn't, but he phoned and said he'd be along."

"And Eric?"

"I can't answer that, Eric breezes in when he feels like it. But judging the way you left it last week, I'd say he's probably giving it a miss."

"Yeah, sorry about that."

"Hopefully you've got it out of your system," said Bob.

"The anger maybe, but how I feel towards Grace, that won't change. Well not for the foreseeable future."

Bob took a swig of his beer, "I take it you and Donna are seeing each other?"

"Yeah, you could say that. Donna's nice," Joe didn't elaborate, much to Bob's annoyance.

Bob finished his pint, "Same again," and walked over to the bar, just as Jim walked through the doors. "What you having?"

"I'll get these, go sit down," it was the way Jim said it that made Bob retreat to their table.

"Jim's getting them in. Something's up."

Two minutes later Jim brought a tray of drinks over, their usual, plus three double scotches. Bob eyed the scotch cautiously, "Looks like you got the taste last week," he joked.

"Something like that," said Jim as he handed out their respective drinks. He sat down picked up his glass of scotch and indicated to his friends to do the same. "I'm going to become a Dad!"

"What!" they cried in unison.

"Georgia's pregnant!"

"I don't believe it!" exclaimed Bob.

"I didn't either," replied Jim, "But it's really happening, Georgia kept it to herself until she was twelve weeks, didn't even tell me. I'm over the moon!"

"Congratulations!" cried Joe, as he held his glass up.

"Yeah, congrats! Really pleased for you both," said Bob. "Wait until I tell Becks."

"I know I ain't been around, but from what I've seen of Georgia, she didn't seem to be the type to have kids," asked Joe.

"Yeah she fooled me too," said Jim. "We talked about having kids but work and our careers seemed more important. Until now!"

"So what's happening with her work?"

"According to Georgia's she's got everything planned down to the smallest of details. She hasn't taken on any new cases since she suspected she was pregnant. Some of her current cases which possibly might over run she's handing over to partners."

"Wow, I could never think of Georgia as a mum," said Bob.

Jim noticed the slightly worried frown on Joe's face. "Georgia hasn't forgotten you Joe. In fact since she's off-loading her case files, she's been making enquiries about Sean Fallon. She figures that if he was capable of framing you, quite likely you aren't his first victim."

"That's good to know," said Joe. "She's done so much for me. I'd understand if she wanted to call it quits."

"No worries on that account," replied Jim.

"As long as Georgia's sure? I'd hate to think that bastard was getting away with what he did."

"As it's you, I'll let you into a little secret. Since the discovery of Terry's confession Georgia began a dossier on Fallon, tracing all the way back to when he joined the police force. It's become her pet project!"

"He must have been a copper for at least twenty odd years. A prick like him must have made more enemies than friends," stated Bob.

Joe grimaced, "That's an understatement, I'd guess."

"Chandler and Lowe have resources at their disposal, not unlimited I'll grant you, but if there's dirt to be found, Georgia will find it," added Jim.

"Tell Georgia from me that I'm grateful for all she's done over these few months. I might not appear grateful but I am. And don't forget to give her my congratulations."

"Right!" said Bob. "Get them in Joe, looks like we've things to celebrate!"

*****

Joe's first day on site went as smoothly as Bob had expected and he was pleased to see his protégée was a quick learner who wasn't afraid of hard work. By Wednesday Joe's first day release at college was a little daunting but he was picking up the basics.

He was seeing Donna three times a week and surprised himself how much he enjoyed her company, so much so that he phoned Grace and asked if she'd mind him bringing a friend the next time he visited Billie at the stables.

"Of course Joe, bring whomever you like, she'll be most welcome," replied Grace.

Her words although said in a friendly manner still cut him to the quick. "Yeah, see you Saturday."

Donna saw the hurt look on his face, "I don't have to go," she said.

Joe smiled.

"Of course you do."

"To be truthful, I'm a bit nervous."

"You nervous, I don't think so. Billie will love you, just be yourself."

"It's not Billie I'm nervous about!"

# Chapter 62

Georgia's pet project as Jim liked to call it was more than that, it had become her secret obsession. Since reading Terry's confession, she'd opened a file on Chief Inspector Sean Fallon. Inside her file was a copy of Terry's suicide note and his detailed confession. But with pressure from her workload and petitioning for Joe's release it had just gathered dust in a drawer in her office, while she concentrated on getting Joe out. Working tirelessly, meeting high up members of the judiciary, arguing her case with the Police Complaints Division she was eventually able to negotiate Joe's release.

It was on the way back from visiting Joe at Durham prison that time with Grace, she suddenly realised how much she'd been neglecting Jim. They'd had countless rows, snide remarks passed back and forth, her unwillingness to marry, the lack of children, the what the fuck are we working for, if we can't pass it on, what's the point, kind of thing. That she didn't want to give up her independence played on her mind, but seeing how upset Grace was on that long journey home, she realised how lucky her and Jim had been. They'd both worked hard and had reaped their reward. Jim was right, she was thirty four, if she didn't stop now; it could be too late.

When she missed her period, the ones that's appeared as regular as clockwork she knew she was pregnant. Not wanting to build up Jim's hopes she kept it a secret apart from her visits to her doctor and the examinations which confirmed she'd reached twelve weeks. Apart from the medical profession she did tell one other person, and he was sworn to secrecy, her father George. Mainly because as senior partner in Chandler and Lowe he would be able to ease the burden on his daughter without giving the game away.

"Georgia, do you know what you're asking of me! If your mother finds out I knew before her; well it just doesn't bare thinking about!"

"Well, don't tell her!" replied Georgia sharply!

Now that the cat was out of the bag, and her marriage saved, *an over exaggeration on Georgia's part,* she returned to the file on Fallon.

Reading through Terry's confession Georgia started a list.

Chief Inspector Sean Fallon.
Inspector John Armstrong.
Arthur Briggs.
Roy (cousin?)
Donald Fuller
Keith Porter

She'd chosen to leave Fallon and possibly Armstrong until a later date. Georgia asked Eric to reach out to his contacts, hopefully someone knew the whereabouts of Arthur Briggs and his alleged cousin Roy. Eric's contacts gave varying sighting, Arthur Briggs was allegedly in Liverpool, Glasgow or Edinburgh depending on the various reports that Eric received, but they all agreed on one thing, within a week of Terry's suicide Arthur Briggs disappeared. Rumours were he'd been killed by the underworld for being a grass, others said he'd fled the country whilst another said he was living in a squat in Whitechapel. None of these checked out

Georgia knew Arthur Briggs was the key, but speculation about his fate wasn't helpful. The mystery man Roy, was just that a mystery. Firstly, extensive inquires showed Briggs didn't have a cousin called Roy. Speculation remained whether Roy or whatever his name was had either moved away, died or was in hiding.

Georgia personally visited Keith Porter and Donald Fuller in Parkhurst on the Isle of Wight. In separate interviews both told the same story, they'd heard Briggs mention his cousin Roy, but neither man had met him. It was plain to Georgia that Briggs had been spinning a line to both of them, a dangerous game, one that Briggs wouldn't have considered if Fallon hadn't been pulling his chain.

Parkhurst had been a dead end, but at least it focussed Georgia's mind on the two most likely culprits. She requested the file of the case against Joe but her request was turned down. After pressure from members of the judiciary she eventually managed to get hold of the file. Carefully she scrutinised the file and apart from no mention of Arthur Briggs's alleged cousin called Roy, she noted there was a gap of two weeks in the investigation, where nothing of any relevance to the case was noted down. Georgia suspected those two weeks were the key to unlocking her investigation.

Georgia needed to speak with Inspector John Armstrong, but unsurprisingly her interview was not forthcoming. Like a dog with a bone she wouldn't take no for an answer. She started making noises that were attracting senior members of the Metropolitan Police who eventually brought pressure on Armstrong to agree to meet her.

Fortunately for Inspector Armstrong he was under the cosh to close a particularly nasty robbery case, but he agreed reluctantly. "I can give her five minutes! My office on Thursday at 10 am sharp!"

Georgia took the tube, getting to London and parking was always a nightmare. Negotiating her way through morning commuters on a busy morning with the rain beating down incessantly didn't do much for her now hormonal disposition.

With the formalities over Georgia acting in her usual abrasive self, demanded to know why there was a gap of two weeks on the case, but was being refused in an equally aggressive manner.

"All I'm asking is an explanation of why there seems to be a gap in your investigation" What are you hiding inspector?" she snapped, causing heads to turn in the open plan office.

"Miss Chandler, against my better judgement I agreed to this interview on a case that's over ten years ago and you ungraciously accuse me of hiding things. You ask for transparency, which I've awarded you. I can't recall, but usually various officers are assign to work cases. Paperwork is scatter amongst the detectives concerned and sometimes things slip through the cracks. I will endeavour to find those two missing weeks and get back to you, but I can't promise anything."

Georgia's impression of Armstrong was of a fat juicy salmon caught on a line. It suggested he knew more than he was letting on.

"That's all I'm asking inspector, I'll expect an answer by this time next week." She could see he was clearly rattled, a few more shakes of the tree and who knows what might fall out.

Georgia's visit to John Armstrong did manage to shake the tree. A rotten apple by the name Sean Fallon. He'd just got off the phone with Jackie about their plans for the week-end, when John Armstrong stormed into his office.

"I've just had that fucking lawyer bitch from the Dempsey case poking her nose in where it's not wanted. She won't leave this case alone!"

"Let her take a look, she won't find anything!"

"Oh no Sean! She won't find anything, you're right, because you kept Arthur Briggs on ice for a couple of weeks. How do I explain my lack of action during that time?"

"You don't, you stall, say nothing!"

"I already did that. She's a fucking Rottweiler."

"You cobble together what paperwork you've got, blind her with science and tell her to fuck off! That usually works."

"Not with this tart it won't. I'm telling you Sean, if this gets out of hand and she really comes at me, I ain't putting my career on the line for you or anyone!"

Sean watched as Armstrong stormed out of his office, the man looked like he was on the verge of cracking. 'That posh tart that accompanied Grace to my house in Wembley, looking at me as if I was no more than the shit on her shoe. She was good then, fiery but with a brain. A brain that helped to screw me out of 40% of what the house was worth,' his brain was working overtime.

"Fuck, fuck, fuck!"

Sean knew she'd be a formidable foe; one that could potentially chew Inspector John Armstrong into tiny pieces, before spitting him out. He needed her stopped!

He'd thought to take Bernie Abrahams advice and let sleeping dogs lie, but this woman was forcing his hand. Not trusting the job to just anyone, he made a phone call.

# Chapter 63

They watched as Grace's BMW turned into the entrance to the stables. Billie came running over the moment Grace pulled up. Joe smiled and held out his arms for her to jump into. Donna laughed in amazement at the beaming smile on Joe's face, before catching the slightest of changes as Grace slid out of her car and walked towards them. Slinked across, was how Donna would like to have described it.

Grace gave Joe a curt smile then held out her hand to Donna, "I'm Grace, I'm guessing you're Donna."

"It's nice to meet you Grace, I've heard a lot about you." To Donna, eye contact told a lot about a person and what she saw in Grace's dark eyes told her plenty.

"Do you ride?" asked Grace.

"Not horses," she said, regretting the words almost before they left her mouth. "Only joking," she added nervously.

Joe gave her a quick stare, before turning his attention back to Billie. Grace smiled politely. "Billie's only ten but she's shown great ability at riding. We're hoping she'll be ready for next year's gymkhana."

"Gymkhana, what's that, I know nothing about horses."

"To be honest with you, until a couple of years ago I didn't know a gymkhana from a gymnasium. It's not really my sport, but Billie loves it," enthused Grace

"How did she get interested in it?" asked Donna.

"She just loved horses from an early age so it was only natural that Eric and I took her to our nearest riding stables to admire the horses. One thing led to another and before we knew it Billie was asking for a horse."

"You bought her a horse?"

"No way! That was out of the question, we compromised and started her on hourly lessons once a week. But once Billie got the bit between her teeth nothing stopped her. She asked the owner if there were jobs around the stables she could do, to earn her a further hour's lesson. So now Billie gets to clean the stables out once a week."

"Good on her," said Donna.

"She's coming out," cried Joe as all eyes looked towards Billie and her pony Abbie.

Joe's face beamed with pride as Billie put the pony through its paces. A rising trot, posting perfectly, before nudging the horse into a canter. As she approached the nursery jumps Donna shielded her eyes.

Grace reassured her that Billie was a far better rider than her years dictated. "I was just like you when she first got up on a horse; petrified."

The October sun beamed down basking the outdoor arena with the last of the summer's warmth, making Donna and Grace's first meeting a pleasant one. Joe and Donna chatted incessantly with Billie, about her horse riding skills, her school work and her favourite pop group. Billie in turn asked Donna what she did for a job.

"Oh, I'd love to do that," cried Billie excitedly.

"Believe me you wouldn't, being on your feet constantly for eight hours. No, you're better off getting on with your studies," replied Donna.

All too soon it was time to go, Joe and Donna, with a promise to return said their goodbyes. Grace watched as they walked back towards the car. She waved as they drove away. She hadn't known quite what to expect in Joe's new girlfriend. On first impressions Donna's lustrous blonde flowing locks would have appeared her crowning glory, but up close it was her sparkling sky blue eyes that shone, eluding a warmth and friendliness that almost mesmerised Grace. That she felt a tinge of jealousy, she dismissed in a heartbeat.

'It had been a standoff,' thought Donna, 'and I came off second best.' The expensive cut to that dark shaggy mop almost hiding those dark mysterious eyes told Donna she would always be the runner-up. She'd made up her mind to hate her, but Grace's disarming charm soon found Donna warming to her; to the woman that could destroy her happiness with just a warm smile.

"She was nice, so different to what I expected. Dark and mysterious, yet charming and warm, stormy and sunlit, all at the same time."

"Very poetic," said Joe as they turned left from the stables.

'Yeah, it was poetic wasn't it,' she thought to herself. They were on the way to meet up with Becky, Bob and the kids at 'The Case is Altered,' near where they lived. It had a pub garden so they were taking advantage of the late autumn sunshine. Seeing Grace had unnerved her slightly, with her dark hair, sophisticated Italian look, her chic clothes, her poise, she was everything Donna wasn't. 'Joe was right,' she thought, 'she is classy; classy but nice with it.'

They pulled up at 'The Case is Altered,' waved to Becky and the kids playing in the garden. "I guess Bob's getting them in. Why don't you join Becky while I get our drinks?"

"Just a lager and lime please Joe," said Donna as she turned and negotiated her way into the garden. Becky smiled as her friend walked over.

"How was it? Or more to the point how was Grace?" asked Becky.

Donna smiled as she sat down next to her, "I hate her! She's gorgeous, classy, sexy in an understated way, but the thing I hate most about her was; I liked her. She had a genuine warmth about her, even an understanding of how I was feeling and….."

"And......?"

"Maybe it's me, I sensed something in her eyes."

"What! For Christ sake tell me," snapped Becky, "The boys are coming." "I believe she still has deep feelings for Joe."

"That's probably your imagination. For fuck-sake, whatever you do, don't tell him," gasped Becky.

Later when Bob and Joe were pre-occupied with the kids, Becky turned to Donna and said, "Have you looked at yourself lately, you're gorgeous, with those wildly abandoned blonde locks, those amazing eyes, not to mention those generous lips. You'd drive any man crazy with desire, Joe's lucky to have you."

"Yeah, he is" replied a fully boosted Donna, "Yeah he is."

"But not classy!" added Becky.

"Yeah, not classy!" agreed Donna, as they broke into fits of laughter. "That's part of my charm."

*****

Grace had become quite famous for hosting the most lavish of dinner parties. But as dinner parties go, it just wasn't up there, intimate music, the finest of wines, but only four place settings, not the usual six or eight. Over the dulcet tones of Barry Manilow an apologetic Grace announced, "Marilyn and Dave couldn't make it, their daughter's got chicken pox. As for Becky and Bob, I thought it wise to leave them out, due to the circumstances."

"No need to apologise, as things stand we'd probably have done the same. And as always it's lovely Grace," responded Jim, as he admired the table display.

"Thank you Jim."

Grace busied herself with the starters while Eric poured the wine. The conversation was lively and varied, as you would expect with couples that had become use to each other's company. They laughed and joked through the meal, with Jim asking for seconds of the crème brulee. It was left for Georgia to bring up Joe.

"How was Joe, I take it he made it to Billie's riding lesson?"

"Yeah, he was there before us, he brought his new lady friend with him," said Grace, as they sat back from the sumptuous meal that she'd prepared.

"Lady friend; you mean the wildcat, Donna!"

"The very same," replied Grace. "Actually she was very nice, I liked her. In fact I was quite taken aback by her easy going friendliness. Billie took to her straight away which is a good thing, if she's going to be a permanent fixture."

"If," said Jim. "I only saw her one time, she wasn't bad but definitely not Joe's type."

"I'd never met her until this morning, and guess again Jim, she's definitely Joe's type. She's gorgeous, blonde with long flowing locks, a stunningly clear complexion and eyes that sparkle."

"Blondes are okay, but I've always preferred brunettes," said Jim.

"Careful," chided Georgia.

"Especially posh birds with pageboy hairstyles," he added quickly.

"Oh Jim, you'd have liked her, she was wearing figure hugging jeans over boots, a casual top and a suede jacket, looking every inch the cowgirl," stated Grace.

Jim made to speak…

"Don't answer that Jim, unless you want to be in the doghouse for the next week. I think you and I ought to leave these young ladies to the wine while we have ourselves a little smoke on the patio," said Eric as he produced two very fine cigars.

"Cheers Eric. I'm not really a smoker, but how can I resist; a Havana I presume?" replied Jim.

"Nothing but the best," grinned Eric.

Both men grabbed their glasses and walked out onto the patio.

Georgia waited until they'd disappeared outside, before she spoke to Grace. "I don't know whether you were pleased for Joe or not?"

"I don't know what you mean," replied Grace coyly.

"You know very well what I mean. It hasn't passed my attention that Joe's lost his boyish good looks and replaced them with a ruggedly handsome man. Damaged I grant you."

Grace tried to interrupt, but Georgia was having none of it.

"Be honest with me, did you find yourself feeling even the slightest bit jealous of that woman you haven't shut up about since dinner."

Grace felt her face flush, "Did I go on about her, I didn't realise."

"Yes you did, don't try to evade my question. I might be pregnant, but I'm still a woman," said Georgia with a malicious grin.

"Of course I was pleased for Joe, she just caught me off guard that's all," replied Grace.

Georgia gave her a knowing look.

"I might have felt something, but Joe and I are history. I love Eric, he's all that I want, all that I'd ever need. He's darkly handsome, he makes me laugh, I feel safe and secure in his presence. We have so many things in common, he loves Billie and we have a wonderful lifestyle together. Yeah I suppose I did feel a little jealous, but that was just fleeting."

Georgia eyed her sceptically, "So when the dust settles, you'd consider asking them to the next dinner party you host?"

"When the dust settles…." responded Grace.

# Chapter 64

As night started to draw in and the November rain poured down, a lone figure bundled up against the weather crept unnoticed into a cul-de-sac in Northwood. Wiping the rain from his eyes he checks out the large spaciously detached houses until he recognises the house he was looking for. He spots the double garage offset from the remaining house and smiled to himself. The rain, the darkness and the position of the garage make it look like a cake walk.

There were lights on in several windows, another good sign. Noise carries farther in the dead of night. Television, music, kettles boiling, all help to muffle any sounds from outside. Double glazing has been a boom for men in his profession. He opens the double door and carefully slides it upwards without causing any noise. Once inside he closes it just as carefully.

With a small torch he explores the interior of the garage, spotting the shiny Porsche 911. He prides himself on doing his homework correctly. Over a period of weeks he's noted the make and model, he'd even bought the manual to familiarise himself with any changes in the braking system. The usefulness of the manual even spelled out the tools he would need to loosen the brake pipe, just enough to make the system fail. Not wanting to leave any tell-tale puddle of brake fluid, he placed a small container under the leaking brake pipe. With the container in place he shone the torch and waited for the brake fluid to almost empty. Once he was satisfied the braking system would fail he retightened the nut with his fingers. Leaving no trace behind he left as quietly as he'd entered.

*****

It was a bright morning despite the rain that fell overnight. Only puddles in the road to testify to that very fact. Georgia rushed out of the house, a half-eaten piece of toast in her left hand and her keys in the other. She was late for an appointment at the Ruislip office and was all sixes and sevens.

"Fuck!" she cried as she realised she'd left her briefcase inside by the front door. The half-eaten piece of toast she crammed into her mouth, and raced back inside.

Grabbing the briefcase she yelled up the stairs, "Jim, give the office a call, tell them I'm on my way!"

Two minutes later she opened the garage and climbed into her car, throwing the offending briefcase across onto the passenger seat. She switched the ignition on and felt the throaty roar of the Porsche 911's engine as it burst into life.

Georgia had come from a family of enthusiastic car owners, cars were in her blood. She'd bought the Porsche just a little under a year ago and it had become her pride and joy. As she drove out of the garage she began wondering whether the car was baby proof. The thought of her baby throwing up all over her lovely new leather upholstery didn't bear thinking about.

She smiled to herself as she drove onto the open road; being late for her appointment she deduced the roads would be less busy. As she turned onto Duck's Hill Road she tweaked the accelerator and was pleased to see she had an open road before her. Observing the speed limit on the urban patch of road; well doing forty five wasn't much above the limit, she switched on the radio. Within a minute she was clear of residential houses and seeing the no speed limit sign ahead of her, she put her foot down. She was doing seventy five as she approached the brow of the hill, instinctively she put her foot down gently on the brake. It felt spongy to the touch, she pumped the brake again as she descended the brow and the brake failed completely.

"Oh shit!" she cried as the car started its descent at sixty miles an hour. Instinctively she tried changing down, but she was going too fast and the gears crunched but didn't engage. Desperately she pulled on the handbrake, only for the car to whip from side to side. Georgia fought with the steering wheel, barely managing to miss an oncoming car before mounting the kerb and hitting the side hedgerow. She braced herself as the Porsche eventually started to slow down. She thought she'd made it, then suddenly she hit something, possibly a tree stump and the car flipped onto its side and careered over the hedgerow, before righting itself as it came to a stop in a farmer's field.

Cars pulled up at the roadside and immediately three men rushed across the field to try to give Georgia assistance. Another driver dashed down the hill to the local newsagent's to phone for an ambulance.

"Oh Jesus!" cried one of the men, as he stared at the wreck of the Porsche. "Give me a hand, she's slipping in and out of consciousness and her breathing's laboured!"

The ambulance arrived on the scene within minutes and two men climbed out and rushed into the field. Within minutes they took charge of the scene. After they gently carried Georgia on to a stretcher and was about to place her in the ambulance she regained consciousness. "My baby! Save my baby!"

Jim was in a meeting at the Civic Centre in Uxbridge when a policeman gave him news of Georgia's car crash. "You need to come with me sir, your wife's been involved in an accident!"

"What!" cried Jim?

"They rushed your wife to the hospital at Mount Vernon, I don't know all the details sir, just that she was involved in a vehicle accident on the Duck's Hill Road in Ruislip."

Jim flew out of the Civic Centre and drove straight to Mount Vernon in Northwood. Abandoning his car at the entrance to the A and E department he raced up to reception. "I understand my wife's been brought in after a traffic accident. Her name's Georgia Chandler!"

For an agonising couple of minutes he waited until a nurse came up to him, "Are you Jim? Georgia Chandler is you're…"

"Partner, yeah," he answered anxiously.

"She's in surgery right now, but if you'd like to wait there's a room…"

"Is she going to be okay?"

"She was lucky, only a broken arm and cuts and bruises, thankfully."

"And the baby?"

"I don't know." The shocked look on the nurse's face, sent alarm bells ringing inside Jim's head. "Let me check. If you'd like to sit down, I'll be right back."

Jim sat, he stood up, he paced the floor, he sat down again, then up immediately as he saw the nurse returning accompanied by a lady doctor.

"You're Georgia Chandler…"

"Husband," he cried.

The doctor smiled, "Your wife is a bit of a handful, she swears a lot. She refused to go down to surgery until they checked if the baby was okay."

Jim smiled, that was so Georgia.

"Thankfully the baby's fine. Your wife's going to be a little sore for a week or two, and she's going to be in a plaster cast for a while."

When they brought Georgia back from surgery Jim was at her bedside. "The baby's fine," said Georgia. "It wasn't my fault, I always slow down before I reach the brow. You know that, you've been with me."

"Yeah, I know, don't worry yourself with it, there's a policeman, who'd like to get a statement from you in a couple of minutes. He reckons you're lucky to be alive." Jim felt himself welling up. "I thought I'd lost you!"

*****

When Fallon found out that Georgia Chandler hadn't died in the crash he was mortified. Eddie had told him that morning that the job went "Sweet as a nut," only to find out she'd survived a few hours later. 'Maybe it's a sign,' he thought. He'd straightened John Armstrong out, reassured him that if he kept his nerve and his mouth shut, they'd weather the storm. 'Yeah, maybe I over reacted, in a few months she'll have her hands full with her brat.'

# Chapter 65

Georgia had her cast removed six weeks after the accident, six weeks of remaining at home, which drove her mad. She'd intended working until the last three months of her pregnancy, but because of the accident Jim had insisted that she took things easy for the rest of her term.

With time on her hands, Georgia sought answers as to why her brakes failed. According to the police the braking system had failed from lack of brake fluid. She explained until that morning the Porsche was running perfectly. The insurance investigator looking into why it had failed and discovered the brake fluid pipe's connection appeared to have worked loose, resulting in the fluid leaking out gradually. It was unlikely that wear and tear of the Porsche's ten months of life, could have caused the leakage. The fact that the Porsche had only recently been serviced caused the insurance investigator to suspect human error on the part of the garage prior to the accident. A fact that would no doubt be denied by the authorised dealer. To Jim and Georgia's relief the claim was settled within three weeks.

It still left a bad taste in Georgia's mouth, both her and Jim had driven the Porsche in the days leading up to the accident and neither found anything wrong with the braking system. If as Georgia believed, it had been a fault caused by the service, surely they would have noticed. The absence of any tell-tale stains on the concrete floor of their garage, led both Georgia and Jim to consider however unlikely, that the brakes might have been tampered with.

The doubt lingered in Georgia's mind so much that Jim paid for an independent crash investigator to take a look. The investigator examined the wreckage of the Porsche, questioned the staff at the garage where the car was serviced and studied the police report of the accident. Then he compiled his report, which he took to their house.

"I was going to post you my report, but as it's inconclusive I thought it better to explain in person," he handed the report to Jim. "To summarise, theoretically wear and tear of the Porsche's ten months of life, could have caused the leakage, but the car would have to have been driven on badly maintained or gravel roads."

"It hasn't," said Georgia abruptly.

"Did you notice, any sponginess in the brakes during the time of the service and the accident?"

Georgia's hormones reacted as she threw a few fucks into the air.

The inspector quickly moved away from Georgia's driving ability. "The second and in my professional opinion the most likely is human error in the servicing of the Porsche which was carried out only two weeks prior to the accident, a fact that has no doubt been denied by the authorised dealer."

His least likely scenario, someone tampering with the car deliberately, was highly unlikely.

"How do you explain no tell-tale leakage in our garage?" asked Jim.

"Do you mind if I take a look?" asked the investigator.

"Sure," said Jim as he led the investigator out the front of the house and towards the garage. Jim opened up the garage door and turned on the light.

"Do you mind if I smoke?" asked the investigator.

"No, go ahead," replied Jim. "Sorry about the missus."

"Don't worry about it, my wife was much the same when we had our first," he offered Jim a cigarette.

"No thanks, never smoked," said Jim. "Apart from the odd cigar at Christmastime."

"Wish I could give it up!" He gave the floor a cursory look, noting the area where the Porsche would have been parked was free from any oil or brake fluid. "To be honest, it's baffled me."

They returned to the house and Jim wrote out a cheque. Then he saw the man out and watched as he got in his car. 'At least it might give Georgia peace of mind,' he thought as he walked back inside.

Georgia having cooled down had stepped outside and watched as the crash investigator drove off with one hundred and twenty pounds of their money. Resigning herself to throwing money at a whim she walked over to the open garage and began to close the door. Her eyes widened with alarm. She was frozen to the spot as she cried out, "Jim, Jim come here, I need you. Jim!"

Jim had just entered the room they used as an office, when he heard Georgia cry out. He flew out of his office and ran through the open doorway and saw Georgia frozen to the spot by the open garage.

"What's up?" cried Jim, "You scared the life out of me."

"Just come here will you," she said in almost a whisper.

Jim walked over, "What is it?"

"That investigator, did he smoke?"

"Yeah, he offered me a cigarette. I told him I didn't smoke."

"What brand?"

"Benson and Hedges, I think," answered Jim.

"Are you sure, think?"

"Yeah, I'm sure, gold packet. Why?"

"What's that?" she said, pointing to a greasy rag up against the garage wall and a discarded cigarette butt lodged in it.

Jim knelt down to pick it up, "It's a roll up, a thin rollup."

A shudder ran down Georgia's back, "Oh my God!" she uttered. "Leave it!"

Jim recoiled and left the offending object lie. He stood up and Georgia clung to him as she began to shake uncontrollably. "I knew it! I knew it!"

"We should inform the police," stated Jim.

"No not yet," cried Georgia as she felt herself recovering from the shock. "We need to think this through. Get the camera!"

Jim laughed and tried making light of it, "You've seen too many episodes of Columbo."

"Just get it!" she snapped.

Georgia had recovered her composure completely when Jim returned with the camera and handed it to her. "Maybe I'm being over dramatic, but bear with me. Georgia then took a series of photos of the cigarette before picking the butt up and wrapping it in a tissue. She left the light on and shut the garage door.

"Not even a chink of light. That I think eliminates it being blown in by the wind," said a self-satisfied Georgia.

The following day she showed the cigarette butt to Eric, "It's definitely a prison roll up."

"How can you be so sure?" asked Jim.

Eric laughed, "I've seen enough of them in my life, that's a prison roll up."

"We had a crash investigator around yesterday, even he couldn't give a definite cause of how my brakes leaked," said Georgia.

"What did he think the most likely?" asked Eric.

"Servicing error," replied Jim.

"What does your garage floor tell you?"

"No puddle, no stains."

"Does the crash investigator know what you do for a living?"

"No, he never asked," said Georgia.

"How much of a nuisance have you been, concerning Joe's wrongful conviction?"

"Until the crash, quite a lot actually."

"Surely Fallon wouldn't go to those lengths!" said Jim.

"I'm not saying he would, but given what's happened I'd cool it if I was you," said Eric seriously. "These people aren't like us, their mind-set doesn't work the way of ordinary people. I'll have a word, if you like, but if I was you I'd leave it."

Georgia took everything Eric had said on-board. Whilst lying in a hospital bed the day after the crash the thought that Fallon could have caused the accident had crossed her mind. She knew she was vulnerable, especially being nearly six months pregnant, but not as vulnerable as Fallon might think.

"Prison roll up, you're sure?"

"One hundred percent," replied Eric.

Georgia wouldn't admit to Jim that she felt badly shaken by the discovery of the cigarette butt. She was a defence lawyer, so it couldn't be anyone she'd put away. She'd interviewed everyone except Fallon. Armstrong the man that arrested Joe, the man that built the case against Joe appeared shaky, but not shaky enough to try to kill her. It was just beginning to dawn on her that someone had tried to have her killed. She could back off, but if it was Fallon pulling the strings, there was no reason to think he wouldn't try again. As for Armstrong, it had been almost two months since she'd given him a week to come up with an answer about those missing weeks.

"I'm calling Armstrong first thing next week, then if I don't get what I'm looking for I'm going after Fallon, himself," declared Georgia.

"Do that and there's no telling what he's liable to do," cried Jim. "Let it go!"

"No! I'm going after Chief Inspector Fallon!"

*****

Christmas came early for Chief Inspector Sean Fallon, when he received the unfortunate news of the passing of Inspector John Armstrong. He'd been sitting at his desk, shuffling papers and answering phone calls when he just keeled over. Coroner's report said it was a cardiac arrest, that one second he was putting the phone down and the next he was dead. Sean feigned shock and sadness, but inside he was singing and dancing. John Armstrong, to give him his due, would have been a tough nut to crack, but who knows what pressure that she devil could put on him. 'Too late now bitch! The one person that could put me away is no longer with us,' thought Sean Fallon as he toasted Inspector John Armstrong with a large malt and a single cube of ice.

# Chapter 66

"Wow! You've got to be fucking joking!" exclaimed Donna, when the Zodiac pulled onto the driveway of Jim and Georgia's house.

"Yeah, my reaction when I first saw it, Jim's certainly done well in my absence," added Joe.

It was nearing Christmas and Georgia had invited them over for drinks, a few nibbles, a laugh or two and there was something she needed to discuss with Joe.

"Why she couldn't arrange an appointment at her office is beyond me."

"Are you nervous," enquired Donna, "because I am. Doubly so now I've seen her gaff."

Joe looked at the many cars parked around the cul-de-sac, then back at the house realising this wasn't an intimate drinks and nibbles affair, but a full blown party. "No need to feel nervous, Georgia must've had a change of heart and is throwing a party instead."

"Thank God for that, meeting Grace and Eric socially will be just that bit easier than an intimate dinner party, said Donna. "I expect Grace will be her immaculate self, as usual," she added, regretting the postscript immediately.

"Donna have you seen how you look?"

Donna smiled, she damn well knew how she looked; she'd spent the best part of the afternoon preparing herself for the evening's festivities.

They were greeted at the door by Becky who'd turned up early to support her friend. "Come on in, change of plan, we're partying," she cried in greeting.

Joe and Donna walked into the extravagant hallway and Jim hurried over, "Glad you could make it. May I take your coats?"

Donna still overcome by the size of the hall, took off her coat and smiled at Jim before handing it to him. "Thanks."

"Whoa, you look amazing!" cried Jim, as he saw Donna in a whole new light. "Georgia's over there," he pointed, "You can't miss her, she's that portly lady with a champagne glass in her hand."

"I'll tell her you said that," replied Donna cheekily.

"Don't! That'll be more than my life's worth," he chuckled.

"See, I told you it wouldn't be bad," said Joe.

They'd just walked into the main room, when Donna couldn't contain herself, "This room's bigger than my mum's house," she declared.

"It's certainly bigger than my cell in Durham!" shouted Joe over the sounds coming from the speakers at each end of the room.

"Can I get you something to drink," asked a highlighted blonde lady, the spit of Georgia, only slightly older, "I'm Pricilla, Georgia's sister, it's my job to make sure Georgia's guests never have an empty glass. Beer, wine, spirits?"

"You must be very popular," laughed Donna.

"Yes, it's a tough job but someone's got to do it," she laughed, "That's why I have a little helper," she pointed across the room, "that's Jessica our other sister, she's good, but not as good as me!"

"I'll just grab a beer," said Joe.

"That's great, I'll have a gin and tonic please?"

"Of course, coming right up," replied Pricilla.

Armed with their drinks they began to mingle. Becky pulled Bob away from some people he knew and came over and joined them. "They're a mixed bag," cried Bob. "Actually they're a friendly bunch when you get talking to them."

Georgia came waddling over to them. "There you are, so glad you could join us."

"Thanks for asking," said Donna. "You have a lovely home, I've never seen anything quite like it."

"Thanks Donna," said Georgia, "We love it."

"I just love the décor, did you design it yourself?"

"I would love to take the credit, but Jim's the one with the eye when it comes to detail."

"Can I get you a top up?" asked Pricilla as she interrupted the group.

"You've met my sister I take it," laughed Georgia.

"Yeah, me and Pricilla are old friends," quipped Bob. "Thanks I don't mind if I do."

"Me too," cried Joe. "What about you ladies," he added.

"We're okay at the moment," said Becky.

"There's food laid out through those double doors, if you're hungry," added Pricilla.

Both Donna and Becky looked through the open doorways at a large table be-decked with a centre piece of dressed salmon, an array of cold meats, smoked salmon, prawns, scotch eggs, spring rolls, sausage rolls, an abundance of salads, a mixture of sandwiches, coleslaw and a selection of sauces and dips, all decorated in a Christmas theme of holly and tinsel.

"Do you mind if we take a look at the display," said Becky.

"You'd be doing me a favour, someone needs to get the ball rolling," replied Georgia.

Donna and Becky smiled and wandered over to the magnificent buffet, while Joe watched them as they negotiated their way.

"I'm surprised you didn't think about an ice sculpture?"

"Don't think I didn't consider it. I know this isn't what you expected, but hopefully you'll understand later. I've a special guest I'd like you to meet," said Georgia, "He's not here yet, but he will be, later."

"I'm intrigued," said Joe.

"You will be, there are things you don't know about, things that concern you, me, Grace and Eric. I'm afraid it doesn't concern you Bob, but knowing how you like to entertain the ladies I'm sure you won't mind being omitted." she said with a serious look. "In the meantime enjoy the Christmas festivities." Then in a flash Georgia waltzed off and began chatting to some posh bloke and his lady friend.

"Fuck me! Now I am intrigued! Another beer, or something stronger?" cried Bob.

"I think I'll stick to beer, I might need something stronger when Georgia gets around to telling us whatever it is," said Joe. "No, second thoughts, get me a double scotch."

An hour later Donna noticed a strained look upon Georgia's face. The explanation came when around nine thirty Grace and Eric put in an appearance. She watched as they made their excuses for being late.

"Usual thing really, we dropped Billie off with Mum and Dad, and were on our way to you when we hit traffic," declared Grace.

"Yeah there must have been a bad accident or something for the traffic to be diverted," added Eric.

"Well you're here now so get yourselves a drink and mingle," said Georgia. "Our esteemed guest has only just arrived so give it an hour and we can retire to the study. Pricilla and Jessica will be filling in while we have our little meeting."

Donna had to admit Grace and Eric looked a perfect fit. 'Or was that wishful thinking,' she thought. 'Oh no, they're heading straight for us. Try not to panic, act casual, make like you haven't a care in the world.'

The usual pleasantries followed as they greeted each other and wished everyone the compliments of the season.

"I can't believe Christmas is here already," said Becky.

"Trust me, it'll be Easter before you can look round," added Grace.

"I understand we have a little treat in store, sometime during the evening," said Joe, as he found himself on the verge of inebriation after everyone had said there pleasantries.

"I wouldn't call it a treat," stated Eric.

Joe had never really bought into the gangster image that Eric cultivated during the Kray era, or was it that Eric stood between him and Grace. Despite how amazing Donna looked tonight, his heart still skipped a beat when Grace walked into the room

An hour later Joe was approached by Georgia who asked him to follow her into what appeared to be a study. Becky and Donna looked on in puzzled amusement, just as Bob and Jim brought them over a couple of refills.

"They left you out too," laughed Becky when Jim handed her a drink.

"I was beginning to feel like Billy no mates until Jim assured me there was a very good reason why they needed to keep the meeting secret," added Bob, "So drink up, the party's still young!"

Joe's first impression when he walked into the study, wasn't the oak desk with some middle aged guy sitting as if he was holding court. Nor the dark green Chesterfield that Grace and Eric were sitting on facing him. But the vast library of books that lined three walls of the study.

Georgia invited Joe to sit down beside Grace, and then stepped nimbly around the study and stood by the side of the man sitting at the desk.

"Sorry for the clandestine way you've be brought here, but I think once we begin you will understand the reason for secrecy. I'd like to introduce you to Sir Hugh Weathersby, Lord Chief Justice of England and Wales. He's here as a personal favour to my father, and myself. He's not here in any official capacity, in fact he's not here at all. The party was a ruse for him to speak to you face to face."

Georgia then stepped back and the Lord Chief Justice spoke, addressing Joe in particular. "I'm here today to clarify a point of law. Georgia thought it would be better you heard it from the horse's mouth, so to speak."

A brief rumbling of approval emanated from the group.

"Mr Joseph Dempsey, the alleged miscarriage of justice that was afforded you and the subsequent release from prison under the terms of years served, does not in law allow for any compensation for the years of loss of liberty. To give its proper title, Royal prerogative of mercy. In laymen's terms it means to change a sentence, but it in itself does not overturn a conviction. You might recall the case of George Davis, who was convicted in March 1975 for an armed payroll robbery and his subsequent release in May last year, after a regrettable campaign for his release championed by his wife."

Joe looking stony faced, addressed the Lord Chief Justice, "Pardon me for feeling aggrieved by what you've just told us, are you suggesting we take action ourselves. Would carving up Wembley Stadium on the eve of the Cup Final next year help my case? Would going to the papers and getting them to print a copy of Terry Richards's confession help! I've lost ten years of my life for something I didn't do. I deserve better!"

"You may feel, quite rightly that you have been unfairly treated and should be compensated for this alleged miscarriage of justice, but as in the Davis case your conviction was deemed as unsafe, and not an innocent verdict. Meaning at this time and in the foreseeable future unless evidence to support your plea of innocence comes to light your conviction remains Unsafe."

"Joe I know you feel angry but the reason for me inviting the Lord Chief Justice was for you to know how you stand in a court of law," stated Georgia.

"However!" interrupted the Lord Chief Justice, "I do hold out a chink of light, very slight at the moment but......" Sir Hugh Weathersby hesitated before continuing, "There has been disquiet over the past few years about certain individuals in the City of London Police and to a lesser extent the Metropolitan Police, who it would appear to be taking bribes, falsifying evidence, and receiving proceeds from crime etc. Nothing proven as yet! There appears to be a wall of silence, either from fear of recriminations from colleagues or fear of being exposed."

"So basically you're saying hold on, there might or might not be a lifeline. That doesn't get me anywhere!"

"Mr Dempsey I appreciate you feeling that you've been abandoned but believe me there are many in the Judiciary and the police in general, who wish to rid the force of this endemic corruption in London's police forces. With two major robberies in the London area in the last two years I can assure you something is being done. On that note I must be away. Thank you for listening. I wish you good luck."

He turned towards Georgia, "Thank you Georgia, as always a pleasure."

Eric, Grace and Joe sat there in silence as Georgia saw the Lord Chief Justice out. A couple of minutes later she re-emerged.

"You might wonder why I asked Grace and Eric to sit in, I'll get to that in a minute. Joe I wanted you to hear from the Lord Chief Justice's own lips the reason why your case is so complex. I wanted you to know I've been breaking my back over your case for more hours than you could ever contemplate. Certain things have happened of which you're aware of and some that you're not! And why I'm excluding myself from your case!"

"Well that's it then!" cried Joe. A growing rage built up inside of him. He stood up, "I've heard enough, they fucked me once; by Christ I won't stand by and let them fuck me again!"

"Joe, stop, listen…." cried Georgia.

He was nearly out of the door…. "Joe! Please come back and listen to what Georgia has to say," pleaded Grace.

He stopped as his hand was about to open the door. He looked straight at Grace…

"Come and sit..." she said almost in a whisper.

Joe said nothing as he slowly returned to his seat.

"Thank you Joe. Some of this you know already, I started another file on your case, one that started with Arthur Briggs and finished with Sean Fallon. I came up zilch on Briggs, he seems to have vanished off the face of the earth, likewise his cousin Roy. I interviewed Keith Porter and Donald Fuller and neither man had met the mysterious Roy, who incidentally isn't a cousin of Briggs."

"You went to Parkhurst!" exclaimed Joe. Despite feeling the effects of the alcohol, he started to realise the extent his friends were prepared to go for him.

"Unperturbed I requested an interview with Inspector John Armstrong. You would have thought I'd asked for an audience with the Queen. On my second time of asking he agreed but was very obstructive to say the least, especially when I requested his files from your case. It was only when I produced a court order that he relinquished them."

Georgia paused while she took a sip of water, "Sorry about that. Where was I, oh yeah, his files though apparently in order showed a gap of two weeks in the investigation. Which Armstrong couldn't explain? He appeared shaken but said he'd look into it. I told him he had a week! Unfortunately my brakes failed, and I ended up in hospital."

Joe could see by the serious look upon Georgia's face that there was more too it.

"The accident was, all though I can't prove it, a deliberate attempt on my life!"

"You're kidding!" exclaimed Joe.

"I've never been more serious in my life!" Georgia took the chance to take a sip of water. "The official reason for my accident was mechanical failure, possibly the servicing two weeks prior to the accident. It wasn't! There were a number of factors that didn't add up. Jim and I couldn't put our finger on it, until I noticed a cigarette butt in our garage. Bear in mind I stopped smoking six years ago and Jim has never smoked, it was unusual. A specific cigarette butt, a roll up, a thin roll up."

"A prison roll up!" interrupted Joe.

"I must admit, the thought that someone was out to kill me, frightened the hell out of me. But I was a hundred percent sure that Sean Fallon was behind it or should I say I suspected. Which made me more determined than ever to lean hard on John Armstrong. I was going to use everything I'd learned at law to bring him to his knees, unfortunately before I could get another interview with him the bastard experienced a heart attack and died. Everyone connected with your case, have either disappeared or died apart from one person. I was going to interview Fallon but Jim and Eric believe I should leave well alone. I'm sorry Joe, I truly am."

"I'm sorry too," replied Joe. "I never realised… You've done more than enough Georgia. I'm afraid I don't have much faith in what the judge was saying. In my experience bastards like Fallon always seem to survive."

Eric stood up and walked around the room before standing beside Georgia, "I take your point Joe. I put the word out amongst my contacts in the manor where Sean Fallon had spent most of his time on the force. I was looking for any dirt anyone might have on him. I also put the word out about any ex-prisoner with more than a basic knowledge of mechanics, meticulous in his craft and more importantly with a connection to Fallon. So far I haven't heard a whisper. But believe me someone out there will know something."

Joe acknowledged Eric's efforts then turned his back and walked out of the room where he re-joined Donna. The look on his face told her it wasn't good news. "That fucker's going to get away with it!" snapped Joe.

"What do you mean?" asked Donna anxiously.

"I'll tell you about it later. Right now I need a stiff drink."

"I'll get it, a large scotch, will that do?" said Donna.

"Yeah, sure, anything to take the edge off."

Grace seeing the anguish and frustration in Joe's face came over and put her arm around him, "I'm sorry Joe, I'm sorry things didn't work out. Eric hasn't given up, and who knows perhaps the Lord Chief Justice is right, maybe one day Sean will get what's coming to him."

"Yeah, maybe," said Joe harshly, then he softened his tone. "You know it's not the compensation, the loss of ten years or even seeing Fallon getting away with it; it's that I lost you. Everything else is nothing compared to losing you."

"I'm sorry Joe, things are different now, I've changed, and you've changed. We have to look forward, not back. Donna's a great girl. She's young vibrant and absolutely gorgeous, look after her." Grace slowly moved her arm away and had begun to walk across the room to Eric.

"You're right, I know; but there's one thing missing, she's not you."

Grace looked sad as she slowly turned her back and moved swiftly into the crowd. Donna had seen Grace go over to comfort Joe and had held back. She felt a lump form in her throat, and began to wonder if it was all worth it. Steeling herself Donna put on a brave face and walked back over to him.

"Get that down you," she cried, handing him a large scotch.

Joe took the offered glass, then he looked around at his friends. All of them had made it in their own way, he could feel himself drowning in his own self-pity. He quickly sank the scotch in two gulps. "Let's get out of here!" he snapped.

He felt himself sway as he walked into the large hallway.

"Are you alright to drive?" asked Donna.

"Yeah, sure I am. Get your coat," he slurred.

Donna felt the world falling in, he would never have spoken to Grace the way he spoke to me, tears welled up as she found her coat, and she began to cry. She couldn't help it as a decision within her began to emerge.

Joe didn't seem to notice how upset he'd made Donna. He walked across to the Zodiac and climbed in. Donna with the door open stood there wondering. When he drunkenly dropped the keys in the foot well, she slammed the door shut and walked around to the driver's side, where she opened the door and snatched the keys out of Joe's hand as he finally managed to locate them. "Shove over!" she snapped aggressively.

Shocked by the aggression in her voice Joe scooted over. Donna fortified by a few large gin and tonics, turned the key in the ignition, switched on the lights, pushed down hard on the clutch, then slammed the column change gear stick into first. She'd seen Joe do it countless times, and hoped she remembered where to find second gear. Beginners luck, the Zodiac pulled out of the close and Donna turned left. A few tentative moments followed where she stalled the car. She quickly glanced in her rear view mirror with the expectation of seeing a blue light flashing, luckily enough the road was empty. She glanced across at Joe slumped in his seat and realised he was sleeping. "Prick!" she uttered. She turned on the ignition, stuck the car into gear and lurched off, a few kangaroo jumps then finally as the car built up speed she began to relax.

As she finally got the hang of the Zodiac, she reflected on the decision she'd made and cried all the way back to her mother's house in Northolt. Pulling up to the curb Donna realised she couldn't leave Joe to sleep it off in the car, much as she felt like it. Fortunately her mum had gone to visit her sister and wouldn't be home. A fact Donna had been counting on, spending the whole night with Joe would have been a lovely way to top off the evening. Instead, she climbed out of the Zodiac and opened the passenger door and attempted to wake him. It took her half a dozen shakes before he finally came too.

Groggy and disorientated he looked up at Donna, "Where are we..."

"We're back at mum's house. I can't carry you so you'd better be able to walk," she snapped at him.

Joe staggered to Donna's front door, falling over once, "Look at the state of yer!" she raged. "Get in!"

Donna thought about leaving him on the couch, leaving her decision to the morning, but felt that was the coward's way out. She looked at the time, it was nearly one o'clock when she put the coffee on. She told herself she wanted to get him sober enough for him to understand they were over. Then the idiot could let that sink in while he slept on the couch or decided to drive home. She managed to get two mugs of coffee down him before he started to come round.

"How do you feel?" asked Donna.

"I feel like shit," he moaned.

"Good, you deserve it," she responded.

"How'd we get here?"

"I drove us home."

"Was I that bad? I don't remember much."

Then it all came out, "I bet you remember her! I bet you remember everything about her, her clothes, her makeup; her hair. Joe I'm sorry, I thought I could do it. I did my best but it just wasn't good enough, we're done. You can sleep it off on the couch or you can drive home it's your choice."

The sudden realisation of what Donna was saying began to register. "I don't want that..."

Donna wasn't finished, "The trouble with you is, you live in some fictitious dream world where you think you're the Count of Monte Cristo. Mercedes isn't Grace, Danglars, isn't Fallon and Eric isn't Fernand Mondego. The sooner you start to realise .........."

"You read it!" said a shocked and nearly sober Joe. He slowly rose to his feet and held her in his arms.

"Of course I read it you idiot, I love you."

"You're right I'm an idiot, I couldn't see what was in front of me. Well not anymore, you're young vibrant and absolutely gorgeous, and I love you," *paraphrasing the very words Grace had used earlier.* I'd be a fool to let you slip away."

A look of devilment crossed her face as she wiped her eyes, "And don't forget I'm a great fuck!"

No more words were needed as she led Joe towards the stairs. At the top, they kissed passionately and clawed at each other's clothing, the dress, the gorgeous dress that she's worn that night, cast aside as they fought their way in to her room. In the process of falling onto the bed Donna attempted to undo her suspender belt. His hand stopped her, "Leave them on," he gasped, as his hand feverishly tore at her knickers. He kissed her more urgently as his lips explored her neck, then ventured to her shoulders and beyond. She gasped in pleasure as his mouth found her breasts, lingering long enough to tease before his lips kissed the small paunch that had always turned him on. She quivered as his mouth ventured between her legs, his tongue searching, Arrrggghh," she cried as she reached her first orgasm. "Put it inside me," she cried urgently. Joe kissed her wet patch as his mouth started on its return journey. He kissed her gently and looked into those mesmerising lustful blue eyes. He kissed her with such passion, so full of love before entered her. She groaned lustfully as she felt him inside. Their animal lust took over as they thrashed about seeking maximum pleasure, neither wanting their lovemaking to end before the ultimate climax.

When it was finally over they lay in each other's arms, their ardour extinguished. Donna looked into Joe's eyes and asked. "Do you really love me?" He kissed her softly upon the lips and looked down into those amazing eyes that spoke volumes. "I meant every word."

During the next few days Joe went over the events of the weekend. He'd been blind to Donna's feeling and nearly lost her. That he'd told Donna that he loved her, spoke volumes, prefixing the very words Grace had said only hours earlier haunted him. Was Grace right? Donna was young, vibrant and absolutely gorgeous and he was a fool if he couldn't see it, but for one precious moment at the party he'd sensed there was still something there between him and Grace. He knew he was clutching at straws? What worried him the most, was he settling for second best. He hoped not!

# Chapter 67

The week leading up to Christmas was unusually busy in Eric's antique shop. Over the years he'd developed an eye for bargains, even spending time looking around junk shops and the antique fairs that had been popping up all over the country. He'd learned to diversify and due to the sixties explosion of pop music and pop art he'd become an expert on what was hot and what was not. In fact he'd given over at least a third of his shop space to an assortment of pop culture, whether it was reproductions of old movie posters, Andy Warhol's pop art paintings of Marilyn Monroe to postcards of the Beatles and Elvis to 1950s/60s comics. Pop culture included movies, music, sports, a two foot high wooden Mickey Mouse and basically memorabilia. "Junk," as Jim had said when he visited the shop.

"To you maybe, but to others priceless," countered Eric. "It's going to grow, just wait and see."

"I'm yet to be convinced," said Jim, as he rummaged through old reproduction movie posters, "Oh shit!" he cried when he came across a poster of Rio Bravo. "Well I can't say no can I. How much?"

Eric laughed, and charged him twice what he'd paid for it. Amongst his more pricey items was his collection of old guitars, Fender's, Gibson's, Gretsch's, and Rickenbackers. Most he'd picked up for a song, some cost a little more and others left behind at gigs in some of London's hot spots of the sixties.

Eric had a busy week selling amongst other items an antique coffee table, a very decorative vase, along with the odd porcelain figurine. His overall profit that week was made up from the odd collectables from his pop culture. He'd thought not to open on Saturday as it was Christmas Eve, but realised there was always a late punter that had left it a little late to get his wife something different.

It was nearly closing time when a man of middle age walked into the shop and started to browse. Eric had seen him peering in the window of the shop earlier.

"That Fender Stratocaster, how much?" asked the man.

'Obviously a panic buyer,' thought Eric. "It really needs restoring to its former glory, but it's a beauty. It's a Sunburst, with as you can see a cream pickguard. Let's see now, a new Stratocaster could cost around two fifty depending where you bought it, possibly three hundred. As its Christmas I could let you have it for a hundred and twenty."

"I don't want to play it, it's for the wife, she wants to hang it on the wall in the music room," said the man, his tone slightly icy.

"Nice present, comes with a case," said Eric.

"Ain't interested in the case, I'll give you a ton."

The man was playing him, and Eric knew it, and as it was nearly closing time he wasn't in the mood for games, "I'll tell you what, you can have the Stratocaster and case for a hundred and ten, final price."

"You drive a hard bargain, Mr…" he smirked.

"Sullivan, Eric Sullivan."

"You've got yourself a deal," said the man.

"I'm sure your wife is going to love it," said Eric, eager to close up.

"I'm sure she will," replied the man. You've a nice town, lived here long?"

"Long enough," stated Eric.

"Let me guess, East End."

"A long time ago," added Eric, tired of this game of cat and mouse.

"Not that long, I'd wager."

Eric didn't answer as he took down the guitar and placed it in the case. He handed the case to the man and held his hand out for the cash. Neither man smiled as they did the transaction.

"Have a good Christmas," cried the man, a smirk of a smile upon his lips, as he turned and left the shop.

Eric watched as he walked away. 'Call it sixth sense, call it what you like,' thought Eric, he'd just come face to face with Sean Fallon. 'What was his game?' Was he sending a message?"

As Sean Fallon walked to his car, he smiled to himself. Sullivan wasn't as he'd expected, the man was too fly to be intimidated, nonetheless Fallon was pleased with his visit, he'd found answers he hadn't even contemplated.

Eric kept the visit of Fallon to himself. It was Christmas, there was no point in letting the sick fuck play with Grace's head. There was more important things to think about, namely Joe. He was coming round at noon to give Billie her Christmas present. 'Something we've all got to get use too,' he thought. He hadn't seen Joe since Georgia's party, but hoped he was in a better mood. Grace had told Eric what Joe had said to her after the meeting with the Lord Chief Justice. It had been nearly four months since Joe's release and Eric was hoping to put any animosity behind them. Judging from what Grace had told him, there seemed no chance of that happening soon.

Billie looked out of the window and saw the maroon and grey Zodiac pull up close to the curb. "It's Dad and Donna," she cried excitedly.

The usual Christmas greetings were exchanged, then Joe presented Billie with two presents. "Open that one first," he said.

Billie excitedly ripped open the present, a Girls World hair styling set, with makeup accessories.

"That's from the two of us," he said. "Donna picked it," emphasising the two with a warm hug across Donna's shoulder. She smiled up at him warmly, and Grace sensed that something had changed between them.

"The other you might think is a bit daft, I just wanted you to have….. Billie had already begun to open the present. "I never got to buy your first Teddy. I know it's daft but I saw it and knew I wanted you to have it."

"Dad, it's, it's…. I love it. It's the best present anyone ever bought me." She jumped up and gave him a big hug. The warmth in Donna's eyes spoke volumes as Grace looked on.

"Would you like a drink?" asked Grace. "A glass of wine, perhaps?"

"Yeah, why not," replied Donna. "What a lovely home, not a bit like me mum's." There was no side or pretension in her voice, Donna was now her own woman.

Grace handed her a glass of wine. "You live with your mum," said Grace.

"It's supposed to be temporary. I was living in a flat until me and my ex split."

"Oh, I'm sorry I didn't mean to pry!" exclaimed Grace.

Donna laughed, "History, nothing more. We're thinking about renting a flat once Joe feels more settled in his job. Perhaps in the springtime."

Grace smiled back at her, she was happy things appeared to be working out for Joe. She hoped Donna was the right woman for him. She was of course, but part of Grace still held feelings for Joe. Deep, hidden feelings.

Joe played with Billie until Eric came over with a drink, "I'm afraid it's lager, but it's wet and cold," it was his attempt to break the ice between them.

"Cheers Eric," he took the offered glass then excused himself from Girl's World. "Donna's idea," he said referring to the present. "Can we talk?"

'Was this round two,' thought Eric, "Yeah sure, let's take a walk. Joe followed Eric into the garden. "I'm sorry you didn't get the result you were looking for," said Eric.

"Nah forget that. I'd long ago given up on the justice system. I just want to apologise, we used to be mates. I was out of order, I should never have spoken to you the way I did."

"So we're alright!" asked Eric.

"Yeah we're okay. I've done a lot of soul searching since the party, nearly lost Donna into the bargain. But we're good, I mean real good. Thinking maybe sometime in the spring about renting ourselves a flat, we'll see how it goes."

Eric extended his hand towards Joe, "In your shoes, I'd have felt the same. Donna's a great girl. Just make sure you look after her."

Joe looked slightly shocked by the relieved tone in Eric's voice. In reaction he grabbed the extended hand and shook it. "I will, you can count on it. Merry Christmas Eric."

"Merry Christmas Joe."

*****

Twenty minutes later they said their goodbyes and turned the car towards Eastcote. Becky and Bob had invited them over to mark Joe's first Christmas since leaving prison with a Christmas dinner with the Walker family.

"It's going to be noisy," warned Donna as they pulled up to the curb outside Bob and Becky's. "Her kids can be noisy bleeders."

"That's okay, I use to be one," joked Joe.

After the pre-dinner drinks, the customary, "Look what I got," from the kids, the tearing open of wrapping paper, the thank you's from the kids, they settled down to a lovely Christmas dinner. Bob as usual asked how it went at Grace and Eric's. Donna answered, "Yeah it was great, I felt really comfortable for the very first time with Grace."

There was no explanation needed, Donna had spoken to Becky at length the day after the party. *"I want chapter and verse," demanded Becky.*

*"Let's just say I'm knackered." Donna had replied.*

"So everything went well?" asked Bob.

"Yeah, I'm finally getting my head together," replied Joe.

"Good. This year we're going to be busier than ever and if you carry on the way you're going you can be a big help to me later in the year."

"How's that?"

Bob looked at Becky a smile appearing on both faces.

"You're having another baby!" exclaimed Donna.

Becky and Bob laughed, "These two are more than enough!" responded Becky.

Bob, now beaming with mischievous excitement said, "Jim's going to be really pissed off."

Before he could get the words out the kids shouted, "We're going to Disncy!"

"Well we're spending a day or two at Disneyland, but we're doing a fly drive through California, Nevada and Arizona. Cowboy Country! Jim will really flip, us going to America before him."

The laughter exploded. "Nappies verses Mickey Mouse!"

"That's great, I never thought you were that interested?" asked Joe when the laughter and excitement died down.

"It's not me, it's those little horrors, Disney this, Disney that."

"Yeah, but didn't you say you wanted to see the Golden Gate Bridge," chipped in Becky.

"Oh, and we're not taking in Rodeo Drive and Hollywood," added Bob sarcastically.

"I always thought it was expensive to go to the States."

"It used to be, but they brought in these ABC and APEX fares, whatever they are, basically it means it's in reach of the likes of us," said Bob.

Crackers were pulled, drinks flowed, laughter exploded, and there were no tears, before bedtime. It was almost midnight when they said good night to their guests. Becky remarked, "They looked happy, let's hope it lasts."

"I think it will," replied Bob, "I kind of envy them, don't you?"

"Yeah I know what you mean; starting out," sighed Becky, "We're okay though?"

"Of course we are," replied Bob. They locked up, then gave one look at the battlefield of crockery, glasses, pots and pans, the carcass of the turkey and various assorted pieces of pulled crackers and opened boxes, looked at each other, and said, "Nah!" before switching off the light.

*****

Georgia felt decidedly uncomfortable as she sat around the large dining table at her parents' home. George Chandler having partaken of a couple of large brandies, wielded the carving knife, *with which he'd miraculously managed to carve the turkey without drawing blood,* like a conductor's baton as he articulated his way through his usual Christmas speech. The benefits of family as he proudly gazed at his three beautiful daughters, their respective husbands and his three grandsons, giving Georgia a special mention for the soon to be grandchild.

They stayed just long enough to make their polite excuses, then after the ritual of saying goodnight they retired to Jim's car. Once he started the car Georgia let out a groan, "Thank God that's over, I never intend going through another pregnancy ever again"

"No need to worry about that, does your dad have any inclination that you're having twins."

"No, only mother knows, although I think Pricilla might have her suspicions," said Georgia, adding "I think Jessica was too pissed to notice."

"She was at that!" laughed Joe. "Right let's get you home, then you can put your feet up and I'll make you a nice cup of tea."

"Can't wait."

With soft music playing in the background Jim and Georgia snuggled up to each other, the flickering reflexion from the open fire the only illumination. "This is what I need," murmured Georgia, "the comfort of our home, a warm drink and you."

"Wow," whispered Jim, "I've never heard you like this; it's nice." He kissed her ear gently. "What's brought this on?"

"Hormones, I guess. It's just this year, Terry's suicide, Joe's release, the work I put in that nearly cost me my life, and these little ones." She held his hand and together she rubbed the bump that was their road to the future. "I'm glad I'm pregnant Jim. I might live to regret it when these two start to run me ragged, but what the heck. I'm so happy to have you by my side."

Jim snuggled up closer and kissed her gently upon the lips, "I'll always be at your side."

# Chapter 68

Before he knew it Christmas was over, and Joe found himself with time on his hands. Donna was back at work on the Wednesday while he had the rest of the week off due to the building game taking almost a fortnight off over the Christmas period. Too much time to think, thought Joe. A lot had happened in such a short space of time. Looking back on the last few months, he realised he had a lot to be thankful for. So why did he still feel the way he did?

His friends had shown him kindness and understanding beyond what he'd thought possible. He listed all the positives in his life since his release from prison, and there were many, the most positive was of course Billie and Donna. Yet in his head the negatives still outweighed the positives. Ten years in prison for a crime he didn't commit, the lost years of Billie's childhood, the degradation of those prison years, the criminal justice system that couldn't admit they'd got it so wrong, the corruptness of the Metropolitan Police and the fact that Sean Fallon would go unpunished, these gnawed at his very soul, but the loss of Grace distressed him the most.

Donna's ultimatum had stopped Joe in his tracks. He'd gained so much, he had a chance to start over and he nearly threw it away. There were injustices in this world, some deliberate while others were just life itself. He knew he had to bury the past, he only hoped he had the courage to leave it buried.

Joe realised as he sat down with a pint in the George on Thursday lunch time that the festive season wasn't like it used to be. With Christmas Eve and New Year's Eve falling on a Saturday, the usual Friday nights were curtailed. It was just as well, he and

Donna were still in the honeymoon stage of their relationship. A Friday night at the cinema beckoned.

Joe and Donna met up with Bob and Becky for a meal at the Plough in Ruislip the following evening. Originally they had a reservation for eight, but Eric and Grace couldn't make it because they had a prior engagement, much to Joe's relief. The thought of sitting across the table from Grace on New Year's Eve would only have brought back painful memories of that fateful night when Grace came through the doors of the George. 'Things could have been so different' he thought regretfully. Then Jim and Georgia cried off because Georgia was tired because of her pregnancy and didn't want to be a party pooper. Joe made Jim promise they'd all meet for a New Year's drink the following lunchtime.

Jim and Georgia's opt for a quiet night in on New Year's Eve was partly because the twins were in a lively mood. But mainly because Jim had been showing Georgia more care and attention since the accident, which Georgia lapped up. The accident had made both of them sit up and review what was important. Georgia had taken an indefinite leave of absence, while Joe's business ventures had allowed him to take one hand off the tiller. Relaxing in the comfort of their home, Jim and Georgia re-kindled their love for each other.

Missing New Year's Eve was a big deal; things had certainly moved on for Jim and Georgia. Although Jim had promised to meet up for a New Year's drink with the boys the following lunchtime.

Donna was the first one to cry off the following morning, telling Joe when they finally woke that her mouth felt like a sewer and she was not getting up until well after noon.

"I'll pick you up once the pub shuts," said Joe as he kissed her softly, and left her mum's house to go home to freshen up.

Joe was the first through the doors of the George. He wished the bar staff a Happy New Year before ordering his pint, then he sat down. A trickle of customers came through the doors after Joe. By twenty past, he was getting worried that he was the only one with stamina. Bob burst through the doors a minute later. "Sorry, no bus, cancelled," then he ordered his pint and Joe's second.

"No Becky? I thought she was coming today?" asked Joe.

"Probably the same reason Donna cried off. Mind you with two kids it was going to be hard."

Eric arrived earlier than usual, ordered a double scotch, smiled across at the boys, "Drinks?" he asked.

"Yeah cheers!" cried Bob and Joe.

"Good to see you and Eric on friendly terms," remarked Bob under his voice

"Yeah, like I said Christmas Day we came to an understanding, actually before that I came to terms with the situation."

"No Jim?" asked Eric as he brought over their drinks.

"Not yet anyway," said Joe.

"You're early, New Year's resolution?"

"Nah, we spent the night at the home of one of Grace's old school friends. They're off playing tennis at her friend's club."

"Billie too!" enquired Joe.

"Yeah, she insisted, loves tennis, almost as much as horse riding," answered Eric. "Can't stand tennis."

"You're not like Jim then," remarked Joe.

"No, soon as breakfast was over I took off," added Eric.

"Whoa, talk of the devil!" exclaimed Bob.

Eric got back up and bought Jim a drink.

"Cheers Eric," he said as he grabbed a chair and sat down. "Had some plans I needed to look over," he added.

"Couldn't you have waited until tomorrow?" asked Bob.

"I could've! I didn't realise Monday's a bank holiday."

"Must be all that posh wine you're quaffing, must addle the brain," said Bob.

It was pure devilment on Joe part as he looked straight at Bob, "Are you gonna tell him?"

"Tell me what exactly!"

"I was waiting for the right moment," snapped Bob his eyes crinkled mirthfully." I was going to tell you without an audience…"

"Tell him for Christ-sake," said Joe.

"You know how much you love Westerns, well me Becky and the kids are off to America."

"You're kidding; right!" exclaimed Jim.

"No, I ain't. We're off sometime during the last week in May," said Bob, "Becky's sorted it"

"You fucker," replied Jim grinning like a Cheshire cat. "We was thinking about it ourselves, but then Georgia dropped the bombshell that she was pregnant. Not that I'm complaining. I think being a dad tops going to the States."

Bob thought about it for a moment, "Actually no!" then added, "To be honest nothing beats the feeling of being a Dad for the first time."

Eric just smiled.

Joe, who'd missed out on most things fully understood what Bob had just said, albeit it was slightly different due to the circumstances.

The talk that day was mostly Jim asking where in the United States?

Bob saying, "We're flying TWA to Los Angeles, spending four nights there, Disney, Universal and Hollywood, then driving up the Pacific Coast Highway to San Francisco, spending three or four……."

Eric looked at Joe, "Why'd you have to set him off?"

"Believe me, having to listen to him raving on about it during Christmas dinner was even worse!" he laughed.

As Joe drove back to Donna's his mood was a little on the melancholy side as he reflected on how things were the same but different. New Year's Day 1967 his world was just about to be turned on its head, but not in the way he visualised.

Prison was to be his future, ten years of a living hell; ten years without kindness. Prison had changed Joe in more ways than anyone would ever know. In the concrete and steel world he'd inhabited he learned how to fight, to trust no one, to stop from going off his head and above all the ability to survive. Fast forward to Sunday 1st January 1978, there was Bob, Jim and Eric, still meeting in the same old pub, it was as though nothing had changed. But life was entirely different. He knew in his heart he still loved Grace, that he would always love her, yet the person she'd known was not the person he'd become. He could see it clearly now, Grace; wonderful, beautiful Grace, was a brief encounter on his road through life, it was a hard pill to swallow, but Grace wasn't his destiny; she never was.

He'd met Donna so briefly on that fateful New Year's Eve, if Grace hadn't re-entered his life what if anything would have happened between them? Was Donna his true love? Joe reached the top of the Ruislip Road and began his descent into Northolt. At the roundabout he took a left. As he continued his journey he was beginning to understand why he loved Donna with a passion he'd never found in Grace. Donna was his soul-mate and hopefully his saviour.

"What's up?" asked Donna.

"Nothing's up, just the opposite," replied Joe. As she got into the car he leaned over and kissed her, "Happy New Year," he said softly.

Joe wasn't the only one soul searching. Bob decided to walk home, or at least hopefully get to the next bus stop before the infrequent bus reached it. Life had been good to him and Becky, a nice house, two beautiful kids and a job that he really enjoyed. Being his own boss was everything to Bob and the new contract with Manco Contractors was giving him the stability, he'd always craved. With the holiday of a lifetime a few months away, he wondered how come he'd been so lucky. When Bob and Joe were growing up, you could have laid odds on Joe coming out the winner, but two simple twists of fate changed everything. Joe met Grace and within a year he lost his freedom along with the woman of his dreams, whereas Bob had a casual fling with Becky, the sexiest woman he'd ever wish to meet and within a few short years he was a family man with a thriving business.

Just at that moment Bob reached the next bus stop as a bus approached. "Lucky or what!" he exclaimed as he jumped on board.

"How was it?" asked Georgia.

"You know what, that fucker Bob has only booked a family holiday to America!"

"Nice!"

"Yeah, I'm only kidding. America can wait. It's great that Bob can take his family away, but nowhere near as important as my wife giving me the greatest gift ever. I'm going to be a father, not just any father, I'm going to be the father of two boys, Newton and sons!"

"Not so fast Buster, they might be girls!"

Jim laughed, "Boys, girls, who cares as long as they're healthy."

Georgia could see the love in Jim's eyes and knew she'd made the right decision.

Grace spotted the troubled frown on Eric's face the moment he walked through the door. "What is it? Why the frown?"

"Ah, it's nothing," he said.

"Has Joe been at you again?"

"No, nothing like that, in fact Joe and I seem to be getting on better than ever."

"There's something troubling you though, what is it?"

"Grace to be honest, it's nothing."

The look on her face told him she wasn't buying it.

"It was just something Jim said. Bob dropped the news that he was taking the family to America for a holiday this summer. You know how Jim has always loved America, well he seemed a little shocked, put out maybe, but then he said, I think being a dad tops going to America!"

Grace smiled at Eric warmly. He wasn't the type to wear his heart on his sleeve, but having a child of his own was his Achilles heel.

"Then Bob added, nothing beats the feeling of being a dad for the first time! Daft I know, I just felt left out, even Joe has experienced that feeling. For one moment I felt like an outsider looking in."

"Well if you're an outsider, then so am I. Come here you big softy."

# Chapter 69

He was slumped partly over the step stile and hedgerow, his discarded shotgun lying by the side of the path. On first impressions it appeared as though the man had slipped on the slippery wet step and lost his footing, discharging the loaded shotgun at the same time. To the local coppers it looked an open and shut case, the half empty bottle of Scotch in the side pocket of his Barbour coat clinching their suspicions. It was only when they retrieved his wallet and the identity of the victim was revealed that they thought to notify their superiors.

Detective Inspector Paul Langley dragged himself out of bed, ignored the ringing of the telephone and glanced at the clock on the side table. It was 10.45 am. He'd been asleep for no more than four hours as the banging in his head testified. He snatched up the phone, "Hello!" he snapped. Not recognising the voice on the other end of the telephone an edge of impatience crept into his voice, "This better be important, it's New Year's Day, for Christ-sake!"

The young constable cowered by the fierce tirade, spoke hesitantly into the phone, "I'm sorry to interrupt you sir, but we have a suspicious death!"

Langley toned down his voice, "Go on, what's suspicious?"

"On the face of it, it looks like an accident with a shotgun. It appears the gentleman was crossing a stile, slipped and discharged his shotgun which killed him."

"Why didn't you inform the detective sergeant that was on call?"

"I did sir, but because of what we've found, he ordered me to call you." "What did you find?"

"His wallet. By all accounts it belongs to a Chief Inspector Sean Fallon from the Met. Apparently he lives locally. St George's Hill area."

"Nothing's been touched I take it," snapped Langley.

"Apart from locating his wallet and half a bottle of scotch from his coat pocket, no one touched anything."

As the detective inspector put the phone down he murmured to himself, "If you believe that you'll believe anything."

By the time he arrived, the forensics team, for what they were worth, had done a cursory inspection of the body.

"Looks an open and shut case Guv," said Sergeant Lomax, "apart from who he is."

Langley called over one of the forensics team, "What can you tell me," he asked.

"We'll know more when we get the body to the lab."

"Give me something!" he snapped impatiently.

"Best I can tell you, considering plods had their size elevens over the scene, I'd say it is what it is, a freak accident. Slippery wooden stile, a half empty scotch bottle, last night's partying and a discharged shotgun, pretty conclusive I'd say."

"The fact he's one of ours, how does that factor into your equation?"

"Even policemen have tragic accidents."

Detective Inspector Langley wasn't satisfied with the pathologist's answer, it was too glib. Langley was old school, he believed a full autopsy on a high ranking officer needed to be carried out by a more competent pathologist than the one assigned to the case. Unfortunately none were available until Wednesday morning. So he was stuck with this particular duty pathologist. Being dragged out of his bed with the worst of all hangovers, to a suspicious death, one of their own, wasn't the start he anticipated to the New Year.

It was Monday morning before the Met were notified. Alarm bells rang at the mention of the victim's name. Chief Inspector Sean Fallon was neither liked nor disliked in the Met. A good thief taker, an exemplary record, tipped for promotion in some quarters, but choosing instead to retire this March. There were rumours, there always are when a high ranking police officer dies by, *allegedly his own hand.*

"Fallon wasn't the type to take his own life."

"What was he doing crossing a farmer's field with a loaded shotgun?"

"Lives there, you dummy"

"Fancied himself as part of the country set!"

"St George's Hill. Costs a lot of dough to live there."

"He made a lot of enemies!"

"Crossed one too many, for my liking."

"Fitted up a few!"

"Was about to spill his guts."

"Some say he was about to rat on his own."

"I never liked him!"

"For fuck-sake he was one of us. Give the man a little respect."

"Maybe so, but if you lie down with dogs you get fleas."

"There was talk he crossed someone big!"

The rumours that he was bent, that he took bribes, that he looked the other way all re-surfaced. It was left to a member of the Flying Squad to silence the furore. "Would you be saying these things if Fallon walked though those doors at this very moment."

The station went silent. "No! I didn't think so. Now keep your speculations to your selves and show the man some respect!"

Detective Inspector Paul Langley of the Surrey Constabulary out of Woking stated that as a high ranking police officer Sean Fallon should be awarded the courtesy of a top pathologist rather than a bleary eyed junior. A sentiment shared by members of the Surrey Constabulary and also the Metropolitan police force. Consequently a second post mortem was carried out on Tuesday afternoon.

By late Wednesday Inspector Langley received the full autopsy report; it didn't make for good reading. The contents of the stomach were consistent with the victim having digested a bowl of cereal which suggest he ate breakfast, putting the time of death somewhere between 6 am and 11.30 am. His lower intestines indicated he'd ate a steak meal some time during the course of the previous evening. Alcohol found in his bloodstream suggested he'd been drinking heavily, but found little trace that he'd been drunk when the incident happened. On examination of the head wound, the previous pathologist had figured the entrance wound had been fired from an upward position consistent with an accidental discharge of the firearm as the victim lost his footing, slipping off the wooden stile.

Detective Inspector Langley phoned the chief pathologist, catching him as he was going off shift. "Whilst photos of the incident suggest the pathologist's assumption is correct, I have to confirm, with reservations that my findings are almost consistent with my colleague."

"What reservations," asked Langley?

"My reservation being the entry wound, due to the nature of the wound the firearm might; and I emphasise might, have been discharged from a slightly different angle. I can't be sure, mainly because only partial fragments of skull could be found, but I concur with my colleague that Chief Inspector Sean Fallon died as a result of death by misadventure, and I shall be recording it as an Accidental Death."

"So there might be reason to believe foul play?" asked Langley.

"I appreciate you wish to leave no stone unturned inspector, so due to the high rank of the cadaver I will hold back my findings until after the week-end, allowing what investigation you might deem necessary. I would suggest a second visit to the site of the incident. A wider search of surrounding hedgerows for as many fragments of skull that might have been missed. That would I'm sure settle any reservations I might have."

"I'll get my men on it first thing."

"You appreciate I can't hold off indefinitely, the coroner will need to be informed," said the pathologist. "I understand," said Langley.

Detective Inspector Paul Langley arrived early on Thursday morning and gathered his team together. Plans were afoot, to strip the bones from Sean Fallon, his reputation was about to be torn to shreds.

"As you're aware I was called out on New Year's Day to attend a suspicious death of one of our own. I received the autopsy report late yesterday afternoon. According to the report it is highly likely an accidental death, but if there's even a slight hint that something doesn't smell right we need to explore the possibilities. If you have to, use a couple of PC's to search for skull fragments. We have until Monday, the clock is ticking."

"If it's an open and shut case, why are we spending time chasing our tails?" asked Detective Sergeant Gordon Lomax."

"Because I say so sergeant!" snapped Langley. "And I'll remind you it was you that got me called out nursing the mother of all hangovers."

A murmur close to laughter emanated from the guys in the room.

"I want everything you can find on Chief Inspector Sean Fallon," demanded Langley. "And I mean everything. Starting from his first day on the force, right though until the day he died. Everyone has skeletons in their cupboard, the inspector won't be the exception. But remember he was one of ours, everything you find out must be kept confidential."

"Has anyone asked why the inspector was in possession of a shotgun on a farmer's land," asked a young detective constable.

"Good question Hargreaves, has any of you shower even thought to ask this question," enquired Langley as he looked across at the blank faces. "Sean Fallon had the required licenses to own and discharge a shotgun. He had permission to use said weapon on the farmer's land. Together with his dog he helped his neighbour to rid the farm of pests. According to his widow Jackie, he took Rusty his retriever with him every Sunday morning. It was his idea of sport and relaxation."

"So, a creature of habits!" exclaimed Hargreaves.

"Don't get ahead of yourself son!" advised Langley. "We'll come to that if or when things about Fallon point us it that direction. At the moment these are general enquires until we can build up a picture. Now get out there and find me something I can get my teeth into."

# Chapter 70

Sean Fallon's death made the front page of the Wednesday edition of the Surrey Comet. No name, just a man's body had been found slumped between a country stile and a hedgerow. First reports stated that a man in his late forties had apparently died from a single shotgun wound. His name has yet to be released.

By Thursday morning it had reached the tabloid press.

**Suicide or Gangland Execution,** was the most eye catching headline, closely followed by **Death stalks the Countryside.**

*Chief Inspector Sean Fallon 49 was found dead on New Year's Day. The deceased's body was found in a rural environment slumped across a country stile with a recently fired shotgun lying close by. It is believed to have been an unfortunate accident. However our reporter claims that a reliable source stated there might have been an ambiguity as to the cause of death.*

Georgia was the first to hear about Fallon's death, when her father rang from his office and asked if she'd read the paper. "That copper chap, he's been found dead."

Georgia found the sensational headline on page four, **Suicide or Gangland Execution.** Her first though after reading of his demise was a feeling of relief, followed by a very dark thought. She immediately phoned Jim, "I'm reading it now," he answered.

"You don't think….." whispered Georgia.

"Don't be daft, he wouldn't be that stupid!" stated Jim.

The news spread like wild fire, "Have you seen the papers?" asked Bob as he entered the room where Joe was chasing out the walls.

Joe looked up, "When do I find the time to look at papers, I've a hard taskmaster for a boss!"

Bob looked at him seriously, "I think you'd better read this!" Then he handed him a copy of the Sun, subconsciously watching his friend's reaction.

Joe put his tools down and began to read, "What the fuck!" He read, then re-read the article, before addressing Bob. "That's all I need! I guess they'll try to pin that on me too!"

"Joe, it says here it was an unfortunate accident!"

"Let's hope you're right. I'm glad the fucker's dead!"

"You can get off, if you want," suggested Bob.

"Why would I do that, it's not like I'd grieve for the fucker is it?"

"Nah, I guess not. I'll see you later," said Bob.

Eric received a phone call just as he was opening up the antique shop. "Good morning, Eric's Antiques!"

"Eric it's Georgia, have you seen the papers, Sean Fallon's dead!"

"What! I don't usually read the papers. What happened?" Georgia read out the article in the Mail. "Freak accident, I don't buy it," he added.

"Well that's what I thought at first. I've rung a source at Fleet Street, someone that's in the know. It appears to be legit. The prick went out with his dog intending to shoot a few pigeons, but ended up shooting himself instead. Good riddance! At least I'll sleep well in my bed tonight," said Georgia.

"I guess I'd better lock up and go home. Give Grace the news before anyone else does," said Eric, "Thanks for the head's up."

Ten minutes later he pulled onto their drive. Grace came to the door wondering what he'd forgotten.

"I need you to sit down!" he said as he stepped inside.

A worried frown crossed Grace's face, "What's up?" she cried as she backed into the kitchen and sat down.

"Sean's dead." Eric handed her the paper he'd purchased after he locked up.

Grace read, then re-read the article. "There must be some kind of mistake, Sean was always careful around firearms."

"Maybe, but you can be too familiar. Complacence sets in."

"Sean's dead!" It was clear Grace was in a state of shock, "Does Joe know?"

Joe rang Donna during his lunch break.

"Hi!" she cried when she heard his voice, "This is nice you ring...."

Joe cut her off in mid-flow, "Fallon's dead. It's in the papers. He shot himself by accident, if you can believe that."

"What are you saying?" asked Donna.

"According to the papers, they're saying he slipped on a stile on New Year's Day and the shotgun he was carrying accidentally went off. Fucking killed him. Donna, I'm glad, I'm fucking ecstatic, the fucker deserved what he got, accident or otherwise. Fucking Karma!"

"Otherwise? What are you saying?"

"A cunt like Fallon has many enemies. I dare say when they get around to it, the filth will start knocking on doors!"

*****

Late Thursday afternoon Inspector Langley called his key men into his office, "Things have come to my attention that suggest Chief Inspector Fallon could have been murdered"

"What things?" asked Sergeant Lomax?

"Skull fragments recovered from the scene today have been examined by forensics and found one section of the frontal lope appeared to have a half circular shape consistent with a 22 calibre projectile."

"Could have been murdered! Are you saying forensics aren't one hundred percent?" questioned Lomax.

"That's exactly what I'm saying. Forensics isn't an exact science just yet, but if there's a chance one of our own was murdered we need to leave no stone unturned."

A hush came over the room, as the officers took in Langley's word

"You did say starting at his first day on the force, didn't you Guv?" said Hargreaves.

"Not literally you tosser!" cried Langley.

Hargreaves ignored the insult, he'd been working under Inspector Langley for a little over six months and had gotten use to his rudeness and profanity. "It might be nothing, but I found a disciplinary report in the archives dating back to Fallon's probationary period. He was found to have gone missing off his beat on more than four occasions. He got written up but no disciplinary action was taken. Sounds strange, don't it Guv?"

"We are talkin' fifties, they did things differently back then."

"Yeah I know, I've an uncle, ex-copper who knew Fallon, said he was sweet on some prostitute and even wanted to marry her, until he discovered she'd been playing him. He wasn't the type to take things lying down. Rumour has it he beat her to within an inch of her life."

"Rumour! You said it! Not fact, fucking rumour," cried Langley.

"What do you want me to do with him," laughed Sergeant Lomax.

"Nothing, Hargreaves has just shown us the character of the man. Rumours are just facts that can't be proven. Keep at it."

Encouraged by his superior officer, Hargreaves piped up again, "This might be rumour, but it is mixed with facts. Fact one, Detective Sergeant Fallon was ear-marked for promotion, fact two, a death in custody on his watch, fact three, he was passed over."

"Wipe that smug look off your face Hargreaves, when you're as good a detective as Lomax then you can look smug."

"So from what Hargreaves seems to have uncovered we can assume, Fallon wasn't averse to breaking the rules," contributed Lomax.

"You could say that sergeant. But what Hargreaves has uncovered is motive! First thing tomorrow I'd like you to pay a visit to Fallon's widow, offer our condolences and then in a roundabout way, find out any relevant background information into their relationship. Just don't make it apparent we're treating her husband's death as anything other than a tragic accident."

"Yeah, you know me Guv, discretion is my middle name."

"It had better be, and while you're at it dig into his finances. Houses in their own grounds in Surrey don't come cheap."

Langley then turned his attention back to the detective constable. "Tomorrow Constable Hargreaves, find out everything you can about the first Mrs Fallon!"

It was early Friday evening when an excited Hargreaves came racing into the detective inspector's office just as he was packing up for the day.

"Sir, it might be nothing, but I've spent the best part of the day looking into the late Chief Inspector Sean Fallon's first wife. It makes colourful reading."

"Enough of the dramatics, get on with it," stated Langley, as he glanced at the time. He and the wife had a dinner engagement with friends in a little over an hour's time. "Make it quick Hargreaves I've places to go and people to see."

"An uncontested divorce even though Mrs Fallon was pregnant with another man's child. From what I've found out about Fallon's character he wasn't someone to take something like that lightly."

"Fact's Hargreaves, not conjecture!"

"Grace Fallon received a fair settlement, considering the affair. As part of the settlement Sean Fallon received an undisclosed package from his wife's solicitors."

"Did you find out what the package contained?" asked Langley.

"Not at the moment sir, but here is where it gets interesting. Fallon's now ex-wife begins co-habituating with the father of the as yet unborn child. A few months into this relationship the man, Joseph Dempsey is arrested for the attempted robbery and kidnapping of a B.O.A.C. employee's wife during an attempted robbery of the airlines warehouse at Heathrow."

"Yeah, I remember it, late sixties if I'm not mistaken," added Langley. "Go on."

"Joseph Dempsey and two others were sent down for it. In Dempsey's case twenty years without parole. Dempsey always protested his innocence, and was released from Durham a few months ago."

Inspector Langley pricked up his ears, glanced again at his watch. "Is this going to take much longer?"

"Now here's where it gets interesting. He was released on the grounds the conviction was unsafe, and his sentence was commuted to time served. A friend of Dempsey, who incidentally worked alongside him at B.O.A.C had left a death bed confession when he committed suicide, completely exonerating him."

Hargreaves couldn't help himself as he milked the situation for all it was worth, fuck Langley and his places to go, people to see. "Not only did this Terry Richards claim to be the real culprit, he pointed the finger straight at Chief Inspector Sean Fallon. Basically stating the robbery and kidnapping was a set up. Instigated by Fallon, doomed to fail and that he, Terry Richards was being blackmailed by Fallon to frame Dempsey."

"So what are you getting at Hargreaves!"

"Motive sir! Framing his ex-wife's lover for the alleged crime."

"A bit convoluted, but interesting," stated Langley. "Certainly a motive."

Sergeant Lomax strolled into the office and caught the tail end. "I might be throwing a spanner into the works."

"Can it wait sergeant!" said Langley glancing again at his watch. "Not really sir, Mrs Fallon and her husband Sean Fallon lived a comfortable lifestyle, expensive house and lovely grounds I might add, plus a villa in Spain courtesy of Jackie's divorce settlement from her first marriage. All legit, but they had a number of investments which although not illegal were, let's just say open to interpretation. After visiting Mrs Fallon I got the feeling there was more to her than met the eye, so I did a few discreet enquiries about the dutiful widow. She'd been having an on off relationship with Fallon's immediate superior Superintendent Charlie Wainwright."

"Fact or rumour Sergeant Lomax?"

Lomax scrunched his face up, "Very reliable source but without pushing it I'd have to say rumour!"

"Tread carefully sergeant, I don't want to open a can of worms if I don't have too," warned the inspector. Getting involved with the top brass wasn't on the agenda, no way was he seeing his career go up in smoke.

"From what you've collated it seems that Chief Inspector Fallon was a nasty piece of work, and in essence not worth spending any more time on than necessary, but the law is the law. Sergeant Lomax, you and Hargreaves pay a call on Mr Joseph Dempsey first thing tomorrow, just a gentle enquiry, shake the tree see if anything falls out. After that call on this Grace... whatever her name is," ordered Langley.

"It's Sullivan, sir."

"Good, now you've got all your ducks in a row, I'll bid you goodnight."

# Chapter 71

Donna awoke bright and early; Joe was picking her up and taking her to see Billie ride. Because of her job she couldn't make Saturday's that often, so she was looking forward to the extra day off, only marred by the news of the copper's death.

'Joe's been touchy, it's as if he's waiting for the knock on the door.' She hated herself for thinking he might have done something reckless. Who knows what untold damage ten years in prison could do to someone. It was an uncomfortable thought, having to second guess herself. She couldn't help herself as her mind kept returning to New Year's Eve. *Joe had been relaxed, he laughed and joked with everyone, not drunk like herself and Becky but merry. It was three minutes to midnight when he suggested they took a walk outside.*

*"Here's hoping this year will be our year," he'd said as they left the pub just before the countdown. The night air felt cold but somehow invigorating as they walked into the pub garden. It was a clear and silent night broken only by the sounds of their footfall crunching on the frozen ground. Alone in the centre of the garden he took her in his arms and kissed her. "I don't want to do the rounds of kissing everyone, I just want to be alone with you," he said quietly. They stood there with their arms around each other listening as the faint noise from inside the pub alerted them as the old year disappeared. He kissed her again; a long lingering kiss, then he'd looked into her eyes and said, "Let's go." They left by the side gate, crossed the car park and located the Zodiac.*

*They nearly made love there in the car park, but for a couple of early leavers, "Hold that thought," he'd said. The Zodiac's engine came to life and within minutes they were racing back towards Northolt. Their love making was intense and lasted until around two thirty in the morning. Exhausted from their efforts they fell asleep in each other's arms. Donna only waking briefly to find Joe getting dressed. She glanced at her alarm clock, "You're not getting up now, are you; it's not even nine o'clock!"*

*"Yeah, I'm meeting Bob and the boys at twelve, and I promised mum I'd look in on them. Besides her breakfasts are legendary," he laughed.*

'Perhaps it's my imagination,' thought Donna, 'Joe, she'd found to her cost, was an early riser. Worrying for nothing.' The year was one week old, New Year's Eve was now just a memory. All thoughts evaporated as Joe pulled up in the Zodiac. His smile made all her worries disappear.

"Dressed to kill, I see," said Joe as Donna wearing the faux fur coat he'd bought her for Christmas walked towards him with a seductive sway.

"Wait until you see what I'm not wearing under this coat," she purred.

It was only when he looked down and saw her hip hugging jeans and boots that he realised she was joking. "You nearly had me in a tail spin. I'm not sure the riding stables are ready for you just yet," he laughed.

Donna looked at Joe as they drove to the stables and realised her doubts were unfounded. Within fifteen minutes the entrance to the stables came into view.

Billie was pleased to see them, and cried out as Joe and Donna climbed out of the Zodiac. "Donna's here!" she exclaimed.

"Relegated to second place," he laughed. "Sorry we're a bit late."

Grace smiled, Eric nodded and Billie waved before racing off to the tack room. "It's been a strange couple of days," remarked Joe.

"It certainly has," replied Eric.

'Egg shells or what,' thought Joe

Nothing more was said on the matter as they watched Billie put Abbie through her paces.

"Wow, she's good!" exclaimed Donna as Billie cleared three fences.

As the training session drew to a close Grace broke the ice. "How are you holding up?"

"I'm fine, I never knew the man," he said rather curtly.

"No, of course you didn't." said Grace feeling a little foolish. 'It's strange really,' she thought, 'throughout their time together Fallon had figured prominently, but Joe and Sean had never actually met.'

"Sorry," responded Joe, "that was uncalled for, I'm okay. Can't say I'm sorry, because I'm not. How about you?"

"It's strange really, I loved him once, but now I feel nothing," replied Grace, before changing the subject. "Billie's in training for the Spring Gymkhana, so she's having extra tuition on Wednesdays after school."

"I get Wednesdays off, would it be okay to come and watch once in a while?" asked Donna.

"If you really want to!" replied Grace. "If she's still doing it after the Gymkhana, maybe we could do lunch."

"I'd love that!" exclaimed Donna.

"That's great," replied Joe. "Tell me, is it my imagination or has Billie grown taller since I first met her?"

Grace laughed, and for a moment Joe was lost, "I think she's having a growth spurt, either that or Abbie's grown taller."

"You'll let us know the dates of the Gymkhana," said Donna.

"Yeah, soon as we know the exact dates you'll be the first to know," replied Grace.

After Billie's lesson Donna said she'd like to try her hand at learning to ride.

"Rather you than me," laughed Grace. "Have you seen how tall those horses really are?"

Donna walked over to the still mounted Billie, and looked up. "Wow, forget I said it," she giggled and Grace laughed along with her. 'How funny,' she thought, 'the woman that I believed to be my worst enemy was in fact a fun loving person that was good to be around. That she's asked me to meet her for lunch sometime makes me slightly nervous, but excited at the same time.' She kicked herself for her dark thoughts of the morning, all was right with the world after all.

As they all walked happily to their cars, an Austin Westminster loomed into view and drove slowly into the parking area of the stables. A tallish young man in his mid-twenties unfurled himself from the driver's side, while the other occupant of the car, a man in his early forties climbed out.

"If I'm not mistaken, that's old bill," declared Eric.

"Excuse me ladies and gents, would either of you two be a Mr Joseph Dempsey?"

There it was, Donna's world started to crumble.

"I'm Dempsey," said Joe in a resigned matter.

"DS Lomax and this is my colleague DC Hargreaves," said the shorter of the two. I wonder whether you'd mind coming with us. We've a few questions we'd like to ask you."

Joe felt his hackles rising. "What if I do mind?" said Joe in an aggressive manner.

Grace sensing trouble spirited Billie back to the stables. She made a hand sign that she was going to make a call. Eric nodded his understanding. Promptly she asked if she could use the phone in the office.

"Georgia, two policemen just pulled up at the stables and asked Joe to go with them. They want to ask him questions."

"Tell Joe not to do anything stupid, and tell him to say nothing until I get there."

Leaving Billie with the stable owners she reassuring her daughter there was nothing to worry about, she hurried back.

"Look, we only want to talk," said Lomax.

"About what," answered Joe?

"I think you know quite well what we're talking about," said Hargreaves.

"Look," intervened Eric. "Do you have a warrant?" The look on both the detectives' faces said it all. "I take it you haven't, then Joe doesn't need to speak to you right now, but hang on."

Grace, looking slightly flush and breathless re-joined the group. She put her hand up while she gathered her thoughts. "What is it you want?" she demanded.

"We only want to talk," said Lomax.

"I've just spoken to Mr Dempsey's solicitor and she advises Joe to say nothing until she gets here."

"How long's that going to take?"

"Ten minutes, maybe a little less," said Grace.


Georgia arrived in nine minutes, and didn't look happy. "What the fuck are you doing?"

"Charming!" exclaimed Hargreaves.

"If you wanted to speak to my client, you should have paid him the courtesy to call first. I'm Georgia Chandler, of Chandler and Lowe."

"We're here on routine enquires into the death of Chief Inspector Sean Fallon."

"Basically we're here to cross the I's and dot the T's," added Hargreaves. "Nothing more, just a fact finding mission."

Georgia looked at Joe, "Are you happy to speak to these gentlemen, here or wherever."

"Here's fine."

"Why do you feel you need a solicitor present?" asked Lomax.

"If you've read anything to do with my case you'll understand. Having been fitted up by Sean Fallon, I don't trust coppers!"

Sergeant Lomax managed the briefest of smiles. "I've read your file and I can understand why," he replied.

"Where were you between the hours of 6am and 12 noon on the first of January this year?" asked Hargreaves.

"I was in bed with…."

"He was in bed with me until around eleven," cried Donna.

"Is that correct?" asked Lomax.

"I don't know exactly, but it was around that time, then I went home and freshened up before meeting friends at the George in Ruislip at twelve o'clock."

"Can anyone corroborate where you where?"

"I can, he was with me and two others, Robert Walker and James Newton, until approximately twenty past two," replied Eric.

"For the record could we have all your names?"

"Eric Sullivan, this is my wife Grace."

"Grace Sullivan, you're ……." said Hargreaves.

"We need to speak to you as well, Mrs Sullivan," interrupted Lomax.

"About what?"

"About your ex-husband!"

"There's a lot to tell, none of it good. But if you gentlemen want to know what a nasty piece of work he was, then make an appointment!"

"We'll do that Mrs Sullivan, our boss is a stickler for detail. Now young lady your name?"

"Donna Douglas."

"You understand it's a criminal offence to give a false alibi," said Hargreaves.

"You asked me a question, I answered!"

"Thank you, Mr Dempsey, I think that's all. If we need to speak to you again we'll be in touch," said Lomax.

# Chapter 72

Georgia was hoping mad, "You should have seen them Jim. Two country coppers out to make a name for themselves. If Grace hadn't had the good sense to phone me, I don't know what could have happened. From the look of Joe he wasn't going with them, at least not without a fight, but luckily Eric intervened, which fortunately bought Grace enough time."

"They didn't have anything on him though?" said Jim.

"No, nothing. They were just fishing. They weren't too impressed when I showed up."

"I bet they weren't," smirked Jim.

"They asked all the usual questions. Where were you at such and such a time? Joe told them and Donna confirmed it," added Georgia. "That was it apart from asking Grace if she wouldn't mind speaking with them about that prick of an ex-husband."

"What's that about?"

"From what I could gather someone's taking corruption in the Met seriously at last." Georgia waddled over to the couch and plumped herself down, "Ah that's better; these two fuckers are really restless today."

"You realise once they pop out you've got to stop swearing," said Jim.

Donna's day off had started out great but went downhill rapidly once those coppers turned up. As they left the stables Joe turned to her, "Why did you lie for me?" he asked. "Did you really think I could kill him?"

"I wouldn't blame you if you had, but no, beneath that hard exterior I don't think you've got it in you."

"So why lie, why perjure yourself?"

"Because I love you! It seemed the most natural thing to do."

"Be honest, part of you thinks I might have done it."

"No, not for a moment," she said.

It was a fraught weekend coupled with anxiety and tension. Even in death Sean Fallon was still able to ruin his life. Living with the uncertainty of wondering what comes next left both of them distraught. Over a couple of drinks in a local pub on Sunday evening Joe told Donna his fears.

"Seeing those two coppers, it felt like it was history repeating itself. Their cocksure manner when they asked me to go with them. I knew, I just knew that if I did as they asked, they'd find some way to stitch me up. Once they get you in the system there's no way out."

"Joe, it's an understandable fear, especially now, but it will pass. You've got me. I'll never leave your side, even if you told me to go. I'm not going anywhere."

It was his moment to step up; "Donna, I'm pot-less, I've nothing to show for my thirty three years apart from my old Zodiac, oh' and my prospects are pretty shit, but Donna Douglas, will you marry me?" The moment he said it, he wished he could take it back. And there it was; Grace. It wasn't that he didn't love her, it… It was too soon.

Donna sat there totally shocked, while he mumbled something about getting her a ring next payday. "Yes, yes, of course I'll marry you."

"That's fantastic!" cried Becky on Monday morning when Donna phoned.

"I wanted you to be the first to know. We'd had such a shitty weekend, then Joe up and proposes, I'm over the moon."

"When?" asked Becky.

"We're not sure, but probably June," cried Donna.

"No not June, early May or July. We're away in America," said a panicking Becky.

"Nothing's set in stone, it'll be a Registrar's Office do, nothing fancy," added Donna.

"That's what you think," laughed Becky. "My oldest mate, getting married, it'll be great!"

"We're going flat hunting in the spring so we'll set the date then."

It was the following Wednesday when Grace received a call from the police.

"Good morning, I'm Inspector Paul Langley from the Woking division of the Surrey Constabulary. I'd like a word with Mrs Grace Sullivan if that's at all possible?"

"I'm Grace Sullivan, what can I do for you?"

"Firstly Mrs Sullivan, I'd like to apologies to you for the clumsy way my officers handled their meeting last Saturday. My instructions were to ask Mr Dempsey in a sensitive way questions pertaining to his whereabouts, to eliminate him from our enquires.

"I quite understand," replied Grace.

"On Tuesday our chief pathologist re-examined the wound and concluded that the entry wound appeared consistent with an accidental discharge."

"Well thank you for informing me, but shouldn't your call have been directed to Mr Dempsey rather than me," stated Grace.

"Right after this call I intend doing just that. The reason I called was two-fold. My officers mentioned you would be happy to meet to discuss the background concerning the late Chief Inspector Sean Fallon," said Langley.

"Why would you want that? The man is dead. You've just stated he died from self-inflicted wounds."

"No Mrs Sullivan, I stated it appeared he died from a self-inflicted wound. I'm sorry I gave you that impression."

"So what is it I can help you with?" asked Grace.

"I'm a career copper; in the job for twenty seven years, been divorced twice; because of it. I suppose you could say I'm married to the job. Sad, I know but it's my world and I'm proud of what we do. When your ex-husband died under what appears suspicious circumstances I felt the need to investigate those circumstances. Unfortunately during my investigation I uncovered a number of anomalies concerning the chief inspector. I hate corruption of any kind especially within the force. The London City and the Met have had more than their fair share of bad apples. I suspect your ex-husband is one of them. Basically any background information you could give me would be appreciated."

"Let me stop you there. In light of what you're not saying, I feel that I would like my solicitor present when we meet. Does next Friday morning suit?"

"That's fine with me, I completely understand. Friday, say ten o'clock."

Grace phoned Georgia right after the phone call with the inspector. "I've just been speaking to Inspector Langley, the man that's investigating Sean's death. He wants to meet me this Friday. He led me to believe it was an accidental death, but as the case is still ongoing I'd like you to be present when he comes."

"You did the right thing," replied Georgia.

Grace's meeting with Detective Inspector Paul Langley was very informative and enlightening. Grace gave him chapter and verse about the verbal and physical abuse she suffered whilst married to Fallon, the underlying threats to her person, the London Fertility clinic, and added it was a matter of record that an accusation about the framing of Joe supported by Terry's confession was ongoing.

Georgia recorded the whole conversation, whilst learning a little about the investigation into the corruption in the Met and City of London police. Inspector Langley was guarded about giving too much away but Georgia sensed an official inquiry was imminent.

# Chapter 73

The open and shut case just wouldn't close. The more Hargreaves and Lomax uncovered, made solving the case even less likely. Since his death more and more people had come out of the woodwork. Tales of double dealing, intimidation, alleged assaults and frame ups, all added to the file.

Between Christmas and New Year's Day a number of bodies were found under suspicious circumstance in the London area, most had no connection to Fallon, but others had distinct possibilities, namely a known villain called Bernie Abrahams. He'd been found shot dead in his London flat, four days before Fallon died. It was only while trawling through Fallon's cases and known associates that Abrahams name came to light. It seemed more than a coincidence that two men of different backgrounds, known to each other, should be found dead within the space of a few days.

Langley's suspect list was growing, there was Superintendent Charlie Wainwright, *he didn't want to go there,* Joseph Dempsey, a man with a grudge, but an alibi, *tenuous maybe*, and now a gangland hit, *most likely*. The more they uncovered about Chief Inspector Sean Fallon, the dirtier he appeared.

It was becoming a hot potato, a case that originally was filed as an accidental death had somehow morphed into a murder hunt. So much time and effort had been thrown at uncovering the cause of death, all on the vaguest notions of one man. Finally financial restraints, and pressure from above caused Inspector Paul Langley to finally admit the skull fragment with the circular half circle the size of a 22, was probably nothing more than his wishful thinking. The death of Chief Inspector Sean Fallon was finally put to bed. The coroner recorded accidental death and the case was officially closed on the twenty first of March 1978.

"About fucking time," cried a rather large and portly woman about to burst. "They took their own sweet time closing the case," said a very irritable Georgia, when she heard the news.

"Let's be honest, it didn't seem likely that a copper like Fallon would end up shooting himself, by accident. My money's on it being a gangland killing," replied Jim.

"I don't really care. All I want is for these two fuckers to find a way out! I don't think it'll be much longer!"

"I'm just glad it's over," said Grace when she heard the news. "The strain that inspector put on Joe and Donna was so unfair."

"That copper was a piece of work!" exclaimed Eric. "A high profile chief inspector drops dead on his patch and he tries to make a name for himself."

"He was only doing his duty," stated Grace.

"I've never like them, never trusted them either."

On hearing the news that Langley had finally closed the case, Joe snuggled up to Donna, "At last! Finally we can get our lives back on track."

"I just feel relieved it's all over," said Donna.

"You say that now, but three times that bastard Lomax interrogated you, like the fucking Gestapo!"

"Joe we need to forget about it and concentrate on looking for a place to live."

"Thank God!" cried Becky, "Poor Donna's been through the wringer."

"Yeah Joe ain't been right since that fucker killed himself. Why those coppers had to keep hounding him and Donna beats me. He was whacked by the mob, everyone knows that!" exclaimed Bob.

"You've been watching too many episodes of Hawaii Five O," laughed Becky.

Bob ignored Becky's quip, "Fucking coppers, they're a law unto themselves!"

# Chapter 74

Georgia gave birth to her twins on the 24th of March at the maternity wing of Hillingdon Hospital. Jim wasn't allowed at the birth, he had to make do pacing the corridor outside the delivery room. Contrary to Georgia's fears, her labour lasted five and a half hours and both her little ones slipped out with only a minimum of fuss. Jim rushed in to see her and was confronted with a boy 6lb 8oz and a girl 6lb 1oz. Both mother and babies were fine.

Jim couldn't contain his excitement, "They're beautiful!" he cried, as he looked at the twins, before planting a kiss on Georgia. "I love you Georgia Chandler."

"I love you too James Newton. You might think about making an honest woman out of me."

"Did you say what I thought you said?"

"Yeah, I suppose I did. Must be too much gas and air!" she smiled. "Well! Ask me then!"

"Georgia, will you marry me?"

"Yes. Kiss me," she said sleepily. "Now fuck off and have a drink with your mates."

"We're here to wet the baby's head. So get them in!" said Bob, the moment Jim walked into the George. "So what was it? A boy or a girl?"

Jim ignored him and concentrated on getting the round it. Then balancing a tray of drinks he brought them over and placed them on the table.

"Well what is it, boy or girl," repeated Bob impatiently.

Jim hadn't sat down, his face a picture of pride, "Yes" he answered.

"What's that supposed to mean?" cried Bob.

Joe laughed, "Got it! Or at least I think I know."

"Jim couldn't contain himself any longer, "I've one of each!"

"Twins!" exclaimed Bob. "Well blow me."

"No thanks!" exclaimed Joe.

Eric walked in and stepped up to the bar. Jim on seeing him jumped up, "I'll get that."

Bob took the moment to ask Joe how things were going.

"Yeah, everything's okay."

"It's just I haven't seen that much of you lately. How are things between you and Eric?"

"We're okay, and I'm good, but I still have feeling for her. They won't go away overnight."

"But you and Donna, you're doing alright?" asked Bob.

"Yeah, we're fine, good as gold, but there's nothing to say you can't love more than one woman."

Bob left it at that, just as Eric and Jim walked over.

"Have you got names for them yet?" enquired Eric as he sat down.

"He'll probably call one Clint and the other Josey," laughed Bob.

"Great idea," replied Jim, "What do you think Georgia would say?"

"I think you already know the answer," said Joe.

"Nah, Eric, we banded a few names about, I'm just glad they're okay. You know it's just hit me, I'm a Dad; I'm finally a Dad!"

"Strange isn't it. Friday nights were all about drinking, getting your end away and live music. Now we're sitting here talking about fatherhood and holidays," mused Bob.

"No one mentioned holidays, Bob," said Joe.

"Yeah where did our youth go?" added Jim.

"I at least know where mine went; down the pan for ten years," said Joe. "While you lot were swopping your youth for domestic bliss I was slopping out three times a day."

"Yeah sorry Joe," cried Bob.

"Nothing to apologies for, I've just got some catching up to do."

"Yeah. I heard you and Donna are looking to rent," said Bob.

"Yeah, we've looked at a few, they're either too expensive or they're shit holes," cried Joe.

"Ain't you got anything on your books?" asked Bob.

"Not at the moment," replied Jim. "It's a pity you didn't ask me a couple of months ago. I had one, perfect for you and Donna. It was just up your street. Pity. I'll ask around."

"No offence Jim, I doubt I'd have been able to afford it anyway."

"Have you thought about buying your own?" suggested Eric.

Joe laughed, "You're forgetting I work for these two."

"What, Fagin and the Artful Dodger," laughed Eric.

"It's a nice idea, but house prices, they're what, fifteen grand for an average semi?"

"You'll not get much change from seventeen grand. The market's flying at the moment," added Jim.

"On my wages," said Joe.

"Rough calculation, I'd say you'd need at least three and a half, possibly four grand deposit," suggested Bob. "But I could rejig your yearly wage, which might bring it down a bit."

"Where the fuck am I gonna get four grand?" snapped Joe, before adding "It's a thought, I'll bear it in mind. Now whose round is it?"

Predictably by closing time Jim was the worst for wear when they poured him into a cab, while Bob staggered off to the bus stop. Eric hung back. "Are you free tomorrow around ten? I've something that I think will interest you."

"Whatever it is Eric, if it's dodgy I ain't interested."

"It ain't dodgy Joe, I've been legit for years. There's something I'd like to talk to you about. It might help you with a mortgage."

"I'll think about it. Where?"

"My shop, around ten."

# Chapter 75

Joe phoned Donna at the salon just after nine the following morning, "Instead of looking at shithole flats, what about us taking on a mortgage and buying a house?"

"Sounds great, but aren't you forgetting we haven't got the money, well not enough for a deposit," said Donna, " Look I got to go, Mrs Burton's just walked through the door, ready for her shampoo and set; old bag. We'll talk about it this evening."

Joe couldn't understand why Eric had asked him to meet the following morning, it all seemed a little suspicious. Yet here he was outside Eric's antiques shop. With a sense of foreboding he entered. The tiny bell rang, announced his arrival. As his eyes adjusted to the darkness and the musty smell of old books he looked around at all the bric-a-brac, the oak writing desk, the stuffed owl, the Andy Warhol prints, Eric appeared from the back room.

"Ah, you decided to come. I wasn't sure."

"Me neither. You know this is the first time I've ever been in your shop."

Eric quickly moved passed him and locked the shop door turning the open sign around at the same time.

"You said this wasn't dodgy. I ain't going back inside," asserted Joe.

"It's not. Believe me what I've got to say, you'll be glad of the privacy." Eric gestured for Joe to follow him into the back of the shop, "Take a seat," Eric pointed to a couple of chairs and an old desk.

Joe unsure of why he was there sat down across the desk from Eric. "Okay Eric what's this all about?"

"Right, I'll get down to business. Are you aware, it was me who found Terry's confession and suicide note?"

"No, to be honest, I thought the police had found it when they took Terry's body down," said Joe.

"I found it in the loft lying next to a joist. Plod hadn't looked hard enough. I read it and realised the importance of Terry's confession. I also realised if I handed it into old bill, it might never have seen the light of day."

"You could have destroyed it!" exclaimed Joe.

"I could have, it would have made my life that much easier, but that's not who I am."

"Grace could have chosen me over you!" Joe instantly regretted his outburst.

"She could have, but I trusted her love for me was strong enough to cope with any guilt she might have felt."

Joe felt a knife had pierced his heart, "Why are you telling me this?"

"Because, I want you to know, despite our differences I still think of you as a friend."

"More acquaintance than friend," stated Joe, "So what's all the cloak and dagger shit?"

"The cloak and dagger shit as you call it started a few days after Terry's suicide. I was going through a backlog of mail when I came upon a letter that made my blood run cold. I recognised the handwriting immediately, it was Terry's."

"What the fuck was…." Joe stopped in mid-sentence.

"Inside the envelope were two letters, one addressed to me, the other to you." Eric held out the letter.

Joe took it and felt his hand trembling. He unfolded the letter.

*To Joe,*

*I won't start this letter begging you to forgive me, I know it is far too late for any of that shit. I want to explain my reasons of why I betrayed you. I don't expect you to understand, I just need you to know the truth. Like a fool I always wanted to be the big cheese. The odd crumbs I got from Eric didn't satisfy me. I wanted it all, not just for myself, but for Heather and the kids. I made a contact with a villain from the East End, a real London gangster, or so I thought. The rest you probably know.*

*I was a coward, I played fast and loose with Heather, but believe me, she was my world; I couldn't lose her. I knew that when I was confronted with those explicit photographs. There hasn't been a day that's gone by when I haven't thought about you, and what I'd done to you. Every time I looked at Heather and the kids, I told myself it was worth it, but the thought that I'd stole your happiness, your time with Grace and seeing young Billie grow up tore me apart. By the time you read this, the deed will be done, like Judas Iscariot, a fitting end to such a wretched life.*

*I'm sorry.*

*Terry.*

Joe looked up from the letter and looked across at Eric. "He did it for love! Is that what he's saying? I'm supposed to feel sorry for him, is that it?" said a grim faced Joe Dempsey.

"You need to read this one," said Eric, as he handed the second letter over. It was addressed to Eric Sullivan.

*Dear Eric,*

*By the time you read this I'll be dead. I'm sorry to hand you this burden, but you are I believe the best person to administer my wishes. Firstly a little explanation. One thing the court and my confession left out was the small matter of ten thousand pounds. Knowing that the gang were eventually going to get caught I asked for ten grand up front plus the incriminating photos. I destroyed the photos and hoped it would all go away. I took your advice and buried the ten grand, intending it for Heather if I got sent down. But as you know Fallon had other ideas.*

Joe stopped reading, "Your advice! What did he mean by that?"

Eric had been expecting the reaction, "You know Terry, always talking big. Kept on about gold bars. I must have said, too much heat, the old bill would turn your drum over quicker than you could blink. So if you're idiot enough go ahead, just bury it somewhere safe, until the heat dies down."

"You didn't k…"

"Know," snapped Eric. "Of course I didn't. What do you take me for! Why would I hand this letter to you, it's addressed to me. I could have destroyed it, even acted on it, but I didn't. I'm doing what that fucker asked of me, that's all."

"Okay, steady on, it's just…"

"Forget about it, read the letter."

*The money is still there, where I buried it. I placed all the notes in an airtight container, placed the container inside a bigger one, and used industrial tape to secure it. Then I drove to the woods, paced out an area, taking note of any distinct landmarks, buried it three feet under with the intention of returning a year or so later. I never went back, until a week ago. It's still where I buried it. Ten grand isn't much compared to ten years of life. Eric when you deem the time is right, get Joe to take the money and do with it as he wishes. These are my map references.*

*Drive up Duck's Hill Road until you reach the car park on the left at Mad Bess Woods. There is a sign marked footpath. Follow the path for approximately two hundred yards, a large oak diverts the path to the left. Stop at the oak and look directly right, you should see a clearing covered with ferns with another similar size oak in the background. Look towards the oak and walk in a straight line towards it. Twenty five yards into the ferns stop. Give or take a foot that's it.*

Joe stopped reading and looked at Eric, "Is this some kind of joke! Is that fucker laughing at me from beyond the grave?"

Eric knew it wasn't a joke, "I don't think so."

"So you want me to go into the woods, dig a hole, for what!"

"Joe, I feel it in my bones, the money's there!"

"Okay, supposing I go there and find it, the money might be papier-mâché."

Eric was growing tired of Joe's outbursts, "That's possible, but you won't know unless you look."

Joe gave it a minute to sink in, "Alright, we find the money, it ain't papier-mâché, what about it being out of date. Remember money changes every few years. Decimalisation must have changed it."

"Look Joe, I thought I could help. Ten grand could get you a good deposit and change."

"Yeah I see where you're coming from," muttered Joe.

"Hey, you've nothing to lose.

As luck had it the heavens opened just as they pulled into the car park at Duck's Hill Road. As the rain pelted down both men sat in silence. Eric lost in his thoughts. He knew Joe was probably right, one, they could dig and find nothing, two they find the box and it's filled with papier-mâché or three, the money's intact but it's ceased to be legal tender.

Joe was trying not to believe. If the money was there, if it was intact, if it was legal tender, he felt a sudden excitement. Suddenly there was a break in the cloud and the rain gradually began to stop. Both men got out and Eric popped the trunk.

"You knew I'd say yes," remarked Joe as he looked down at the spade, a pick a shovel and a small axe.

They easily located the large oak and looked expectantly for the second oak. The ferns wet from the rainfall glistened in the sunlight, but the oak was nowhere to be seen. Joe raced through the wet ferns desperately looking for a sign of the oak. Then though the wet ferns he saw a fallen tree, he cried out to Eric. "I've found it, looks like it must have been hit by lightning."

"Stay there, I'll use you as the marker." Then Eric paced out twenty five yards. Deep amongst the ferns he found where he believed the spot to be. Joe walked back over, he'd missed the spot by three or four yards. They checked the line, they rechecked the yardage, and then they began to dig. The deeper they went the wider became the dig. "Fuck it," said Eric once they'd reached their depth. "We need to go left a bit," he said in frustration.

Then suddenly Joe's spade glanced off something. It's a fucking root, give me the axe."

Eric passed it to him, and Joe swung the axe. A sound like cracked brittle plastic caused both men to stop in their tracks. Excitedly both men clawed at the earth like gold prospectors, until they could see the tell-tale cracked Tupperware box. A few frantic moments later Joe pulled the box from the earth.

Gathering up their tools they quickly made their way back to the path. They approached cautiously as they reached the car park. The rain had eased off but the clouds were still threatening. Loading the tools into the boot of the car, they clambered back inside the Jaguar.

Eric produced a knife and handed it to Joe, who was cradling the Tupperware box like a baby. "Open it!" he cried.

Joe took the knife and cut around the outside of the box, and opened it. Wrapped in more industrial tape was the smaller box. Feverishly Joe sliced of the tape before looking nervously at Eric, "Well papier-mâché or bust!"

Wrapper in tight bundles of plastic bags tied together with elastic bands were bundles of what appeared to be ten pound notes. "I think we hit the mother-lode," cried Joe excitedly.

Back at the antique shop Joe stacked the money on the table and looked it over. He was mesmerised by so much cash. All used notes. Eric picked up the phone. "Who are you calling?" he asked suspiciously.

"Someone that either turns your dream into a nightmare or reality."

"Hi Fred, just a word, I've just sold an antique clock, for a hundred quid, the man paid in tenner's. I noticed one of them was the older version, are they still in circulation?"

Joe pricked up his ears.

Eric listened intently then put the phone down. "You're in luck, the new ones came into circulation in 1975 and are alongside the c series which are due to be taken out of circulation sometime in 1979."

"So it's real!"

"Yes Joe it's real. You're rich."

"We're rich," said Joe handing him a wad of cash.

"It was meant for you. I don't want it.

Joe started to protest….

It's yours, let's just say it's in payment for an old debt."

Joe didn't push it, the thought of what this money would do for him and Donna was all that mattered.

"Just be careful about how you flash the cash. Stick it in a building society or two. Tell no one, not even Donna. Now bugger off, I've a shop to run."

Joe, still in shock stashed the money into an old bag and stood up. "Thanks, I'll do that.

# Chapter 76

'Tell no one, not even Donna,' thought Joe as he drove home. He should have felt elated, over the moon, true the money could solve a lot of problems, but it could also create many more. His mind was in turmoil. Everything about the morning had felt unreal.

A sense of foreboding began to creep over him. He was driving with a wad of unexplainable cash, if he was stopped for any reason the spectre of Fallon's murder would surely crop up. Even in death that bastard was still there. Would Fallon's unsolved murder continue to affect his future?

He realised he couldn't hide the money at Donna's so he had no alternative but to stash it at his parents' house over the weekend. Eric's idea of opening a building society account come Monday morning seemed the best option. He'd drip feed an account, a couple of grand shouldn't raise too many eyebrows. The bulk of cash he'd hide in the loft when his parents were out.

After he'd hidden the cash he drove to Ickenham and popped into the Coach and Horses for a pint and a chance to think. The Coach seemed the least likelihood of bumping into anyone that he knew. With his pint in hand he sat down at a table in the corner. His head was spinning as he took a sip and began going over everything that had happened that morning. Life was finally looking a hell of a lot brighter, accept Eric's curve ball had thrown his life into disarray.

He told himself to stop worrying about something that might not happen and concentrate on the positives. He had enough money to put down a deposit on a house. 'A two bedroom terrace, nah more like a three bed semi,' he mused. The very fact that he now had the means to break free, no more spending time at

Donna's mum's or his parent's house, he and Donna could buy the house of their dreams. He took another sip. It all felt too good to be true.

"Who turns down five grand!" he cried out loud. Fortunately his outburst had not caused anyone to look in his direction. Joe began to relive the moment when he'd offered Eric half the money. 'Yeah, no one,' he thought, 'it doesn't matter how wealthy you might be, no one turns down free money. Sullivan had turned it down, saying it's in payment for an old debt. 'An odd thing to say. An old debt, I suppose I took it to mean him and Grace, but maybe I was wrong? On the surface it seems an innocent enough remark, but then there was Terry's written words, *I took your advice and buried the money.*' 'Am I being paranoid, or is it my imagination?'

It was nothing just a throw away remark, that's all it was, yet it was taking on mammoth proportions. 'What if Eric knew about Terry from the start? Nah, Eric was a lot of things but he's as straight as a die.'

Joe didn't like where his mind was taking him. 'But if that were true, how would Grace react? Grace, it was always Grace,' he thought. He was letting his mind runaway with him. 'Would she leave Eric? Would she want me? It was fantasy, nothing more. The seeds of doubt wouldn't wither. 'I've got Donna, we're getting married. What if Grace needed me?' It was irrational thinking, but until he knew for sure, how could he and Donna get married? Then he shuddered as another thought flashed though his head, 'Eric had kept both letters, what if he was setting me up to get caught with the money. I'd probably get banged up to finish the rest of my sentence. Perhaps Eric feared that Grace wanted me.' He needed to talk to someone, but who?

His first thought was Bob, but he was too close, in fact they were all to close. 'Fuck,' he thought, he couldn't confide in Donna that was obviously out of the question, more pressingly he felt he needed to postpone the wedding at least until he got his head straight. He took a sip from his glass, "Ugh!" the beer was warm and flat. More importantly Joe was none the wiser as he left the pint and made for the door. He was sure of only one thing, Saturday night wasn't going to be all moonlight and roses.

Donna wasn't happy when he broke the news, "I've been thinking, do you really want us to live in a rented flat, paying money that could be put away for a deposit."

"What are you trying to say Joe?"

Joe chose his words carefully, "I was talking to Eric last night, he reckons if we postpone the wedding for a year or so, we should be able to save enough for a decent deposit."

"So Eric's put this idea in your head? Well fuck Eric!"

"I'm trying to look at it constructively. According to Georgia there is also the possibility of compensation," he lied. "Who knows we could be looking at a nice nest egg, in a couple of years."

"A couple of years," said a despondent Donna. "You want me to wait a couple of years."

"Getting married is a big decision, I know it was me asking. I love you, that's why I want to do it right. Who knows it might be a year."

The discussion consumed most of the evening, with Donna crying, "You don't love me. It's her… It's always been her."

Joe replied, "I've told you it's you I love. That ship has sailed," not the most tactful, he thought regretfully. "Forget it, we'll rent a flat, then get married as planned."

"But that's not what you want," she cried.

Frustrated and angry Joe snapped, "You're right, it isn't what I want! You might be happy in a flat in Northolt, but I want more! My friends are all settled with their fancy houses, I want that for us, I've ten years to catch up on!"

Donna looked crestfallen at Joe's outburst and said nothing for a few minutes. Joe in turn apologised for raising his voice, but added. "Since the moment I was released from prison, my family, my friends all of you have been falling over yourselves to help me. Do you know how that makes me feel? I'll tell you. I feel like an old lag, released from prison, a no nothing nobody."

It all came flooding back, from the overflowing slop buckets to the wanton violence of a typical prison day. The fights, the billiard ball in a sock, the boiling water and sugar, the improvised knives and razors, the law of the jungle. To survive you had to be as bad as the next man.

"Well I'm not that man, I'm a somebody and I intend making something of my life. I'm an innocent man, fitted up by a corrupt copper and an establishment that should have known better."

"I'm sorry Joe, I didn't know you felt so bitter. I thought it was just Grace."

"It was my whole life, it was stolen from me." Joe hadn't realised until that day how much resentment and anger were still eating away at his insides.

"Okay, we'll do it your way, said Donna. "I love you Joe, probably more than you know, but don't play me for a fool."

"You're not a fool, I love you very much." replied Joe.

It was true, he did love Donna and in reality, it made perfect sense to wait. A nice house in the Ruislip area, living amongst his peers. The money would give him the chance to level up, a real chance to rebuild his life. More than that, he needed the time to get his head straight. Only yesterday he had nothing. True, he had a gorgeous woman that loved him to bits, friends that had given him a chance to start over, and now in less than twenty four hours he was handed a wad of cash that could insure his and Donna's future. But, was that enough?

Joe pulled up at Donna's on Monday evening. "Get your coat, I've got something I want you to see."

"What!" exclaimed Donna?

"You'll see," replied Joe with a smile.

"Where are we going?" she asked. "Why the mystery?"

They drove straight through to Ruislip, then drove around the area looking at houses, "This is what I want you to see, our future. One day soon we'll have a place like these."

"In your dreams and mine," replied Donna.

"That's where you're wrong, I'll explain it all over a drink." Donna couldn't understand why they spent another ten minutes looking at houses they couldn't possibly afford, although Joe's enthusiasm was infectious. Then they pulled into the Swan car park.

"Why the Swan," she asked.

Joe laughed, "You'll see," then he sat her down at a table, where he smiled cheekily and went to the bar. Returning a couple of minutes later he said, "I took the liberty of ordering salmon and cucumber sandwiches." He put the drinks down and saw she was still bemused.

"You agree, living in any of those houses would be a dream, your words."

"Yeah Joe, but I'm looking at reality, even if we save for a year, even two we ain't gonna have enough to get one of those you've showed me."

He smiled at her, then reached into his inside jacket pocket and waved a building society book in front of her.

"What's that?"

"That sweetheart, is a building society book and that if you look closely is a deposit of two grand. I told you I was serious."

Donna looked incredulous, "Two thousand pounds! Where did you get two grand?"

"Mum and dad. Well actually Dad, he said provided I added to it each month and didn't dib into it, we could call it a wedding present."

Donna was in shock, she couldn't take her eyes off the building society book. "Is this for real!" she barely managed to get the words out.

"Best you believe it."

"We must go around there and thank them properly," she cried excitedly.

"No, they'd hate that. Dad gets embarrassed, and I don't think he's told mum," lied Joe. He hated lying to her but it killed two birds with one stone. If things turned out okay he'd be able to add at least another grand, maybe two.

The following morning Donna was on the phone to Becky, she'd cried her heart out to Becky all Sunday, now everything had changed.

"Wow!" exclaimed Becky. "It's a pity you're having to wait another year, but it means he's serious."

"Of course he's serious, he loves me," she cried excitedly into the phone.

By the following weekend they broke the news.

"Lucky bastard," said Jim, "I guess it makes sense, paying rent is like throwing money down the drain."

"Says you, with all your rentals, replied Joe.

"Exactly," stated Jim.

"I'd still have liked to have been Matron of Honour," added Becky.

"Nice to have great parents," said Bob.But it was Eric's wishes that resonated the most.

"Glad you took my advice."

"Thanks," replied Joe with a knowing look. Behind the smile Joe's mind was still in turmoil. At least the Old Bill hasn't felt my collar, he thought, 'it's been a week, if Eric was doing the dirty on me, he'd have done it by now, but there was something about Eric that didn't sit well.

# Chapter 77

He'd thought he'd eased his conscience, until the phone rang in the back of the shop.

"Hello 'Eric's Antiques.'"

"Nice to hear your voice Eric, it's Heather."

"Oh hi Heather it's nice to hear you too. How are things?"

"I'm fine, still miss the rotten bastard, but I guess time will take care of that I suppose. Anyway enough of that, I had a visitor call on me yesterday, it was Joe, Joe Dempsey."

"Joe! What the hell did he want?" he snapped."

"Wow Eric! No need to bite my head off."

Sorry Heather, I've been under some stress lately. What was it he wanted?"

"That's the point, I'm not sure. He said he had some business he needed to attend too and that while he was up here he thought he'd pay me a visit."

"That's possible I suppose."

"Why'd you say that Eric?"

"No reason, just my suspicious nature, you know how that works."

"Yeah, I do," replied Heather. "He said he was sorry about Terry's death, but I took that with a pinch of salt," and in that moment it all came flooding back.

*Heather had just finished vacuuming the front room when the doorbell rang. Opening the front door she stared at the man in front of her, "Can I help you?" Then recognition hit her. "Joe," she exclaimed.*

*"Hello Heather, it's been awhile."*

*"Come in, can't have you waiting on the doorstep." She'd thought that since moving away she'd never have to have this*

459

*awkward meeting. Gathering her thoughts, she asked if he'd like a cup of tea.*

*"Love one," he replied.*

*A brief few minutes of silence while Heather made the tea. Then she brought the cups into the front room and sat them down on the table.*

*"How are you settling in? The neighbours, they okay?"*

*"Yeah, they're real nice."*

*"I'm sorry about the manner of Terry's death it must have been dreadful for you."*

*"It was." The shock of Terry's death and the revelations that followed had taken a toll on her. She'd started to build a new life for herself and the kids, what she didn't need was the reopening of barely healed wounds. "If it's any consolation Terry had a terrible time after you got sent to prison. He had a nervous breakdown, of course we didn't know it was connected."*

*"Of course you didn't," replied Joe.*

*"What's that supposed to mean!" snapped Heather. "If I'd known Terry was guilty, I'd have made him give himself up," she added.*

*"I'm sorry, I didn't mean to imply."*

*"Of course you did Joe. I don't blame you, I'd have felt the same."*

*Shocked by the abruptness, Joe began to say he was sorry for upsetting her. "You're right, I did think there was a possibility at first, but not now.*

*"I should hope not," she replied defensively. "So I guess this isn't just a social call."*

*"Your right I do want something. You might be able to help me, you might not."*

*"Anything, if I can," replied Heather cautiously.*

*"I wondered whether Terry would have confided in someone else, he was close with Eric," asked Joe, knowing he'd worded his question a little to near the point.*

*"Eric wouldn't have stood by and let you take the blame,"* she blurted out.

*'Maybe too convincingly,' thought Joe. He'd picked up rumours that Eric and Heather were friendly. "Terry was a friend of Eric's, we all were, but he had dealings with him."*

*Heather remained silent.*

*"You know what I'm talking about."*

*"Yes,"* she sobbed, *"but Eric wasn't mixed up in that business."*

*"No, of course not, but Terry must have asked his advice over the years. Eric seemed to be in the know, if you get what I mean."*

*"It's possible, but unlikely."*

*"Why unlikely?"*

*"I knew Terry was a bit dodgy, yeah he had his head in the clouds about being a big man."*

*"A big man like Eric,"* persisted Joe.

*"What's that supposed to mean?"* she said angrily.

*"I'm sorry, I didn't mean any offence."*

*"My Terry, my Terry didn't have the guts to come clean, if he had we might have had a chance. There was nothing big about him."* Heather started to cry, *"I think you'd better go!"*

*"I'm sorry to have upset you, that wasn't my intention. I'll see myself out,"* Joe kicked himself for questioning Heather so abruptly and clumsy.

"And that was all he had to say?"

"More or less, I just thought you should know. He seemed more interested in you than Terry."

"Thanks Heather. Come the summer Grace and I will give you a call and pay you a visit."

"That would be nice. I'll look forward to it."

Eric knew this day would come, that one day he'd have to face Joe with the truth. His biggest fear was of losing Grace. He'd remained silent and destroyed any hope of happiness for them.

'But that was before Grace and I got together,' he reasoned. 'I was grieving for Gloria, I had my own problems. I tried to get Terry to come clean. Grace loves me I'm sure, but how strong is that love?'

He thought about confronting Joe, ask what he was playing at, act the indignant innocent, and tell him he was clutching at straws. 'What was up with the man? His obsession with Grace had to end. He has a beautiful girl friend and an assured future. I can't give him his life back, but the money should go a long way to ease that pain. Thanks to Heather I'm forewarned, best leave it for Joe to make the first move.'

# Chapter 78

It had been a long drive for nothing, thought Joe. He still had his suspicions, but that was all they were. 'Perhaps,' thought Joe, 'the money was Eric's insurance, that he'd given me the means to step up in the world, knowing that if I made a move on Grace he could bring my world tumbling down.' "Fuck!" he shouted. 'I'm being irrational, I'm trying to fit pieces into a jigsaw that don't fit!' It was true and Joe knew it.

He realised since finding the money apart from postponing the wedding and convincing Donna that opening up a building society account was worth waiting, he'd done nothing but stew over his suspicions. Heather hadn't been able to throw any light on it. It should have been the end of it.

Then Joe got to thinking. He'd been looking at it from the wrong direction. Those men that were convicted alongside of me, must have known about Terry and Sean Fallon. 'Both dead,' he thought, 'so that doesn't help, but Donald Fuller and Keith Porter might have some answers. They're in Parkhurst, getting them to talk wouldn't be easy, they were hardened criminals, but what the fuck so am I!'

Knowing that he couldn't ask Georgia to fast track a letter to a prisoner he had no choice but to ask Bob how to go about the procedure as he'd written to Joe, albeit Joe hadn't replied. Bob explained how he went about it, then asked who and why?

"Donald Fuller and Keith Porter, the why is my business."

"Shit Joe. I think you're making a big mistake, besides they might not want to speak with you."

"That's a chance I'll have to take. If they don't want to talk, I'll leave it, I just want closure Bob, nothing more."

Two weeks later Joe received a visiting order from Donald Fuller. He was a little surprised, he'd thought Porter seemed the more likely. "Be careful Joe, whatever it is you want to ask him, he'll want something in return."

"Yeah Bob, I know. One last favour, I need a couple of days off, so cover for me, will yah."

"Yeah, but now whose putting themselves on the line," Bob quipped.

Thursday afternoon Joe was face to face with Donald Fuller.

"I was shocked and surprised when I got your letter, curious even," said Fuller.

"Yeah I thought you might."

"I guess you want to know why we put you in the frame."

"Nah, I already know. Survival. I reckon Sean Fallon had a hand in it," said Joe.

"Then the rumours are true, you put pay to that fucker." Joe could detect admiration in Fuller's voice.

"Think what you will."

"Jesus! Prison must have done a number on you. Are you coming for me and Porter next? Poor fucker's quivering in his cell as we speak. Bring it on."

Joe laughed, "I ain't interested in you or Porter, you're nothing to me. What I want is any background on Arthur Briggs, his cousin Roy anything on Sean Fallon."

"Well there ain't much I can tell you, Arthur just disappeared, so I reckon he's dead. He weren't smart, if he was alive he'd have shown up by now, as for his cousin Roy, never met him, reckon he's a ghost too. So looks like a big old negative. But then you already know that. So what's it worth for the facts, the rumours of the late dearly departed Sean Fallon, need to ease your conscience."

Joe just smirked, "Do you know why your prison sentences haven't been added to since it broke that I was fitted up, well I'll tell you. Five and a half years from now you're eligible for parole, well a word or two from my solicitor and myself, could make the difference between you getting out or having an extended stay at Parkhurst. Your choice."

"You do that, I'll come for you, you can bet on it."

Fuller's tone was full of menace but Joe's reply showed no fear, "You know, I'd welcome it, so bring it on."

Fuller smirked, then grinned, "Okay, it ain't much, but it's all I got, it's only rumours mind. Nothing to do with your case, but it might be of interest. You heard of Bernie Abrahams."

"Yeah, sure read about him, he's an old gangster from the East End."

"He was, he's dead. Word is Fallon did it. But here's the kicker. Seems Bernie was Fallon's mentor, more maybe."

"More maybe! What's that supposed to mean?"

"Check out Somerset House. That's it, now fuck off."


The following morning Joe turned up at the North Wing of Somerset House and looked at the imposing and sprawling structure of the buildings, and questioned why he was there. On seeing an official looking man stand about doing nothing he asked directions to the Registrar General of Births, Marriages and Deaths.

The official looking gentleman looked perplexed, "That department is no longer with us."

"Is this some kinda joke," spat Joe.

"No sir, the register for all births, marriages and deaths certificates were moved in 1970."

"So where are they now," asked Joe with a slight impatience in his voice.

Unruffled by Joe's demeanour, the official replied, "It's at St Catherine's House formerly Television House in Aldwych. It's now called The General Register Office."

"Thanks a bunch," cried Joe as he left the building wishing he'd never started on this journey.

Two hours later after going through more bureaucratic bullshit Joe found what he was looking for, and more, much more....

# Chapter 79

Joe grappled with his new found knowledge, it wasn't what he'd been looking for, no mention of Eric's involvement with Terry or the others. What he had was a direct link with this Bernie Abrahams and Sean Fallon. Maybe enough for Georgia to put pressure on the courts to get his case reopened and the possibility of a pardon. A pardon could give him grounds to claim compensation for wrongful imprisonment. It was a long shot but worth a go.

His first thought the following morning was to take what he knew to Georgia but instead he found himself at the door to Eric's antique shop. The itch wouldn't stop, he'd exhausted all possible leads so he thought it was best to confront his fears. Luckily it was early and no one was inside as Joe entered the shop to the familiar sound of the bell just inside the door.

"Can I help yo…Oh Joe I thought you was a customer."

"No such luck, I couldn't afford your prices," replied Joe with a cheeky grin he never felt, before coming to the point. "Two things have been bothering me."

"Yeah I guessed there might be. Heather phoned me, said you weren't happy about something."

"Cut the crap Eric," said Joe as he locked the door and turned the closed sign around. "Something you said about repaying a debt and Terry's note, about taking your advice. I can't get them outta my head. If I'm wrong I'm sorry."

"I don't understand, I explained to you when we counted out the money that it was payment for an old debt."

"Yeah, that's right. What old debt?"

"The bad blood between us when you found out I'd married Grace, I just thought the money could help you get on your feet.

You and Donna seem to be happy and Terry wanted you to have it. I could have taken it, but because of our circumstances I couldn't do that."

"You could have taken half!"

"It was your money Joe."

"Yeah, I can see that now, but I didn't just go to see Heather, I took a trip to Parkhurst, spoke to Don Fuller, hoping to find out who else was involved in the Fallon fit up. It seems everyone involved are either dead or disappeared."

Eric smiled, "Sorry Joe, I didn't think anything I said to you would send you off to Parkhurst. For Christ-sake, that was a bit extreme."

"Yeah, you're right it was a bit extreme. Neither Fuller nor Porter knew why Fallon wanted them to say I was the man behind the robbery and kidnap, they just though their sentences would be reduced, I guess."

"So you come here, with these insinuations, expecting me to confess to something I know nothing about. I know you've an axe to grind but don't take it out on me because of Grace."

"Grace, yeah, there's always Grace. I wonder how she'd feel if she knew she'd married Fallon's half-brother!"

Eric's face turned ashen, "What!"

"No point in denying it, I've seen the records. No wonder Grace was attracted to you. You're the flip side to Fallon, alike in so many ways, a little dangerous, a little flash but outwardly a decent human being."

"What is it you want?"

"What I want is my life back!" exploded Joe. Seconds later he added calmly "But I know that's not possible."

Eric slumped against a display table, "What is it you want?

"The truth Eric, all of it."

"You won't get Grace back. The truth will destroy her. It'll hurt Billie and it would hurt you as well."

"I know that Eric. I lost Grace all those years ago, but I didn't know it until now. She loves you Eric, but the penny dropped when I saw the records. I have the full story now. I could destroy your life but telling Grace is not my intention. I wouldn't do anything to hurt her. Yeah she loved me but not in the way she loves you.

"What do you mean, not in the way she loves me?"

"You'll figure it out."

Joe looked down at the floor lost in a moment of thought, then he slowly looked Eric in the eye, "I'm done!" then he turned away and walked slowly towards the door.

"Joe, wait! You don't have the full story!"

Joe stopped and turned around slowly.

Eric took a deep breath, "I know you love Grace with all your heart, just remember that what I'm about to tell you if it got out it would break her heart."

He motioned to Joe to step into his office at the back where he'd sat when they counted the money a few weeks previous. Eric opened a draw at his desk and brought out a bottle of scotch and two glasses. Joe motioned that he didn't need a drink. Eric ignored him and poured two generous glasses.

"Sorry there's no ice, but I think with what I'm about to tell you, you're gonna need it."

Joe looked puzzled as he took an involuntary sip of the fiery stuff.

"Despite what you might think, Terry never asked my advice or confided in me about any part in the robbery and kidnap plot. If he had I'd have made him admit his part in it or I'd have told you. That said, you poking around in my business, bothering Heather and going to Parkhurst, what's that all about?"

"Eric, like I said, I'm done, it's over."

"It might be for you, but it ain't over for me…" Eric took a gulp of whiskey then looked Joe straight in the eye. "You see, I killed Sean Fallon!"

468

# Chapter 80

"What?" cried Joe, "It wasn't your fight?"

"Oh, but it was," replied Eric. "It all started that Christmas Eve."

*"It was nearly closing time when a man of middle age walked into the shop and started to browse. I'd seen him peering in the window of the shop earlier.*

*"That Fender Stratocaster, how much?" asked the man.*

*'Obviously a panic buyer,' I thought. "It really needs restoring to its former glory, but it's a beauty. It's a Sunburst, with as you can see a cream pickguard. Let's see now, a new Stratocaster could cost around two fifty depending where you bought it, possibly three hundred. As its Christmas I could let you have it for a hundred and twenty."*

*"I don't want to play it, it's for the wife, she wants to hang it on the wall in the music room," said the man, his tone slightly icy.*

*"Nice present, comes with a case," I said.*

*"Ain't interested in the case, I'll give you a ton."*

*The man was playing me, and I knew it, and as it was nearly closing time I wasn't in the mood for games, "I'll tell you what, you can have the Stratocaster and case for a hundred and ten, final price."*

*"You drive a hard bargain, Mr…" he smirked.*

*"Sullivan, Eric Sullivan."*

*"You've got yourself a deal," said the man.*

*"I'm sure your wife is going to love it," I said, as I looked at my watch I was eager to close up.*

*"I'm sure she will," replied the man. You've a nice town, lived here long?"*

*"Long enough," I stated.*

*"Let me guess, East End."*

*"A long time ago," I added. I was getting tired of this game of cat and mouse.*

*"Not that long, I'd wager."*

*I didn't answer as I took down the guitar and placed it in the case. I handed the case to the man and held my hand out for the cash. Neither of us smiled as we did the transaction.*

*"Have a good Christmas," cried the man, a smirk of a smile upon his lips, as he turned and left the shop.*

*I watched as he walked away. 'Call it sixth sense, call it what you like,' I thought, I've just come face to face with Sean Fallon. 'What was his game?' Was he sending me a message?"*

"Why didn't you tell anyone?"

"It was Christmas, I didn't want to spoil it for everyone. Then a couple of days after Christmas I learned through the papers that Bernie Abrahams had been murdered. I'd known Bernie since I was a kid, he was a sort of friend of the family. So I took a ride up the smoke and visited my dear old Mum. She told me everything. I knew that if Fallon wasn't stopped Grace's life would be in danger. So I stopped him in the only way I knew how."

"It was still dark that cold and crisp New Year's Day morning.....

*Jackie was sound asleep as Sean climbed out of their king-size bed. Despite falling into it at a quarter to two, the moment his head hit the pillow he was out for the count. Unfortunately Sean's body clock woke him a few hours later. He looked at Jackie and knew she'd be asleep until lunchtime. He smiled to himself as he shuffled his way into his bathroom. A quick shower, followed by a swift brush of his teeth and he sought out his country apparel. He'd really gotten into the country gentleman way of life and New Year's Day would be no exception. He'd regale the locals at the Horse and Groom with his daring tales of blags and bank robbers, fast cars and faster women. (Not when Jackie was in ear shot.)*

*But first, his Sunday morning ritual, a quick bowl of corn flakes, swilled down with a cup of steaming hot tea. Rusty his golden retriever nuzzled up to him demanding his walk. He pulled on his green wellies, slipped on his Barbour coat, took a half bottle of scotch from a cabinet and put it in the side pocket of his jacket. Then he grabbed a handful of 12 gauge shells and stuffed them in the other pocket, before unlocking the gun cabinet concealed behind a pantry door. He gazed at his small collection of shotguns and selected an over and under Beretta, his favourite, he broke it open and loaded in two shells.*

*With Rusty excitedly running rings around him they left the house around 7.40, the quiet of the countryside awaiting them. It was still dark as they made their way along the hedgerows that bordered their property. Ahead Sean could see a faint chink of light. With the Beretta in the safety position in the crook of his arm Sean set out to murder some pigeons. Not because they were pests but because Sean had a fascination with watching the birds fall out of the sky.*

*It was cool and crisp and the sound of the frozen ground making crunching sounds, helped to ease the effects of the celebrations of the night before in the Horse and Groom. As he walked he gave thought to the events of the previous few days. He'd truly regretted killing Bernie Abrahams. The man was well into his sixties, still fit with probably another twenty years left in him, but he was a danger that couldn't be ignored. It was a pity about Eddie, he'd always been useful, playing Arthur's elusive cousin Roy his crowning achievement, a good mechanic too, but a loose mouth if he was ever cornered. He'd meant to be staying in Brighton, but the lure of the Smoke during Christmas was too much for him.*

*With loose ends all tied up, Sean was looking forward to retirement, Jackie had suggested two weeks in the Greek islands.*

'Why not,' he thought. Pleased with himself he could just made out the stile fifty yards in front of him. Quickening his pace, his breath billowing out of his mouth like a steam train, he wasn't as fit as he once was, as he thought about the resolution he made each year, but never kept.

He slipped on the step as he started to climb over the stile. "Fuck," he cried. He replaced his foot carefully on the step and was half way over the stile, when a cold voice commanded him to stop.

"Move a muscle, you're dead."

Sean froze, half on half off. He could throw himself over the stile snap the shotgun into locked position. 'What is this, the Wild West?' he though in the briefest of seconds before he cautiously turned towards the voice.

He smiled, "I should have known, the apple doesn't fall far from the tree." He looked straight down the barrel of a 22 calibre revolver at the antique dealer.

Eric moved forward and stood parallel to the hedgerow and the stile that Sean was perched upon. "You should have left us alone," said Eric. "You'd won your little game, but you wouldn't leave it be."

Sean smiled, his hand clutching the open shotgun, weighing up his chances. The gun in Sullivan's hand steady as a rock. Sizing the man up he could see the antique dealer wasn't an amateur out of his depth. Hopefully keep the man talking was his best chance. "I came looking for answers, but on seeing you I had all of them wrapped up in a blue ribbon. You're the spit of Bernie, when he was your age."

"Why'd you have to kill him?"

"Bernie was my mentor, he saw in me what my parents never could. He saw my potential. But how could I compete with you, Mr Squeaky Clean; the would be gangster, that doesn't get his hands dirty. You're his son, his blood!"

472

*Eric remained unfazed, Bernie Abrahams had struck up a friendship with Eric when he'd been nothing but a street urchin. To a street kid, being friendly with one of the kingpins of the underworld was the ultimate kudos. When news of Bernie's death reached him, he looked for answers. He'd found them when he called on his mother. She was inconsolable and told Eric that Bernie was his father. They'd met shortly after his mother came over from Ireland. She was young and pretty and very soon they fell in love. The inevitable happened and she became pregnant. By this time she knew Bernie Abrahams was a gangster. He asked her to marry him, but she refused, stating she didn't want her son to follow in his father's footsteps. They stayed close but the relationship ended.*

*"Yeah, I know." Eric kept his eyes fixed on Fallon, he sensed he was about to move. In an attempt to keep him off guard, Eric added, "Your mother died in childbirth. She was the first person you destroyed."*

*Fallon looked shocked. "What are you talking about?"*

*"Your mother died in childbirth and you were adopted."*

*"How do you know this?" asked Fallon.*

*"The same way I know Bernie Abrahams is your father!"*

*"What!" exclaimed Fallon? The truth slowly dawned on him. The tough talk, the way Bernie inserted himself into his life.*

*"You shot him, you shot him down like a dog, your own father," Eric expected Fallon to move, but instead he remained motionless.*

*Fallon looked at Eric and knew his chance was moments away. Steadying himself on the stile, his right hand close to the trigger, he knew his gun, he knew in one fluid motion he could bring it up and end it. "We're brothers, we have the same blood flowing through our veins. We're so much alike, you and I!" He laughed, more to himself, "We even married the same…" Fallon saw a flicker of doubt in Eric's eye and made his move, he flipped the shotgun hard, locking it in one swift movement, but it was too late. A 22 bullet smashed into the right-hand side of his forehead close to his temple and turned his frontal lobe into mush.*

*Sean Fallon was dead, yet he remained perched motionless, almost upright on the stile just as he had a minute earlier. Eric stared up at the prone figure in disbelief. He'd hoped that Fallon knowing he'd murdered his own father and that they were half-brothers he'd have shown some remorse.*

*Eric was shaken, yet his instincts to survive kicked it. He knew not to panic. He knew he needed to think it though. Panic would get him caught. He glanced at the shotgun and an idea began to form. He's seen Fallon slip on the step, the gun could have gone off by accident. Eric picked the shotgun up off the ground, measured it from trigger to tip of the barrel against Sean's body, then aimed the gun at almost point blank range and fired. The impact sent Fallon flying like a rag doll over the stile and hedgerow. Wiping his fingerprints off the gun he grabbed hold of Fallon's right hand and pressed it against the trigger and trigger guard. He cursed himself for being so methodical, but remembered the one thing that Bernie Abrahams had instilled in him, 'don't get caught.'*

*Satisfied he'd covered all his bases, Eric walked calmly away.*

"It was over, the nightmare was over..... Or so I thought. I hadn't reckoned on a swede basher from the sticks trying to make a name for himself. I'm truly sorry I might have caused you some discomfort."

"Discomfort Eric, that ain't the half of it! You don't know how much heartbreak you've caused me!"

"Believe me Joe, I didn't want to tell you, but with all this suspicion going on in your head, then getting in touch with Heather and now you tell me about Parkhurst you'd left me no choice but to tell you the truth, no matter how vulnerable it's made me. I didn't know about Terry. I hope now you believe me?"

"I believe you. Like I said earlier, I know Grace loves you. After what you've just told me, you've just extinguished any flickering flame that I might have to win Grace back. Like I said one time, we're not friends."

Still in shock from Eric's revelation, Joe rose from his seat, looked the antique dealer in the eye and then without another word stepped out of the back office. The tiny bell rang as Joe opened the door and walked away.

May 17th 2020

Revised February 14th 2025 ©

# About the Author

Michael Kennard makes his home in the Oxfordshire countryside, where he spends his retirement writing, travelling, socializing and playing snooker. Tennis and golf a now distant memory. Having written several novels, *all hopefully reprinted in the near future,* his latest novel a change of genre is packed with his familiar brand of intricate plots, storylines and unforgettable characters